C0-AVC-541

ALSO BY GEORGE MINOT

The Blue Bowl

om love

om love

A NOVEL

George Minot

ALFRED A. KNOPF NEW YORK 2012

THIS IS A BORZOI BOOK
PUBLISHED BY ALFRED A. KNOPF

 Published in the United States by Alfred A. Knopf, a division of Random House, Inc., New York, and in Canada by Random House of Canada Limited, Toronto.
www.aaknopf.com

Knopf, Borzoi Books, and the colophon are registered trademarks of Random House, Inc.

Library of Congress Cataloging-in-Publication Data
Minot, George, 1959–
Om love : a novel / A Novel. — 1st ed.
p. cm.
ISBN 978-1-4000-4274-6
1. Yoga—Fiction. 2. Manhattan (New York, N.Y.)—Fiction. I. Title.
PS3613.I6604 2012
813'.6—dc23 2012018976

Front-of-jacket photograph © Hugh Chatfield
Jacket design by Kelly Blair

Manufactured in the United States of America

FIRST EDITION

FOR KRISTIN,
GIULIA AND MILO

Then he shut his eyes. Like the clouds on the wind, he was in no hurry. If things took time, he didn't mind. He stopped thinking and gave himself over to the flow of time. At this moment, time's natural, even flow was the most important thing.

—MURAKAMI, 1Q84

om love

1. Second Avenue

A turquoise crumb.
Her sleeping cashew body.
A pink flag on lower Broadway.
A red dot. Third eye. dot om. on Astor Place.
On the mental map of our quavery Lower Manhattan.

~

We went everywhere on our bikes.

Amanda was afraid I'd be hit by a car and killed. She thought I was too aggressive. Dipping. Dodging. Wheedling through cars at intersections.

I thought she was too slow and spacey. We plugged along at her speed. Pulled apart by our natural paces.

Riding along together she'd put her hand over mine where I held the handlebar. We'd ride along like that.

~

Clues are always there from the start. Glimpses. Revealing later reality.

The eulogy in the introduction. Words encoded eyes. The book in the leaf.

But you never believe this great new love will ever end.

Any more than you believe you might die.

The *teachings* notwithstanding.

Nonattachment. Life.

Written wobbly.

Impermanent.

On water.

Love.

The old RamAnanda was a funky old place with purple sweating walls. Dark. Grungy.

Rows of bodies undulating in unison. Twisted into crazy pretzel knots. Everyone breathing together.

Eyes roved around the room. Met and glanced away. Or were fixed in that impersonal zone of yogic concentration.

Not too fierce, not too soft . . .

The teacher's voice led you through the class. One *asana* (pose) to the next. The basics. Refinements. Assisting you now and then. Maybe. Hopefully. The touch everyone craved.

Up the broad stairs on Second Avenue between Ninth and Tenth Streets. Between an Irish pub and a Brit-themed bar. Those red telephone booths outside. But no phones.

You pushed the buzzer. The door was shared with a Thai restaurant nobody went to above the British place.

Someone upstairs let you in. The lock clicked. The door gave.

Inside it was like a haunted Victorian mansion. Wide creaky old staircase on the right. Maybe a bike locked to the bottom of the banister.

Or someone's dog leashed to the chunky newel post. Sitting there in serene doggie meditation.

The stairs went left at the top. There on a stool sat a cute barefoot girl in cutoff sweats. Beastie Boys T-shirt. A spaceship on it.

She calmly checked you in for class. Face friendly. Hair a raggedy blond helmet. The cash register was a Batman lunchbox.

This was Amanda. So named by her Marin (California) mom thirty-three years before.

Feet together at the front of your mat.

A loose cluster at the top of the stairs before class. Or at prime time the line swelled. 6:15 weeknights. 10 a.m. and noon on weekends. Spilled halfway down the stairs.

Regulars heyed. Hugged. Chatted. Newer people took it all in. Smiles. Hands-in-prayer greetings.

The sixties smell of incense. The chanting at the end of the class finishing up in the room.

Loose cotton Indian outfits. Shaved heads. Sanskrit tattoos. Street ink. Piercings. A diamond bindi stuck onto (*into?*) some girl's forehead.

String around a left wrist. Red God thread.

These things gave the place a cultlike feel. To the outsider.

Though most of the people didn't seem soft in the head. This wasn't some strange beaming cult.

It was a mixed bag of downtown New Yorkers. Lost and found fringe dwellers. Among the accomplished. Committed denizens of the art ghetto demimonde.

Habituated urban animals. Stray cats. Epicene dudes. Cute scared squirrels. Lone wolves.

That giraffe supermodel. Creature-mouthed. Careful-eyed. Tiptoeing tall-ly in. Gingerly among the mats. The supine others.

Half-naked. Seals on our rocks. Prone. Limber. Endangered species. Protected. Safe here. Spent survivors. Starting again.

Innocent upstarts. Fresh-limbed lambs to the slaughter.

Players. Strangers. Fond familiars. Merging.

The famous and the smudges.

It was mostly women.

That little peek of thong showing above low-slung waistbands.

Where did they all come from?

The characters converged around the *om.*

We kept coming back. Happy to have found this place. This practice. There was definitely something to it. This peace.

Yoga means union. To yoke. Union of body. Mind. Spirit. Your lower self with your higher Self.

The teachings at the beginning of class sometimes seemed hokey or stupid.

All matter is music.

Something to be endured to get to the actual practice.

Everything is imagined.

Selections from the Yoga Sutras.

Yogash chitta vritti narodha.

Sometimes the Sanskrit without translation. But you'd hear it all again and again.

Yoga is the cessation of the fluctuations of the mind.

Bhagavad Gita. Other spiritual texts.

Followed by explanations. A personal story. Rambling associations. A sermon. *Everything is vibrations.*

They often went on too long. But there was almost always something good in there.

Om is the ace of all sounds.

Some redeeming kernel of insight. Fresh outlook. Illumination.

Om is the sound of God.

Some of the talks were really good.

Be the mountain. Whether the sun shines and plants grow and rivers flow all over you.

The practice at the beginning was broken down. The different *asanas.* Each distinct. Doable. Easy. (Seemingly!)

Or shrouded in stormclouds it rains and snows and floods and everything freezes and dies.

Like words. Phrases. Lined up one after another. As when learning a new lexicon. Like these words. Cleanly drawn. Clear clauses. Start simple.

Shoulders relaxed. Exhale. Gaze straight ahead. The tip of your nose.

Easy at first. To follow. Digestible. Some difficult. Awkward. But doable.

Exquisite intro alphabet. Of this elegant intricate body language. Mind. More.

You repeat and refine the basics. Assimilate. Until you get them down.

They grow. On you. In you.

The teachings became integral to the practice. You felt you were enacting the teachings.

Be the same still mountain self and mountain peace no matter what the external conditions.

Working them into your body.

Your life.
Clearing the way.
Creating insight.
Growth.
Gentleness.
Strength.
Clarity.
Instead of just thinking about these things.
Or not even.
Letting the life knot soften.
Instead of tightening further.
Turning it around.
Letting love.

The bright headlight moon races our car in and out of the trees without moving. Over the water many melted moons slide along in a wobbly connected body of mercury moonspill separating and coming together between grasping branch fingers.

Mum grips the steering wheel as if to keep it from vibrating or coming off, her mouth set. Her Tanzanite ring she wears for fancy occasions stands out like a relic or talisman from a different life or world. The diamonds catch the white moonlight, blue over the black water. Almost home, Dad asleep in the front seat, chin to chest, passed out.

Mum was driving us home after a Fourth of July beach party across the harbor. Boats, fireworks, families. Rowboats full of ice and beer, bar inside, buffet, music by the pool, smoking on the beach. Cherry bombs, firecrackers, the odd, too-loud M-80 explosion.

Sister Kate wasn't old enough to drive yet, but old

enough to get what was happening. I was, too, almost, but so also didn't. Welly was oblivious, between us in the back seat.

The radio I remember was on because I remember Mum turned it off in a minute. It was the summer of that song, *Everybody here is outta sight..* But that song wasn't on. It was WRKO (Boston), the song, I'm sure, was that long Queen song, like an opera song, I used to sing, whispersinging, in my mother's ear sometimes. *Mama! Just killed a man..*

The car clung pleasantly to the lineless road pulling us smoothly homeward over the little hills and contours, familiar in your bag of bones body swaying slightly away from the curves. When I was little I'd lie down in the back seat and guess or know where we were from the fleeting trees or a gap of sky or lamppost.

Mum drove pretty fast, like she was pissed. (As in pissed off, not pissed like Dad, as in wasted.) But her face, from the side, from the back seat, was more like the moon that lit it, impassive and central and floating along without moving, than like Mum pissed off. So if there was tension there in the car, it's gone now.

The practice was a lot more than the intense workout. Or the scene. That drew a lot of people there in the first place. The practice had its magic. Like any workout.

But unlike any other workout. It was way more.

You felt this was a beautiful thing to be doing. Not just with your body.

But with your life.

The teachings worked their spell. Subtle. Yet powerful. Not just in your mind.

But in your emerging *subtle body.*

The real (inner) life. Within your ordinary (outer) life.

You felt really good after practice.

In and out of your body. Mood becalmed. Mind clear. Anxieties allayed. Evaporated. Sweated out of you. For now.

You left there feeling a certain vital something. Something you knew you needed. Everyone needed. The world needed.

Grace.

Not to mention all the scantily clad babes padding around the place.

This amazing roster of New York's hottest.

Doing downward-facing dog.

Rows of them. Around you.

Take your pick. You wish.

Butts thrust in the air.

Breasts hanging.

Performing all kinds of showstopping positions. Unabashedly.

In the safety of this place.

Fertile field of budding yogaholics.

Demented contortions.

Like Twister.

Beach Blanket Bingo.

Kama Sutra!

Breathing. Sweating.

Ecstasy expressions.

Little bleats and moans.

Who could resist?

Whatever got you there. (As Scott put it.)

It's all good. (Inane motto of the nineties.)

Ultimately the practice was its own reward. You were on the path. Determined to stick with it. Or already addicted.

Plus there was that certain someone who took the Wednesday 6:15 class with Jonquil . . .

Inhale. Arms over your head.

This was at the very end of the millennium. Tummies exposed. Maybe a piercing winked in a belly button. Fleshy hooked fishy. Bending over.

Fishtail diving under the waistband. Top of a flowery tattoo branded on a lower back. Upper butt dual assets.

Alluring advertisement. Stamped invitation to get in there. Juicy peach.

Holy hidden buttonhole Batman. (Brahman.) (*Bad man.*)

The top and bottom few buttons of shirts undone. Reveal the tummy. Abdominal girl-curves. Hips.

Bell-bottoms were back. In hip-hugging solidarity with this long-neglected erogenous zone. Supersexy. Finally freed.

The delicious belly swell. Pelvic cheekbones. (Parenthetical.)

The new jeans were on the rise. Engineered. Suddenly everywhere. Overnight.

The first generation with an eight- or ten-inch folded cuff. As if they appeared too suddenly. Grew too fad-fast.

Braids were in. (Always cute.) Twin tails. Flapping on a bike.

Swinging in rhythmic Rollerblade velocity. Bodies bells in different parts of the city ringing toward each other.

The yoga nation in downtown Manhattan rode bicycles.

And didn't eat meat (much).

And they didn't care about money. (Just worried about it!) (Both the yoga-poor and the superrich.)

Or read the paper. Really.

(*It's all bad.* A would say.)

They were onto something else. Living in the moment. This new path.

They'd leave their shoes at the door. (Egos, too. Supposedly.)

Sit on the floor cross-legged. At potluck vegan dinners in little apartments.

They went to India.

Exhale. Hands beside your feet.

The road dives down in a tricky tight turn to the right where I wrecked a car not too many years later, the wall was fine, made by Italian immigrant masons, nice serif bookends, between them the long sentence curve along the back of the beach at the back of the cove. The road follows the wall, the wall follows the road. The opening in the middle has heavy green wooden double doors that are always open except during big storms. So you can see the beach and cove fleetingly when you pass by there. The sound of the car's engine louder against the near wall lifts away for that split second you pass the opening and instantly returns.

Without saying anything Mum stopped the car there, as if dropping something or somebody off at the opening, which framed the cove, the moon wiggling in molten slow motion on the water in her four- or six- or eight-headed train, beyond the harbor, the headland houses bunched in the dark blanket of trees, their lights spilling golden drips, brush-tip touches, strips, melted over the water.

Mum got out of the car, without explaining what she was doing. With an expression and manner I'd seen in her face and bearing before, but not often, she looked at us with a kind of eerie smile. Kind of kidding, kind of not, her eyes full of emotional meaning and moment. But not heavy, but light, to cherish and impart, as if this were the last time she'd see us, and we, her.

It was the expression she wore sometimes when we were little, scaring and entertaining us in bed at night. Once, in summer, in her airy, see-through nightgown, hair teased out with her brush to an electric, frizzed dandelion glow around her head, she was part fairy, part witch. She danced around in slow spooky circles, the room dim, arms doing this underwater thing, hands weaving, and when she got near the end and closer to us the witch part got stronger, her expression less fairy and more menacing, the thin, not funny smile not funny.

"Stop it, Mum!"

And she answered, sort of purred, not joking, her voice as gauzy and ghostly as her floating nightgown, but dead serious, "I'm not your mother."

"Did you call?" Amanda asked the next person in line.

Beefy bald guy. Falling-down pants. Big baby. Massive head. Already sweating.

"Uh, call?" Dude didn't know the system here. "Uh, no—"

"You should call and sign up at least an hour before class," she explained. "Class is full, but I'll put you on the waiting list."

Pickled lips a little o.

"Don't worry," she added sweetly. "I think you'll get in. Check with me at five past. Do you need a mat?"

Inhale. Look up.

6:15. Rush hour assailing the city. Full swing at the yoga center. Like being on the subway.

Mostly women. Familiar and not. Lots of people know each other. Hugs. Heys. The chatter. The hum. (*Om.*) The party hubbub and din.

Milling bodies. Crowded club. Wall-to-wall people.

Crammed in the banistered passage. At the top of the stairs. In the coat and shoe room. The narrow corridors. Waiting for the changing rooms.

The three tiny louvered bathrooms. Side by side. Like the Brit phone booths down on the street.

The sort of kitchen area. The chain of lesser rooms. Leading to the big room.

Steadicam curiosity nosily penetrates the dim. People lined up against the wall. Sitting. Squatting. Like an audition.

Waiting to get into class. Get a good place. When the 4:00 lets out. The placid stream.

Poached faces float by. Blissed out. From another world. Wrung out. Blessed by those carousing endorphins. The calm rush. *Shakti.*

How do you go from not knowing anyone. To knowing almost everyone?

You show up. Don't look down. Let nature take her course. People blend. Human nature. Divine? Souls merge. Grow together. Glow together.

People were happy to see each other at RamAnanda. Like friends everywhere.

But here the social climate also had a strange chill.

You sensed by degrees. Especially for a place that preached love.

We are all One. We are not separate beings. We are all the same.

And for a place that espoused *satsang.* Hanging out with like-minded people.

I.e., people on the spiritual path. (*Sadhana.*) Other yoga people. (*Yoginis!*)

I.e., keep coming to class. (Keep paying.) And to the workshops. Group meditations. Chanting. *Kirtan.*

Certain people didn't say hello at RamAnanda. It was weird. Aside from normal friends greeting each other. Girl-women girl-laughing.

But with some insiders it was the cold shoulder. Many.

Why? Was this a yoga thing?

They would glide by you without a glance of recognition. Let alone a nod. A smile. A measly little *hey.*

What was up with that?

This after you'd chatted many times on your mats. Practiced together. Chanted together. Assisted each other. When class went to the wall. Or broke up into partners.

It took me a little while to figure it out. Let alone accept. This chilly vein. Running through an otherwise warm and uplifting place.

The frozen vapor trail left in Jonquil and Frankie's astral wake. Crystalized in the adopted attitudes of the adopted underlings.

Frankie and Jonquil couldn't look you in the eye. Like normal people. And say hello.

Many didn't notice or care. Most just practiced at RamAnanda. And got on with their lives.

Maybe noticed Jonquil and Frankie were a little weird. East Village yoga hippies. But whatever.

But some were more deeply involved. Attached to Rama as a home hive. Almost cult.

Where friends all came buzzing (*omm*-ing) together. Big replacement family.

There were lots of stray yoga chicks out there. Guys too. But mostly gals. From broken families. Scattered lives. Looking for guidance.

For meaning. For a guy. Looking for a home. Of the heart. Looking for love.

Jonquil would say *Looking for God.*

Jonquil and Frankie walked through Ananda looking down. They wouldn't look you in the eye or say hello.

So the inked and pierced flock of RamAnanda chickies also padded around looking down.

Shy. Or beginner-minding their own business.

Wouldn't look you in the eye. Wouldn't say hello. Like this was cool. The yoga way to be.

Amanda walked around with her face tipped slightly upward. Like a satellite dish. Receive the signals. Slightly upward-facing face.

She'd look you in the eye. Smile. Send out good vibes. Ready with a wisecrack. She'd say hi. She didn't buy into that weird coldness.

Socially anyway. A people person.

But of course she was caught up in it. The whole neurotic human web. She worked for these people.

She had worked for them for years. They were in charge. Her sort of surrogate remote parents. Aptly apart. Coming and going.

She was always there. She ran the place. In her bare feet.

Exhale. Jump back.

She walked away from the car, a silhouette of her shape and her dress, the moon just above her head like a headlight coming at her. A beam from the mother ship issuing a command. Her shadow shape obeyed, walked over the sand, barefoot, over the dark moustache of seaweed, to the water's edge. Without pausing she kept going, walked away from us into the water, as if onto the water, into the silver memory. We watched as she walked out deeper. The bell of her dress filled around her. She tipped forward and to the side and like a ladle dipped into the water.

After a moment her head came up, in the silk moonlight spill, like a dark oil-slick seal's head, then with maybe an underwater kick or two she went under, again, and this time stayed under, and stayed under, was gone.

I finally bought a mat after renting one for a dollar each time.

It's declaring your commitment. Buying that first mat.

Amanda helped me choose which one. She basically told me which one to get.

Dark blue. Medium thickness. Like hers.

She assigned me a cubby. Showed me how to fold the mat.

Except that mine was always sopping wet after class. So I'd drape it over the banister overlooking the stairs. With others.

She'd put it in my cubby for me next morning when it was dry. Folded not perfectly.

Push-up position. Chaturanga dandasana. Head lifted. Inhale. Arch back. Upward-facing dog. Urdhva mukha svanasana.

I always looked forward to seeing her.

Before class. (Hubbub.) After. (Ditto.) During. (*Samadhi.*)

I loved practicing near her.

Exhale. Downward-facing dog. Feet shoulder distance apart. Inhale one!

Until much later I didn't realize how much my practice was wrapped up in Amanda.

Or no.

I knew then. But not how much.

Even when she wasn't there. Or when my attention went elsewhere. If you know what I'm saying.

Inha-a-ale. Exhale two.

We often had little to say to each other.

"How're you doin'?"

"Good. How're you doing?"

But that was fine. We always liked seeing each other.

She was definitely one of the main draws of my daily yoga habit.

Inhale. Arms straight! Exhale three. Look at your belly button. Your crotch.

Some people get into yoga gradually. Warming up to it. But I dove totally in. True addict that I am.

After one Basics class in the back room I went timorously into the big room for an Open class with all the hotshots.

That was it. I was hooked. Practiced every day from then on.

Knees straight. Exhale four. Heels down.

Today I was going to buy a Year Unlimited pass. I was now ready for the next level of yoga commitment/addiction.

I didn't exactly have my rent covered. But I had my priorities straight.

They were offering a Valentine's Day special on Year Unlimited passes. I counted out twenties. Gave them to Amanda. She counted them again.

"What, you don't trust me?" I said.

She smiled. Kept counting.

Inhale. Back straight. Lower back. Butt high! Moola banda! Exhale five.

While Amanda counted my cash this other girl I had a crush on came up the stairs.

I felt v uncomfortable. Suddenly nervous. Scrambled. Divided attention/affection. Guy-guilty.

I didn't even know her name. Yet. She didn't look at me. Or at anyone. It seemed. Dark hair. Smart dark eyes. Serious expression. Really pretty.

In fact stunningly beautiful. If atonally masked. In a way that seemed somehow uniquely designed and suited for me.

Except she hadn't seemed to notice me. Yet.

On the inhale jump forward. Feet between your hands. Look up. Flat back.

Met glances. We'd practiced near each other. But not beside.

Hadn't spoken.

And yet already it was clear. I felt ready to cast my lot with her..

She was another draw of my daily yoga habit. I always hoped she'd be there.

Once or twice a week I'd see her in class. Rita's. Or Virginia's or Frankie's.

We both liked to set up our mats in the first or second row. Near the teacher. Back to the window.

Exhale forward bend. Paschimottanasana. Chest to knees. Knees straight.

We weren't scared but it wasn't funny, we didn't know what was happening, so it wasn't scenic or lyrical, the scene, until after she came back up through the surface. And not even then, but only later. Over the years it became more beautiful, poetic, the more it returned to me, revised and refined by memory's supersubjective fiction-making machine, ever redesigning the past, to emerge mythic, moment-perfect.

She swam a bit, sidestroke, slowly, a fingertip moving along a silver sill. She stood, leaned and pushed and swam again. Then rose and walked back out of the water toward us, a seaweed monster from a bad late night movie, dripping shadowstuff and molten money.

Back at the car we could see her face and it had that expression again, or still, except now there was a deep satisfaction added, and also maybe amusement she wouldn't let out, but let it glow better by keeping it in and mixed with the mystery. She opened the door and got into the driver's seat, sopping wet. Kate leaned forward to say or do something to Dad, maybe shake him, wake him, show him this lesson or something.

But Mum turned, and though her expression and placid purpose alone stopped Kate, she put a finger to her mouth, meaning *Shhh,* and said only, as if it were a gift to him and special secret to us, "Don't wake him."

The two halves of the room faced each other. Like opposing teams. The day's incarnations. Mixed race. Mixed sex. Mixed up.

former club people	East Village ex-junkies	survivors
Brooklyn hipsters	12-Steppers	Midwesterners
transmigrated to Tribeca	Seattle/SoHo	Croatian sculptor chick
native New Yorkers	Jersey girl (incognito)	Southern peach
what does that guy do?	stockbroker!	"designer"
artists (intended)	writer (supposedly)	musicians
supermodels	director	producers
grips	stylist	that Scandinavian girl you see everywhere downtown
therapist	body workers	carpenter artist
hedge fund manager (quietly)	unemployed & unashamed	graphic designers
"working on a script"	what's that guy's name?	unemployed & unhappy
editor	dot-commers	
waitress/actress	teacher	

a few doctors	regular models	the odd lawyer
dancers	former dancers	transgender (preop)
between jobs right now	metrosexual (gel)	doesn't need a job (trust fund)
architect	store clerk	office slaves
wonder what she does?	former athlete	fireman
who's she?	fashionistas	"consultant"
perspiring actors	early adapters	actress/waitresses
yoga teacher	holistic types	students
tech guy	gallery gals	old guy
big movie star (corner in back)	generic desk jockey	entertainment lawyer
child star actress (adult now)	clothing designer (new yoga line!)	her friend

Eclectic downtown hothouse. Humid mixed gene pool. Upwardly striving. Sexy democracy. Downward-facing. Lost and found. Reconnecting. Hopefully.

In this little sanctuary in the big city. Safe and sound. On a floating island just off the coast of America. Plot revealing herself.

Seekers. Spiritual materialists. Perspiring actors. Identities throbbing. Melted. Stars beside sponges. Melded.

We are all souls looking for God.

A hip-hop mogul. Shaved head. Practicing beside the guy behind the juice bar. Skinny-ass dude. Sandy dreads. Dreamy expression.

Surrounded by girls on mats in outrageous positions. That strategic little peek of thong above hip-hugging waistband..

Inhale stand. Hands together over your head. Arms straight. Shoulders relaxed. Look at your thumbs.

Rose was one of those methodical people. Who'd come in and put her mat down before changing out of her street clothes.

Get a good place. Then go change.

So I got to see her cool clothes. Good taste/fashion sense. Simple. Classic but street. Something sexy up her sleeve.

God in the details. Every detail a signal. God is in the girls.

A crescent of pierced holes crept up the apricot cusp of her left ear. Soundless ellipsis. . . .

She was already past piercings.

Colors she liked I liked. Dark solids. Red. But dark. Also yellow. Surprisingly. I liked on her.

This one time in the changing room. Curtain stalls. Like voting booths. Always a line to get in. Before and after class.

She was two in front of me in line. Then beside me in the next changing room. There was a space beneath the plywood dividers.

People undressed and dressed fast. Clothes would fly around. Drop to the floor in the adjacent booths.

I dropped my soaked shorts and knew they were in the visual vector we shared under the divider.

Right then she knew I was naked. No big deal after all the near-naked shenanigans. Heated proximity.

Variations on vulnerability. Proxy erotic. Arched open emotion. Prone. Tied up. Week in. Week out.

If she noticed.

In the next instant she threw down her sweater. Like a poker player. A blood red burgundy I could live inside. You can go home again. Sip and see nature incarnadine.

Did she throw it down on purpose? Her gauntlet.

Isn't the answer to questions like this always *yes*?

I liked that she was so quick. Decisive. Game.

This could be nothing. Or it could be everything.

Mind the mind. Imbibing itself.

Game on!

Exhale arms by your sides. Stand straight. Chest/heart open. Shoulders down. Mouth closed. Breathe smooth. Tadasana. Mountain pose.

The day I was buying the Year Unlimited pass (Valentine's Day, 1998) we weren't yet greeting each other.

Except in that tacit way. In the big room. In the practice.

As sort of yoga teammates. Energetic affinities established. But still tacit.

I'd actually made her a Valentine's Day card. In case she was there today.

I make collages. Constructions. Assemblages. Compulsively. Constantly.

One of the things I do. Part of my art. Manual preamble. Conjure the dimension. Ramble on in.

Render daily!

This one was a turquoise crumb.

Plucked from my yoga shorts. (Black Calvin Klein underwear. Midthigh. De rigueur.)

(Guruji wore them! Up to his ribs. And tank top. Tucked in. He taught like that.)

(Until 2000. When he graduated to Adidas. [*Adi* = unto + *das* = god].)

The turquoise crumb was taped onto a card-size piece of red paper. With clear packing tape. Shiny.

The tape squished the crumb. Sealed it fortuitously. Found form. Found in the process of making it.

I'd made this weeks ago. (Before I got my new mat.)

My idiot/artist's delight. When the tape flattened the mat crumb into a perfect little heart shape.

This definitely meant something! A sign. A valentine. There are no coincidences.

For Rose. (Her name. Not on her mat.)

Or for Amanda?

Rose.

Amanda.

Rose..

Mat crumbs were the scattered residue of our tandem bouts. Amid puddles of sweat. They'd stick to your body. Your shorts.

So-called *sticky mats* only stay sticky for a month or so of serious use. Then they start to wear out. Wear in.

The two worn spots. Landing strips where your toes land when you jump back. Again and again. Shedding mat crumbs.

Everyone. Every mat. Has a different pattern of dual worn-out spots. Every foot. Each side.

Irregular fat footprints. East side. West side.

You could analyze. People did. The imbalances. Imperfections of your practice. By the way your mat wears out.

The shape and depth of these amorphous spots. The pattern within. Going threadbare. Too much weight on your left foot. Big toe.

Goes to your pelvis. Tipped pelvic girdle. Sacrum strained. Bad girl. Lower back. Spine uneven. Shoulder strain. Seventh cervical. Sporadic pain.

Hands in prayer behind your back. Hurts. Etc.

That chronic sore wrist. Right side. Tendinitis. Not carpal tunnel!?

It's all connected. On and on. Your left side's your father. Pain is fear.

Don't these people have a job?

Today I had the card with me.

This was their job. Mine too. More in a way.

At least for two hours a day.

The plan was to slip it covertly to Rose. Or semi-covertly. If she was there. If the opportunity slyly presented itself.

Or job replacement. Real relationship. Life replacement.

The real yoga. A way of life.

Part of the whole New York package. New century/era spiritual awakening.

If you really live it. The way they say.

Or just adjustment. Necessary retooling.

Or not *just* at all. Bill. But serious business. Slow down. Vital tune-up. Stop. Get realigned.

(Your spine. A. Your life. B. With *God?*)

Starting now. You are here. Each time a new beginning.

(Because out there you forget! Lose the red God thread.)

Otherwise the bold approach.

Before I saw her coming up the stairs I thought of slipping it to Amanda.

But when I saw Rose coming I froze.

"I'll make out your pass after checking everybody in," Amanda told me. "And give it to you after class."

Amanda took class too.

She was set up in her usual place. In front of the big claw-foot radiator in the back row. Leos both.

Heating up. Between the two windows onto Second Avenue. Behind me. One over. (I was in the middle row.)

Rose was in front of me. One over the other way.

I felt pierced by their diagonal (divine!) proximity. Lifted. The whole time.

Energetic arrow through my adult child's valentine heart.

Beside me was the thick guy with the bucket head. Pickled liplets. And some spluttering invisible girl.

Amanda had a beautiful practice. Strong. Grounded. Smooth. Graceful. Juicy.

Without the dancers' *look-at-me* presentation. Their little floral hand flourishes. Overarching the back while bending forward.

Chest too puffed. Projecting outward. Swanning. Even in mountain pose. (*Tadasana.*) Standing position. (*Ta-daaa!*)

Amanda did the poses pure. Nothing added.

Her motions linking them (*vinyasa*) were fluid. Seamless. Appeared effortless. She was amazingly flexible. And solid.

Not like the strong oak that gets knocked over in the storm. And not the supple grass that gets flattened by the flood.

I was grunting and sweating the whole time. She was gliding easily in her element.

The yogi is like the willow tree. Both flexible and standing strong . . .

She was one of those rare people you see practicing and think *I want to be able to do that.*

Her round body somehow hidden. Generalized to a form. Muscular lovely dolphin. Under her cutoff sweats. Loose shirt.

Sometimes during practice she'd shed her shirt. Reveal her torso. Narrow shoulders. Danskin top. Spaghetti straps.

Rounded trapezii. Sloped like a swimmer's.

Nice little bump breasts.

Strong defined baguette arms.

Bigger bread biceps. (Like *me mum's.* (*hmh.*))

All upside-down.

I looked at her in downward-facing dog (*adho mukha svanasana*) (five breaths).

She was my *drishti* (point to which the gaze is unwaveringly directed) (ultimately and always on God) (not on some chick).

I stayed a little ahead of the count. So I could see her doing her *surya namaskara* (sun salutation).

Inhale arms over your head. Hands together. Look up at your thumbs. The almond of air between them.

The teacher spoke constantly. Leading the way. In words. Counting the breaths.

Jump back. On the exhale. Push-up position (*chaturanga dandasana*).

Amanda leading (me) in action.

Upward-facing dog.

Arch back. Howl at the moon. At your failures. At your father.

Down-dog . . .

Rose had good natural grace. Concentration. Dancer's poise. Without the flower puff.

Warrior one!

Same level practice as me. Beginner but strong.

Virabhadrasana. Hold for five breaths.

Going places. On the stationary mat.

Stand on your mat with your legs apart.

Like a surfer.

Arms overhead.

Now stargazing.

Front leg bent.

The teacher walked around assisting people.

Further. To a right angle.

Rita's *Cherman* accent.

Further, Beelly!

Aiming the hips forward. She straightened your arms. (You thought they already were straight.)

At the same time making you relax your shoulders away from your neck.

How can you do this without scrunching them up? And they kept saying it was all about the *breathing* (*pranayama*).

Back foot at an angle. Outer edge to the mat.

The refinements were endless.

Hips face forward.

(*Ujjayi.*) Breathing. Out your nose. Audible. Open channel. In the back of the throat.

Like Darth Vader. Smooth. (*Hnnhhhh.*)

Mouth closed.

In-haai-il.

Jonquil strung the instruction *inhale* out. In a weird singsongy way. That many of her follower/fledgling teachers copied.

Lots to remember. Forget.

Hands together overhead. Aiming a (peace!) gun at heaven. Look up at your gun, girl. *Hold.*

Rose held her hands apart for some reason. Some other system. A beat behind. Sometimes. Her way.

Both sides. (Whatever you do on one side. You do on the other side. Always.)

Then into warrior two (*virabhadrasana*). Arms out. Parallel to the ground. A baseball umpire indicating safe.

Rose worked those black and yellow striped bumblebee shorts I came to love. Short!

Rose was a natural beauty. Breathtaking. Took care of herself.

Seemed to know just how she looked. But seemed to care more about more important things. Her composed appearance was just part of a whole refined whole.

But she definitely loved clothes. Our chosen plumage. Sexual signage. And class and niche.

Composite presentations. Advertisement for self. Signals. Assumptions. Also protection. Shields and shell. Ward off aliens. Artists.

Her Carhartt hat. Black pleated skirt. *Classique.* Stripped down in the room. To those bumblebee shorts. To the physical essentials.

Dark smart eyes. Handy hands. A dancer. In college. I bet. As a girl. Coltish boy-girl. Bound in the budding strong bundle woman body.

Inner power subdued. Tamping her soul into her cool cannon ambition. Mouth firmly set. Projecting projects into the world. Work in progress.

Lovely face! Distorted upside-down. Hanging there between her legs.

Head filling with blood. Eyeballs unglamorously bulging. Birthing herself.

Strong snub feet vs. Amanda's champion high arches. Her/their presence invading/pervading my all-over-the-place mind.

Back to the breath. Back to Rose. Her mystery life. Crammed with promise. Smoky moody. Sex-skinned future. Riding with me!

Slender neck. Erect. Elegant. Not too swan. Nor egret. But robin. Or—

I had to keep myself from looking at her too much. I couldn't believe everybody else wasn't staring at her the whole time.

Or maybe they were.

Mats are like flying carpets.

We'd surf. Bend. Into. Out of. Our addled psyches.

Push. Sweat. Breathe. Travel. Through mental clouds. Arching. Over undulating emotional terrain.

Shrouds of consciousness. Your inner movie. Voices. Running unedited away. Losing the plot.

The practice is a flying journey. Elemental passage. Through time out of mind. The essence of your ages. Your riddles. Distilled.

Your buried conflicts unburied. Released. Bit by bit. Into stillness.

Beyond words. Ineffable.

Pure energy. Mortal volition. Losing the pilot. At last. The plane. *Aaahh.*

But if words can approximate. Indicate the experience.

Psychic air. Above all else. Drill deep access. The found flow.

And if words can help thaw the frozen iceberg

of emotion in us all. Love. Then here come more words!

You forget where you are. Let it all fall away. Open into the dimension.

Words like birds flying in formation over the interior landscapes. In pairs. Single artist spies.

Your problems. Engines of action. Reaction. Resentments. The many muscles and mouths of your appetites. Appeased. Assuaged. Desire. Atomized.

You are profoundly right there. Pure. Dissolved. Into the music.

Everyone around you is off on her own penetrating trip. Also.

The teacher's words leading you into the practice. The practice leading you into that real realm.

Beyond words. Beyond information. Our era and ethos. Eros. Rose.

Yet you're all moving in powerful unison. Rose my inspiration. Amanda my other engine. Angels around me. Leading me in.

You come up for air and awareness of where you are.

You think not only now *This is a beautiful thing to be doing.* But *This is a beautiful thing being done to me. Through me.*

All parts. Time layers. Of your life. And inner life. Seemed included. Wedded. (Yoked.) As in dreams. As in love.

You do the *asanas.* Or do the *asanas* do you?

Forward bends go into your past. Work through your old shit.

Backbends are about the future. Unlimited opening. Abundance abounding.

Such a wild chaos the mind reveals itself to be. Schizoid. Ricochet Rabbit. Bouncing all over the place.

We're all like cities. Our minds. Crazy busy. Metropolitan bodies. Fleshy vessels. Chemical cocktails.

Racing on emotional ether. Love's fumes. Visions. Unreality. (*Maya.*)

Pain equals fear? Desire ends in pain.

Move into the fear. Stay calm. Breathe.

Memories. Pretty words. Money. As unreal as love?

Karma means action.

Again and again the teacher brought you back to points of concentration. Inside the effort. All different *asanas.*

We went to the wall. Frankie's class.

Frankie was a woman. Frankie and her partner Jonni were the famous Frankie and Jonni.

Getting famous. Like they wanted. Like RamAnanda.

The lesbian yogini couple who created RamAnanda. And all the Rama yoginis.

Frankie liked taking us to the wall. After a vigorous sun salutation. Many. Rigorous music cranked up. Get the heat (*tapas*) going. The *prana* (life energy).

Go to the wall.

I wanted to be near Rose. But I didn't want to follow her. (I wanted to follow her!)

Everyone lined up right beside each other against either wall. Mats touching.

I gravitated toward the uptown wall. Where she seemed headed. In her firm Rose-daze.

But she was too slow. There were no spaces left. So she gravitated to the other wall.

I went toward Amanda. A few over from the

door. Our eyes didn't meet. We were in practice mode.

We weren't men and women in here. Sweating. Half-naked. Milling. Moving around among other near moving bodies.

In extraordinarily erotic and vulnerable positions. Legs spread. Backs arched.

Endorphins rising. Wailing. Within. But calm. Cool Customers. Wide open. Crowded together. Hot. Sweaty. The ritual mystery. Sexless orgy.

We were serious yoga practitioners. Practicing yoga.

Frankie told everyone to get a partner. Someone near you. And near in size.

Friends blended. Familiars gravitated. Strays stayed put. Others panicked. Blundered. Broke forcibly through rigid test tubes of fragile self.

Fragile tubes of rigid self.

Met or avoided searching glances. Negotiated partnerships with a nod.

I went right for Amanda. She turned to me.

First person first. Stand facing the wall. Leg distance away. Hands on hips.

Right foot flat on the wall. Waist height. Leg at a right angle. Knee straight.

Standing leg straight!

Twist to the right. Right arm extended to the opposite wall. Standing twist.

Partner stand behind. Turn the person's torso further. Shoulders. Twist from the hips. Shoulders relaxed. Breathe even. Knees straight. Gaze soft.

Amanda dutifully touched my hand. I instantly became stronger. More focused.

She placed a hand on my shoulder. On my back. Gently but firmly. It felt good! Right. And turned me further. And I could turn further.

Then we did the other side. Standing on the right leg. Twisting the other way. She touched my standing knee with her foot.

It was a little bent. I straightened it. And lost balance.

We smiled. She held me up. Like a woman with a drunken dance partner. (My mother with my father.) (Hers with hers.) I regained my balance.

Then I assisted her.

Her body was strong and soft. Familiar. And new. Excitingly. Not too soft. Not too hard. Pliant. Responsive.

I twisted her further. She twisted further. Easily embraceable. It felt natural touching her. It felt good. All sweaty.

"Thank you," she said demurely. Sweet.

We separated. Dragged our mats back to our original places.

After class Amanda found me on the bench. Putting on my shoes.

Amid the almost subway hustle. Meets club mingle. See. Be seen. And school feel. (It was a school.)

Rose had dressed and left fast. Or hadn't changed yet. She had disappeared.

"Here's your pass."

Amanda handed me an orange laminated card.

On the back she'd made an *om* sign.

Girly. The wacky 3. Curled cat's tail. Sticking out from its big butt cleavage. The floating little boat hat. Its dot.

In exchange I could have slipped her the valentine card I made.

I should have. It was laminated with shiny clear packing tape.

Her card was orange. Mine red.

This was perfect. The perfect moment. But I hesitated.

And then. Of course. Rose appeared. Right then. Behind Amanda.

In the passage from the bathrooms to the coats and shoes.

I balked. Froze. Choked.

Amanda exchanged words with someone. Followed that lifestream into the next room.

Rose came out. Went down the stairs.

I left.

Plodded home. Over to Avenue A. Along the park. Down to Houston. Down Ludlow.

The Year Unlimited feeling its new place against my bank card. In its paper sleeve. In one pocket. The valentine in the other.

On the back of it I'd made a question mark. Close in form to the *om* symbol Amanda made me. Ditto the heart.

In the dead letter office of my pant pocket. The minute romantic mystery of *Who's it for?*

Instead of *Who's it from?*

And the question mark asked. Asked itself. Asked me.

¿Why didn't you give it to her? *¡Stupido!* To one of them! ? . .

Rose was the one I was thinking of.

I also had a crush on Amanda. Looked forward to seeing her every day. Loved. In fact. (If an emotion can be a fact.)

But the serious crush was on Rose. Who of course was more elusive. Imaginary.

One day I left just before Rose. Not by chance! This was well before Valentine's Day. We'd talked a little before class. Lying on our backs. On our mats. Side by side. Doing warm-up stretches.

It was like being in bed together. Or on the beach.

When I stepped outside after class it was snowing. Lightly. Everywhere.

It was noon. The monstrous engine of the city had slowed to a gentle *om* hum. Subdued by the spell of the snow. Ambient padding.

My own spinning engine had been calmed as well by the class. Amped and well spent.

It was the first snow. Or the first in a while. It was lovely.

The door opened and out came Rose. She stood beside me at the top of the stairs. Taking it in.

The slo-mo spew of polka dots. A couple of taxis sleighing by.

"Nice," I said.

"Yeah, it is nice," she softly agreed.

Zipped up her cool coat. Charcoal wool. Collar up.

Walking home in the snow I took a different route than usual. At Second Avenue and Fifth Street I noticed Rose walking half a block ahead of me.

It was like she appeared out of nowhere. It was weird. I'd been thinking about her and she appeared! How that happens.

(*Especially when you just left the same place together a few minutes before!*)

I crossed the avenue when the traffic paused so it wouldn't seem like I was following her.

In a couple of blocks I was abreast of her. In the diagonal snow she turned.

Her Carhartt hat pulled down over her forehead and ears. Self-contained consciousness. I wondered if she skied as a kid. Like I did.

I waved. She waved back. Mine was a lifted *How* hand by the shoulder (like an American Indian in the movies). Her arm shot up like a basketball player's.

Small smile.

Humid base lodge. Hot cocoa. French fries. Tons of ketchup. Huge plate glass sweating. Girls smoking. Hats off. Fat boots unbuckled. Puddles of snowmelt.

Please let her be something halfway intelligent. Whatever child's God I was talking to.

She doesn't have to be a writer. For instance. Or even a magazine writer. Just working for a magazine..

She's young. Bright. Self-possessed. Beautiful.

"What do you do, anyway?" Rose asked me.

Putting on our shoes. Chatting almost easily. She. Another time after Rita's 10:00 class.

"That you can go to yoga all the time . . ."

"I'm an artist," I answered. License for anything.

Her knowing expression. Wary. Not the usual hedging lift toward impressed. *Do you show? . . .*

Which I liked. Her head bobbed a little. Like one of those toys stuck on a car window.

"What do you do?"

"I work at a gallery." Her head slid evenly side to side. In that way girls do now. Car hit a bump. Indicating her job was maybe a concession.

"Oh yeah? Where?"

"The Woog Gallery."

Ding.

"I used to show there. Back when he began. In the eighties . . ."

She had a poker face. She was in high school then. Or not even.

"Then in the nineties in the Projects Room."

"I run the Projects Room." She sat up straight. Perked like a bird. Alert top student. But keeping her cool. This one.

"I had the inaugural show in the Projects Room."

"No way."

"Yup. 'Ninety-two."

All downhill since then!

I was probably her age when I first showed with Woog. Back when he was in the East Village. Like all the hot new galleries then.

Storefronts. A living room. Anywhere you could cram 'em in there.

Before they moved to SoHo. Before they moved to Chelsea.

She could go back and look at my slides. Hear stories of the old days. Get my whole career online.

Fabulous unconscious rise. With the wave of the eighties. The vague decline. Humble dwindle. If she got that far. Recently mostly omission.

It was not a good time for me. Recently.

But you keep going. Ride it out.

You reconfigure. Wait it out. Lie low. Work it out.

Do your work. Live life. Go to movies. Get sick.

Wait for love. Find new worlds. Rise up. Do new things.

You take up yoga. For example. Stop running. Start healing.

Or get on this new high hamster wheel. And suddenly you feel better. Lighter. Right again.

Out of the ashes the phoenix rises. Out of the mud the lotus.

Rita would walk on your back after bow pose (*dandasana*).

The room would hear the cracks. Like a lock tumbling open.

We were working out the deep kinks in the mind/body.

Knots. Lifelong compressions. Strains. Spurs. Stains.

Absorbed unholy taints. Emanations. Melancholy links. Leaks.

Burrs of anxiety. Pain. Fears. *Psoas.* Buried hard. Tight.

Unspent emotion stored deep in the tissue.

Dead light in the recesses of the flesh.

Embedded poison. Lethal bacilli. Industrial seep. Distilled in our blood. Marinated into the bones.

Settled in cells. Dark seeds. Colonizing our musculature. Lymphatic city. Metropolitan metabolism.

Sapping the will. Drawing our faces. Dimming outlooks. Eating enthusiasm. Vitality. Crimping everything. Devouring youth.

Forming habitual movements. Reactions. Postures. Restrictions. Attitudes.

Toxic stuff polluting our minds. Thoughts. Vision.

But we're used to this. This is what we know. Habit mind. This is who we are. This is who I am.

Pancha. Habitual thinking.

Miasma. Death serum. Causing cancer. Gloom. Fatigue. Antinature. Anger.

The layers over the years. Tapping vital energies. Killing spontaneous joy. Sucking lumens. Bloom and life.

Instead this internal parasitic clusterfuck. Capitalism's chemical residue. Everywhere. In us. Invaded. Our era. Seen and unseen.

Inhabiting our inner organs. The soft machinery. Inhibiting our amazing blood-murky processes. Miraculous minutiae.

Pink dark hotel of pent agonies. Silent flax of flesh.

So much loss! Pain. Fear. Frustration coursing. Rage unspent.

The psychic toll. From the first brutal blows of infancy. We wail in agony. In protest. Scream in terror.

We are not cats. Stretching. Hanging out. A life of sleep and meditation. Rent free. Food free.

We suffer severe emotional twists. Below the conscious level.

We're wound with mortal urgency. Housing our wounds. We have to work.

The body tightens. And the heart?

We duck in fear. Lie low. Worry. Stuck. We escape. Weep.

It never stops. We don't want this.

And yet we keep it all.

Why?

We stash away our pain. Hoard it within.

Like it's precious. We cling to it.

Who will teach us to let it go?

Rita. For one.

Where else do our buried feelings go, if not into our bodies? Are they gone? Or just filed away in the computer memory banks of our brains? Sorry, kids . . .

She'd draw out her talk.

Lower your legs into halasana. Feet pointed, today. Knees straight, Bee-lee!

As we struggled upside-down in plow pose (*halasana*).

We practice yoga because something's wrong. Knees bent now beside your ears.

Chins crunched into our necks.

We're all here because we want to change. Squeeze your ears with your knees! So you can't hear me!

We were agonizing. Spines fisted. Relax. But flex. Strong. At the same time.

Why is it so hard for me to give up this life I don't even want?

She wasn't even counting. She was just talking away.

We have to work to free ourselves. It took years—all our lives—to get us all tight and knotted and bottled up like we are so fantastically.

Practicing by Buddy. Good strong guy flow. Buddy-boy.

It'll take the rest of our lives to undo it. Many lives.

Rose's fallen arches. Feet together and open like a book (*baddha konasana*).

Every day to polish the mirror of our souls. Every day to free ourselves. See and remember who we really are.

Amanda's tiny twin ankle freckles. A carob colon. (:)

Our true selves. Our real Self.

Juice after. Lucky's. Carbs. Berries.

Which is divine.

I lingered after practice one morning. Waiting for A to come out. She was ten or fifteen minutes behind me in her practice.

She had a pink towel (Jonquil's) around her neck. Like this was a regular gym where people worked out. Like Crunch downstairs.

(A would become for me. As in this instant. A representative of the real world. Also advertisement. Special A among ordinary people. And the mainstream things they do.)

"You're a bad man." She said it with a pretty good Indian accent. That lilt.

She sat beside me.

"How was practice?"

"Good. Nice hot one. Not that much pain."

We half-laughed.

"You are not the pain," I intoned. Semi-Indian accent (bad).

"You *are* the pain." She liked this. So so did I.

(Was this our/her first flip-quip? where you flip the word or what the other just said and make it into a quip about them. You'll see.)

"Oh, wait," she popped up. Sailed back to her office. Came back more than a second later with a flyer on orange paper.

"I don't know if you're busy or if you'd be into this, but on Friday night we're having this annual dance thing with my African dance class, like a class and dance party open to friends . . ."

"Okay, yeah . . . Thanks." The flyer had the word *womyn* on it. Harvest moon. "Sounds good." So now I have to do African dance, too?

"What is it, though?"

"Don't worry, you don't have to dance if you don't want to. You can just watch."

"No, I love to dance. I just have a hard time with those African dance steps."

"Don't worry. Lots of people don't know what they're doing. You'll be great. And this class will be easy, for outsiders . . ."

The flyer said six. I got there just past.

Stone church on West Fourth Street. Washington Square Peace Church. (Where they had Vietnam protests.)

Not far from kindred Judson Church. Where they also dance. (Like St. Mark's in the Bowery Church.) (If you catch the trend here. what is sacred around here.)

The golden dusk pure harvest. People sitting on the steps. Mostly women. Milling around inside.

It wasn't even close to starting. No Amanda.

A chair rack slid against the far wall. The clatter of a folded metal chair falling on the floor. A squeal. Followed by a few more sliding and crashing. Laughter. Female.

Amanda emerged from behind the barge of chairs. came toward me like a boatless boat cutting across the cove floor. Wind at her back. Her chest a lifted shield. She was the bowsprit. "Hey, you came!"

"Yeah, I was just about to leave." I laughed.

"You can't . . . It'll be fun."

Women of all ages. Colors. Shapes. Sizes. Talked in groups. Or were busy with preparations. A few guys too. Everyone seemed happy.

"I just have to help some more with setup," she said. "You can just hang out on the steps or whatever. Go eat a Big Mac, and I'll come and sit with you in a few minutes. Don't leave!"

"No, I'll help set up. What are you doing? What can I do?"

"Folding up chairs." She nodded thataway. "And we have to move these tables."

We moved tables together. Conjugal exercise. Pressed together in the corner they still took up too much space.

I suggested we fold up the legs. Stack 'em.

"I knew you were smart," she said.

"Genius," I warned her.

Mostly women. All smiles. All saints. Paid at the door. greeted each other. Hugs. Kisses. Laughter.

They wore. Or changed into. Dance clothes. Colorful. Skimpy. Tight. Loose. Waistbands rolled down. Hair bound up. Back.

Hips. shoulders. Faces. Breasts. Bare feet. Ready to rumble.

The drummers. All guys but one. Assembled where the minister used to stand and deliver the service.

Hat appeared in front of the drummers. (Harriet.)

Strong black woman. Ageless fierce upper forties. Tight braids. Warrior eyes. Mini microphone headset. Like a telephone operator.

Black Danskin outfit (V-neck. sleeveless. midcalf.) Highlighted her exquisite neck and limb articulations.

Dancer's body. Defying middle age. Refusing the sag and muddled form. Sheathed in loose drawstring shorts. African print. To the knees.

Dancers lined up in rows. Filling the floor. Amanda was in the front row. One of the hotshots.

She told me to get anywhere. Just follow along as best I could. I got behind her and followed her.

This was easy during warm-up. The first half hour.

Stretches (some yoga. yogish.). Arm and head movements. Crouch. Work the shoulders. Torso.

To the bubbling beat. Simple steps. Sample the stew. Brewing. Grew more complicated.

Hat led facing everyone. Moving in a cool cat-smooth crouch. Belted out instructions over the sound system. The drumming heated up. Like water boiling.

Everyone massed together in the back. By the door. the same rows moved forward. One after the other. Following Hat's slinky set moves.

Dipping. stomping. spinning around. Up up up to the front. To the drummers. Melt away to the sides. Head back to the back.

Hands touched the floor. Fingertips. palms. In front of the drummers. When they got there. In supplication/ thanks. Or hand to heart to floor to heart. To floor.

Quickly got more complicated. The arm and head and hip movements. The steps. And got faster. Forget it.

I stuck behind A. Impressed! Lost. She was great.

The drummers. In loose African garb. And street clothes. Black jeans. Muslim hat. One guy superskinny. grinning. Not great teeth. Were off in the drumming planes. Inspired. Pulsing. Layered away.

The rhythm got faster. The dancers sped up and let go. Lift-off. Shedding Western self-consciousness with the dripping sweat.

The high olden days hall of the church. Hulking dim in the day's last glimmer. The season's last living light. Golden century. Suffused through ugly blood and brown beer stained glass.

Filled with a thumping orgiastic stampede of wild ecstatic women. Equally gorgeous gay men.

A far cry from the sober Episcopalian worldly intentions of the original church's founders. Congregants. top-hatted. Bushy sideburns. Hoop skirts. *Clop.*

Stepping from a carriage. Light snow. Like feathers. plumes blown from the horse's nostrils. His glossy black eye. Straining. Seeming to see *backward.*

I thought if Amanda and I had children they'd come here. Like the kids scrambling and bouncing around the margins. Dancing right in front of the musicians.

Far cry from touch football along the Charles River. While parents drank bloody marys. at noon.

Heinekens. Tomato bisque from a plaid Thermos. Ate picnics from baskets. On tailgates. Station wagons. Wood sides (fake).

Deviled eggs. Dash of paprika. Cucumber sandwiches. White bread. Moist with mayo. Crusts cut off.

BLTs. Toasted. Wax paper bag. Before Harvard football games. Sculls row eternally by. Graceful. Silent. Pulling along.

Stroke! curved oars cutting the skimming water bug barely-a-boat's reflection. Feathering back just above the water's surface. Into the dark arches of the bridge. Shaped like footballs. With their reflections. Smell of cigar smoke..

The drumming and dancing followed Hat the leader into the building repetition and rhythm.

At a critical boiling point the rows broke up spontaneously into free dancing. Arms and legs and shaking butts all over the place. Feet. The beat. Weaving. Ecstatic. They made a circle.

Hat in the middle kicked and ducked. Rolled into a sort of vibrating wobble. Shoulders and breasts shaking like mad. Quick little fussy steps. Strutting tight coils of orgasm unsprung.

Hat beckoned the skinny girl with branch tattoos on the backs of her legs. In her every minutest movement the skinny girl with branch tattoos on the backs of her legs shadowed Hat.

Everyone started clapping. Whooping. Dancing in place. Hat moved out of the circle. Panting. Swirling. Slick with sweat. Absorbed into the wall of mostly women. And the girl went into a reeling solo.

When she was done she returned to earth and picked someone else to join her in the center. Amanda.

She stomped and boogied with the branch girl. They smiled. On. Off. On. Off. Quickly when their eyes met. Arms almost flapping together. Shoulders in deft shadow dialogue. Torsos working. Shimmy. Hips making eights. Sometimes sort of stomping. Knees high.

Then the branch girl slipped back into everyone else and Amanda was alone and went slower. More undulant with the hips and butt. Arms out to fly.

Her eyes closed and her head dropped as she went into a rumble with the garrulous drums. Jive-talking. Bapping away. Bubbling. Slapping. Ba-*pap!*

Everybody clapped her into her hastening runaway groove. Faster. Louder. But she kept it. Didn't let it run away. Kept it cool. No rush no need to do anything tricky or escape her rapt element.

"You're a great dancer," I told her afterward.

We sat on the stone steps of the church in the copper marigold streetlight. Stagelike. Because New York is a set. For a love story. Millions of them. (Us.)

People were leaving. Most touched her and said goodbye. A bunch of times she got up to hug. Kiss.

At the bottom of the steps appeared this guy James. Enter James. Her old boyfriend.

Until when I didn't know. But his loving. Sorrowful? accepting expression said not long before they'd broken up. We knew each other from *ashtanga*. Sort of.

He didn't come anymore. To the new Rama. He and A came to a dinner I had in the spring in my studio for yogi friends. The first of many.

They hardly talked during dinner. They didn't seem like a couple. She sat beside this guy who also did *ashtanga*. One of the teachers. Jules.

Effervescent gay guy. Brimming with tart fey cracks. Or giddy. Or just goofy. Silly. Sweet.

During dinner. Dessert. They held hands for ten minutes. Amanda and Jules. James didn't seem to mind. Or notice.

He sat erect in his chair. Chest oddly puffed. Heart center open (?). Mild (stoned?) expression pasted on his face. Said only that golf was yoga.

He praised the food. Amanda said almost nothing the whole meal.

James and I nodded and then didn't speak as Amanda greeted good-bye a clutch of babes heading out. Waiting and watching her he said "Gotta love Amanda."

When she was done he asked if So-and-so was here. Amanda said yeh. Inside. He went in. Ungainly lumber. Exit James!

We chatted a little longer. She said she had to help clean up. I said I was going to get going. Thanked her.

The sweat-wet sunflower of her hair clung in petals to the side of her face and strong stem neck. She looked calm and beautiful and a little savage in the lake.

The frenzy from the dance still leapt in her eyes. Her eyes glassy. Dazed. Glazed blue in the copper light. Her pale blue shawl.

As I drew away. Looked back. She raised her hands in prayer near her chin. Her hands in prayer against the shawl wrapped around her shoulders. The blue shawl against the stone steps of the also stone church. Her not-stone face. Fills the screen.

Her hands in prayer. For me. I did the same back. (First time. Outside of class.)

You know one of these moments when it happens. The heart registers. Fixes the sappy copper old gold sepia. Remembers the tableau. Files for life.

Love! the disappearing act, the details. The cat lying long, happily crushed between us in bed like a pillow, staying there all night, no matter how much we move, he's not moving, wheezy breathing, he's still there in the morning, white hair all rumpled, in the sun. A pigeon coos heartily out on a ledge, unseen, almost purrs, almost a baby, wing tips tap four quick times as he flies off, a faint fifth. On the black fire escape railing a black squirrel twitches his tail, stops, stands, puts up his dukes like a little boxer, looks in the window, looks left, right, and leaps away into the fresh-money leaves. A song arrives in a car, the beat first, *thwumping,* getting louder, then the woman's voice gets clearer, louder, subsides, salsa this early, rappa, horns and the rhythm bouncing up the street, fading blending into the gentle roar of morning cars sweeping uptown on the avenue. A truck booms, day is declared, relative silence resumes. Children chatter in their daycare T-shirts to their knees, teeter and bumble along the sidewalk hand in hand, in pairs, the teacher repeating the same singsong theme, the city samples, a persistent lilting patience. The trees out the window lightly laugh, shake with shifting light and shade, up and down the street, the billowing park canopy. The Mexican guy at the Korean corner deli cuts flower stems and bundles them fast in red rubber bands in his special way like hard hair in a ponytail. The women in their mirrors getting ready for the day, I look fat, I feel fat, I'll skip breakfast, do I look fat in these? I'll skip lunch, just a juice, just coffee and juice. Just coffee from Mud. The Macedonian guy with the bushy mustache selling roasted honey nuts from his stainless steel pushcart on the corner of Lafayette, sugar not honey, a bit burnt, superseductive aroma, warm pretzels, big salt crystals encrusted, in winter, first hot spring day it's Italian ice, the Mister Softee truck arrives, *You're Mister Softee,* his swirly head, vigorously ringing his bell after the not-very-catchy melody scratchily tinkles and screeches through the mounted speaker, the bell like a bicycle bell, hand cymbals along with the harmonium, first notes, first *omm* of the day, creaky first *asanas,* getting some heat going, *prana, vinyasa,* warming into human pretzels, a juice on the bench after, watch people pass by, girls talking with girls, the things girls talk about. Guys, new students, timid to start, cute, looking around, the one wearing socks, the salmon curtains drawn, long tall gowns holding morning light, afternoon a longing, long elsewhere blues, practice in full swing, that song "Hallelujah" (Leonard *There is crack in everything* Cohen. Buddhist. *That's how the light gets in.*) sung by Jeff Buckley, one of us, gone, downtown peer, died young, like his dad, fell off the riverboat, they say not drunk, no drugs, some come and thank her after the class, the one who always has a question has a question, holds back till last. She thinks maybe a movie later, a meal, dance class and sit some, the bath up to her neck, the hot water continuously running, just the right temperature, the day done, a good day, good enough, a friend calls, she's delighted, she's down, they talk about a guy again. Plans for the beach for the weekend, a week in Costa Rica, or California next month, or new jeans at the Barney's Warehouse sample sale, go early, go see some music, tonight or tomorrow night, *You can't see music!* she cries, she laughs into the phone, and *Fat is not a feeling!* into the mirror all women share, what they gain and negotiate there, their automatic knowledge we guys will never get, we just see that need-to-know, the patient seemingly sure way to move into the future, the next moment, like it's waiting for you, doodling round little hearts in her Light On Yoga, the silence and sensed breath of supernature like a big cat outside inside the city, in the rhythms of lives, imagined and felt, the on-again off-again romance, heartbreak report, empathetic wisdom and light comedy flickering in faces, seen and unseen, open and shut heart spaces, flashing in your eyes, emerging, blinking, from too-long sleep, the emotional stasis, holding patterns, adolescent safety, the gossip, small worries, worst fears, merging with others in subtle sport, release, the yoga mats, different colors, mostly blue and green, lined up in the humid dark room, softly lit from the ceiling, the human smell and incense, small-orbit emanations of sweet summer-scented body products (organic), mingling. Verbena, jasmine, names of the women in their Lululemon outfits (many named Maya, spelled different ways), so similar but each distinct. The guys like trees among the flowers, hairy animals, a bear, a deer, the feel of each body, assisted, so different! Everyone standing at the front of their mats in *tadasana,* poised, a doe, mountain pose, goat, minotaur, vulture, to dive, ease, step off into outer space, delve, within, the labyrinth, the sensed river waiting, conjured, minds rushing still, racing around, the mountain will come to Mohammed. Light traffic breathes out on Broadway, flows like the energy in our bodies, the potent river current feel, you're carried in the stream, fast subtle eddies, the Russian River where she went as a girl with her family, her freckled loud cousins, and swam with her brother. Swung out on the rope and splayed, shrieking, let go into vertigo, splashed into the streaky brown current, color of café au lait, clotted with cloud, elongated, reflected ribbons and swirls of sexy blue skin sky peeking through. She tries to hold her breath underwater to sixty, counts fast, flowing sideways, cheats. Tries to hold her brother underwater, they spit water at each other, identical demented grins, spew fountain spouts out their mouths, she slow-dances with her dad to Van Morrison, "Moondance," on the porch outside after dinner, dark, while inside they were doing the dishes, the TV on, a car chase crashes and squeals away, as the fire they cooked hot dogs and burgers over rolled over and lays down, spread out and broken into orange embers, the flame gone down for good after popping up and then sitting down again a few times, lively die-hard dancer-trickster, the embers still glowing strong, hours after they're all asleep, pulsing in the morning under a barely breathing white pelt of superdelicate papery ash, like something underwater, deep-sea life-form, deep peace, do not disturb, move, don't breath a word, asleep in another world, all these things spell Amanda.

~

The altar. In the far dark corner away from the street.

A lit brass Dancing Shiva. One knee raised. The leg turned just so. Ready to karate-kick if you come any closer motherfucker. Arms everywhere. Aureole of squiggly fire.

A boatlike incense holder. Incense burning. Tiny orange soul glowing in the dim. Rising thread of smoke. The Nag Champa blue box. The celestial subcontinental smell. Minus the inconvenient squalor and rot.

A vase of orange marigolds. Another of roses. Gold-framed photographs. Floor to ceiling. Gurus. Rock stars. Bobby Kennedy. Martin Luther King. Nelson Mandela.

Smaller ones lower down. Dead friends.

How dare they tell you you cannot be the most gorgeous, intelligent, vibrant human being you can be!?

Inspirational quotes like that. Unattributed. Or wrong. Or wrongly attributed. Streaming around the place.

Be that change you want to see in the world. Gandhiji.

Cracked-open hearts circulating. In safety and hope.

The yoga safe house. Where the yoga crushes abound. As everywhere in life. Maybe more so here.

The yoga room is a hothouse of writhing energy. Affinities. Energetic affinities flourishing.

Body and soul. Exposed and alive. Poised and aware.

Each needing and seeking nourishment and care.

Human seeds. Soft-shelled. Sexual-spiritual sprouts and shoots. So many emotional tenderlings.

Tall girls. Small girls. (Women.) Fewer guys. Far more women. Same tight pants. Midcalf. (Not with slits yet.) (Before Lululemon.)

Bud buttocks. Bending over. Breasts like fruit you shop. *Stop it.* Abounding. All around. All types. You get used to it. You get into it.

Flowers and full plants. Pulsing in the moist musk. Abundant garden variety. Paradise for a wolf. Tomcat. Single cell artist spy.

The sensual insouciance. Sweat and near-naked bodies.

Right leg bent. Ninety degrees. Arms overhead . . .

The accepted code. Assumed and dissolved barriers.

Don't look.

As in the city. On the subway. Don't stare. Rule of the wild.

Look and look away.

Pretend this is not ridiculously sexually revealing. Titillating.

Act like we're all just bodies. Single sex. Doing our thing together. One gender under God. (*Brahman?*)

Not men and women. Mingling in this lubricious and steamy almost-orgy. Controlled erotic ritual.

The seductive repetition. Day after day.

Transfixing *asanas.* Connected like words. Living sentences.

Internal effort. Athletic prowess. Erotic magnetism.

The familiarity of faces. Constellation of heads. Solo planets. Some have gravity. Some are unseen.

Ruddy moons. Lips and longing eyes. Going deep in.

Minds languorously opening. Eyes closed. Holding on. Letting go.

Shedding stories. Tensions. Visions. Toxins. Worse.

Tasting something sweet. Somewhere lovely. Behind consciousness.

This new thing. And ancient.

And always there. The familiarity. Compassion.

I know this. I know you.

Softened lives. Gentle faces. The intimate interflow.

Learning yoga's like learning a new kind of language. Body language. Life language. Mental. More. Get into it.

Like learning to read. A new kind of reading. Novel process.

With newfound senses. Attuned. Emerging subtle body. Soul.

A new kind of text. Spirit. *Asanas* the alphabet.

You start slow. Easy.

Short movements. Simple phrases. At first. Simple. Clear. Concise. You get it. (Like this.)

You get used to the first phase. Assimilate this new language. Process. Breathing. Awareness.

Awkward. Stilted. Also appealing. At first. The easy read.

Its simple rhythm. Elegant lines. The building blocks. Broken down. The music and magic of repetition.

Then you progress. To something more complex. Deeper.

When you're ready. By degrees of growth. Opening.

Something shifts. like this. Into the next phase.

When the dimension deems. a new element arrives.

A small change. but significant.

Different now. But also the same. but deeper. something more. maybe more intimate. apt. noticeable. nice.

Like this the practice evolves. in you. You evolve in the practice.

You do the poses. Or do the poses do you?

The practice is a breathing alphabet you build into *asanas*. The *asanas* build into you. Moving toward longer living sentences. where *asana* clauses animate. pause. combine in *vinyasa*. Deeper meaning. Later.

Here now. A new sensation. within the familiar. to work with. work in. go with.

And these people are a part of it. This change. in you. this dimension added. this personal downshift. sidestep. uptick. is collective also.

Also sexual. Because yoga's like sex. without the ecstasy. over the top. But something close. kindred. calmer. bliss. but diffuse. delivering. the dimension.

Sex is like yoga but with the full play. power. mystery mess. of the other. the lesser or greater god. (lust or love.) (or *God?*) depending.

A yoga crush may or may not turn into a real crush. Just as an energetic affinity. With a yoga brother or sister. May or may not turn into a real friendship. Or a yoga crush. Or a real crush.

But they often do.

Advice to guys out there whose wives. girlfriends or boyfriends are into yoga. who are talking a lot about some yoga teacher? or yoga *friend*.

If you want to hold on to your partner. Get yourself a mat. Restructure your schedule. your life. And get in there to those yoga classes.

Same goes for women. Gals maybe more so. (Consider nature. the ratio. free radical odds.) (and the NY ratio.)

There's nothing innocent. or minor. or *only yoga.* about yoga.

If anything it's the other way around. Yoga is not the

fad of the day. or of the decade. Like jogging or aerobics the decades before. Jump on the bandwagon.

Or it is that. But it's also more. Way more. For the real practitioners. of the real deal. Drink the Kool-Aid.

(Even for those who don't really know what they're doing. Yoga transforms in spite of you.)

The yoga clarity feels like a fresh planet. What we need!

It's like being early for once. Again and again. Instead of late. in a hurry all the time.

The harried rush. Flushed away. Left behind in the disappearing flux.

Everything leading up to one's arrival here is suspect. Under review. in the new magnifying now.

Breathe in. Soulful scrutiny. Dark shadow stuff. Painful feelings.

And sacred. Because it led you here.

Breathe out. Release. Light. Hope. Calm kindness. Love.

There are lots of different kinds of yoga crushes.

DIFFERENT KINDS OF YOGA CRUSHES

-Across-the-room yoga crush

-Close-up crush

-Yoga-buddy crush

-Mystery crush (Who's that guy/girl?)

-Rarely seen (similar)

-Fresh crush (new person/fresh meat)

-Like-the-body yoga crush (but not the face)

-Like-the-body-and-face (but not the personality)

-The ol' don't-know-why-I-like-that-one-but-I-do crush

-The personality/energy (but not really the body)

-Love-the-body (but . . .)
-Love-the-body-and-face (but . . .)
-Dig the whole body/face/person/soul package (but why can't she be smart?)
-Like/love-the-practice yoga crush (energetic)
-Like-the-elusive-presence (spiritual crush?)
-Yoga teacher crush (prevalent)
-Teacher-student crush
-Not serious crush (but there)
-Your friend's friend
-Your girlfriend's friend
-Girlfriend's girlfriend (etc.)
-Gay crush
-Gay-hetero crush
-Hetero-gay crush
-Lesbian crush
-Any permutations of the above. Secret or obvious

And on it goes. and on..

I had a yoga-teacher crush on Rita. I admit. At first. Kept me coming back.

Along with Amanda. others.

Whatever gets you out of bed. as Scott would say.

Big part of the practice appeal. But was it her? or the practice?

It was her in the practice.

Sometimes I imagined it going further. Into actual life.

Maybe our limited conversations only needed time. familiarity.

Or more. A kiss. or less. Or more!

Dissolve the barrier. Lubricate ease. Access nature. Transform spirit. beyond yoga stuff.

I'd sometimes run into her outside practice. On the

street. In front of the green vegetables at Commodities. roots. in bins.

We'd kiss and hug. Lit to see each other. Curious how strong our connection was. without really knowing each other. In the usual way.

She wore clothes. Jeans. A black-and-blue North Face shell. Hair neatly back in a braid. taut.

Her teeth white and long. Scary in her protuberant smile. Bursting out of her skull. Like a horse. Or quasilascivious.

The possibility flashed on and off. at first. But that didn't last long.

But the practice attachment did. Once I got to know her a little there was no way.

But the intimacy was real. I loved her as my yoga guide. honor her here.

In Buddhist iconography we come across the image of two women, one on either side of the Buddha. Or a chair. Or a tree. (Early versions of the Buddha.)

They represent the guides (*bodhisattvas. angels*) on the path. (*Dharma. Sadhana.*) Those who lead us there.

Amanda's voice came down the stairs.

"No Rollerblades up the stairs."

I looked up at her.

"Busted."

I started to go back down.

"Kidding!" she gleefully shouted out. lopsided grin. looking down from up the stairs. over the banister.

This was a healing time for me. I'd been sick. lost.

I'd been half-asleep. dreaming. alone. waiting. coiled. burrowing. dawdling. cycling. downwardly dwindling. Stuck.

Working but not really. All process. nebulous production. direction. low actual output.

Puttering in my studio. Sort of stumped but bumbling along. bruised grace notes blooming in my head. imaginary. imagining imaginary things. My father in his basement.

I hadn't shown in years. Okay. Now I was awake again. Climbing back into life.

RamAnanda's underground reputation was growing.

Aboveground. going mainstream. Other yoga centers were popping up everywhere and growing as well. In New York. LA.

Across the weird wired new virtual country between. (our ears.) dot-com. Before that bubble burst. but also kept going. e-everything. i-stuff. (made in China.)

America was learning to *om.* (*made in India.*)

Frankie and Jonni's dream coming true.

(*Ka-ching!*)

RamAnanda was known as *the* cool place to practice. hands down. Hippest crowd. most intense classes.

Hands together over your head!

This was before yoga was everywhere. in magazines. in ads. in movies. in every dot city.

Before yoga mats were a de rigueur accessory. (Let alone the yoga mat shoulder bags.) Seen carried on every other block. like so many personal battering rams. to battle the mortal ills. slings and arrows. lovers and bills.

Urban. postmodern. The millennial malaise. post-everything. The feeling something was really wrong. seriously out of whack spiritually.

This was the beginning of the yoga boom.

2. Lafayette

The new RamAnanda was totally slick. Upscale address. just down from Astor Place. The Public Theater. Indochine and Blue Man Group.

The balconies and French-door garret windows of that blackened building like Paris. fluted Corinthian columns eaten away like sugar. a bit burnt. by acid rain or ozone. or time.

Above Crunch. Big bike rack on the sidewalk shared with the Crunchies. You can see in. their plate glass storefront. frenetic aquarium workout scene.

TVs all over the place. news on. sports. unheard music thwumping. gals on treadmills in exercise bras. boytoy guys. etc.

Elevator up to the third floor. No Rollerblades In Lobby. Sometimes the elevator would stop on the second floor. doors open to suspended punching bags. new. blue.

CRUNCH emblazoned on them in a punched starburst. immaculate room. black rubber floor. no one there. Like an enviable Jeff Koons installation.

Or more Damien Hirst. except carcasses implied. live. are us. you. Or so the doors would open to beefy guys in boxing gloves pounding away. grunting. sweating. carnivorous slime.

Another brilliant William Winslow living art installation! So conceptual it was never made. seen only in the fleeting perception. exists in the mind only. here. now. later. never.

Antiyoga realm in there. Like a slaughterhouse. except lab sterile. padded. no blood. they the meat. you. human menu. hanging from hooks.

Wry comments from the elevator (refrigerator) packed with pacifist yogis. yoginis. and maybe a silent (American) Indian. big round dude. braids. going up to the tribal office.

Flyers in the lobby sometimes for ritual dances. drumming circles. Chief from *Cuckoo's Nest.* some chief sage. his nature name. Falling Elevator.

And the nicotine/caffeine-anxious-but-clean pre-yogis. at noon and six. heading up to meetings (AA/NA). something wrong written in their faces. urban-eaten. defeated. one calm one. (innate yogi).

The doors opened at the third floor to a fully stocked yoga boutique. A catalogue come to life. It was like a joke.

Statues of Krishna. Ganesh. Hanuman. Shiva. Brahma & Co. lined up above the bookshelves. little and bigger. the whole holy roster. in order of height.

Full CD rack. vertical. rotating. chanting hits. Ambient "meditation" music. ocean sounds. Racks of clothes. mats and mat bags. those flat wooden incense boats you think you could use. etc.

Whispers. fears that they were *going commercial* were garishly surpassed.

Reception desk to the left. outfitted with three computers. (wo)manned by bright bewildered young yogini chickies. open wet mouths. Amanda's charges. freshly minted RamAnanda T-shirts. black.

New green antitheft rental mats. RamAnanda towels. also green. folded behind the girls.

They even sold. not kidding. RamAnanda water. their own label. a cobra. along with various juices. in the Fresh Samantha cooler.

On the long bench people shed shoes. milled. laughed. looked around. Checked out the big coat/shoe room. Racks with hangers you can't take off. Cubbies to the ceiling.

Opposite the purple wall a fountain. travertine tile. water nimbly raced down the uneven surface. mesmeric. pleasant fountain trickle. bucolic plash. burble. into the trough people dropped pennies into. Wish for love.

And the pretty big dressing rooms. Curtains over opposing entrances. men. women. A flash of white flesh. when the curtain opens for a second. camera aperture. between classes. a bent-over bottom. (*Look/look away.*)

No Shoes Beyond This Point. computer printout page. taped on the fluted cast iron column. painted ceiling turquoise. mottled sponge technique.

A world unto itself. like a set. for a play. for a game show. RamA Las Vegas. the joke going around.

Tonight was the big gala opening. Floating faces. familiar bodies. all the fishies swimming around in their new purple tank. nosing every corner.

Elements carried over from the old place. A chakra chart. color-coded. Painted relief of Arjuna on the field of battle. rows of bows and arrows. Charioteer Krishna. blue-faced. confused.

Same altar photos from *the old place.* Frankie and Jonni's pantheon. Their personal yoga/rock-and-roll hall of fame.

Ensconced in a big fancy altar. high wide alcove. recessed lighting. elaborate frame. florally jigsawed plywood painted gold.

Already it was *The Old Place.* The sacrosanct sanctuary so readily abandoned.

So much intention cooked into those walls. the living psychic lung. oasis inner space. the quiet place. supercharged with Shakti. concentrated energy. spiritual exertion. libido. cosmic reach. a living temple.

The new practice rooms were impressive. One wall all new double windows. onto Lafayette.

White propeller fans under the wavy cement turquoise ceiling. Black box speakers nestled in corners. snugly snaking wires. well-clamped.

Shiny new oak floor. big open space. Except at the back there was *a stage?* What was that about?

Two feet high. thirty by thirty feet. easily. Sticking out like a barge. The surface was a flesh-colored single sheet. (Caucasian.) some kind of heavy-duty linoleum/urethane flooring.

Coltish girls soon discovered you could slide in your socks on this surface. really far. with a running start. Much dissent/discussion about *the stage.*

"It's a totally ugly waste of space."

"No it's not. You can practice on it."

"It cuts off the room."

"It's like a big truck parked in the back of the room."

"Who would want to practice up there?"

"I would!"

"You *would*."

RamAnanda was like a sitcom. dot-com. an excellent smash-hit HBO series. with streaming realistic dialogue you overhear. underdressed babes and countless subplots blooming. serious but also feel-good. real good. Like Rama. real.

The removable wall separating the two practice rooms had been removed for the festivities. Heavy solid-core wood panels. stained. interesting wood-grain patterns. opposing book symmetrical. all sexual. (Rorschach.)

There was also a smaller practice room in the back. one wall all mirror. For Basics classes. Pregnancy classes. Baby and Me. HIV.

And even smaller rooms for privates. on the way back there. And offices. from which Amanda emerged. floating. on cue. theme song rising from the big room behind me.

Her flowing baby blue dress. from India. to the knees. barely sleeves. slits on the sides. same cotton/silk material skirt underneath to bare ankles.

Her (always) bare feet slapping. like a cavewoman. surveying her scene. her girls. chicky-fluffy hair belying all-business eyes. striking blue. enhanced now by the sky-blue lift of her outfit.

Just as her lovely face. gently upturned. rare among ordinary others. was enhanced by my enhancing gaze.

"What's up with that meditation room?" a girl-voice averred. I softly yeahed.

Amanda shrugged. "Let's go in." led the way. our plotline clear.

The scene's obvious offering was a big plastic sort of

igloo parked at the corner of the lobby. Stoop to go in. stupid little Disney door.

Not exactly peaceful inside the meditation hutch. like being inside an enlarged model of a stomach. The fiberglass walls were not sound-insulated.

In fact they seemed to pick up sound. conduct and reverberate. the various voices and noise in the lobby. like being inside a big ear.

"Om shantih," Amanda sort of bellowed. loud low vibrato whisper.

She often mocked this whole yoga thing. Answering her phone *"Namaste."* (not cell yet. next year.) when she knew who it was. (Caller ID.)

Tonight was the big gala opening of the new center. A few days before was the more somber. less avidly attended closing ceremony at The Old Place.

Devoted to Ganesh. the fat elephant deity. candy addict. his little mouse friend close by. Remover of obstacles. expediter of transitions.

The gals were all dressed up. India/ashram style. for the festivities. saris. bindis. Played hostess in the lobby. showed people around.

In one of the back rooms an actual Indian woman was doing those henna temporary tattoos. (*mendhi.*) blood brown. five bucks a pop.

She came from Jackson Heights with a gentle stick-figure priest guy. loose white pants and shirt. performed a blessing earlier. attended by invited RamAnanda insiders. chosen yoga babies.

Sanskrit invocations.

Sita ram sita ram sita ram sita RAM!

Incense. sandalwood. camphor and various burned

offerings. Over the chemical new-beginning smell of fresh paint.

Amanda went off and then rejoined me for the opening chanting. building slowly. led by Jonni. Over an hour.

Shiva shiva shiva shambo-ho . . .

Followed by this big gentle bear of a man wrapped in sheets and prayer cloth. rough ropes of spiritually unwashed (*sadhu*) hair piled in a crazy beehive knot on top of his head.

Thumping one of his crossed legs against the floor like a swaddled amputee. this feral performer. head lolling. eyes shut. rolled back.

Channeled the music. ecstatic. savage. anima animal. ethereal/divine radio. rousing. transmitting signals from that other civilization. spirit dimension. crumbled centuries. rhythmic drones.

He rolled around in place. as he played his *sur bahar* (bass sitar). upright stringed instrument. a gourd with a shotgun. like it was alive. and wild.

And he was trying to tame it with his strange movements. hitting it. stroking spasmodically. with love. and keening. sacred Sanskrit invocations. incantations. bellowed. mumbled and moaned.

And instead of taming it. it possessed him. its raw spirit energy. electrocuted with magical music. which infused the room. the many rooms of the minds present.

I tipped toward her ear. She smelled nice. fresh.

"Who is this guy?" Like all pretty girls. "He's pretty incredible." Like her ear was a flower.

"That's Bhagavan Das. You don't know him? Yeh, he's great. Part of the family."

We sat. half lotus. on folded blankets. My knees hurt after not very long. lower back. Even though leaning back against a column. which helped. and being with her.

Boisterous finale. roundhouse rounds. Everyone seemed to know the words. this way of singing/ chanting. rocking a little in your seated position. get into it.

Pick one of the verses and stick with it. rise with it. into the building hastening frenzy hilt. of this woven crescendo dome of sound.

Then the abrupt halt. From which flowed the lovely long silence. aural dark mystic river. peace. a shuffle. a cough.

Eyes closed to the glorious vibration. palpable. single placeless spirit. here now. not a concept but felt. if you were into it. and felt it.

Frankie stood and spoke. low. serene. severe. also elegant in her folds. Hair slicked. parted like a book. long nose. look. hands. vision.

"It pains me to look at her," Amanda leaned into me. breath a warm cup of tea. jasmine. *mu.*

"Why?" I asked.

Though the answer was clear. A band of anguish seemed to bind her jaw to her forehead. spoon cheekbones. fierce evident skull. *memento mori.* the pain a big part of the teachings. hers anyway.

"I just think she's not very happy." *I'm the intuitive type, B.*

Amanda's compassion touched me. It felt good sitting beside her.

So different from Frankie's maybe sadistic psychic

intensity. The rest of the room nicely irrelevant. and also part of it. this big soft dimension. holding us.

These yoga gatherings made me a little uneasy. Who were all these weird people?

What was all this chanting and Hindu ritual? *Hare Krishna!?*

I didn't believe in this stuff. But I believed in sitting beside Amanda.

First up in the stage show was a tall teacher. Kim. elegant rare shorebird.

One of those women other women say she's so beautiful. Isn't she beautiful?

But guys go yeah. no. look at each other.

She slipped out from behind the black scrim. Then from the other side this shiny shaved-head gay guy I'd practiced near a bunch of times in the front row.

Fellow yoga addict/achiever. longest lowest *omm* in the room. booming at the end of class. and the beginning.

They took their places. eyes met for that moment of mutual performance/soul-assurance. The music that came on was rock-and-roll.

I knew this song.

The dim room a crop of heads. everyone sitting on the floor. freer in this new vibe.

I liked this song. But what was it?

The two dancers moved around and on each other, in and out of *asanas.* like a sex manual. (*Kama Sutra.*) I didn't say to A.

Folding together. stretching apart. attached. in all these careful extreme ways. undersea waves. They were good.

It was that Patti Smith song "Holy." Allen Ginsberg's words (was it?) sung in her taunting haughty punk style. fed up. fuck you. But singing. well. not just yelling at you.

The strong shiny gay guy held Kim up and she did some incredible backbend bow contortion. up over his head. her head. eyes. near her negligible perfect butt.

As Patti Smith spat it out. holy everything. holy New York. holy Los Angeles. holy cock. holy asshole.

This was a spiritual path I could believe in.

This girl Kim was one of the *ashtangis* (ashtangess). meaning she did *ashtanga*. a whole different level.

If this was a glimpse of later. where this path is headed. I'm getting out of here.

Peek in the room where they're doing *ashtanga*. it's a whole different world. vibe. exertion. concentration. body language. *dense.* daunting. nobody talking. intense. *italicized.* but calm.

The next guy in the show was no *ashtangi.* Blond sun/body/self-worshipper from California. solo show-off primadonna. the tats. the pecs. the whole package.

Stupid golden hair that doesn't go with New York. I'd seen him around. you couldn't miss him.

A explained he was Jonni's latest adopted yoga pet. Recent import. big plans for little buff guy.

Totally gay but didn't know it. yet. totally devoted to Jonni and Frankie. Their next triangle project. perfect.

He had this aerial lift thing going in his circus act. slo-mo levitating jump-throughs. handstand to crow to side crow.

He seemed to do the whole thing without touching the ground.

"That's not yoga," Amanda said. not derisively. "It's magic."

And I believed in sitting beside Amanda. and practicing beside Amanda. or near.

Consider all the efforts you make in a life. constant, unending. to find a place where you feel you fit.

When you find it, this is something supreme. to be embraced. Mysterious elements line up. within. without. beyond.

We return. When it keeps working. we keep returning.

The yoga practice rewards you. You stick with it. go deeper in. because it worked before. gets better. because it feels so right.

Like any addiction. Like love.

Frankie or Jonni or Rita or any good teacher might take it a step further and say.

It is *love. The higher love you never got. Everything we do is toward God.*

A shrine sprang up, the way you see them sometimes on a sidewalk when someone who shouldn't have dies on the street there by freak accident. random violence. another urban incident. statistic. bad luck. sad story. It grew around the big black cube sculpture at Astor Place you can push and rotate if you push hard enough, as the wayward teens sometimes do, gathered on the median triangle island where shirt-flapping skateboarders hop the curb with their slap, scrape and scoring sounds, stopping traffic, checking each other out, darting about, and watched by baby-faced goth kids, black-clad stoners, heading in the wrong direction together, like bats hanging out afternoons and all day on weekends and into the lurid orange-amber overhanging Astor night. It grew to a garden of flowers in their cellophane wedges and deli paper, like the vast art installation outpouring aproned outside (empty. conspicuously) Buckingham Palace, pouring out, when Lady Di died, but local Saint Amanda proportions, lots of candles and cards and whatnot clustered and littered around. candies. Little statues of Hanuman and Dancing Shiva and a big fat Ganesh someone left. a picture of Guruji. one of Amma. a black-and-white print of Anandamayi Ma, very cool, which I wanted to take, looked like a film still from her life I should make, at least write, at least imagine, seated there looking out-of-this-world stoned and sexy. *om* stickers and a Hello Kitty plastic lollipop mirror. Sai Baba, his big fro. a Barbie doll with the hair cut like Amanda's, it was kind of creepy, too voodoo, someone made a yoga outfit for the barefoot Mandy/Barbie, tank top and little cutoff sweats. one day in uncomfortable seated position, not the best lotus (*padmasana*) ever. Next day she'd be in down-dog. next day a headstand. Then someone brought a Ken, dressed as a fireman. a little surfboard appeared under his arm. around Big Ganesh's neck a string of mahogany Buddhist prayer beads. the red tassel. Many notes, a few photos, yoga cards, some drawings. streaked and swollen and disintegrated by rain. but replenished daily. Someone kept the shrine orderly and clean. many girl hands. women without children. without men. (yoga instead of sex. yoga world instead of family.) plucked and tossed dead flowers. New flowers arrived every day. for a long time. Someone. guess who. painted a big splat red dot on four faces of the big black cube. It actually looked great. much improved. like the Japanese flag, but on black. cubed. signally potent, formally complete. Saint-marking the place. what happened. Announcing the great absence. Gone to India.

Over the street entrance on Lafayette. below the big gorilla hand squeezing the word *CRunCH.* atop the turquoise word *RamAnanda.* sat a big red *om* symbol.

First morning of practice at the new center was a murky low-ceilinged London morning. Buddy and I arrived at the same time from opposite directions.

"Auspicious day," he said. In we went. and up.

The partition wall was back in place. all the panels with opposing wood-grain patterns. People sniffed suspiciously around the stage like dogs.

Which way do we face? The room was virgin. no teacher. vibe. spirit. yet.

No Amanda. Long Kim by the altar wall already well into her swan practice. as if she'd spent the night here. in her deep attainment. just kept going.

The east windows a wall of prerain suspended light. Maybe ten of us for the opening chant. led by Frankie. still crusty with sleep. Marigolds still there. also tired.

Then everyone went off into his and her own adventure. the long sentient swim through still space. inner/outer. breathing. different for each person. It was like being inside the hold of a new ship. liner. chamber of the sea. a shell. a safe harbor shelf in the mad city mind. the self.

The Old Place had a creaky floor. the old ship groaning. speaking.

This pristine new floor was eerily silent. as if less soulful. less interested. interesting. less listening.

Buddy and I liked practicing together. in sync. at least at the start. today especially. We pulled each other along nicely. created a smooth strong mutual energy together.

Amanda came in after fifteen/twenty minutes. in a slash kind of mood. dragging her mat. late in the standing poses. rested/tired. young/old. there/not there.

Face a little puffy from sleep/not enough. hair wet from a shower/bath. drying in licked petal/sprouts.

Slapped her mat down behind me and Buddy. And there was that feeling. You knew.

Ashtanga you do at your own pace. the pace of breathing. a walk through the park. picturing sky. go into the sky. No talking in the room. just the layers of breathing. and consciousness.

The bump sound of jump-backs. gentle occasional murmur of the teacher walking around. assisting here and there. A joke now and then. a laugh.

Fast people need to slow down. (New Yorkers. Type A.) Slow people need to speed up. (California.)

Tense people need to relax! learn to.

Strong people need to get flexible (guys). the more flexible (you gals) need to get stronger. You work toward the balance.

Yoga means union. (Don't forget it!)

You go on your own. every day (except Saturdays and moon days). advance at the pace of growth. *Ashtanga* is a fixed progression of *asanas.* unvarying. the traditional model most led classes are based on. improvised around.

Start with the standing poses. (Up-dog/down-dog. *Surya namaskara A, B.* Triangle. *Trikonasana.* etc.)

Get those down. remember the sequence. The teacher goes around assisting you where you need it.

At first you go only so far. When the teacher decides you're ready, he/she gives you another pose. after maybe weeks or maybe months. then another. the next. when you're ready.

Your practice lengthens. From under a half hour at first. to an hour and a half. after maybe a year. two. full primary series.

Two hours! primary plus first part of second series. maybe five years. You build up to it. over months. daily practice. except Saturdays and moon days (full. new). over years.

People used to come back from Mysore (India). practicing with Guruji. excited. *I got a new pose!*

For the rest of the year they'd practice up to there. get that pose down.

Return to India. hopefully get another pose..

When I first started *ashtanga* I watched. awed. the people who'd been practicing for maybe ten years. Crazy positions. refinements I couldn't even guess at.

Strength. smoothness. concentration/relaxation. The unbelievable things their bodies could do. like second nature. like circus performers. contortionists. with intention.

I wondered *What do they still get out of it? What, really, are they doing?*

Now that I'm one of the ones with a deeper practice. at it for a while. I look at the people just beginning. struggling. sweating, grunting. distracted. arms and legs and minds all over the place.

And I wonder *What are they doing? What do they get out of it?*

"We're all down in the mud. Who are we kidding?"

Rita had a healthy fed-up realist streak of spiritual skepticism. For a yoga teacher. At RamAnanda.

Her classes were intense. She began with a talk. Like all RamAnanda classes.

Her talks and the practice were a revelation. To this someone new to the practice.

The birth of the subtle body!

Everyone sat on their mats.

In a comfortable seated position.

Half lotus. Butts propped on a folded blanket.

Pert buns. Other forms. Sack of potatoes. Can of beans.

Rows on the two halves of the room facing each other.

Rita sat by the wall in the middle of the room. Between the two sides. A book beside her.

She'd apply the teachings to everyday life. Her own life. She'd talk about her relationship.

Because your life should be your practice. Otherwise what's the point?

How she and her boyfriend try to practice *mindfulness.*

You do asanas and get a good workout. You get strong, sit on your mat and get calm, sense grace, feel God, whatever. Good.

And how impossible it is to do this. In actual real life.

But then you go home and argue with your boyfriend. Or say something mean. Or avoid him so you won't argue . . . What is that?

We held our positions on the mats. Knotted. Erect. Aching. Dying to get out of it.

We call it gardening at night, when we argue at night . . .

Waiting. Trying to go deeper in. Tendons waiting for her little speech to end.

Nonattachment doesn't mean avoidance, people! It means the opposite.

A sustained forward bend. (*Paschimottanasana.*) Maybe fifty breaths. Sixty.

Fearlessly facing the things we need to face. Embracing our lives.

Long shoulder stand. (*Salamba sarvagasana.*)

All the tedious details and difficult conflicts down here in the mud.

Students would squirm with restlessness. Pain.

We live in New York City at the end of the twentieth century, people!

We are not sadhus in a stinking diaper eating bhang and a chickpea a month and living on a pole or sitting in meditation forever beside the river.

Knifesharp knee pain. This isn't yoga. This just hurts.

We are yogis in the Western world. I don't care about all this philosophy that says the things of the world aren't real! That's not real. This is the real world, people!

Your lower back would kill. You breathe through the pain. Into it.

Remember why we practice. It's all about love. Self-love. First. Not selfish love. But the divine right there within you. You know it's there! So you can spread that love . . .

Amanda's eyes closed like an angel's.

We don't practice yoga to be good at yoga. We practice yoga to be good at life!

Into and not into her talk. You and everyone.

Samadhi means same as the highest. We feel this when we practice. We're in touch with our real self, our higher Self—

Into and not into the practice.

She'd pick up the book beside her and read from a marked place.

After attaining the pure, nonreflective Samadhi, the Yogi gets "wisdom-filled-with-truth." This is the meaning of ritambhara. What is this actually? Patanjali continues by saying,

Okay, stand at the front of your mats with your feet together!

And the *asanas* would begin. Another class.

The choreographed continuum.

One *asana* to the next. One class to the next.

The breathing.

The intense workout.

The soaring something.

Another dimension. It was like diving into the water.

We were all little fishies. Swimming together in the school every day.

Moving together this way and that. Copying one another. Enhancing. In aqueous unison.

And at the same time everyone off on his and her own acrobatic thing. Exertion and access. Adventure. Of the mind.

And after class we'd *scatter.*

And return the next day. To do it again.

Amen.

Namaste.

It's like a drug. Except it's good for you.

(*Right?*)

Neither sport nor dance nor therapy nor religion.

But touching all those. Except better.

Exquisite exercise. Where we live.

Body prayer.

Active meditation.

It's a gift to your life.

A lovely discovery. Potent and subtle. It's like sex.

Amanda.

Rose!

Rita's departure left a hole in the RamAnanda community.

In the yoga-hearts. lotus blooms. in the mud. daily lives. of her abandoned fishies. slapping about. gasping. expiring on their mats.

If not on the schedule. or in attendance. The new place was booming right from the start. Classes were full. even off-hours during the day.

Amanda was now on the schedule. purportedly filling in for a few classes. for now. though she technically was still only a TT (teacher trainee). From then on she was always on the schedule. quickly shifting to the better slots. rising to her place as one of the main teachers.

The chants. the teachings. at the new place. at the beginning. were all about new beginnings. Jonni spoke about expectations.

So often they ruin experience for us. *Future tripping,* she called it.

We imagine how things will be. then believe it. count on it. And then are disappointed.

Expectation is a resentment waiting to happen.

Saturday Rose came to Frankie's class. A glint of gladness to see me.

My brother and sister were in town. I dragged them to the class.

They hadn't been bitten by the yoga bug yet. though

Kate was starting to get into it. going to classes now and then. up in Cambridge. To *Bikram*. where they crank up the heat in the room. better than nothing.

Started by a starfucker yoga teacher in LA. now owned a fleet of Rolls-Royces. a whole yoga empire. (not really yoga. but a good yogoid workout.)

Is trying to copyright the *asanas.* (So he'll *own yoga.* and all the rights to all the *asanas*!) Sponsored a yoga world championship.

And guess who won?! His winning quote was "I am the serenest!"

Rose a few rows away. looking good. tired. the weight of the world pulled her eyes down. shoulders. She soldiered on. dragged her ass in there. slapped down her mat.

And of course I felt like it was my job to lift her. After class we put on our shoes side by side. walked down the stairs and out together.

Sister Kate was already outside. like a rapper she'd swiftly hand-signaled *cell phone* (thumb/baby finger. to mouth/ear).

Brother Bob was lagging behind. This was the family/sibling dynamic.

Me in the middle. the glue. my role. my art. my problem. the hole. I explained to Rose that Kate had four girls back in Boston. and all hell broke loose when she left.

Her husband was a softie with them. It was a *Daddy holiday!* whenever Katie left.

In fact brother Bob was already outside. standing. sort of sunning/meditating. lurking. eyes closed. leaning against the building. When I spoke he opened his eyes without expression.

I introduced him to Rose and he smiled double-wide. Rose is a babe. Bob a bit of a lone wolf.

His steadily balding head a balloon slowly inflating with years. debt. flight. doubt. fear.

She asked him what he did. His answer might have amused me. except he was my brother. "I have different projects going."

Hands deep in khaki pockets in a certain shifty way. shoulders hunched. arms straight.

He was a venture capitalist. so-called. trying to ride the miracle e-wave. with other people's money.

But his life. fabulous invisible mountain range of finance. hushed finesse. speculation avalanche. was crumbling around his ears. squinting. one eye shut.

Exquisite October light. sharp shadows silkscreened over the architecture. long triangles. his chipped tooth from fifth grade. recess.

Cheevers makes the save! with his face. the little triangle chip. He used to stick a straw in it. sort of whistle through it. *lithp. Pleathe. Thtop it.*

He already talked that way. then when he chipped his tooth it was like an excuse. explanation. He lived like that. still.

His wife had left him. again. He was fabulously in debt. juggling. scrambling.

But it wasn't real debt. he'd explain. it was possibility. seeds. rubbing his stubble with the knuckle-backs of his fingers. his signature distracted upward strokes. pained little wince.

A musician between songs. trying to figure it out. waiting for it to come to him. Defendant waiting for the jury. It was complicated. (always.)

I saw Rose saw him. Soft nod. knowing expression. also sympathetic.

How could I feel closer to her. whom I hardly knew. than to my own brother? my sister. my flesh and psychopathology. strange movable home-head. you always want to move out of. and always come home. are already there.

Sibling sameness and otherness. So many of the same entries. images. etc. in the mixed-up personal misinformation encyclopedia of the psyche.

Sister Kate gravitated back. as she wound up the phone call. finger raised. one last point. negotiation. dramatization of how it is with us. between siblings.

Apart but in sight. holy but far. loop back. then spin and lean away again. gyroscope leaning away. but holding. there and not there. hologram family.

"Damage control," she rolled her eyes. amused surrender. just like Mum. Acceptance! Where do they get that?

Rose was heading uptown. walked with us for a bit. We were going to Angelica for lunch.

When we parted she said a soft "Seeya."

And to Bob. and I liked this. "Good luck with those projects."

She was barely out of earshot. she had a nice walk. hip-hugger bells. ringing away from me. when Bob goes "You have two girlfriends?"

Before class I'd introduced him to Amanda.

Kate read the menu carefully like it was a test. Bob went straight to the answer key on the back. vegan glossary.

"What are all these things?" *Arame. gomasio. seitan. umeboshi. tempeh . . .*

The menu had the answers ready. The vegan roster. entering the lexicon. (slowly. at last.)

Kate closed her menu. decision made. I thought she was going to say what she was getting.

One of the specials. bad pun/koan title. We Only Harvest Sunflower Seed Croquettes (millet-quinoa) (pr. *keen-wah*).

But what she said was "You guys, Dad has cancer."

Rita had her following. Her boy-fishies. Aspiring eels. Shiny-slick. Me among them. Her classes were full. She was my yoga bootcamp drill sergeant. My first teacher. *Hari om.*

But Jonquil and Frankie were the main draw at RamAnanda. They were the founders. The driving force. Stars of the show.

They'd started out in the late eighties in a basement space on Avenue C. Three students became five. Six.

Before this was India. Studying yoga with different teachers (gurus). Also upstate.

They were strange people. Hippie lesbians. Socially maladroit. But also appealing. Kinda cool. Kinda not.

Something special showed. Even shone.

Adept at the practice. Steeped in the teachings.

Good teachers. Naturals.

Maybe they weren't so good in an everyday encounter. But get them in a room with mats on the floor.

People on the mats. Seals on our rocks. Awaiting instruction. Slapping tails. Flapping fins. Open needs.

Then they knew what to do.

Cat. Cow. Upward-facing dog . . .

They made no bones about stressing the spiritual side of yoga. Indeed that was their mission.

Jonquil was meek as a mouse. In appearance anyway. Outside the yoga room.

In reality she had a double demeanor. She appeared to move close to the ground. Quickly along the edges.

A pert little woman who always wore pink. Not everything pink. But something she wore always had to be pink.

Even if it were only the woolly caterpillar hair elastic she'd wear around her wrist. Like a sweatband. Or around the forearm. Or bicep. Where a cobra tattoo snaked around her upper arm.

Multiple earrings. Diamond zit on her nose. Short hair mouse gray. Cut to a rigid military brush cut. Always trim and clean. *Sir yes sir.*

Steel dark ice eyes. Dark eyeliner. Sometimes some pink on the hidden round of the upper eyelids. Her eyes were habitually downcast. So the pink was revealed.

She couldn't look you in the eye. Except when she was teaching. When she had the power. When you couldn't look back. She had eyes like a wolf.

In reality she was a lion. I.e., when she was teaching. Her eepy tender little mouse voice was replaced by a bold tenor bullhorn. The schizophrenic shadow sister. Stepping out and enlarging.

Where did *that* come from?

Her real self. Or so she'd say.

Her compact field mouse body became a field commander's brisk swaggering machine.

Striding the rows of her writhing foot soldiers. Twisted. Prone. Wounded. Breathing? *Breathe!*

Like some rock stars who are tiny. Or movie stars.

Who came to her classes. And whom she loved more than other people.

Other people were mere mice. (Because she was a mere mouse.)

Stars were where it was at for Jonquil. Outsize. Eroticized. She loved the stars. And she wanted to be a star. A yoga star. And so she was. Becoming one.

Her given name was Joanna. As a teen hippie lesbo-feminist she changed it to Johnna. Psychedelic Haight-Ashbury runaway. Grateful Dead. Jimi. More Janis than Joni.

Became Jonquil when she morphed (not that far) from tripped-out tie-dye flower-power druggie-hippie into a flowing robe flower-power hippie-healer type.

Boulder days. Herbs. Crystals. Drumming circles. Sweat lodges. Prayer circles. Chanting. Yoga. India.

Where she met Frankie. More Shiva than she. Became Jonni.

Frankie looked like a man. Tall. Elegant. Handsome. Like Fred Astaire. But severe. Dark hair perfectly wet-parted on the side. Retro. Sharp.

But Frankie was a woman. Technically. If not really.

If you liked her look she was lean. Epicene. Androgyne.

To some she was way too skinny. Self-starved. Gaunt. Like a hypodermic needle. *She's sick.*

Dried out. Brittle like she'll break. Snap in half. In backbends. (If you got to see her. In *ashtanga*.)

Her walking-around demeanor was as fierce as Jonni's was meek. As fierce as J's was teaching.

Whereas Frankie's teaching demeanor was enlightened-soft. A radical tone shift. Her compassion zone. The caring gentle core of another militant radical feminist general.

Heavy beetle brows perpetually pitched in a disapproving frown. Like an angry saint. Bristled as she drove a point home.

Her full mouth pursed when she paused. Striking hollow cheeks. Her cheekbones said more than her sermons.

Her long veined arms. Man hands. Bone hips.

Renunciation embodied. The focus on the Other Thing. Finely braided muscles articulated devotion. Ribbony ripples. Each controlled or casual movement.

A living ad for her message. Walk the talk. Sit it.

Frankie was ardent. Earnest. But also caustic. Verging on cynical.

Sometimes scathingly funny. And the acerbic New York edge gave worldly credence to her otherworldly sincerity.

The clearwater spiritual teachings didn't seem softheaded coming from this jaded warrior of the real world.

Jonquil took Frankie's classes. And Frankie took Jonquil's. Always back-to-back. Frankie and Jonni. Always their mat in the back-row corner by the door on the Second Avenue side.

They tried to show there was nothing New Age about yoga. Indeed yoga was ancient wisdom. Revival. Awakening of the spirit. Abiding. Sterling. Universally true.

But something about their act seemed distinctly *New Age*. In spite of them. And indeed because of them.

Quirky assertions.

Bad actions are bad. Bad words are worse. Bad thoughts are worst of all.

Seemingly stupid. Or in fact very wise?

Curious airy interpretations.

You are not what you think.

Facile quantum spiritual assumptions. or profound.

The witness inside consciousness watching your thoughts and feelings is God within you.

Slick phrases.

As in the practice.

Mixed into the message.

So in the life.

Ridiculous titles of workshops. On flyers. At Omega.

Pranayama Weekend: Breathing with Your Higher Self

Their eventual injection of peace and love and *om* into the money mainstream. In this in no way were they from another planet. Another plane.

Meditate. Levitate. Talk about it. Astrally project however mightily they might. .

They ran a business. They were teachers. Good teachers. They had an act. And they had their act down. They were pros.

They taught that yoga was not a sport. But a spiritual path. A way of life.

They knew what they wanted to say. And how to get it across.

Bob Dylan. #1 guru.

(I agreed with them there.) (Even if Bob didn't. Wouldn't.) (Part of the Bob appeal.)

And what they gave was authentic. Impassioned. If maybe not exactly the Vedic tradition. Or not strictly. Not only.

But Sanskrit strands. Stripped down. The gift of yoga. Passed along. Appealing. Seemingly authentic. If adapted. Easy to use. To us now.

Jaya guru de-va-a-a . . .

Conveyed through the practice. Repetition. Refinement.

Ommm . . .

Beatles a close #2. Saint John. St. George.

Nothing's gonna change my world . . . Harrison.

And through their continuous talks. A bit of performance thrown in. Harmonium. Chanting. (*Kirtan. Bhakti* yoga.)

Jaya Ga-nee-sha . . .

And some good old rock and roll. (Old.)

Jim Morrison's mystic slurry mumble.

Crank up the class. Crank up the heat. (*Tapas.*)

Generate some *Shakti.* Spiritual energy.

Van Morrison's slurry mystic mumble.

They truly believed in the spiritual power of yoga. And their talent and duty to spread it. Teach it.

Create community. *Satsang.*

And they taught great yoga classes.

Strenuous adventures. Sweaty. Adroitly choreographed workouts. Continuous movement. (*Vinyasa.*)

A full-body conversation. Strategic holds. Each class. Each breath a piecemeal conversion.

And the mysterious *ashtanga.* More advanced. Early morning. Intense. Complex. Calculus instead of this easy math.

Intimidating. But appealing. When you caught a glimpse. Like seeing your future. Pulling you there.

There was a reason their classes were packed. That people kept coming back. RamAnanda was booming.

Amanda pretty much ran RamAnanda. She worked for Jonquil and Frankie. She was one of the original few over on Avenue C.

Back when she hit bottom. And rose in undersea slow motion through the (yoga) motions. Through the seasons floated back to the surface. Turned back to life. On a leaf. (Lotus.)

She rolled out of bed on Avenue B and onto a life raft mat on Avenue C. Yoga saved her. Jonquil and Frankie.

Twisted. Bent back toward the light. A plant alive again. Lotus girl. A soul saved.

The teachings healing. Trickling in. Something. The practice. Its recursive magic. Absorbed. Transformative.

Ha *means sun.* Tha *means moon.* Hatha *means sun and moon.* Yoga *means union.*

First she swept up. Folded mats and blankets. For class credits.

Of mind. Body. Spirit. Masculine. Feminine. Darkness. Light. The eternal yin-yang.

Are the kinds of things they'd say in the classes. They stuck or didn't. Something sank in.

All the sayings. The traditions. Take your pick. Just because they're cliché doesn't mean they're not true.

Then she worked the door. Really the top of the stairs. And office work. For pay. She was the staff.

RamAnanda got popular. The community swelled. Around us. Among. We were the core. Rose with the level. A staff grew under her. Barefoot. Bushy-tailed.

By the time I went there she pretty much ran the place. She didn't teach yet.

There was a new teacher training program. In its second year. The first bunch of teacher trainees (TTs) had been recruited from among core (hardcore) regular students.

Now they taught. At RamA and elsewhere. Health clubs. Private lessons.

Someone asked Amanda if she was going to do the teacher training program. It seemed weird she hadn't already.

Her practice was better than most of the new teachers'.

"Why does everybody have to teach?" she replied. "Why can't anyone just practice anymore?"

Which I liked.

When you like someone do you like what they say because you like them? Or do you like them because you like what they say?

We were sitting on the bench after class. People streaming by would greet her. She always had a wise-crack ready. Or it just came out.

"Don't ask me. I just quit!"

Which I loved.

At *ashtanga* one morning in the good gray flux continuum Amanda needed to be dropped back. Frankie had left the room. Michael was making tea. small talk. out in the hall. I stepped up.

Doing backbends. wheel. (*Urdhva dhanurasana.*) near the end of the practice. last before finishing poses. you do three yourself.

Then you stand and get dropped back. supported in the arch. lower back. upper butt. to go deeper in. Walk the hands a little closer to the feet. arms straight.

I stepped up.

"I trust you." She smiled.

She showed me how. my foot between hers. I supported her lower back/held the top of her butt with both hands as she dropped back. the first. top of head to the floor. hold for five breaths.

I was afraid I wouldn't be able to support her for

this. but it was no problem. she was self-supporting. solid meets supple. Then four times. back and up again. smoothly rhythmic.

She was basically humping my thigh every time she came up.

"That okay?" I asked.

"Yeah, you're great." Face flushed.

The fifth drop-back, arms back. hands to the floor. into a human bridge. wheel. elevated bow. walked her hands to her feet like a circus act. trained chimp. upside-down. no prob.

I didn't try and reach down to pull her hands to grip her ankles. though they were right there. didn't want to slip.

But then she grabbed her ankles herself! one. then. garbled grunt. head red. about to burst. the other. Nice! Freak!

Michael came back in the room right then. blowing on a Chinatown mug of tea (Pearl River).

He put it down. beside the coconut. (symbolizing ego. crack it open.) garish Ganesh. little shelf by the door. semialtar. where teachers left keys during class. CDs. a mug of tea.

"I'll do that," he said. testy. terse mouth. thighs flexing as he strode over.

Amanda popped up. her head a beet. grape eyes (green. bled blue). bulging. big lemon wedge grin.

We lay splayed in *sivasana*. drenched. drying. dead/ deliciously dying. on our two blue life rafts. magic carpet mats. off in the astral zone. our own inner trips. near sleep.

Meditation's expanding inner chapel spell. molten

energy. morphing thoughts. radiant unconscious possibility. minimanic synaptic afflatus. images tumbling. separate but also symbioticosmically connected.

(Is the kind of exaggerated way I hyped it to myself.)

It was nice lying beside her. why not simply say.

We both felt it. I knew. you knew. towels draped over our corpses. neck to knees. arms a bit out. hands upturned. curled open. nearly touching. Later she said she knew. then.

Feeling the other there. the gentle thrum. proximal pull. subtle thrill. body electric. liminal. Enjoying those swimming endorphins. minds leaping. dopamine dolphins. subsiding. oneiric. subliminal. erotic. etc.

Out by the fountain after practice. gulping. licking itself. A talking to zap-haired Dina. I sat by them. put on my Rollerblades.

"You guys," Dina teased. meaning Michael. Only the teacher's supposed to do assists.

She leapt up as Sarita passed by. handed her a few sienna cards from a pack in her hand. Amanda already held one.

"Nice drop-backs."

"'Hanks."

"No, thank you."

"No, thank *you.*"

"You've got a good touch."

Amanda handed me the card she held. Another event.

"Dina's doing a slide presentation of her trip to India. Part of this whole India-theme thing, I guess, they're doing at this place over in the meat-packing district. You should come."

"All right. When is it?"

She snatched the card back and read from it. It was

on Tuesday. tomorrow night. We already had a plan for the next night. Wednesday. a grand group performance. friends involved.

Next morning we practiced side by side. in sync for a while. pleasant overt symbiosis. till she pulled ahead. *Sivasana* emo-osmosis again. eroto-.

We made a plan to meet that evening after the 6:15 class. which I took. might as well. Taught by Jen. sassy-ass drill sergeant. makeup. dyed black hair. China chop.

A had to work till then. Rose was in the class. a few away. friendly, but not too.

She wore (she didn't always) her bumblebee shorts. Once class started friendliness was a thing of another dimension.

We all became walleyed fishies. swimming in our own sweat. moving faster and harder.

Up-dog. down-dog. harder. faster. twisting. holding. deeper. further. To Jenifer's relentless insistent dominatrix commands and blasting tunes. saturnine/sappy.

I don't know if you could really call it yoga. but it was fun. She kicked our ass. Like she was training us. seducing us. challenging us not to be yoga pussies.

And of course everyone wanted to prove to her. to each other. *I'm not a yoga pussy!*

After class we walked west and uptownward. checkerboard style. to the dead meat district.

Warm clear night. warm for late October. but not for a California girl.

This happens all the time in palimpsestuous New York. The place we were going to was two doors down from where I used to live.

Before my paintings actually sold. The easy eighties. Before they didn't. before I stopped painting.

I held her forearm to stop her in front of 414 West Fourteenth Street (414W14). The door was different.

"I used to live here."

Clean new meat store. white bright fluorescent light. chopped corpse. Art! but already old hat.

"You did not."

What a surge when I got that lease! The first night in there I pounded bricks. with a five-pound sledge. out of a bricked-over window facing south. Living symbolism.

In the smashed indigo mouth. brick teeth knocked out. the sacred downtown skyline. dark blue. beyond condensed West Village rooftops. supine. all dressed in black.

Home-heads of SoHo. lips of building lit. outlined blocks. Tribeca rising. tessellated lights behind. the downtown towers. like crossword puzzles. figure it out. clues abound. everywhere in the addled city psyche.

The local glows. our packed fort of humanity. bunched asleep. safe and lovely. beneath the abiding robot peace sign of the World Trade Center twin towers. some actual stars. above.

Such energy back then. I could hardly contain myself. I couldn't. I didn't.

Now I had to do yoga for two hours every morning just to get the engine started. keep those demons downsized.

And then take a nap. before getting going.

And where did all that money go? And the easy flow of it.

Arrived like magic. remained in character. and vanished like magic.

This India Night event was happening next door to an old neighborhood transvestite bar with an excellent survivor/archival jukebox. r&b. obscure soul. funk. classic seventies and sixties rock. solid gold. feel old.

A liked this detail. Nodded thataway with her eyebrows. *Let's go.*

This place and Florent. his maps of imaginary cities over the booths. (all ports?) were the only places still here from before. plus the holdout packers.

Everything grew up around them. It was not yet all upscale and trendy. French bistros and airy architects' offices. lofts. Hotels. expensive clothing stores arriving. by night. like us.

The meat was still there then. Pastis not yet built. (Marble floor. field of fans design and installation. by William Winslow and co.) The disgusting death smell still hung and made you gag. The cobbled streets were still slimy.

Like the junkie tranny hookers servicing drive-bys way west. under the rusted high line. before it was the High Line. dark loading docks. weedy. smeared makeup. nobly wobbling on stilettos. wasted. the seedy chic noir cobbles.

"Around the corner from here's a famous s&m sex club. The Meat Locker."

"Sounds charming."

"It's unbelievable. What goes on in there."

Her arched eyebrows inquired. surprised and amused I knew.

"All kinds of rules and codes—like a yoga center. All types in there—businessmen, construction guys, closet kinky people—all joined by this passionate interest. *Need,* really. Wednesday nights are Pig Night. Only men. I didn't want to see that."

"You went there?"

"It was a project, with a friend."

"Oh, a project. With a *friend*."

"Yeah, a soundwalk of the neighborhood. Cool series. It's all about debasement, of course. That's what they get off on. They were debased as kids, and now they *need* it to get off."

"In de basement."

"Yeah. There were all kinds of things going on in there. The rooms got darker and smaller the deeper you went back. And more depraved."

"In da basement."

"Yeah, right, nice, yeah." I thought she'd heard enough. so I let it trail off.

"So then what?" But she wanted to hear more.

"So the guy who ran the place showed us around. He had his slave, a naked fat guy in spiked leather straps, dog collar around his neck, on a leash. Following him around on his hands and knees. Every once in a while he'd kick him, and the guy would wince, go *Oww,* then *Thank you, master.*"

"Shut up." Sly side of her mouth.

"I'm serious."

"Yeah, nice, right, yeh." She got me back.

Amanda waved to a cluster of characters arriving. One of the girls. flinty eyes. nose ring. made a face of amused nosy interest. flirty brows lifted. at what I was saying.

"And there was a guy with his balls nailed to a board. Everywhere in the shadows guys had their dicks out, jacking off. The rule is, no actual sex. Just acts, watching, and jacking off. Except in the dark back rooms . . ."

"Well, I hope this place is as exciting for you," she

said as we entered the space. club/gallery/happening kind of place.

Techno-Asian beats from a good sound system. speakers everywhere. chased coy little semisexy melodies around the connected darkish rooms. dot-to-dot.

Too-sweet incense mingled with cigarette smoke.

Yoga babes with tummies showing mingled with your standard issue New York dudes in their twenties. thirties. fresh upstart faces animated. long sideburns. fair youth voices fairly booming.

That buoyant fleshy brio of their freshly minted lives. unconscious confidence. careers. fortunes on the sure rise.

While their leavened bodies began. already. that long slow inverse crawl back home. the unseen decline. from brief stud six-pack abs. to so-what six-pack baby fat. little gut. love handles. swelling slowly or quickly into chronic long-term middle-aged pregnancy. (pregnant with their own deaths.)

"Come over here!" A bunch of friends saw Amanda.

"Look at this," I said. A video going of some crazy festival ritual in India (*Kumbh Mela*).

A massive mosh pit. everybody writhed and slammed around together. ecstatic. lashing each other with powders and paints. splashing incredible bright colors. shredding and spreading the spectrum.

It was a few days in spring. someone was saying. this holy festival when identities and caste distinctions are put aside. shaken up. like Mardi Gras.

Everyone mingles in this orgiastic chaos of music. color. movement. contact. trance-like dance. writhing knot of fleshy undifferentiated humanity.

Our crowd was a little more tame. standing there talking. holding drinks. Two out of ten were guys.

Maybe four out of the ten drinks were alcohol. the middle way. moderation. part of the new deal.

Meditation. not medication.

Plus lots of recovering alcoholics. addicts. in the yoga community. Yoga Sutras layer over the 12 Steps. (easier softer way.)

New addiction. better for you. Temperance the rule this time around. (if not exactly moderation!) (*ashtanga* is proudly hardcore.) not-so-gentle middle way.

I'd carried A's bag on our walk over. Now she put it on the floor. squatted there to pull out a tall bottle of Evian. like a clear skyscraper. classic baby blue cap.

She offered me some. I declined the Chrysler Building. She glugged about a dozen floors.

Claire was there. hips roving side to side in front of Dina and Sarita and someone else. nodding slowly. pony-tail. always. shy girl-smile coming slyly in and out of play.

Amanda led me to the next room. The music guy. going through the selections. all deejay serious.

We walked the rooms. In back was a bigger room. dimmer. deftly lit blue. No chained sex slaves. just a few tables and chairs. candles in glass.

Not many people back here. the music softer. it was nice. wandering in a warm cave and coming upon a cool lit pool. a candle floating there. little lady private dancer.

No big thrill. but better than that. far broader. the pleasant field of being with Amanda.

A beelined it over to her friend Sarah. I'd seen her often. but we hadn't really met yet. Soon to be known as Sarah1.

With her was a tall good definition of *handsome guy*. professional alpha. winning smile. white teeth. seen him around too. but less often. We talked knees sometimes in the men's room. y'know.

"They're like a brand-new couple," A whispered. Sarah heard her and bulged her eyes shut up.

"You guys wanna join us?" Sarah's pulsing face said go away.

"Let's let them be," I muttered.

"No, let's invade them." A slid into the chair between them.

On the way over A said she was hungry. She was talking to the right guy.

I told her I had some food. We give what we have.

I carry my canvas bag everywhere. filled with whatever you need. If I can't fit it in there I don't need it. is one of my guiding principles. the simple life.

I took out two blue-lidded Tupperwares. two plastic Chinatown bowls.

Two pairs of chopsticks. red enamel dots on the ends. in their woven sheaths sister Kate gave me for Christmas.

And two salmon-colored napkins with little gold leaves on them. from India. from that place on Spring Street. also a gift. from someone no longer in the picture. as my mother used to put it.

"Wow, you come prepared." Sarah1 looked genuinely sad.

"You don't get any," Amanda said. very much in the picture.

One container was filled to spilling with a nice pilaf of millet and brown rice (golden rose) with diced bok choy stems. plus greens. and toasted Mexican pumpkin seeds (*pepitas!*). tamari-roasted.

The other had fruit. sliced apples (Stayman Winesap! from upstate) and grapes (red, seedless. organic. California. non-union.) washed and plucked.

On a hidden bed of cashews (some roasted. salted. some raw and not salted. The girl at the cash register didn't like it when I mixed them in the same bag. but I did it.)

She was right, B. They're different prices.

"*Zowee*—this is the best apple I've ever had," Amanda beamed.

"It's a winesap," I explained. "From my guy at the farmers market."

"You're a winesap," she wisecracked back. Maybe the first? or not yet..

"Wow, you lucked out, Amanda," the guy said. Tree. for Trefon. he looked Greek. American. Also his height and oaklike bearing. "Where'd you get this guy."

"Picked him up off the floor. He was, like, lying on *myyogamat?*" Valley girl voice.

I didn't know Amanda was so funny. sassy. until we started. like. *talking?*

"Passed out."

"Poor guy. In a puddle of sweat."

"That was tears." My joke came out strange. as in *not funny.* Tree broke the not-really strangeness. or just wanted to jump in on our play.

"That was vomit and piss." Even not funnier.

"Lovely," Sarah intoned. her low droll deadpan drone.

"Help yourself, you guys," I offered. "There's plenty."

But they didn't. really. Tree took a token smile of apple. white and red as his good-guy grin.

"Wow, good," he enthused. Sarah was force-fed a few falling bites by Amanda. rice/pepita. The two chewed.

"Mmm," Sarah1 felt obliged to mrmr.

But A was way into the food. "This is *good!*"

Good! It was me. my love. going into her. via her stomach. seat of the soul. ancient love technique. enter via the eternal verities. thine appetite eyes. her happy mouth. into her blood. coursing cosmos. eros. her opening heart-head.

Ingested delight popping out her wet mouth. ingress. in welcome smacks and yums and buttery wisecracks.

Our delight drove the other two away. after first it drew them in.

We didn't eat all the pilaf. But we ate all the grapes. and every last chubby little cashew.

"'Slike peanut butter and jelly!" Amanda purred. Slumped in the plastic spoon-round chair across from me. content and comfortable. sated and looking at me. Fond and superfamiliar. easy.

Dina's slide show ran on a continuous loop in an open room near the entrance. A few chairs sat empty. A bunch of people sat on the floor in front of them. cross-legged.

Amanda too went right to the floor. I pulled a chair up right behind her.

She sat beside Jules. He pouted his lips out fishy style. they fish-kissed hello.

They held hands for a while. He smoothed his hand over her back the way you would a cat.

And she responded like a cat. leaning a little into him. She rested her head on his shoulder. for a while. recharge. safely.

The slides were good. for someone else's slides. She was a pro. our Ms. Dina.

You could feel her avid eye and eager imagination

leaping out to capture and savor the life and colors jumping out in kaleidoscopic mulligatawny India.

Rickshaws among cars. A cow.

Bright elaborate daily powder drawings on concrete in front of ramshackle houses.

Toothless grins. Rheumy eyes.

Women wrapped in vibrant saris. jasmine in their hair. Mad markets. Bright fabrics stretched over rocks to dry on the riverbank. quilted as far as the eye can see.

Yoga girls doing poses in front of desiccated stone temples. atop hills of stone stairs.

A leg straight back. body parallel to the ground (warrior three). like a figure skater. hands plowing forward in prayer..

It felt nice. so near A. I was behind her. leaning forward. nearly touching. How much did she sense me here. keenly rapt. keying on her?

Completely, B.

If Jules could touch her like that I could touch her like that too.

I touched her back. up near her shoulder. Not a graze or incidental leaning against her. but a definite hand on her.

She felt really good. I kept my hand there. and took it from there. Stroked her a bit. slowly. lambskin soft! under the silky hair. as if a surprise. And so it begins.

Found and softly traced the ease and acceptance. prodded the twin muscle snakes along her spine.

It's different touching not in yoga. just touching her.

Duh!

Her neck was surprisingly narrow and frail-seeming. though strong. trapezius bands bundled pretty tight. I prodded gently. played the tendons of tension. a little harder. loosened a suggestion. And so it goes. toward the only solution.

I pushed in her lower back. palming a shoulder. make her sit up straighter.

She turned her head and smiled. slumped again. It went from massage to petting to both. kneading. softening to strokes. caresses. We're in.

Walking on Gansevoort leaving we passed a couple. he a disheveled tall shipwreck. distracted. She a shipshape beauty. precise haircut. efficient stride. both in black.

In a split second you take it all in. Every day in New York. night. the layered human density. maze of desire in motion. the thousand glances meeting. flashes and signals. picked up and sent out. faces and meanings.

She caught my eye. I caught hers. and I imagined loving her more than Amanda. a whole life with her. Instantaneous.

The awful way that happens when you're with a beautiful woman you're kind of falling in love with. Guys know what I mean. And you see another. better.

Amanda seemed to pick up on it. and didn't seem to mind! She elbowed me discreetly. But not what I thought. A New York sighting.

"There's Monica Lewinsky," she whispered.

A chubby ordinary-looking girl crossed right in front of us. almost bumping into us. almost pretty. short. full lipstick mouth downturned. not wearing the beret.

I never would have noticed her. But the amazing thing was not that there was Monica Lewinsky.

But that the sharp-looking woman walking in the

other direction and passing us with the rumpled tall guy said the exact same thing as Amanda at exactly the same time.

A didn't notice. but I did. and the woman did. and we smiled at each other. kept going. off into our separate stories. maybe similar. but totally different trajectories.

Like two open books. briefly face to face. Where they touch. fleetingly overlap. the dialogue's the same. and the scene and characters.

Maybe what she said next was also the same as what Amanda said.

"Poor thing."

Which I thought was sweet. compassionate. But more what she meant became clear when she spoke again. once way out of earshot.

"She's gotten fat."

As we ambled east omnivorous night inhaled the hurrying people. everyone trying to escape. sucked them into bars. restaurants.

Melting down into the subway entrance at Twelfth Street and Seventh Avenue by St. Vincent's. the perforated Overbite Building. tinily tiled. contested. the usual developers. (overbiting.) vs. preservationists. (us. in spirit.)

And spat as many out its ubiquitous urban mouths. the doors of buildings. the other subway entrance across the bounding avenue. swarms. disgorged from the New School.

Foaming out of movie theaters. life again. this again. blinking. at the whelming tidal resumption of the real. versus their own dubious devices. within.

Glimpses of lives inside the ground floor apartments.

Buildings different personalities. but similar. like the people passing. also the blocks.

Spiffy and pedigreed (brick) beside a haggard brownstone brother beside a vine-infested goldmine. Doors different colors. stoops and stairs.

A wore sandals that had seen better days. her long ankles were lovely. bone. spoon. I asked her about her job.

"I love it and I can't stand it," she began. Conversation is good because it distracts the other speaking so you can look at her closely.

"I love it because of the people. My friends come and see me all the time. It's great. And I love the yoga . . ."

Her eye and then head turning followed some wacky guy on his tricked-out red bicycle sliding by like a one-man parade. mounted radio.

Reflectors and polished chrome. a horn. a bell. streamers and upright American and Puerto Rican flags rippling from the handlebars.

You see this guy around downtown. Lower East Side. The Puerto Rican Day parade for him lasted all year. day and night.

"That guy's great," she said.

"Yeah, he is."

"Reynaldo . . ."

"You know his name?"

"Yeah . . . Reynaldo."

I bumped her gently back to the shadow she slid from. or into. "What don't you like about your job?"

I'd noticed her telling and not-telling expression back there at the slideshow when one of the girls who also worked at Rama said about Jonni "She's a crazy psycho bitch."

Now she sighed a big exasperated sigh.

"I've learned a lot from them. More . . . They saved my life. And I'm totally grateful."

"That's great . . . That's beautiful."

"But Jonni's . . . not always easy," she put it diplomatically, "I just don't seem to be able to please her," as if Jonni were there listening.

"Yeah, she seems—*eccentric* . . ."

"Yeh. No matter what I do, I can't do anything right."

"*Mhn.* Sorry you have to put up with that."

A black-clad crowd. (adult) children of the radical chic. too cool for school. their (our) New York religion the old game of distinction. gathered outside St. Mark's Church. for Danspace or the Ontological Theater (R. Foreman).

We were in old RamAnanda territory. new cultural capital. home turf. for both of us.

At the corner of Tenth Street and Avenue A we paused to part. Spiritual capital.

"So tomorrow night the Grand Group," I said.

"Tomorrow morning *ashtanga*." Gradual accrual. speeding up.

"Yep." Or not so slow. I kissed her. on the cheek. "So shall we have dinner first?"

"Let's just play it by ear, see how it goes . . ."

Passing people passed.

"I'd rather make a plan. So we know . . ."

"Are we fighting already?" She smiled.

We were a couple. conducting our relationship on the street corner. Tenth Street and Avenue A.

I always imagined we'd get married at St. Mark's Church, which we'd pass every day on our bikes, on our way home, evens run east, stop at Lucky's for a juice. large. *You're a Reggae Rumba.* where we went sometimes to dance performances. get the holy men to come and do their thing, as we did for this unwedding now (how funerals, memorial services, seem like weddings, the wedding party, or are the same, in the unconscious, as ritual or psychic event, in the life, in significance, the same people and depth of existential emotion, moment. but are opposite), have the after-party there, too. Indian food to live Indian music, ragas, the bubbling tablas. simmering away. and sitar and singers. Eat with your fingers, sit on the floor, flip on the sound system, pipe in the Bolly-pop, first, then bring on the funk, then the rest, *¡womp!,* dance all night, everybody, our chosen and gifted extended family of friends our gifts. Walk out of there in the small of the night, bushed, elated, my hand on the small of her back (as my father *pshaw*ed at my mother for wanting, for saying so) then arm in arm, hip to my thigh to her long thigh, nice feel, keep walking side by side up the avenue, nice fit, down the sidewalk, through the intersections and rooms and days and nights and on through all the passages and dimensions of the rest of our life together. the long walk marriage. (back to where we came from.)

St. Mark's Church sits back at an equilateral angle from the corner of Tenth Street and Second Avenue, unchanging, apparently observing, at a placid historical-philosophical remove from the racing flux. It is made of squarely cut gray bluestone, symmetrical, handsome, pretty big inside, and empty, for years, of pews or altar or anything ecumenical, just a big floor, like the Peace Church, like Judson Church, for dance, nice open space, for Danspace and other performances, but it was packed, not overfull, they said there was no way, but it was full, it was packed, in the end it was perfect, the way the right things sometimes work out right. often. (always?) in the art box. (anyway.) All the people we would have had to our wedding and wedding party were there, of course, and hundreds more, she touched this many, so many, good God, who goes by many names, I knew maybe half, maybe half of those by sight only, though many of the unknown knew me and acted familiar, and they were right, we were all familiar, wonderfully one, Amanda's family, it was horrible beyond words she had to miss this, but she was there, as many said, her bighearted spirit presided powerfully, gently, in her way, beyond words, everyone was happy, as she would have wanted, with hugs held long and crying together in pockets, laughter breaking out of it in lively eruptions, heartbroken little spurts.

That guy was there. huge head. looking lost. but now he was nothing. zero nemesis reading on the alpha scale *CRUSH-YOU* radar. But still I felt like, *That guy?*

"If she would have seen how many people are here who loved her," Sarah2 said, taking in everybody, the room, everyone seated on the floor, except on the sides, "she never would've died."

"She didn't *mean to,*" Sarah1 tartly replied.

"Whelp!" Sarah2's face, eyes, choked, bulged with grief.

We kept the ceremony short, as short as we could. It started late, in honor of Amanda. Sarah1 sang, slowly pumping her harmonium, leaning in, after leading all in a resounding single collective *om*, looking up, mouth pressed, head bowed back down, unable at first to rise out of that low safe kind of moan-humming zone, everyone waiting for her to crack, and she didn't, instead she got on track, her voice broke through lovely to the near heavens our emotions inhabited already, together and singly, merging and building as our voices followed hers in swelling heartflight through the familiar cadences and mysterious Sanskrit birdsong never more meaningful and wonderful and natural as now. Felix played his cherished beat-up old acoustic guitar, almost a hole worn through where his hand had strummed for decades of lonely nights and private transportation successfully transformed in the end into entertainment, success, soulful song, access, balm and that mysterious gift only music can attain and impart. Some girls sang with him, and also with the Das trio, next up, with their godmen instruments, who chanted and sang in alternation then shakily holy together, weaving *Go-pa-la . . . go-pall-la* . . . and wavering exquisitely in their practiced spirituality of imperfection, repetition, silence.

Maria sang and I read my eulogy, a catalogue progression, really, of details imagined or sort of lifted from Amanda's life, spirit, sifted through me, amounting to a free-floating poem (abstract expressionist), the fragments hopefully indicating the hopelessly ineffable whole (and the unspeakable hole), which ended with the words *All these things spell Amanda,* an offered prayer, to God, to love, in the disappearing details.

My voice caught on the middle *man* syllable of her name, and I sat and couldn't speak for a minute, a half an hour (a year and a half. my heart. a decade), but didn't have to, I was done. couldn't really sing along to Sarah's closing, keening, heartbreaking *Jaya Ga-nee-sha.*

Like vapors from the lasting heat under the ash layer names rise in rows from the rows of the souls assembled, credits roll, on the air, handwritten in each person's hand, as on the chalkboard in the back of the room at Andy's where you sign in, take your place, begin in the finishing room until your name, next up, is called, and as you enter the big room, your name, like Amanda's, is crossed out.

The India Night thing was our predate. A always maintained. To me it was our first date. or second. or fiftieth.

Amanda maintained that our first official date was the next night. the Grand Group. So all right. here we go.

We practiced near each other that morning. our daily ordeal and transportation. the gradual accrual commute. though I got there almost an hour before her.

When I left I said (softly) "I'll call you later, okay?"

"Yeh, 'kay."

"What's your number?"

She told me her extension. She was in *navasana,* where you balance on your butt bones (*sit-bones.* they call them).

Make a V with your body. diagonal legs straight. feet pointed (moonward). arms straight ahead. parallel to the floor. palms facing each other. back straight!

I toed her lower back. straighten it. She swatted me away.

You do this five times. hold for five breaths each time. between each one you cross your legs. lift yourself off the floor for one breath. like an amputee. hands beside your hips. pressing down. arms straight. tilt a little forward.

As I left she pushed up and plumped down in one funny little movement. sort of a sack-of-potatoes collapse.

I laughed. her practice was so strong and beautiful this little lapse was cute. you had to make fun of her.

"Don't laugh," she said after me.

"I'm laughing."

We met after work at Tsampa. this Tibetan place I like.

A quiet low-lit sanctuary on Ninth Street. before the dogleg to St. Mark's Books. (Wanamaker Place.)

Between a popular Japanese place below street level. lit. and a raucous Spanish bar and I guess restaurant (*tapas*).

Tsampa (barely pr. the *T*) is run by three Tibetan sisters. one more beautiful than the next. all married to the same guy. (who owns the place. whom you rarely see.) This is still done in Tibet. and among Tibetan exiles.

You see the monks in here. quietly eating. crimson robes. saffron sash. bare arms. heads shaved. or hair bristle-short.

A large photo portrait of the Dalai Lama on the long wall. exposed brick. presiding impishly over the middle tables. our *maya* zone. candles flickering. minute souls.

Another photo of a Himalaya (*him-áll-a-ya*) lake. black and white. surrounded by glacial moraine.

Easily unnoticed amidst the rock rubble. scree. a heap of bundled cloth: clothes. a man. me. you. asleep beside the lake. dead? or deep within (y)our highland dream.

There were only two people in there when I arrived. hungry ghosts. at one of the small tables. When A arrived there were eight or ten.

She wore the usual. jeans. shirt. Ditto B (me too).

She smiled through almost visible sparks and zapping live-wire strands of her winding-down day still zipping around her head.

Which wore now as well the candle's competing warm gold calm down Hollywood glow.

She rooted in her nasty backpack. pulled out a sock? scraps of paper. Kleenex. receipts mixed with crumpled bills, etc. Pulled out a CD.

Held it across the menus to me. It was Krishna Das. devotional chants.

KD did *kirtan* regularly at RamAnanda. Part of the original RamA family. toured. was getting pretty big. in that (still small. back then) sector. Select yoginis singing backup.

"He's great," she said. "Do you have that?"

"I don't. Thanks."

I gave her a book I like to give to people I like. love. (*Light Years*. James Salter. trim quiet masterpiece.)

Seems to skate over life and love. celebrate the details. the full sweep. elevate. while revealing. loss. an elegy. sanctifying the quotidian. life. love. (the purpose of art. religion.)

A novel, I told her, that wants to be a poem. Not the best reading recommendation. for her.

So I didn't add that the poem at its heart aspires to prayer. and the prayer to music. and of course music intends. evokes. pure spirit.

She looked at the back of it and put it on the mesclun mix of bills and paper scraps beside her.

"I just ordered some momos," I told her.

You're a momo, she shot back. (Not yet! Our repetition retorts were not yet in place. But no doubt budding. Or maybe already spontaneously combusting. popping out.)

She asked and I told her what was good. She got what I got. Tsampa plate. your basic classic macro(biotic) meal. (Rice. beans. greens. seaweed. tofu. nutty nice tahini sauce.)

We talked about yoga stuff. her hammies. people. my knees. It was nice.

I asked for the check before we were quite done. Pointed out the time. She was blithely unconcerned. I led us outside. A cab came flying down Ninth Street. I flagged him down. lefty *Sieg YO!*

There was a line outside the Grand Garage still. good. Waiting list still waiting. just starting to be let in.

The girl (cute. quick player eyes. curly long hair.) (into threesomes. I learned later. from Buddy.) checked her lists. let us in.

It was full. but there were two free seats near the middle. not beside each other. So I asked the six between the seats if they'd move one over.

No one liked the idea. but they did it. and then no one minded when we moved in. thank you. thank you. thanks.

"Hnnh?" Amanda mrmrd about twenty minutes into the show. the usual exquisite performance barrage.

A storm of signals. mixed-media playground. dream illogic. cartoon animus. high-tech. antic chorus. barebones. low-tech. looping movements.

We're in a war movie. inside a ship. wait. it's a burlesque club. also. they go together.

It's about coupled realities. continuously peeling off in different directions.

Chilled counterpoints. mysterious drops. shifts. strains. morphing quixotic music.

A little song and dance. a section of straight scene. poignant. tame. perfectly rendered. classic stage acting. stand and deliver.

For a swelling moment. poise. penetration. they get you. spilling over into meta. ironic asides. psychotic stops.

Catch you off guard. sting your expectations. a game. Push you over. then catch you. or maybe not. when you fall for it. I loved this stuff.

"What's going on?" Amanda said at intermission. perplexed. slumped a little dejectedly.

"You just have to go with it." My bird hand alighted on her shoulder. but my actual hand didn't.

"Think of it like a dream . . ."

I wanted her to like it more. I wanted to stroke her back again.

You should've, B..

"I never get these things." Resigned. exhale. stumped. still.

"Think of it like visual music," I tried, "the different elements mixing . . ."

"I like Kristina, though," she said. Kristina was the star.

Practiced at RamAnanda. good practice. sexy ripe pear body. pale. red heart lips. drooping brooding gaze. then suddenly Betty Boop. little red pout.

Shy in person. normal. but what a fabulous chameleon ham she was here!

"Yeah, she's great."

When they took the stage for the second part Kristina smiled at Amanda and waved. On with the show. this is it.

Dark lips. eroto-ammo. comical diva. mercurial facial expressions irresistible. inwardly amused. delighted. fleeting. demented. delighting.

She sang and a man's twangy country-western voice

came out of the sound system. eyebrows archly arched. parted porno mouth. minstrel eyes expand. the whites. roll. a manic little head toss. tic.

You could just watch her the whole time. I kind of did.

I loved the show. Afterward Amanda said she was glad she saw it. but liked things better she could understand.

She kinda got that there were maybe two different endings. but didn't like that.

One where Kristina dies and is carried off in a Welsh miners' dirge. it's sad. surprisingly. feels real. brass band. cold but soulful. majestic. calm. very cool.

The other your happy ending. campy family/cast photo that won't stay still. the camera lingers. everyone horsing around. like the end of the show. *The Brady Bunch. SNL. Bye!*

"Why can't they just decide and stick with one story, and one ending?"

I skirted. skipped. the real answer. that that's the whole point? That every moment posits its givens. is invented anew. its apparent reality. branches into another. aping out of it. creating and defying expectations.

(But what about the other branch. every branch of the way?) The hint to the meaning was in the name of the show. on the program.

Pathological Curve. Which had to do with fractals. particle physics.

The program briefly explained Parallel Universe Theory. A dizzying radical theory of quantum mechanics.

In particle physics a new reality is created every nanosecond. (*Veddy Vedic.*) Where do the alternate branches go? The theory says they're still there. somewhere. in a parallel universe.

Instead of getting into this I attempted another answer. know your audience. couched in her kind of language. logic. short and easy.

(Like I keep trying to make this map. this full sweep deep account. Keep it simple. But I can't!)

Nothing too deep, she and her friends liked to joke. their play motto. (but also no joke.)

"Because it's like declaring regular life's not enough," is what I came up with. As in *Art is for those for whom life is not enough.* I didn't add.

Another one they had. not entirely a joke either. that I never tired of hearing was *What is it we're supposed to surrender to again?*

Disgorged from this cramped mind-set. (parenthetical. *italicized.*) egested. with the rest of the audience. space/mind-travelers ejected. blinking. spent. from the crazy brilliant collective dream journey. *sent.*

We repaired. resumed. by instant degrees. relieved. our pixelated identities. but still kept. happily. some of the otherly spell. Voices ghosted off around people. sidled up the buildings. as they dispersed.

"Why can't they just do it so you understand?" Amanda tried one more time.

"Maybe they're showing the way life is. The way the mind works."

"Not mine. I'm a simple girl. I like a good story with a good ending."

The cobblestone street scene was lit an effervescent magnesium lime by a couple of tall streetlamps. nosy armless aliens stooping. necks bent. harmless. to watch. see through us.

Into our baffling earthling stories. rituals. pathological curves. we humans from earth. in our clothes. in our thoughts. our thoughts cloaked in feelings. both clothed in words. or naked unseen.

Souls glowing together. walking slowly. along our converging plotlines. under the tall hatless hat of night. hello up there. Downtown around us down here appealingly empty.

Old run-down SoHo. exquisite graffiti and grit. palimpsest. on a classic old SoHo door. endangered species. all of this. us.

We pass between a building on Grand Street (Yohji Yamamoto) and a mound of garbage in black garbage bags at the curb. like big raisins. bloated. The feeling a rat will run out any second and up your leg. up under your pantleg.

Posters. peeled and newly glued. battered loading dock. The triangle roof shape and square like a child's drawing of a house on the side a building where the building beside it is missing. used to be.

You walk through New York. especially at night. imagining you're tracking your future. somehow feeling or working it out. and everything you see adds up to a long visual nostalgic swan song.

Tragic without seeming tragic. hopeful rather. the pleasures of merely circulating. seeing. because you can't see life passing. even though it never stops passing. you can't see the world ending around us. can't really believe it's really happening. Not here. now.

Especially if you're walking along with Amanda. and everything seems great.

Nearing my building (Ninth near B (*Loisaida*) (*Lower East Sider* pronounced by a Lower East Sider)) I asked her if she wanted to come up and see my new apartment. Rita's apartment.

"*Hyeah!*"

I'm sure I explained. on the way up. at the door with the key. by way of warning. apology. disclaimer. that the paint job. the interior generally. were hideous/hilarious. were not mine!

The slate floor in the kitchen I didn't hate. But the dropped ceiling and recessed lighting. and the useless sheetrock boxed window situation.

Amanda was into the bathtub in the kitchen. right where you walk in.

(Fast-forward to her in there, splashing around. getting her book wet. *Light on Yoga*. greeting me getting home. soaking and making wisecracks. music requests. while I cooked.

Hey, B, gimme a taste. only her head and knees out of the water. face floating. the hot running the whole time. Her mouth agape like a chick in a nest.)

(But not so fast.) (Though it was almost that fast!)

I took her ratty baby blue backpack. stained with street. her day in it. she said.

And she didn't miss a beat when I made some stupid remark about fitting a whole day in that backpack.

"My whole life's in there."

I hung her whole life on the hook by the door. her jacket. I showed her around. Like welcome to your new home. your future. (Good luck!)

The front room (soon to become the Lake). overbuilt woodwork. TV and stereo boxed guiltily away in a corner cabinet. badly stippled gross green with the stupid sponge technique.

Not much of mine in there yet. Some books. boom box. CDs. a few *New Yorkers*.

Futon on the floor. half up against the wall. open tortilla. waiting. for a couple of meaty bodies to wrap and fold themselves juicily into it.

She stood in the room. gave it seen size and moment. a woman's appraisal. benediction. The woman you want. you want her vote.

This was a railroad apartment. rooms in a line. one leading to the next. doorways lined up. like cars on a train.

Lower East side tenement. whole families in here. well-recorded crowded histories. dissolved and gone. now ours. next in line. to imminent oblivion. unseen but always under way.

The bedroom past the kitchen was dark. also dapple-painted. dark blue infected. infested with *purple.*

I showed her the lights on a dimmer. shooting upward from another box situation. at the head of the built-in platform bed you could barely fit past.

One of these lights was a regular light. The other was purple! I brought it up and brought it down. way low.

"Oh my God," Amanda said. sounding more serious than amused. grave. enthralled by the creepiness. "That is hilarious."

"Mood lighting," she added. We liked that. The sex light.

It was a pretty nice apartment. anyway. in spite of Ken's insane obsessive beaver mania to box. botch. anally wrap and wreck it.

We sat at the kitchen table. U-shaped. linoleum. Attached to the wall. held up by a piece of two-by-four. a couple of (#8) nails he couldn't get out banged back against the wood. pointed ends exposed. (*What the fuck? Ken.*)

Everywhere I looked I saw things that needed to be

fixed. or finished. or torn down and gotten rid of altogether. as in my life.

Except for Amanda sitting here. no apparent inclination to leave. (*Here to stay!*)

Our near-each-other magnet happiness. easy. lazy. hungry. made for a kind of third happiness greater than us. that we settled into. form-fit. to bask in. and behold. while you bask. and form it. and ride.

(Adumbrating. immediately! its shadow opposite. creating. the Third Thing. of the Theory of the Third Thing. imago. to come.)

She asked me about the apartment. I told her the deal. sublet for the rest of Rita's lease. ten months. till the end of August. Then I could take over the new lease. supposedly.

I didn't get into the details. Not at the moment. i.e. the extra money Rita also wanted. "key fee." but no guarantee..

I must have offered her cider. We were tired.

The silent kitchen. late suspended hour. expectant stillness. apparent arrival.

A tipped in her chair toward me. I touched her neck. nape. cotton and organic flesh. tenderness.

Massaged softly. crept up into the silky northern border. where twin muscle bands meet skull. hair. the whole central nervous highway converges.

Under delighted inspecting detective fingertips.

Moved to the edge of my chair to palm her shoulders. like holding. molding a clay vase. the clay still soft. indeed alive.

Gently prodded around. loosened the knots in her neck. shoulder slopes (trapezii).

Sort of clawed my fingertips in under her collarbone.

from behind. squeezed. pulled back. apart. her shoulder blades came compliantly together. her chest opened (heart chakra).

I softly reminded her to keep breathing. She laughed a puff out her nose.

The room was getting the massage too. and the message. The barrier was gone. seemed never there. teased out. and with it time.

She shifted in her seat. My curious hands inquired further. read carefully her living braille body. the braless warm opening invitation. easy answer. Her skin took my touch by the hands into the private welcome event unfolding.

Skiing. sort of. under language. softly over welcome svelte warm snow. melting carnal intro. to the deep source communication. tissue meeting itself anew. inventing our crafty top sport collusion. coming your way. right now.

Her upper arms like me mum's. hmm. She moved forward to let me go further down. *mmh.*

I kneaded downward. first the slope from neck to shoulders. then down the spinal staircase. either side. to the flesh smile above her pants. under her shirt.

And this was sex now. officially. you knew. when I touched her skin there. her offered form. up under her shirt.

Her head lolled forward. really relaxed. eyes gently shut. I can't keep saying like an angel. Her head came up again as I went under her shoulder blades. then rolled to the side and I kissed her neck.

She moved her head to lightly lock my face there with her hair and head. We were in business. breathing together. out of mind. or deeper in.

The chair legs hiccupped and burped (on the floor) as I moved it closer.

My clawed fingertips plowed through the golden California hilltop. worked her scalp pretty hard. softly combed the shorn corn silk. which elicited her first little sex sound. the pleasure motor starting up. vibrating. one low note in her throat:

"Mmmm . . ." Almost *omm..*

I readjusted my position. held her head in both hands. heavy. fragile. extremely valuable egg. frangible. her neck a touchingly vulnerable stem. extremely touchable.

I looked at her. she opened her eyes. enlarged her gaze. Letting in my own lost and found soft focus. her mouth smiled and stayed open. that erotic soft rictus.

My hand on her forehead. the other holding the weight of her head in the back in my hand.

Speaking can wreck it. or can break a tension and ameliorate. save and improve the moment extended. usher in the show. light up the erotic circus.

I spoke. but we were already fine. way saved.

"Before Freud came up with free association for psychoanalysis he used to put his hand on the patient's forehead like this and say, 'Tah-*rye* to ve-*mem*beh . . .' "

She was tilted toward me in her chair. almost tipping over. we stayed like that. (for two years!)

In the middle of the apartment. of the city. the good night. our lives. her girl-smell. heating up.

Our mouths softly negotiating. grazing that great feeling. arrival and home release. a nibble. her neck. sending the shimmer/shiver sensation over her skin. wind over savor water.

The poem flow of images unleashed. bodies in transit. barely touching. proximal sweet pull. game on. barely begun.

My mouth stayed where she held my head with her head tilted to stop the clock. and movement. and my free-falling life. diving into her hapless mouth. happy.

My mouth moved. my parted lips met. sex in itself. greeted. in this supercharged context. grazed the downy coast of her cheek.

Her mouth was open a little. still. like she had an eye in there looking out. She turned to see and I kissed her mouth.

It opened and our mouths made a hollow between them. almost not touching. arching wide open.

It was weird. It was like when you gum your lips over your teeth. be a toothless old geezer. both of us.

I gummed her lips. no. wait. she gummed mine. no I lipped hers. but wet. mine over hers over mine. oiling our. little power struggle. it begins. pure play. for now.

Except what. really. is more serious. What. really. matters more?

Mouths open still. as if competing. like who can open their mouth further?

Like a lesbian kiss. was this?

Subtle body. subtle lips. subtle kiss.

I closed my lips. I'm a feminist. let her win. maybe get hers that way. But it didn't work. her mouth stayed open. like a baby bird being fed. agape. a lip. a grape. an egg.

The egg it just came from. the robin's egg room around us. enveloping.

So I fed her. but how? How did she want this. my tongue met the hollow. no go. negative space. a nonkiss. kiss.

I forgot what I was doing and she ate me slowly eating her slowly also. at the same time.

We were still warming up. minds melting into slow time.

She touched my shoulder. turned. To touch me but also to hold on and not fall.

We both turned our bodies more. front to front. not very comfortable in our chairs.

It was as if till now we'd been facing the camera. still were. filling the frame.

I turned further. shifted. embraced and held her for both of us. Her head lolled back into the kiss/embrace. classic shot. that perfect fit and feeling. R-rated so far. Adolescent fiction.

Now her mouth was consuming our delectation. trying to steal my new food? fresh face. strange close-up. blurry one big cyclop eye. new monomania. new life. meal. her taste.

Her mouth was no longer stuck on the wide-open thing.

Now we were really in business. meaty infinity eights. 3-D. 4.

"It's not very comfortable here," I said at last. the only words in how long was it? An hour. more. since Freud spoke.

"Let's lie down."

I led her by the hand into the dark lair. Lying down with her was another felt degree of fond deeper found dimension. building. home.

The lengths and toes of our alliterative bodies settled amiably together. arranged and pressed into the longing. dissolving. the craving. our thighs. delivering. happily. opening.

I toed off my shoes. one knocked on the floor. slid hers off. Held her hip. held her head.

The kissing was the main thing. at first. Mouths more open than I wanted. again. or more than I was used to.

It's like we were kissing. but the kiss was missing. in the middle of it. But this was great!

Our bodies probed the next level of strange lovely familiarity. We stroked and pressed and felt and found. The way it goes.

Side by side for the longest time. like we were hiding in a canoe together. undulating.

Our mouths couldn't get enough of each other. the first kiss. continuous. gingerly grinding. the soft swim.

The waves. the current. the carnal water moved through our bodies. the ranging delve and dive. floating river kiss.

The kiss voluptuously returned to the source kiss. to lick and consume and thank it. resume. the hollow swallowed by wet nibble and eat. this delectable feast. funnest dulcet graze. almost sound.

The kisses within the kiss. roving tongues. and then wait. and the lower body free press! nice moves. open licit scrimmage.

Like competition here also. springs up. hip vs. hip. jeans against jeans. adolescent friction. the hips against the pelvis. bump. oop. to *aah.* pelvis vs. thigh. More blood sport down here than the more articulate artful water play above. of the mouths. breathing each other.

Our heads. the lighter osculatory exchange. winning the play. genital hum and glee. easy way. nature's hard/ soft target. best and highest say. triple X intention.

My pleasure meets and greets and makes hers. which meets and makes mine. world's greatest invention and personal discovery. this please go zone. divine collaboration. animal grind. lingam and yoni. yearning to be felt and free.

As great as the long loss before (and after). greater. the original way. to fill the big huge hole in our heart. the greatest show on earth.

The marathon wrestle begins. power struggle. wriggling play. power takes over. kidnaps your will. your whole life. the way it happens.

Of all the things the mouth does. strange portal orifice. rimmed in lurid sexy red flesh-pads. supersensitive. mobile. labile. ever ready. So much of our lives passes through our mouths.

Every moment fueled with another breath of air. cool on the way in. another expelled. warm on the way out. warmed by the body.

And so many moments fathered by busy verbal flight. word upon bird-rustling word. rushing out. hushing. feathered. chasing more of the same airy connected hustling bodies. if you think about it. meaning meaning.

Shifting formations of sound. millions compressed in continuous streams. bubbling. somersaulting burbles of thought. vanishing. wishing away.

Garbled. swallowed. murmured. lost. propelled into the otherness out there. on little wings of sound. hope. luck. air. love.

Expecting our feelings to be seen. met. felt. embraced. chasing and pressing our desires into the world.

Expecting our fine feathered emotions to work their same strong spell on others. on the world. as they do on us. Expecting our feelings to fly! and win love.

Our mouths open to our bodies. where we live. after

all. it's all there. the years and people. the endless movie. our undying habits. old tricks.

Predilections and opiate strategies. intricate unconscious arsenal. twisted custom tools. assumptions. ways of seeing and saying. strained mental musculature.

Hopes. in spite of the evidence.

Unspooling repetitions. dim mysteries. hidden dammed weaknesses. damned. doomed. Spare me. spare you me.

The struggle. anxiety. lifelong loneliness. serial disappointment. entrenched. the whole psychic battleground. buried. trapped in the body. freed now. so easily!

Entrained metaphysical questions. the quest for meaning. the problem of living. your thousand sideshows.

Complexity channeled through the mouth. suspended. The whole show chastened. into flowing animation. draining. pulling into the current. of this awesome subtle potent flux.

Answered with the touch of another mouth. *No problem now!* the one you want to touch. and you want to touch you.

Empty crowded house. crammed with junk. ideals. memories. our fears. loss! pain. rage. the wounds. the whole world within.

Mercurial shadow armies. massing. all the needs. we must feed and inspect them. food in. words out. import. breath in. export. breath out. air. smoke. language. laughter. song. more food. succor. sex. more words. more love. more. *more.*

The amazing human mouth. does so many amazing human things. its underappreciated duties cover the crazy spectrum of all life's activities.

Our mouths salivate. om. sing. hum. wail. sigh. smack. purse. sag. yawn. etc.

Part snake part slug. part sexual organ. the slithery slippery tongue tells all. slides around. tastes and shapes the world and sends out all we have to say.

The mouth does its work. Houses all our stories. the names of our friends. secrets. life plans. places. Behind the serried pearly whites. guarding the entrance to language. all possibility.

You cannot possibly quantify. catalogue. describe. explain. only open your mouth. close your eyes.

But the busy mouth tries! And gets its rewards. Immediate satisfaction. please. now. it gets to eat. taste. often. Asks for more.

And of all its tasks and tricks. what ours were doing now was by far its favorite thing to be doing. moving around the other moist mystery mouth.

Supersmooth. at first. where dry on dry. seamless satiny border. tongue and dart. tickle-lick it. (clit.) lick in. (here we come.)

Wet meat movable goal. open. enchanting. alive. the mute eat. gradual. mutual. pry. *May I?* tongue tongues tongue. wait. probe. *I must.* ply the fleshy gate.

Through our mouths we compose and present ourselves. Offer ourselves. pray.

She tastes good!

Entry to inside. her domed inner life. her amazing mouth. which I always loved to look at. always loved to look at. always loved. now more so.

Open to me! melting. welcoming me. om! welcoming her. *Yum.* melting the welcome. in your mouth.

My lips reading her reading me. reading her mind. reading mine.

Tongues touching. like children. prodding eyeless sex

animals. blindly going at it. like dogs. pups. dodging. slippery. slugs.

We give ourselves away. to the other. to the tumbling fall. the morphing images that come with it all. the feeling. weightless ride and bloom in the free-fall rise. reflecting back and forth and back..

The opening. meeting and blindly greeting my own. grazing the beginning. touch by tongue.

Finding the weird fun way in. from all her heart's knocking-around wanderings. into my heated home. the ongoing epic movie. unedited. long wordy story! sorry for the mess. but come on in. you are welcome here.

Inchoate ensemble. unseeable museum of me. my foibles and larks and hallmark tricks on full display. pulling focus. the best and the worst hidden away.

Silent film. for now. for her. but it doesn't stop. it opens up! more.

Out-of-control plotlines. inspirations. chimeras. transportations. intensities. convolutions. savage repetition.

Nearly insane involution. converging and seeing and rampantly combining. continuously. if never really coming together.

But not coming apart. promising big things! rarefied varieties. step right up. exquisite neurotic forms. half-sensed curiosities.

Secret fractals and saints. pundits and crystals. flowers and soldiers. wounds wrapped in newspapers telling what happened. what didn't. what won't.

Chiseled-in-stone patterns. guilt. avoidance. failure. abandonment. fear. shame. etc.

.loss.

The feckless defects. the wobbly structures. long

abiding longing. the classic mistakes. did I say repetitions? disappointments. the different ages. beliefs. attitudes. delusions. stages. hopes.

.loves.

Styles of being. ways of not. all the people. music. mental wind. on escapist walkaway water. imagined outcomes. buoyant boats. exploded planes. the trillion efforts. a lifted finger. the little gesture. effects scattered. gathered. scattering.

Floating cities. coy floating candles. reflected. the wobbly train of the moon. making many moons. connectedly elongating.

All the tries. the places. the storms and quiet corners. arrival. faces. emptiness. lassitude. worse. tangled. overgrown scenes of love and loss. where we go.

Neglected gardens. entire alps. agonies. silver murmuring seas. heaving. laughing. islands. bobbing. sinking. lapping.

The inner realm. where we live. and flee. consciousness and the welling unconscious. as if they're different. as if mind and body are different.

The realm meditation claims to tame. aims to touch. to lead to the end of suffering.

The lines in your hands. the faces you see. maps of the future. moving away. and on it goes. Only traces escape the velvet black hole. or enter.

A true portrait of a person. All the days. people. places. things. industries of loss. of hiding. piecemeal growth. yowls of rolling unmet yearning. unnumbered species of hope. put out there. each labeled with love. loss.

Each eye. each chakra a god. brightly tattooed on

the holy human blueprint. masterful genome. mandala. made flesh. Amanda!

The buzzing blooming confusion. the swarming civilization of the mind. colonized by instinct. inhabiting the body. Hers meeting mine. *Good luck!* Here we go.

We think we're just kissing when we kiss someone!?

We're out of our depth.

If love is anywhere near. you're stepping off your own known planet and slipping through the black velvet mouth into another parallel universe. where real life begins.

You look like yourself. but you're not anymore. You're inhabited by the other. or rather you inhabit the other dimension you create together.

You're both in that parallel common dimension now. When you fall in love you even look different. You even begin to look like each other.

You're not living on food and sleep. and the usual friend-love. what you do. You're living on a different fuel. erotic love. People say you look different. you look great. whatever it is. they say. you should bottle it..

And as in yoga. so in the life. the practice (in yoga). ultimately the real practice is alone. And when we're alone (in life) we feel like our life is just practice. for later. waiting for the real thing. when love is there. the real life.

And when love comes along it feels like that. like now real life is here. this is what I've been waiting for. my whole life. for this now. Practice is over. This is it.

We're no longer practicing alone. waiting. Now we're living. *we.*

And same with the practice. when you practice with

someone. others. it's totally different. it's almost effortless. relatively.

You're pulled by the mutual/collective energy. the slipstream effect. the quicksilver team. No longer alone!

And of course the real practice is life. love.

The real play is sex.

She stretched long. *Leela!* arched back. wildcat! her exposed tummy. jean-clad hips upward. sexward-facing cat.

I pressed her crotch explicitly with my hand cupped. she opened to it. cunt compliant within. not a word. pressed back. opening to me.

I slid on top of her. up on my elbows. (*Chaturanga dandasana*. sort of. sunken. into her. but light. lightly holding myself up. into sex the morphing surfboard.)

Grazing her face. those live rubber lips with mine. riding her dolphin hips. with mine.

Gazing into the grainy huge close-up of her face. faintly fully there. in the grape dim. I reached over and found the dimmer for the mood lighting. push-clicked it on.

Wrong light! the regular light came on. violently bright. sudden buzzkill antilove glare. Her face curdled. scrunched up.

I clicked it off. hit the other one. lowered the garish stage light from *totally gross* (A) grape through mauve to violet to violet barely. airily.

Bathing her photo face in developing solution. preserving (forever!) the moment. interexpanding. the limned rose-gray form. grainy lineaments of her still face. and form in rapt repose.

Tasting. easing. feeling our way. each other. into the borderless place. the no-rules. the suspended locution.

continuous inner location. of a dream. no pace. just flux. barely coming up for air.

Swimming together. the liquid slow sexy swim. dolphins muscling the shifting dreamscape. undulating. like being swallowed. while also swallowing.

Plummeting through the dimension. as you create it. it you. you both. selves and moment dissolve into one binding sensation unbounding. arrival. sensational.

This exalted vital force. delivering you home. at last! you almost can't believe it. but you feel it. you are more than yourself. you are more than welcome here. the pleasure place unbundling. encrypting. you need this like nothing else.

And you are needed here. this furtive center. warm. meant movement. wanted. felt. almost whispers almost words. breathing together. jazzing apart. the cosmic swim. falling. subjective. reeling.

Feeling meaning. welling glee. fetal amnesia. meaning feeling.

Our fingers skimmed each other's skin. rode rougher over the rougher clothing. she felt around under my shirt. on and off. she pushed it up. I took it off.

I pulled at her pants. she lay there letting me. I undid the Levi's button. zipper down. she lifted her hips. wriggled as I pulled off her pants. one leg. free of the foot. the other as if by itself.

No underwear! A pair of pants is only a pair of pants. negligible layer of fabric and fashion. cotton protection. But what a world of difference! when they're off.

She went for mine next. fair is fair. unzipping further and tugging down. kneeling with her knees hip distance apart. I pulled off her little nothing shirt. starting flag raised. number one entertainment. Ladies and gentlemen. *And they're off!*

We felt not just natural with each other from the start. We kissed some more. mouths open. luscious pause. delicious promise. skin on skin a revelation. a startling feast.

It wasn't as if we'd never had sex before. either of us. but it was as if neither of us had ever had sex before.

We felt made for each other. our bodies extended together. no rush. to blend. anticipation part of the game. so much more to explore. mildly possessed. more. blessed. a single writhing eight-limbed beast. taming itself. (*Good luck!*)

I didn't expect this to happen. at least not tonight. didn't know it'd feel so great. so totally right. And we had barely begun.

Amanda closed her eyes. in the deep purple dim. she opened them. I could barely see her eyes locked on my eyes. the expression. relaxed. serious?

She moved against me. I loved the way she moved against me. under me. beside me. bestride. on top. side to side. the continuous loop. lascivious variations.

Kissing the whole time. touching and not touching. my upward-facing hard-on. rubber madman. flapping around. her knee raised. my thigh against her pussy. her pussy riding anything near it.

Grazing my cock lightly a few times. mostly her hands searched my sides. back. legs and butt. like learning me. washing aloneness away. over and over. imparting a blessing. a balm. on my flesh. my inchoate wound.

I stroked her hair. neck. back. painting her. her hip.

etc. sometimes we almost stopped. her little bud breasts fit in my palm. perfect perfect butt. full peach form. open hips. those long thighs! against mine. moving. teaching me her.

I couldn't get enough. her narrow shoulders. strong back. two round halves. elegant feet. lovely ankles. her lower back. where it rose to her butt.

I turned her over and stroked her whole backside. long river runs. eights. from her neck to her feet. her curves and curvy sides. (side bodies.)

Her calves. supple slappable filets. into the pussy now. moist nest. waiting. sweet rest in there. wet welcome. opening. slick strokes. lips part. we both like this. a lot.

Her clit like another nipple. soft circles. hey there. slow gain. in a little. a little around. and out and in. and back to the body. cruising around. looking for trouble. feeling the love.

My touch gave hers ideas. her hands went over me where my hands went over her. fluid variation response. together and counterpoint. embodied improvisation. music embodied.

Questions and answers. in this best ever test devised between man and woman. lover and lover. her earlobe. silk neck. nuzzle. nip. tickle. trap. you. no you.

Arching acquiescence. vital purchase. rhythmic push. off to the places.

So much of the heart's hidden data transmitted in these sericeous transactions. slick tongue and journey accordingly. and you don't stop.

The touch and the slow win opiate whelm and release your minds. drug the demons. beguile the out-there night. busy downloading day.

Downloading our vital emotional info. coded mysteries encrypted. embedded in the flesh. imbedded in the bed.

Lightening now in the room around her. us. *already?!* crepuscular seepage around the window shade. light blue light invasion. as she pinned me her little brother down on the lawn. big leaky grin.

Let spit drip down. splat on my gob. she licked it off. I gripped the narrow basket of her ribs. squeezed not too hard. bench-pressed her away. she was strong and struggled against me. as hard as she could.

She was strong. wriggled. wrestled. bit my little scraggle beardlet. to moor her to me. it worked. it hurt but didn't hurt beyond that.

She gripped my forearms. fingernails digging in. bucking bronco. dolphin shark. tried to push and thrash my arms away. without pushing too hard.

"I'm stronger," I said. "Sorry."

We hadn't spoken for a long time.

"No, I'm stronger."

"No, I'm the alpha."

"No, *I'm* the alpha."

She grinned her crooked grin, bearing down on me. Saliva welled. a big drool tear. sort of demented.

"Sorry. You wish."

With a surge of last strength she fought. wiggling. thrusting. wrestling down at me. but I kept her away. I levitated her. I liked her a lot. I got me a keeper. I let her free.

But then folded her up in a ball. child's pose. tipped her over. compliant egg. who's your daddy. rolled her back up. pussy protruding between the orb of her butt and her smackwarm thighs together. her heels.

I was dying to fuck her. then and there. the whole time. but was waiting for her to really want me to.

I did!

I was waiting for her to die for it. go crazy. beg for it..

I polished the round of her back and her butt. both protectively egged and provocatively offered. stroked her cheeks. the cleft between.

I made bold and bent and licked her lower back. down to where the runnel of her spine became valley between her buttocks.

With a good load of saliva slicked my tongue over the deep groove to her slick vulva. sliding. pressing. passing her buttonhole. bump in the road.

Split the wet wait with a single long lick. tasty claim and taste. a promise of things to come. it didn't seem she wanted more now.

Are you crazy?

I'm a guy. I'm a slut. I would've done anything.

But I know my emotional rutting technique. when. how to let the woman lead. build it all up to the berry bursting point for both.

Gently father the long touch. stroke her pussy a bit. but more everywhere else. divine any auguries. read the blood and beat and subsenses shifting in the gentle falter. (*Tantra*. kind of.)

Deep inside the satisfaction sensation now. let the grace in the silk tip of my cock and tongue begin to touch and soften her heart's whole hard secret history.

The grinning girl in roller skates on the hot-top driveway on Orange Avenue. arm raised to the disco god. the audience out there.

To the chapped crack leaking dark threads of last breath from her gaunt sharp deathbed head. embrace.

"I knew you were bad," she said, looking back. her smile moist. lopsided. asymmetric gobsmack.

The soft daylight. the sensual languor. torpor. lingering delight.

The shadow stuff arriving already. riding the rushing ineluctable wave. unloading unseen. proliferating black tendrils and bright seeds. both. with love's first licks.

The first night blended with the next and the next and the sweet holy next. We rolled out of bed. drugged with erotic delirium. *Hungry!*

High. that higher state. the oneness with the other.

No real sleep since we first fell in. except that divine enhanced state where you're still ensorcelled together while roaming around REM and the nether rooms.

We went out into our days. the flux. apart. afloat. Walking orgasms. waiting to happen.

Then stumbled back to bed and our continuous wrestle. mingle. antic oneiric jostle. metaphysical pleasure principle negotiations. complex. ontic. ongoing. endless. simple. unseen. Countless ways to see and say it.

On a bright real Saturday morning we came up for air. practice. a bold cobalt New York new day.

A crowd of characters on the steps of Charas across the street. chatting. smoking. something going on there. public school turned community center.

The day offers this first detail clue and hidden reminder of the mystic chain inside the day. beginning again.

And now with your awareness you join the the love poem momentum. Gather as you go.

Rusty orange leaves shaped like paper dolls and cutout bears shaking and shushing faint stadium applause against the Delft cerulean outer space sensed pressing down in the depth of darker blue density the higher up you look.

We walked through the park holding hands. everything eroticized. magnificent.

Frankie's noon class. filling up fast. A led us toward the back. slapped her mat down in the back row. no place beside her. so I put mine in front of her.

Amanda went off to do her Amanda things. Yoginis clustered around her before she made it to the door. bees to queen bee. apparent. Also the honey.

I started to stretch. lie there. ten minutes till class. Like sunbathers on a crowded beach. people wandered the rows looking for spaces.

Checking each other out slyly. they think. Look. look past. make it look like you're not looking.

A few generous souls moved their mats aside to make room. most ignored the seekers. I have my spot. don't look at me. our Western way. blithely automatic American way. yoga be damned.

I reluctantly moved my mat over. My reward (*instant karma!*) (A'd say). in walked Rose. hair half wet from a shower. pulled back.

(Instant karma also the other way. a test. for everything with A.)

We'd had a few semifriendly encounters lately. but she hadn't been around much. at least on Saturdays now. or moon days. when I took open classes. since now I was practicing *ashtanga* every morning.

The one thing I missed about open classes was seeing certain people. women. her.

Her face didn't exactly light up when she saw me.

but her expression did shift from neutral. her walking-around mien. to a softening or that certain subtle something around the eyes and mouth. when our eyes met.

I felt a panic. the zing of seeing her. then of our gazes meeting. and of course of everything with A. with A around the corner.

Rose walked toward me. wearing not her bumblebee shorts. but regular old cotton gym shorts. red. white piping. tank top (gray). tucked in. mostly.

Most of the guys wore these wife-beaters (white). me too. (then also black.) (then in *ashtanga* no shirt.) (guys.) I liked when women wore them.

Someone else snagged the place beside me as she approached. dude with an anvil head. But there was a spot in front of me. (better!)

She put her mat down there. We said hey. eyes said a bit more.

Behind her Amanda came back into the room. talking to somebody. eyes closed an extra second. in that way I love. as she smiled at something. the way eyes are caught closed in a photograph.

She was a happy person. looking at her with others.

She had a solid barefoot walk. not heavy but strong. leonine. with her fluffy mane hair. She spent her life barefoot. like life's a beach. (she wished.)

Rose was lining up her mat equidistant from the mats on either side. staggered forward. to give herself arm room. parallel to the lines of the floorboards. She was like me.

She looked up. about to say something. She saw Amanda get on the mat behind me.

She picked up her mat and dragged it to the other side of the room.

Frankie's talk today was good. She liked to talk about arcana. but also about real-life things.

How yoga can help us. in practical day-to-day things.

Nonattachment does not mean ignoring the nuts and bolts. the problems. the daily details. the unending activities of life.

Because where else do we live?

Frankie looked like a priest. sitting in front of the class. erect. in lotus (*padmasana*). in her black outfit. skin-tight. boy-hair parted like a black book.

It means facing them with clarity. gentle concentration. unfettered focus. untroubled energy. acceptance.

Frankie read from a dog-eared paperback. She looked like Fred Astaire. as ever. severe.

Everybody wants to fall in love.

I wanted to look back at Amanda. but did with radar only. (radar love!)

Everybody needs to feel connected. This is the main force behind all human activity.

Frankie had us in a forward bend. (*Paschimottanasana.*)

At the hollow core of our ego selves lies suffering. A pained awareness of our aloneness and our separateness.

You could tell this was going to be a long one. She read with measured beats. Deliberate pauses. So breathe and relax into it. *Moola bandha.*

The experience of separateness arouses loneliness. anxiety. fear. Worse. The deepest need of man. of woman. is to overcome her separateness.

To leave the prison of her aloneness. This is the main problem of existence..

The solution lies in the achievement of interpersonal union. of fusion with another person. in love.

This desire for interpersonal fusion. call it the biological imperative. or existential mandate. or spiritual purpose. is the most powerful human need. our most fundamental passion.

It is the prime impetus motivating everything we do. the binding force that keeps the human race together. the creative urge. the couple. the family. the clan. tribe. society. civilization..

Frankie looked up. It wasn't clear which lines she spoke she lifted off the page. and breathed out to us through the vibration miracle (as she'd call it) called voice. and which were her own.

Indeed, this need to feel connected. to feel love. is really our need for union with God..

~

Jump ahead, past the erotic circus first phase, past the all-too-soon decline and fall, ineluctable and unstoppable, the erratic Middle Place, after the Disaster Place smoke clears. Take life and the loss into art box. Our love, our story's over, supposedly. but one day I'm in the bath, after practice, minding my own business. the buzzer rings and it's guess who.

"Amanda."

"Who?" We both laughed.

I was dripping on the floor. I got up to answer the second buzz. dripping all over the floor. cats curious. my mother in me peripherally furious. the eternal teen *fuck-it.*

"Can I come up?"

"No." We laughed again.

"Come on." A kid.

I let her in and got back in the bath. leaving the door

open a crack. life was suddenly breathed back into the apartment. into yours truly.

I thought it was a mistake. But who was watching? (God? my mother?) And who was I kidding? I was delighted to hear her boxed voice in the intercom. instantaneously alive. I wanted her to come up. It felt like the most natural thing in the world. really, what I wanted more than anything.

She came in. I remembered another time. She stood on her red painted floor, puddled, woolly in her winter outfit. her striped Gap hat with the strings hanging down. fluffy chicky sweater (poodled). turtleneck. her uniform jeans, their frill, cut off at the ankles. socks striped pink and orange.

"Your socks match your hat," I told her then.

She hated anything ensemble. her mother. but it cutely came through sometimes anyway. like this, details unconsciously matching. or just going ahead. her adorable ragamuffin outfits. Blink and now she wore her same jeans. next incarnation. Birkenstocks. ditto. soles wafer thin black and white stripes. Light blouse with little blossom nonsleeves.

From the horizontal water she seemed so clothed. and vertical. Also naked in her need. appearing like this, presenting herself.

She handed me my towel. helped towel me off. Without a word we made love on the floor. me still partly wet, she very, she still half dressed.

I started with that trick I discovered maybe too late. after she sucked me for a pretty long time, no rush, slick strokes taken hungrily deeper than she usually did. and such abandon! We should break up more often!

Ease two fingers in and out, curve back up to the

inside eave, turnaround lay-up to the hidden g-spot basket, stay. while thumb and third finger ply the clit, play it, vibrato, sort of holding it out for the fluttering tongue. She went wild.

When she came again when we were fucking she made these little puppy sounds I'd never heard her make. exactly. like hiccups that seem to scare themselves and sort of yell and blip up into little yelps. When she came I came. so her sounds seemed to come from my own spasms, and hers, mixed.

"Turns out you're a director." Exhausted, panting, limp. not displeased. It was true. I was telling her what to do. more than usual. nothing to lose. And it worked. it worked great.

"Was I in your ass right then?" Part of the surprise shuffle. our pure act, out, shifting around and in again, and again. back and forth.

"I don't know," she moo-crooned. stoned. still not back yet. meaning it was beyond location. it was everywhere. (which was beyond me. how could you not know that?)

Now what? We were supposed to be broken up.

"How do you do that, B?!" She meant the thing I was doing. She wasn't thinking about *what now.* for us.

I felt like she would take the trick and show her lover how to do it. I said nothing. cool.

And afterward she didn't want to talk. wreck it.

But I persisted. I insisted. which of course drove her away. So I stopped insisting. The spell was broken but also still there. the pull and ache. our potent mystery. and also kind of curse. I went with her down the stairs and outside. keeping it mellow.

And when life won't solve your problems, put them in

the art box. is my strategy. and let unconscious justice run her brutal magic course.

So sitting, boxed, framed in front of the graffitied door beside my building. my favorite doorway in New York. favorite woman in the world.

I didn't want to do this here. in public. even though the early morning was pretty much empty, just some sedate cars and a few characters headed for work. It smelled like garbage. We were right beside the building's garbage. I said it smelled, and got up. She said, *"Please don't go."*

We were both really upset. First it was only me. Then she caught up with me. Calm, both of us, but both devastated. I was too much of a wreck to speak. Besides, I had nothing to say. So she spoke. This worked. I tried not to cry. stopped trying.

"I really love you, B."

I shrugged. My hand rose and fell, limply gesturing *great* for-what-it's-worth resignation. I summoned uprightness out of a little *nnnh* sound and looked into her eyes. Her whole life there, open. My eyes were melting down the mess of my face. I hated doing this in the street.

"Sorry for all this difficulty."

She'd used this phrase in a recent e-mail, too. This was how she saw this phase. *This difficulty.*

I looked left and right up and down the street, the flight instinct. I wasn't going to fight. Tomkins Square Park at the end of the block was a lush smash of shushing leaves. Out of the exquisite green and bright dappled morning sunburst a bobbing band of small children was headed past the dog patch toward us. Wee white T-shirts to their knees.

“Here they come,” I mumbled.

“Who?”

A looked. and looked puzzled.

“Our replacements.”

She saw I was attempting a joke. but didn’t seem to get it. She put a gentle hand on my shoulder. It was all I could do to stand there and not perish.

“We don’t know what’s going to happen, B.”

This was something else she’d said, more than once, in e-mails and in person.

“Yeah, but we know what’s happening now . . .” My voice barely made it out.

She came close for a hug. I backed up a bit.

“I mean—are you still with your new *boyfriend?*”

She nodded minutely yeh.

“But—”

“I can’t do this,” I spluttered. barely words.

I moved to the side to leave. She stepped in front of me, a dance step, blocking me, a football player, and hugged me. I only hugged back halfway, with one arm. But she made it juicy and moving, and I let it go deeper, let slip the locks, then breathed it in. then breathing more relaxed, both of us, together, our heads cradled in the soft shelter of each other’s quivering shoulder and neck. My reluctant arm came around and we embraced all the way home.

The kids were here. Tripping, bumping, bumbling along. holding hands in pairs. Telling us something. The teachers herding them directed them nonstop, using their variously ethnic names. Most of the kids, too, were little chatterboxes. Plump, fresh, beautiful little faces. their mouths and perfect clear eyes. You could see them all as grown-ups, still the same, but compromised, or ruined. Their wee T-shirts said, in green, Children's Liberation Day Care. These little people did me in.

"I have to go," I creaked in her ear. I broke away.

"No, B. Wait—"

But I wouldn't. I couldn't.

Amanda never, or rarely, talked about having children. I thought about it all the time. To me it was our second great given. The first was this. us.

"I'm sorry!" she cried. "Wait!"

I went.

Her eyes were puffy, red-rimmed, watery pleas. I resolutely beelined away, keyed into my building, tried to breathe and bowl my way up the stairs.

Wait for what? This was not unfamiliar. How many times would I be pulled back in. only to be slammed again, blindsided and spinning away, devastated again?

One last time.

I followed the old pull back down the stairs. She was gone. The chain clanged against the hollow aluminum of the streetlamp's base as I resignedly, unhurriedly unlocked my bike.

3. East Ninth Street

Dad woke one night and heard rain. He lifted his head from the pillow and the rain stopped. Rested his head. his right ear. back down. the rain resumed. Lifted his head again. and again the rain stopped.

The effect didn't go away. It didn't happen all the time. but from that night on it might. and it did. happen anytime. and more often.

"It's the damnedest thing," he reported. "Apparently the rainy season has arrived."

Katie was mildly fascinated. "What does it sound like?"

"Rain on the roof." He shrugged. "Rain on the leaves."

"Sounds nice."

"Rain on the pool."

It was funny. but it wasn't. You could peek into his room when he was supposedly sleeping and maybe see him lift his head from the pillow. mouth drawn down. pause to listen. lower it again.

Our first argument involved dancing. I couldn't believe how deep it went. how far and fast. Wow. How loaded. Over nothing. Here we go.

Salsa dancing. which I don't know how to do.

Coming downtown in the subway from a rare uptown foray together. supposedly fun. Amanda stared ahead with a frozen. blank expression. exhausted, elsewhere.

Everyone in the car. representatives from around the world, also off in their own worlds. concerns. daydreams.

At Union Square the announcement over the really crackly, really loud PA system said, "Stand clear of the closing doors, please." in its friendly upbeat robot voice.

Without snapping out of her zombie state Amanda repeated the announcement with uncanny accuracy. like a ventriloquist's doll. perfectly getting the golly-gee tone. the singsongy rhythm of the jolly imaginary guy. Without moving her face. or mouth.

At the next stop the crackly static was louder and worse. downtown degeneration. our stop. Astor Place. Instead of a recorded announcement the driver cut in with his slurred union-required New York accent. world-weary.

"Disaster Place."

A didn't notice. I repeated it. She flatlined, glazed. I thought it was funny.

A bar on Broadway near Houston. Claire and whoever. Like a western bar. wood walls, neon beer signs. Except salsa music. loud. lively dancing in front of the bar.

Most knew what they were doing. We didn't. I didn't.

A watched others. as we/she danced. picked up steps like that.

I felt like a spaz. I'm not. But it takes me a minute. or more. I'm slow picking up dance steps. or at least slower than her. way slower.

I wished she'd be patient. help me. Once I get it down I'm good.

After enough fumbling I stopped. I felt like she wasn't dancing with me anyway.

This guy with a horse overbite shimmied with her. spun her. She knew him. stupid long sideburns. angle-cut. not unlike mine.

She smiled. I left. Just to get air. so to speak.

The fresh night air of Broadway the river. river traffic bouncing along. She came out. She was really pissed off.

"I really wanted to dance."

"You did."

"With you."

"We did. I suck at it."

We were the couple arguing on the sidewalk. outside a bar. already!?

"You could at least try."

She was really fucking upset. She looked like a different person.

"I did . . . I'm sorry . . ."

I felt terrible. I'd lost her. it felt like. Wow. *How?*

We went back inside. without making peace.

Claire was dancing with an old guy. flannel shirt, jean jacket. country guy. Like the bar.

They weren't really dancing. he wasn't. She introduced us. It was her dad. seemed like a good guy.

We tried dancing again. It was hopeless. it was worse. I couldn't do it. I hated it.

A showed me the basic steps. two steps forward. back. swivel the hips. sort of. as you march in place. I tried.

Blading back I went ahead of her on Lafayette. long strides. bike lane. arms swinging rhythmically. pendulous. clanging petulant liberty. I waited at Astor Place, by the cube.

She took forever. deliberately. Slowly pumping along. shoulders slowly rolling. heavy. angry.

When she arrived I kissed her. cold kiss. Didn't work.

It was Saturday night. Lots of cars. kids. the skateboarder and goth teens. infesting the cube island.

Party time. droves of young urban strivers on a mission to get wasted. bridge and tunnel crowd. workforce strays. street people.

At St. Mark's Place I dipped and ducked in and out of cars and characters. No praise now for my happiness in motion.

"Those things are dangerous."

We rolled on sedately. on the surface. through the park. They were all out tonight.

"I don't want you to wear those anymore. You'll get killed."

Into the dark mind of the park at night. the drums bubbling on the far side. At home you could hear them clearly. Lakeside. the natives. into the night.

A movie was always a safe bet. I told her what was playing, and where. read off the times.

She made a face at the French film. She called Moviefone and when he greeted her answered Mr. Moviefone back *Hello!* in his same manic game-show voice.

Of course we/she chose the good ol' Hollywood romantic comedy. It did the trick. I kissed her when they kissed. We kissed.

All day in bed. More orgasms than either of us had ever had. more laughing. They were the same thing. different mouths.

We were living inside our own romantic comedy. triple-X. People saw how happy we were, how well we fit together. how right we were.

Friends saw it. said how lucky we were. People who didn't know us would stop and watch us. walking holding each other. her hand in my front pocket.

We joked and messed around. wrestled. fucked, licked, sucked. fucked more. made love. lay there gloriously beat. glowing. The snailing tongue. a fingertip tracing another new pleasure trail into known silky dreamland. again. and again.

We fed each other. (she) threw the food. (she started it.) Mashed it into orifices. (I finished it.)

Until we had to go outside. Sooner or later you have to go outside. So we'd go eat (Angelica's). Go to a movie (Angelika). Some music. (Angelique.)

For something new and different we headed one night down Avenue B. walking super slowly. drugged with delight. arm in arm. side-bodies Siamese.

"That used to be my favorite bar." We floated past her past. behind the windows. safe now.

And farther down, "I used to buy heroin in that

bodega . . ." Glacial fluorescent storefront glare. muted salsa. emitted louder when the door opens.

Here's where she almost died once. that dive was her favorite bar. lived there. worked there! till they fired her.

There's where she had a crummy crash pad share. could hardly remember. sometimes slept on the kitchen floor.

We went to Gloria's. new then, still just one corner room. My friend did the walls. washes and stenciled patterns. bright Brazilian license. for free food.

The waitress came under our spell. She came into our jokes. said what to get.

Everything near us slid into the warm pool of our brimming good humor. overflowing. It was the funniest time out we ever had. the funnest. Everything opiate, lovely, loose.

The general electric. languorous thrall. gentle erotic thrill of simply being together.

When we left the waitress said, "Can I come home with you guys?"

Amanda catsat one weekend right near there. So *we* catsat.

For another couple. further along the downward path of coupledom. for a little weekend adventure. visit their life, but them not there. poke around. Look at this! joke around. Buddhist books. dirty books. We read from one. laughed and kept going. got off.

Apparently the guy was going after other women. Surprise surprise. He was a good guy. But y'know. he was bad.

Two kids on a stoop outside that apartment, between C and D, maybe ten and six years old. The older one teaching the younger.

The little kid tries, "I smell puthy."

"No," the other says. "You gotta say it like this: 'I smell *pussy!*'"

Dad seemed the same when I visited him in Santa Barbara a month or so after he was diagnosed. He had begun rounds of chemo. gentle doses at first. Followed by rest. when he puttered around in his garage workshop. played golf with three clubs. light canvas bag like a third pantleg.

He was a little thinner. looked better. He wasn't trying to put on a bright façade. He was calm. wry. removed. as usual. kinder maybe. or more circumspect.

Then he weakened. Took to bed. At first it seemed *for now.*

After a certain point TV didn't interest him. videos. and then music. His wife Carla and the day nurse wheeled the entertainment table out of the room. bumping once. he anticipated the second. then twice. on the threshold.

Carla read him different things. but his mind wandered. and they'd stop. Until mock-sheepishly he asked her to read him "The Night Before Christmas." and he was delighted.

She read it every evening. from then on. nothing else. When he was a child his mother had read it every year to him and his brother and sister.

When Kate visited he asked her to straighten the duck etching on the wall. She reminded him he had taught them as children that framed pictures on walls moved. over time. due to the spinning of the earth.

Hence the Spanish Armada series. frigates in flames.

all tilted just the same slight degree on the living room wall in Massachusetts. Unlike the battle-skewed fleet depicted.

On the wall the etching was angled just like the ducks taking off in it.

"Or due to human error," he suggested. forty years later. reminded now. "In the hanging."

"You must have that pattern in the lace memorized," Kate said of the lace canopy that framed his last little corner of the world. like the visor of a cap.

Clearly placed there over him to mock him. the lace covering. fitted onto the mahogany bell curve frame. set on four tapered poles. striated. lacquered. topped by twirled flame finials.

He spent his life living simply. energetically. a man of steady duty. habit. dignity. privacy. intelligence and wit. A gentleman. reviling cruelty. fools. their frivolities.

And now here he found himself in this unlikely sickbed. incarcerated by his own gentle and violent demise. by time and the dangling bell. by merciful God and this other ruthless damn thing.

Ensconced like some sissy prince in what he repeatedly referred to as *this ridiculous bed.* surrounded by women and cups. whispers. pillows. though he only needed one of each. he claimed.

"They missed one right there," he confirmed. pointing at a dropped stitch in the pattern of the lace.

"And the hedge needs trimming," he added. And so it did. leafy shoots encroached upward. somehow comically. the rogue upstarts. nosing into the picture of outdoors in the window in front of him. below the lace fringe.

"And the pool needs to be cleaned, and our pool boy, Ramon, comes once a week, and doesn't like to clean the pool. He likes to play music in the garage, loudly, and take my decoys out of the pool."

A pair of crude duck decoys he carved and painted. expressly for the pool. hoping to attract tired or confused migrating birds.

Perhaps those strays with no reservations in the scarce booked wetlands clinging to clefts. dry riverbeds. low lakes. endangered creeks. losing their last wet grip between the mountains and the drop-off coastline.

Anemic trickles. slow last drips of the vast continental snowmelt. sucked up by thirsty omnivorous human cities. fields of crops. rows of profit. fields of Mexicans. turquoise swimming pools.

Circled ultra slowly. beak to beak. pulling arduously gracefully apart. beak to butt. in the pool's mysterious spindrift eddy. So far there had been no (*known. observed. mind you.* as Dad pointed out) visitors.

While he was at it. for you never knew. he made a couple of (rough) pileated woodpeckers (rare!) and stuck them on the base of the single scarred palm sweeping artfully upward between the garage and the pool.

From his bed he could see in the window a section of this tree. The waist. as it were. of this lissome curve.

The canopy bed had followed him across the country. at Carla's behest. He felt foolish ensconced in it now. helpless. boxed in. trapped. as he kept saying. as if dressed in a nightgown.

For instance the aged heirloom christening nightgown. yellowed. lace papery-fragile. his grandfather had worn to his christening. and his father. and he. presumably his siblings also. certainly his children. and some grandchildren. had worn to theirs.

When over the years the picture of him as a cherubic boy wearing the christening nightgown elicited the inevitable comments he had his chortle and ready response ready.

"That's me when I was a little *guhl* . . ."

Kate served him orange juice in a straw. "They will no longer permit me to hold my own mug," he explained. complained.

Complaining meant he was still kicking. still wry. ironic. still himself.

"That's because you kept dropping it, Billy," Carla bandied playfully. like Grace Kelly in *Rear Window*. their fond modus to the end.

"First they took away my glass and replaced it with a mug, because it has a *handle,*" he explained to Kate.

In fact the first thing they took away was his knife. (Or rather. really. his car was first. after the uncharacteristic accident presaging the decline. motor control. He sailed obliviously through an intersection like Mr. Magoo. his rear hip bumper crashed into by a car obeying the light to his right going green..)

Under pressure of his real-life deadline he was carving a bird for each of his kids and grandkids. but kept cutting his fingers. his hands. But he kept going. hands bloody. When they took his knife away he continued with another knife. Then Carla took that one, also. Then he took to bed. as he called it. instead of just for parts of the days.

"I've taken to bed," he joked on the phone. when he still spoke on the phone. "Like Hugh Hefner."

He sighed into something arriving. significance fading. and seemed to forget it. or glumly remember.

"I've lost my sense of humor," he stated flatly.

Later, when irony had withdrawn. with his vitality

and his voice. he would sort of hum thanks. *Hmm.* when we moistened his lips with ice cubes. (*Hi. omm.*)

One morning Carla found him on the floor in the bathroom. the tiles streaked. gory. His temple covered with dried blood. his ear caked.

He'd gone to the bathroom during the night and slipped. fell. and couldn't get up. *Damnedest thing.*

So he resigned himself to his predicament. and waited there. When Carla finally opened the door in the morning he greeted her calmly.

"I knew you'd come eventually."

Once Carla found him in bed smeared with shit. the sheets a mess. After that she hired Hildy. the day nurse. whom he liked immensely.

"Hildy, my dear, you've convinced me that the time has come at long last for women to take over. We've made a fine mess of things. The world needs you. I hereby relinquish my reins and domain. I'm fully convinced you ladies can do a much better job, all of you . . ."

One afternoon Carla came into the bedroom to find him sitting on the far corner of the bed. like a benched athlete. naked. elbows on his knees. glumly waiting to get back in the game.

"Are you okay, my darling?" They really spoke this way. It was sweet. genuine.

"How much longer do I have to stay here?" he asked the end zone.

"Not much longer, my darling."

We had dinners. friends. we. I. Friday nights or Saturday.

I cooked. shopped. did everything. happily. My department.

Warned the always pissy misanthropes in the apt (apartments are small in New York) below. before. a knock. a note.

Union Square Farmers Market that day. my element. superabundant urban cornucopia. also urban super-expensive. People shopping for people. feeling right with nature. nil carbon footprint. food miles.

The movies were our second bedroom. third. The first was the dark actual bedroom.

Just the bed fit. Narrow window. The crown of park trees above the neighboring roof. toss in the wind. nature out there. also here within.

We collapsed the Ken-built bed frame. fucking.

We met in the closet passage to the bathroom. The Alley.

"Don't think you're just going to just pass me like that."

Pin her there. let her fight back. pull the struggle in. and here we go. again.

"What makes you think I won't cut you?" she threatens. jabs.

The second bedroom was the Lake. Futon raft on shiny turquoise floor.

The TV was in there. VCR. and the music. Two windows onto the street. Charas across the way. big abandoned classroom windows.

So glaring. right there. everywhere. the New York split. social good vs. profit. Personal development. hearts. minds vs. real estate. that kind of development. realty. bottom line. reality.

I bought A a new (used) bike at the workshop on the second floor of Charas. before they closed it down to community use. Big corner room. the high mullioned windows. After-school program kind of thing. Old Geppetto guy teaching kids how to fix up bikes.

Movie theaters were our third bedroom. The Loews on Eleventh Street and Third Avenue. Glass and escalators. a certain Lower East Side view. St. George (Ukrainian Catholic) Church. rooftops to Delancey and past. the Willamsburg Bridge. at night a string of pearls. parabolic. dual.

The guy there I loved tearing tickets. prim neighborhood mouse you still see sometimes. Black. gay. going gray. slightly bent over. Had his little low-volume low-frequency East Village mouse life figured out.

"Thank you for coming to Loews." Ironic? prim little nod.

The Union Square monster megaplex had just opened. Big soft seats. Bounce back a bit. ready for takeoff.

The arms of the seats went up. We'd put the arm between us up. so we were on one big padded seat. our movie bed.

We'd slouch and mold together. intertwine. hold each other. one. We kissed. we talked. during the movie. as ever.

I did Billy Bob's voice in *A Simple Plan*.

"Hey, that's *funny!* He can't hear you cuz he's *dead!*"

"Shhhh," from the usual querulous New York loner nearby.

I did that Billy Bob voice for a year at least after that. With my wool hat pulled down I looked like him. a lot. with my black-rimmed glasses. Got *real good* at it!

And whenever they kissed in the movie I kissed Amanda. Every time. Every movie.

In those early days!

Slow homestretch stroll through Tompkins Square Park.

Evening park peace. under the sage old elms. their cathedral grandeur overarching. limp old money leaves. sexy lithe limbs. graceful evolved avatars. open mind arms. presiding.

Their impressive gathered experience. quietly applied. perfectly executed. amazing water use. carbon storage. filter. more. that miraculous unseen alchemy photosynthesis. the original leaf-light solar technology. unbelievably elegant solution and system internalized. seen and unseen. totally self-sufficient. no ego.

Half-feeling half-thinking these things and our place in the mystery. love and her place in nature. maybe I looked at her a certain way. limping a little. my knee.

"What's up, Old Guy?" Chewing her gum. with that slight openmouthed sass. like me mum.

"I love you." Slight shrug.

"You do not."

Blinking her whole face at me. like a wink but both eyes. sort of full facial squeeze. She did this sometimes. not like a tic. but an emphatic expression. a kind of facial joke. aimed at me.

Her own spontaneous facial italics. automatic. mirthful but also somehow mocking me in there.

She aimed the remote at me to turn me off. shut me up. when I called her seriously forgetful friend Anna a *perforated person.*

And of course she pounced on this. on me. "*You're* a perforated person."

I agreed. said so was she. joking. but meaning it. "I guess everybody is. But you're the one I'm up against."

"Against?" She took offense. like she was looking for something. just waiting. Her whole body stiffened. face hardened downward.

"Sometimes . . . Don't you think?"

"No, I never think. I just act out. Isn't that what you say?"

Wait. How did this just happen. (this happened to us.) this shift. from joking. after making love. about someone else. to arguing now? about us..

(And why did it happen after making love?)

"What's wrong?"

"And I'm the human you're *up against*. Rai-*eeet?*"

"It's nice to be up against you . . ." I tried to wriggle out of it. into her. "Wait—don't move . . ."

"I'm Swiss cheese, is what you're saying."

"Sometimes. Sometimes I reach out and get nothing. You're not there."

"I'm a big hunk-a Swiss cheese."

"Not just you. Everybody . . . Everybody's unconscious. Unreasonable . . . to different degrees . . ."

No reaction.

"Blind spots. Different holes. Different smells . . ."

"That's gross."

"It's like the concept of empty air."

"*Oh* no." Ironic but now she wasn't hurt or whatever. It'd passed. it seemed.

"If you don't want to hear it, that's okay. In fact that's a perfect illustration of it. Better than any explanation."

"You're better than any explanation." Joke your way out of anything. is one way to react. And not the worst way.

But tired patterns are tired patterns. Avoidance. But let it go.

"Thanks, Man."

I ease-wedged three fingers into her still drenched pussy. four. She went *Mmmm,* with a growl-tail *nnn* . . opened up. pushed deeper. suction and squeeze.

"See what I'm saying?"

"Ungh!" No problem understanding here.

Slid my tongue into her languorous mouth. which came alive. almost sucked mine unsuspecting out of its socket.

She wasn't asking. as usual. but I. as usual. explained anyway.

"Empty air is when you want a reaction and there's nothing there."

"_"

No reaction!

"Like in that movie, the Mike Leigh, or Ken Loach, where the woman's totally worried and freaking out about the missing kid, after she finds him, she takes him to McDonald's or whatever and tries to impress on the kid that he must never, ever, go off like that again. While the kid stuffs his face, oblivious.

" 'Do you understand what I'm sayin', sweetie?' This is *veery impor-int.*"

"The kid shows no sign of having heard nor absorbed any of it. Not defiantly, but matter-of-factly, zoned-out—just a kid, utterly absorbed in his food bubble fugue state—the kid says something like, 'Can I have some kitchup, please?' "

"Perfect example of empty air. When you want a reaction from the person and it's just not there. You're left alone with your need, enhanced, hanging there—the psychic negative space, expanding . . ."

A's breathing had changed. How perfect was this?

Her mouth was open. mashed into the pillow. her leak leaking. pooled. both mouths.

She was out like a light. I pulled the comforter up to her neck. tucked it around her shoulders. Her body was warm. soft. a big baby.

Once as a brooding taciturn teen I asked my mother why she talked so much.

"Somebody has to," she replied.

I've become her. Fill the gap. for everyone's sake. conjure. channel something. connection. warmth. verbal life. into the void of the moment.

While also becoming my father. interior man. coolly looping within. naming. hiding. making things. instead of living. more. among others.

Clearing my throat. the sound. inside me. I'm him.

Movie night! We took a cab. rare treat.

She loved cab rides. and always said so. Slumped in the back. chin to chest. watching the city slide by. holy night.

The pleasure of merely circulating. flickering liquid colors. shape-shifting urban lumens. washing over her face. as the boating blocks slid by. Holy New York.

And tonight. bonus. it was snowing. silent night.

The ambient city rumble subdued. in abeyance. absorbed in the immense mind. the falling indigo figments. feathers. and surrounding unseen nest. sensed architectural density. blanketed near and behind.

Souls appeased. at rest. allowing us our peace. the patient snow. forgiving. for now.

"This is my favorite movie theater," she said. in line. on line. no line.

"It is not." We never went there.

An unlikely Loews. up on Thirty-second Street. East Side. Kips Bay. Abutting a box set of chain ubiquity. homogenous. fluorescent. LensCrafters. Starbucks. CVS.

"Is so."

"Why?"

The sickness in one place. the cure next door. Funeral homes should bookend every block.

"Cuz I'll never see anyone I know up here." She who spent all her time with others.

The place was humongous. inside. anonymous big-box multiplex. Could be another city. a mall anywhere. which is why she liked it. I guess.

Yellow. lit. nobody around.

Except the two black girls behind the counter. stretchy synthetic uniforms. hair elaborately braided. lightning-bolt zigs. zags. like Sprewell. (bad-boy Knick.) big bling earrings.

Their dual pear forms cinematically framed. backlit against the bright bank of popcorn. urban unconcerned faces catching the radioactive upglow. candy arranged in colorful orderly rows. leaping inside the lab-lit vitrine. $12 million at auction. easy.

Escalators and other vast floors. carpeted quiet corridors. You got lost trying to find the right theater.

Black wall-sized silhouette depictions of old movie stars. She quizzed me.

"Who's that?"

"Greta Garbo, Man."

"Who's that?"

"Tyrone Power."

"How do you know?"

How do you not? you do not say.

We went in between Veronica Lake and Barbara Stanwyck.

A got fully into the moviegoing experience. Tub of popcorn. huge lemonade. hugged to her. carried like a kid. both containers a bit tipped. spilling. I offered to help.

"I got 'em."

And I had my goodies. Grapes in Tupperware. cashews. rice cakes.

What movie did we see? Slouched and blended into a single two-headed movie-body. Blended into all the movies we saw together. into ours. here.

Feet up on the seats in front of us. in fact *over* the seats in front of us. Knees where your shoulders would go. if you were sitting in front of us..

Holding hands. thighs. morphed together in different shifting ways. She'd move her hand away and I'd reach and put it right back where it came from.

She'd pull it out again. whack me. feed on popcorn for a while. a few falling on her. stuff some in my mouth. without looking. then her hand would burrow back somewhere else in my warm bundle.

"Shhh," she'd say when I talked too much. because I talk in movies. I had to point things out. Or she'd just reach over. without looking. and cup her hand over my mouth. or mash it. with or without popcorn.

What if your life together seems loops of repetition? Pleasant enough. sex. yoga. dreamtime. Is this a blessing? Or stagnation. like a stuck record. in the yoga bubble. in the art bubble. in the love bubble.

We walked home. Silent night. The snow was nice. inside the New York snow globe bubble. shake it up. still coming down. indeed straight down. supergently. as if slowing. hesitant. as it got nearer earth. us.

As if it knew its palliative soft-touch power. the slow snow. to smooth over everything. our earthling playground. roving holy ghosts. devouring and killing everything good.

There was no wind. few people. The city was padded. layered over and shriven. lines crisp. surfaces generalized. choice lines and edges limned. each block etched in fixed perspective. nocturnal chiaroscuro.

Stairs. rows of segment sills. linear strokes. details picked out and precisely highlighted. a near hydrant. its hex-bolt horn. capped by a white thumb. a dumpster. a hooded figure. unmoving. as in a Dutch painting. winterlude.

A muted horn. followed by a few more. a trumpet trill. faraway. light. Amanda's exhaled little *kapalabhati* laugh. like a pigeon taking off. you hear the wings lightly tap.

That quick chain of alto exhalations. four or five *ahs*. in fleet delight flight. softly voiced. each beginning with *h*. Breath of fire. without the fire.

A diagonal railing a violin bow. poised. Conductor's baton. delicately held like a stick of incense. dot of fire. minutely aglow in the dim. moved about with maestro precision. grace.

Like sparklers as a kid. but soft. fragrant punk. straw stick instead of wire. like incense. My father called me *punk. squirt.* (Well before punk.) "You little punk."

"Do your cigarette thing!"

My father describes swift circular shapes on the dark with the orange ember comet of his cigarette. on request. bedtime. magically trailing a short tapered tail. tucking us in. cowboy pajamas. campfire with crossed sticks. lassos.

"It's nice to walk," A said. lashes starred. We were so often on our bikes. (even in snow.)

We sang Christmas carols. as far as we knew the words. which wasn't very far. so back to the refrain.

The horse knows the way..

She veered into me. shoulder block. lost horse..

Deep and crisp and even..

The horse knows the words.

A spat into the snowbank. A whole mouthful.

"Are you okay?"

Waiting for the long light to change at Fourteenth Street. shadow people rose out of the earth. poured up from the underworld out of the subway entrance. (L train.) bubbled into life around us. lively mixed race faces. girls chatting away. guys standing there. waiting for the long light to change.

Moments like now maybe we both could feel. without saying anything. we were getting old. compared to these kids. They were kids.

Williamsburg babies. eagerly calling themselves *hipsters*. jean cuffs folded. heel-eaten or no. just so.

We were the East Village generation. another. hedging the next. almost safe now. back downtown. back across Fourteenth Street.

She spat out another mouthful. splat on the sidewalk. popcorn pureed. a lot.

"Looks like you had a little too much popcorn, there, Mandy."

"I do this all the time."

"Really?"

"Yeh." She smiled.

Her nose had a drip she'd sniff and wipe away. the whole walk. and it would come back again. the whole winter.

She hated winter. announced it regularly. her general disclaimer. not enough sun. melatonin. die-hard California girl. Never really adapted. like with good gloves. warm waterproof boots. *Winter clothes!*

She had her orange Gap parka. orange Gap hat. three stripes. one pink. earflaps. But always seemed to have wet shoes. sneakers. ankles exposed. tummy. wrists. neck. nose.

So her toes were always cold. and her fingers. And she always wanted me to warm them. rub them.

And she liked it. for some reason. when I squeezed her fingers. which isn't easy to do. squeeze a finger. *Hard*. But I did. *harder*. one after another.

It seemed like I wasn't doing anything. when I squeezed her fingers. one after the other. but she always seemed satisfied.

Foot massages would go on and on. in fact kind of replaced sex.

She'd ask me to push her up the stairs. when we went up together. Holding her butt. both bones. sit bones. and between. hand like a waiter carrying a tray.

Up the butt! up the stairs. elbow bent so I could shoulder her weight. It/I was like a ski lift. we.

And she always wanted me to go to her 6:15 class. Wednesday. Prime time. So I always went.

She said it helped her that I was there. helped her feel herself. have confidence.

I liked her classes.

You're just saying that.

And seeing friends.

Girls, more like.

But mostly it was to support her. Sometimes I didn't feel like going. y'know. stay in the studio. NPR on. home. watch MacNeil-Lehrer. But you go. *This is love.* This was my dharma. (path. duty.) I believed this. I did my best. It was my pleasure.

It was my privilege. really. To love her. to serve her. I felt that then. not just in retrospect.

I didn't know how to do it better. what to do differently.

Even when it didn't work. when it was bad. when she shut me out. etc. Especially then. embrace even this. That was hard.

It's easy to love. to be kind and funny and agreeable. when things are going great.

But love means all the rest of the time. to beat the same drum again. and again. repetition. like sex. yoga. prayer. I need that. stay on the beam. drum it in. The magic of repetition. drilling it in.

What the practice is all about. insight meditation. (*vipasana.*) mindfulness. I took this stuff seriously. Cultivate *purusha.* the witness. the higher self. *Samadhi.*

Not just in yoga class. in some meditation hutch. but here in the personal daily life.

It's easy on the mountain (in the temple). Harder in the marketplace. Hardest at home.

One day after her class A told me something Jean said.

Jean was in charge of the teachers. class schedule. who gets to teach when. She and Amanda ran the growing RamAnanda together. They clashed.

Jean was weird. looked like a corpse. no color in her skin. which she smeared with some greasy product. formaldehyde. organic! limp hair. leached. drained of life by a lonely life.

By the job. the endless henhouse squabbles. with A and the others. power struggles I heard all about. Jean was petty. isolated. neurotic. etc.

But perfectly nice to me. She saw me around RamAnanda a lot. bringing A lunch. popping by. with an apple. flowers from the farmers market. taking her class religiously. right up front. right in front of A. etc.

Every class at the beginning. sitting in half lotus (*padmasana*) at her harmonium. middle of the room against the wall. after the initial chanting.

Call and response. (singing. Sanskrit. offering it up to God.) (the Gods. Shiva. Rama. Vishnu. Govinda. Ganesh. Krishna. Brahma & Co.) then silence.

Amanda would ask if there was anyone here taking class for the first time.

She'd look around the room to see. I'd minutely lift my hand. little flipper. *Me!* right in front of her. every time. And every time she'd smile. roll her eyes. shake her head.

I knew what we had. (And not just in hindsight.) The most precious gift in life. and most precarious.

Jean said to her. re me. "There's a man whose search is done."

"She's right!" I told A.

A was less convinced than Jean. or me.

We fly many flags. from ego's fragile stick. (finger. tongue. dick.) snapping. vigorous. limp. Jean's words became one of my private banner headlines.

I liked to think of myself that way. It felt true. and liberating. royal relief.

(And escape and relief from all other duties? I wasn't even close to thinking that yet.)

So much wandering in life. Distraction. emotion. destruction. So much loneliness and wasted time. wasted life.

A was in her prime. I was in there with her. I was watching her. watching her grow and move more into life. And something was happening in me. to me. too.

I didn't distinguish between being in love. and that whole new lease on life. and the effect of the practice. the teachings. the transformative powers. you couldn't distinguish.

They were the same thing. blended so inextricably in this great new feeling you couldn't separate out the love from the practice. Except in the obvious immediate experience of each.

Amanda and me and this whole yoga world we inhabited. the practice. the people. the teachings. the movement. within.

Let alone where she ended and I began.

Where we ended and the practice began. this union we heard about all the time. and experienced. steadily. of body. mind. spirit. called yoga.

Where love ended and God began. why not say God.

We lived in this very cool and pleasant thing we shared and learned and generated together.

Moved through the cracked fractious world untouchable. in our love bubble. lifted.

A was on her bike. aloft. I was on my Rollerblades. afloat. The new Salomons that went like magic.

So smooth. silent. You just stand there and they go. You just stand there and they *accelerate*.

Approaching St. Mark's Church. Say God.

"Was that class any good?"

She always asked me this after her class. with a touching and annoying regularity and desperation. Indeed she'd already asked me. pressing. on the way down the stairs.

And I'd told her the truth. It was great. clearly everyone was really into it. transported and drenched. wrung out.

But she asked me again. It was gnawing at her. as usual. so she was gnawing at me.

(Take someone on. you take it all on. the quirks and the perks. baggage and wreckage. seen and unseen.)

"I mean really. You can tell me, B."

I tried to think of something critical. so she'd believe my praise.

"It was a beautiful class, Man."

I then pointed out a place or two where she slipped up. lost count of the breaths. or the pace. Or lost me. couldn't hear her. her voice too soft.

The part of the talk that seemed muddled. (The same part that seemed muddled when we went over it last night.)

She memorized all her talks. wrote them out. in her crawling swarms and round clouds of notes. and memorized them. And memorized the sequence of *asanas* for the whole class.

Blocked it out in the bathroom each morning. mat at an angle so it fit. Each class was completely choreographed.

I admired how hard she worked. I just wished some of that effort would go into her*self*. into *us*.

We waited for the light. Across the street a girl was changing the display in the window at Urban Outfitters. Brightly colored velvet cushions. retro-sixties-style. one nice leopardskin one.

Her disconsolate face framed between the Second Avenue Deli clock and people in line at the ATM across the street. She was lost in doubting and damning herself. her habitual downward inward spiral.

I kissed her. prime her. her prime! lift or snap her out of it. My role. No reaction.

She rode along the right side. I rode along behind her. Cars passed on her left.

It seemed to me more dangerous to ride on the right than on the left. Especially for someone as dreamy as A.

(This was before bike lanes. on the left.) (We were the pioneers.)

You were farther from the driver. on the right. which increased the danger. Every pass was a hurried distracted multitasking bad city driver's fleeting peripheral guess at the distance.

Whereas when you were right beside him. on the left. there was no way he'd hit you. We'd talked about this.

She said it was because she was left-handed. (?) She felt safer on the right. It felt more natural there.

So there I was minding her business. (My job. The business of a relationship. Minding the other person's business.) Cruising up Tenth Street.

She was going too slow so I passed her. Cut *Hi* affectionately close. bouncing along. crouched down. zooming ahead.

Cars came up behind. The first slowed at First Avenue to go left. The one behind it cut to the right to go around it.

I was gliding fast between this second moving car and the parked cars. He kept coming over. (*Motherfucker!*)

It was a cab. No idea I was there. The last car on the block just ahead was parked way away from the curb.

The careering cab almost sideswiped the parked car. with me between them.

I saw this happening. as it occurred. It happened so fast I didn't have time to panic. just respond. flash-pray.

I straightened up straight. slid one foot in front of the other. so I was only as wide as one leg. down there by my knees. where the cars merged.

It was an act of instantaneous faith/hope. stupidity. instinct. that he wouldn't veer any closer to the parked car.

And athletic. yogic. reflexes quick and smooth. calm. and danger was past.

Sped up Tenth Street toward its next victim. some steamed dumpling floating out of the Russian baths..

New York is a fast-moving maze of hazards and victims. The most famous game board on the planet. Open challenge international invitation to all the peoples of the world. High stakes gamble. *Try your luck!*

You learn to play safe. you unconsciously navigate. the myriad subtle learned reflexes of street sense. That was a close one.

"William Winslow, that is not funny!" My mother!

"I know!" I laughed. "I agree!" And I let out a *¡Whoop!*

"It's not funny."

Now came the adrenaline. after the *almost*. Breathe, Welly. *Whew!* I could've done a standing back flip. back and forth. on wheels.

"That's it. No more Rollerblades." She wasn't laughing.

The next heat of cars came roaring toward us up First

Avenue. We slid along the side. eddied. slow. against the flow of traffic.

"You have to get a bike."

Brother Bob. (aka Gully.) picked me up at LAX. His flight got in an hour before mine.

He'd picked up a rental and was there when I walked into the terminal. Standing among eager others meeting eager arrivals.

Among drivers holding up signs with last names. Gully held a slip of paper discreetly over his heart. scribbled with my old family nickname:

WELLY.

He smiled when I saw it. We hugged.

He felt stiff and not quite there. defensively treed within. an athletic hard hug.

We drove through the endless strip mall of LA. feather-duster palms. streaming shiny new cars infesting the expanse of low shamefaced buildings. run-down. nondescript commercial excuses.

Gully seemed to know where he was going. Seemed preoccupied. seemed lost.

The radio was tuned to a good alternative rock station. The laid-back deejay described the upcoming set with a pleasant casual vagueness.

". . . A little of this. A little of that . . ."

Not far past the crashing seaweedy Malibu headlands. beaches. hideaways. it was suddenly as desolate as Wyoming. out of LA.

Dry grass and chaparral hills. laced with dirt roads. ready to burn. few houses. and then none.

Empty afternoon. cars all new. whipped-up ocean in and out of view. cliffs and carved black rock coast. sunshot expanse to the level horizon line. The Pacific Coast Highway.

Gully was having a crisis and needed to vent. Money. Love.

Their mystifying disappearance was torturing him. And the terror behind that was hunting and haunting him.

Marriage was not working out. Work was not working out. Life was not working out.

I felt helpless. except to listen. to help him. Offer sympathy. assurances. Be a brother.

I felt lucky. My life was good. A's love. Everything we had. I was thinking about her. I was thinking about Dad.

Magnificent eucalyptus trees lined the mountain road up from the highway. trim. well-dressed. Their long leaves tossing and thrashing up high. pummeled by giddy Ms. Santa Ana.

Rounded strips of bark flaked off epicene trunks. in layers. shapes. like maps. palimpsest camouflage. like badly peeling paint.

Perfect straight white horse fences cleanly marked the perimeters of that tax bracket tax break. groomed clod and grass terrain.

No jasmine or jasmine smell on Jasmine Terrace. But orange blossoms scented our passage from car to living room. the hopscotch flagstone path.

Fat clear worms of excess silicone drooped beneath four blue French tiles by the front door. Dad. their street number. from one of their trips. (when they kept returning to Tours.)

"Welcome, darlings."

Kisses. unheld hugs.

"He's still the same. You should come on back."

Kate and Carla had everything under control. They didn't seem in the least upset. if anything they were gently energized. pacific.

"Prepare yourself for a shock," Katie warned as we walked back to Dad's room.

My chest hurt suddenly. the top. my throat. a steel ring constriction.

A strong medicinal smell came from and filled the room. and something else. fungal. fetid. mingled in.

Dad was not Dad but an emaciated old man unmoving on the bed.

The covers were pulled up to his shoulders. his skull revealed. on display. whittled bones jutting between temple and ear to deep sockets. new brow bone.

The collar of his pajamas showed. light blue with dark blue piping. Had he ever worn any others?

His beard was days unshaven. His parched lips were parted. His head seemed shrunken. more pained than restful.

More gone than pained. sunken in the pillow. sunken cheeks. bluish near the bone. weird bruises.

The only thing in the room that moved was his eyes. also sunken. and a few small tassels. suspended in border rows from the bed's canopy.

Not looking and seeing. but roving steadily back and forth. on and off. his gone eyes like beacons. on automatic pilot. In an unwavering way you couldn't possibly simulate.

"They've been doing that for days. It's a sign he's going."

"That's when they said we should make the call." The summons.

His three children surrounded him. on the bed with the lace canopy. Children no longer.

"Speak to him." Kate wet his lips with an ice cube. "He can hear you. They say the hearing's the last thing to go."

What do you say? It didn't seem possible he could hear us. He was more comatose than conscious. He wasn't at all conscious. it seemed.

"Hey, Dad. It's Welly. Just got here from New York. Gully's here, too."

"Hi, Dad," Gully put in. He didn't know what else to say. He shrugged. sad little smile. We all laughed almost.

"We're all here, Dad. We love you," Kate put in for us.

Tea. Sit with Dad. A walk on the beach. Sit with Dad.

A meal. Sit with him more. take turns. Look at old photo albums. A movie.

We slept at a big old semiseedy hotel in downtown Santa Barbara. Spanish-style arches. tiles. We seemed to be the only people staying there.

Gully and I in one room. His stuff everywhere. clothes vomiting out of his suitcase.

Kate spoke for a long time to Jay and the kids. The girls wouldn't go to bed.

This exasperated Kate. They were always exhausted and cranky when she returned from a trip.

It was her unrealized dream that she and Jay would parent the girls from the same page. Not from different books altogether.

"So what," Gully opined. "So they get to stay up late and make popcorn and watch a movie . . ."

Kate was about to respond with all her pointed passion. But she caught herself and just shrugged as if he were right.

She yawned. Wrapped in a nice umber shawl with a fringe. framed in the doorway. pulled it tighter around herself. a kind of self-hug. threadbare.

"Night, you guys."

I called A. left her a message. She called back and talked about her class the whole time. Sarah1 told her afterward she didn't speak loud enough. didn't show enough authority.

Patrick told her about how much the practice means to him. how life-changing. how much she helps him. He mentioned our Knee Club for Men. how I show him hip openers. ankle to knee.

Not a word about Dad. or me.

I let it be. but noticed. Got back into the moment here. (But still wanting to tell her what was going on.)

Patrick had told me that of all the different kinds of exercise he'd done all his life. always extreme. intense. as a marine. boxing. then karate. lifting weights with the fire fighters. *This yoga* was the toughest workout of all. by far.

Away from the practice. and the context. it seems so far. like it never existed. But also ever-present. within. or was it?

When the life is the practice you just do the next thing. and the next thing. steady as she goes. That part I had down. (Like my dad.)

Thai takeout. CNN. The Sunday *Times.* Gully on the phone a lot in the other room.

His keening tone and its disconsolate antimusic could not be missed through the shut door. pleading. whining. hammering away. He emerged flaring. miserable. standing in flames.

Looked at pictures of Mum as a pie-faced schoolgirl. pleated skirt. tam-o'-shanter. worn back and tipped like a beret.

Dad's eyes stopped moving. Then would go on autopilot again. back and forth.

His shallow breathing got shallower. Sometimes his breath would catch. as if the air supply had stopped. or the will. or some mechanism in between.

Winding down. but hard to switch off.

His skin was pink. gray. waxy. shiny. He was really skinny. His knobby knees protruded under the sheets. and his feet.

His capable hands were now another man's. those familiar sausage fingers now tapered and elegant. a pianist.

He used to look like Gorbachev. Now he was Marcel Duchamp. me.

Pictures of Dad in the bathroom. different chapters of his life. In his Harvard hockey uniform. same dark olive eyes. time-leveling.

Strikingly handsome. clean part. same noble lascivious mouth. cherry-lipped boy. now a chapped lizard.

Raking leaves in his Norwegian sweater. its pattern like golf ball dimples. Taken by Mum. seventies Kodachrome. her long shadow on the leaves. their subtler pattern. reptilian.

Dazed at his wedding with Mum. slender version. Dad tux-clad. black and white. grasping by the neck. as if about to hurl. sideways. at his dazed leonine dad. a dark bottle of champagne. (Moët.)

Different man. face fuller. torso. rotund. the race run. winning Carla. wincing. at their wedding.

Dad with Kate's girls. Dad in his workshop. Dad in a boat. belt slung under his round drum belly.

I poked around in his things in boxes in the garage. worthless. to most. hardware store calendar. rusted vise grips. everything talismanic. to me. invaluable.

A compass. like a crystal ball. fitted in a wooden box. future direction notched and numbered.

Diagrams in pencil on the work surface. clues. dusty boat models. unfinished bird carvings. partly painted. pencils whittled down. his old hammer. time-smooth wood handle paint-spackled.

When he was still up and about. but *declining.* as he wryly put it. during my last visit. he described his confinement. guffawed.

"*Ambulatory,* they call it," he cheerfully, ruefully explained. "Which means walking about. As if I'm about to *fall,* so they can take me away in an *ambulance.*"

I drove his car to the supermarket to get some things for Carla. get away. Rounded dashboard. rounded everything. padded.

Moving placidly along. encapsulated. the freshly paved road curving smoothly under classic dappled leaf shadow and light. scabrous eucalyptus columns marching by.

An access of dread arrived like a creature vision standing in the middle of the road. a monster Hulk linebacker grinning. menacing. green.

Sliding through the car and the curve and swallowing whole a sickly sway going through me down the hill.

An antirevelation. or moment of clarity. of nullity. of the utter senselessness of everything. effort. love. art. life. uncentered and random. baseless. amorphous and base.

Sudden dread knowledge. dead certain and fucking horrible to feel and know so absolutely that God just does not exist. not even close. You live and die and that's all. and there's nothing else.

I wasn't thinking about God. or mortality. or Dad. or anything. I was listening to the song on the radio. Otis Redding. "The Dock of the Bay."

And through this lovely-as-hell falling rain nostalgic lullaby refrain the bottom fell out. through me. like a piano crashing through floors from heaven above consciousness. through you. through the earth and molten core to cosmic hell.

An acute inversion. Dread (read *Dad dead*) converging in a single plunge closing in and strangling nature within. While everything around looks the same. goes on. the song. shimmering California. where you go to die. (Dad. father.)

The awful feeling didn't go away. nor the awful truth it carried. You understand why people need to die. if they feel like this. all the time?

But be here now. this. now was the test.

And God was overwhelmingly nowhere near. All that seemed so false and soft. meaningless. powerless. hollow premise. need-based invention. purely imaginary. fad. fodder. nothing.

And it didn't go away. but the plunge eased. defused. or diffused. as if everywhere now. formless but pervasive. atomized. instead of the concentrated lethal dose blast.

The difference is that when death saturates and dominates everything, then you're alive in death, not alive in life. (Which is the real *real*?)

Back at the house of hushed voices the emotional-memory-immersion-workshop ritual. (psychic preparation.) continued with more photos. more evidence.

Albums. of us as kids. Mum's cursive captions. in her felt-tip (Pentel) pen.

Trapped in those frames. locked in that mind-set and pecking order forever. Yearning for escape. from the others? from childhood?

Me and Gull with crew cuts. big white Chiclet front teeth. squinting.

Katie in a white hairband in the back of a boat. same squint. holding a can of 7UP and half waving to the open spacial future. freckled face. pigtails. white feathers of spreading wake pulling away behind.

Mum at the beach. Starlet hornrim sunglasses. scarlet lipstick. hand covering her stomach for the picture.

Looking a lot like Katie now. not unlike. indeed. Amanda.

Not many of Mum. censored. She tore them in half. threw them away.

Nor of Dad. He took the pictures. Or blithely smiled. or pursed the lips. white boat/tennis hat dropped flopped on his head. his round glasses. LBJ. Or wasn't there.

At the helm. on skis. same swayback pose. leaning (belly) onto the chrome steering wheel. onto planted ski poles. atop Mont Blanc. Hat. again. barely on his head.

Washed-out Polaroids. A duck hunting and drinking party in Cheaha-Combee. North Carolina. Charades. other couples. escapades. shoot skeet.

Dad with some garment on his head. mincing. tiptoeing? Arms acting out. fingers pincered and fanned like a pickpocket's. Artful Dodger. Eyes slurred. agape.

"Well. Come in. He's going." Kate's voice was soft. "Where's Gull?"

It was just after four in the afternoon.

Dad's breathing was audibly strained. phlegmy. worse. uneven. The rattle.

He exhaled and didn't inhale again. Then after twenty or thirty seconds he breathed in again.

This happened a number of times over the next half hour. Each time it seemed like his last breath.

His jaw had fallen so he had an extreme overbite. As if a bone had disappeared from the lower part of his face.

We leaned in close. Then he'd suck in one more.

The four of us sat on either side of him. touching him with our hands. our words. his flesh. his family.

We were crying but it was not horrible. It was beautiful. the crying was streaming. otherly sent. soft. gentle and powerful as his dying.

Carla held his hand. spoke to him. I had my hand on his forehead. Kate held his other hand. and stroked the smooth underbelly of his forearm. his slender wrist.

Gully touched his shoulder. his chest. hand flat. reading the last movement within.

We knew he wouldn't last long. There was an especially long pause. We could tell that was it. His breathing had stopped.

But then. after thirty seconds. he breathed! another last breath. sucked from the depths.

And another. after another long pause. We were sure. this time. both times. he was dead.

Then nothing. After four in the afternoon. Sunday. Dad was dead.

After a pregnant suspended minute. stillness. more. Carla leaned in close to his ear and spoke.

"One more breath, my darling."

I felt sorry for her. He was already dead.

But then his mouth moved. a grimace of intense effort wrenched his face. his head lifted a little off the pillow.

The gasping choked sound as he sucked in one more breath was achingly expiring animal. final.

We stayed with him for over an hour. Talking. laughing. crying.

The intensity subsided. spread through us into a wonderful kind of glow. closeness and perfect placement. in the stillness when the music stops.

And his soul. as they say. and it's true. stayed there with us.

Gully felt his chest. "His heart stopped."

We all sat on the bed. touching him. Gully asked if he could shut his eyes. and shut his eyes.

Dad's face was mountain calm. uncharted peace. We kept marveling. remarking.

My hand on his forehead. the whole time. his skin so smooth. his skull. the shape and fit feel. healing my hand.

The others touching him where they were touching him. sending him off. we his family. so this was family. holding him here still. on this raft in between. a moment longer. suspended.

"So lovely," said Kate.

"Looks like a saint," said Gully. relieved. for now. of anxiety.

Composed. thin. these last weeks. days. his features revealed. displayed now. so still. bony brow. cheekbone to the ear. He looked like me.

His skin cooled slowly. The room resolved to a focus and dimension beyond stillness. supreme calmness. serene.

Not heavy and sad. not sacrosanct. like the grandeur

of death. the deep drumbeat. God in a cathedral. great umbral apse and humbling awe.

But the simple magnificence of life. as is. in a quiet California bungalow bedroom. immediate wonder. an ordinary afternoon. into evening. anywhere.

The moment at hand. grace. palpably there.

That energy went into us. pure offering. amplified. like he was in us. was us. already. always. And now this. call it what you will. imparted.

It was not like he died. like he was injected with death. or drained of life. and died. ended. and left. merely.

But instead we were infused with life. his life. when he died. a light clarity and energy. the way he died. an added dimension. power. lasting and limitless.

He reversed the expected awful wrenching exchange. So different from the threatening grief leading up all year. the null void wall. the fear I avoided.

Instead. in the end. the life-giving opposite. departing life imparting life. to life. our lives. and more. The unspectacular miracle of pure God awareness. Presence.

Wonderful trick! an amazing parting gift Dad gave us. and honor. and lesson. abiding. miraculous.

To be with him. accompany him. see and feel him so gracefully go.

To see and feel that dying is the most natural thing in the world. In fact it was incredibly beautiful. easy. There was nothing to fear.

It was no big deal! But at the same time. it felt like no exaggeration to say it was divine. it was (we were) seeing God.

Carla called the hospice people to come and get him. in two hours. We called others to let them know.

Their solemnity. solicitous words. convulsions of grief at the other end of the phone. were from another world than our peaceful place here where Dad died.

How do you tell them *No! It's okay! It's beautiful!?*

I wanted to describe all this to Amanda. and also felt far from her. I waited till later to call.

Times like this pull you up straight. give you the truths in your life. the strength of clarity.

I never really did convey this to her. this blessing. on the phone. or in person. She was busy. (*"busy."*) my moving target. (*Chitta vritti!*)

Like many conversations we never had. we never had that conversation.

My report on my father's death. this account here. instead.

No lamentation over the body of Dad. We lingered on the bed. that raft. this room afloat. this release we spoke freely into.

The last year leading up to this. all the surging grief and fear I ran from. vanished now and replaced by this peace.

We talked about all kinds of things. It was strangely very pleasant. light. even giddy.

First we spoke about Dad. How he went. How he felt. his body hardening. How he looked.

Where he was right now. (Because we knew. he was right there with us.) What he thought of us right now.

"He'd say, *'Shhh, they'll hear you,'*" Katie said. What he said when we spoke about others. hunching down as if to hide.

As if they were right around the corner. Which in the house in Maine. on the wharf on the harbor. they sometimes were.

Carla told us that when Dad was courting her he proposed to her the morning after they'd first slept together.

"You don't have to marry me, my darling," she'd told him. taking care not to laugh. But she laughed freely now. Gully admitted he'd always been in love with his best friend's wife.

The dialogue. the scene. were like a dark-humor one-act play. sitting around the corpse on the deathbed. making jokes and laughing.

We actually mimicked Dad's last breath. Down to the sunken chin. We took turns. refining the sound. competed. for the best *Dad dying.*

This led to comparable renderings of Fred Astaire the cat in the car on the way to Maine when we were kids.

Fred would yowl inconsolably. almost a yell. strange-sounding. We three Winslows could do it well. and we did.

We howled now like aggrieved cats. as if in heat. loud yowling rounds. sitting around Dad's dead body. cooling. howling him to the heavens.

Around seven a man and a woman in ordinary clothes arrived. rang the bell.

We wrapped Dad in a sheet and moved him. on three. not perfectly gracefully. onto the gurney they brought in. He was bony. Not quite him anymore.

They raised the sides. clicked in place. and we rolled him out of the room. lightly bumping over the threshold. twice. down the carpeted corridor. muted.

Past the lit empty living room and open-plan kitchen and out the door. scuttling over the hopscotch flagstone walkway. half lifting. to their car.

It wasn't like a hearse or an ambulance. It was a regular station wagon. like Dad drove. back in Massachusetts. in our childhoods. The rear door was raised.

We push-crashed the gurney against the bumper. the way you bash a shopping cart into the last one in the condensed train of them at the supermarket.

The aluminum legs collapsed and folded back like landing gear retracted into the bottom of a plane. First the front legs. then the back legs. folded under. clicked in place.

Dad the mummy slid right in. The rear door was shut and off they drove. to the silent sea.

We agreed Dad would've liked it that he was taken away in a station wagon.

Carla remarked how wonderful and agreeable the hospice people had been over the past months. She looked exhausted.

He also would have liked that he was cremated in a cardboard box.

Like the cardboard boxes of a life lived. things. products. projects. all now ended.

And that his ashes. in a tough clear plastic bag. were kept in a cardboard box.

And he would have murmured the word *cremains.* wryly enunciating.

Like the cardboard boxes in his garage workshop. like the cardboard boxes in my studio. Cardboard boxes everywhere.

His name written on the box in Magic Marker. product labeled and ready for shipment. *Cremains, indeed.*

The oven was like a huge pizza oven. crossed with a firing kiln. at a place off the highway.

They slid his box in on rollers. Hissing spear tips of white fire piped inward from rows of nozzles inside. A gauge outside like a speedometer told the infernal temperature within.

They said it would take six hours for his body to burn completely to ash. (as long as a last long drive on a last tank of gas. odometer done.)

We read poems and passages. from printouts. from the Bible. Lie down in green grass. from his favorite book. *Peterson's Field Guide to North American Birds.*

A description of the American goldeneye. Plumage. migration. mating habits.

We used to lie in the *way back* of the station wagon for the seemingly interminable drive to Maine. sleeping bag spread over the duffel bags.

Sometimes you'd look out at an unbelievably long hill ahead. or stretch of road tapered behind. a tail flattened on the earth. and it was unbearable how long life was.

Fred Astaire stayed under the seat. yowling away. now and then. If he came out he came out spooked. low down. eyes crazed. buggy.

'Member the time he escaped in the Hojo's parking lot at Kennebunkport? Bolted. running low to the ground. under parked cars. Red Sox bumper stickers.

But mostly he'd stay under the seat and yowl. repeating it. perfecting it. and we'd copy him. repeating it. perfecting it.

When we got to the island and emptied out the car he wouldn't get out.

We'd leave the back door of the station wagon open and leave him in there.

He might stay there all night. still in there the next day. still under the seat. yellow violated eyes. still hypervigilant. black dagger slits. *blink.*

4. Broadway-Houston

And so I got a bike.

An excellent rebuilt retro cruiser from the old guy at Charas where we/I got A's.

Fat tires. one gear. strong triangle frame. A good solid workhorse street bike.

I put one of those big butcher/delivery baskets on the front handlebars. The basket was heavy. and made the bike front-heavy.

This affected the steering. and you couldn't park it with the kickstand without leaning it against something. or it would fall over.

A design flaw I remedied next bike. after this one was stolen.

My canvas bag fit in the basket with plenty of room to spare. for groceries. carrying all A's junk.

Goodies for the movies. which always included a sweater for A. for example. hoodie for me.

Sometimes I'd bring dinner. A grain. a green. a sweet vegetable. maybe seaweed. Chopsticks.

Standard fare was grapes. cashews. rice cakes. cider. water for A. tall Evian bottle.

Maybe a cookie or two from Angelica's. some vegan candies from in front of the cash register at Commodities.

Chewy nougats. sweetened with whatever. for A. com. yum .om.

I put the food (rice cakes are not food. fyi.) in Tupperware. takeout containers. For a good orderly moviegoing picnic experience.

Avoid crinkling wrappers. plastic bags. paper bags. A didn't care about this.

She was one of the people whose deli bag. *and* wrapper. you heard crinkle every time she reached for a bite. She thought I was too anal.

"B, you are too much."

As I set everything up around us. I was just being considerate. of my fellow movie addicts. and of A.

We ate on and off throughout the movie. dreamfeeding. my finger in her mouth. the led-meditation dream.

We leaned into each other. Interlocked. and less interlocked. Her fingers up my sleeve. my hand up under her cutoff jean. frayed cuff. supple calf.

She'd shift. I'd eat a little of this. a little of that. then want to get back in the exact same comfortable position. but it was gone.

But it always came back. but different. which was why we stayed together. or how. Not the sustained intensity. love connection. as in the beginning.

But the next chapter of it. as we pulled apart a bit. adjusted. arms overhead. made room for ourselves. with each other.

This was natural. I told myself. this was desirable. Or were we sadly fading? *Already!* the inevitable pulling apart. threads snapping. seen and unseen.

We had fun. loved our little life together. Did our things. performances. events. yoga events. *movies.* hang out at home. y'know. daily life. the little things. nights. *Living together.*

We also did things with friends. our dinners grew into other activities. We became the center of our growing group of friends. a center.

Martha's Vineyard Memorial Weekend Yoga Retreat. with Amanda and Sarah. Vegan food by Billy!

Wheeling gulls crying like babies. pink champagne moonrise. NY characters in parkas on the ferry.

Practice in the morning. Afternoon beach walk. Chanting at night. after dinner. Charades.

You're a hanging chad.

Intrigues. an expected hook-up. another unbelievable one. *Those two??*

Girls in gaggles. at the end of a pier. trying to get a signal on a cell phone. (which at this time were still optional.)

Scattered on the lawn in front of the Vineyard barn. as from a plane crash. the beach too cold.

Recovering from winter. Record rainy spring. lying in the sacred sun. like dandelions.

You're a millennium bug.

One chilly exquisite Monday morning. as usual we rolled on over to practice on our bikes.

As I veered over toward my place on the side of the RamA/Crunch bike rack she kept going straight up Lafayette with a strange little smile and a toodle-oo wave.

"I'm going to Andy's." she informed me. like a Zen koan. trickster girlfriend. keep you guessing. on your toes. *What the fuck?*

I couldn't believe it. I felt betrayed.

This was more than one of the thousands of threads snapping. This was a thousand at once. like yanking out hair. a hank.

Andy?

Of course I rode after her and demanded an explanation.

"I decided to switch." She shrugged. "You should come, too. He's great."

But so I did go too. Not that day but the next.

Buddy. baffled. followed.

And Andy was great. Andy's.

After spending most of his twenties in India. the '80s. into the '90s. Andy started his own *shala.* (school/room.) in New York. blocks from where he grew up. (Sullivan.) Just *ashtanga.*

The corner of Broadway and Houston. Not that far from Rama. Above EMS. Big corner building crowned by a green copper cornice. leaves like little teeth.

Same building as Angelika! (movie theater.) but opposite side. diagonally down. Mercer & Houston.

So in triangle pose (*trikonasana*) you're pointing diagonally down (*drishti.* sort of.) to the null movie screen in the unconscious dark. (empty mind.)

(Angelika. the sticky rug (as opposed to sticky mat. up here.) growing a fetid fungal really bad smell. worsened by a bad air circulation system. but good indie/foreign films.)

A movie and a yoga class take the same amount of time.

A quiet room on the airshaft on the second floor. solid interior stillness. up the stone stairs.

Past the cheerful Jamaican doorman George. in his jacket and tie and white teeth. always smiling. the greeter. security guy. seated at his post.

Greeted the yogis. especially the gals. all by name. too early. too loud. loquacious. But a good guy.

People came to Andy's after they went to India. Mysore. learned the score.

Maybe learned *ashtanga* at RamAnanda first. often after years of open classes there. then move on to the next thing. *ashtanga.* every morning early. except Saturdays and moon days. (full and null.)

Then went to Mysore. to Guruji. the source. Then to Andy's when they got back to New York.

Amanda of course knew about this progression. knew Andy a little. Went one Sunday with her friend Beth. without saying anything. check it out.

And instantly decided to switch to Andy's. again without saying anything. independent gal. apparently.

Until we were on our way to practice on that chilly exquisite Monday morning.

And like mountain climbers who can only see the piece of cliff they're steadfastly clinging to. the next crack and crag and effort.

(*Tiger above. abyss below. strawberry dangling. eat it and savor. This is your life.*)

Or marathon runners who can only see the piece of road pulling out (from) under them.

Inveterate travelers (fleers. in place.) that we were. only after we arrived at the oasis of Andy's did we realize this was where we were heading all along.

It was obvious. pleasant. this fully realized place. nice Nag Champa smell. and sweat. humid. warm. the welcome new dimension. within the familiar.

Frankie and Jonni never. or rarely. called you by your name.

Andy. first day. first minute. after the initial intro. "Billy!" Pointed to my place. among the rows of new *ashtanga* bodies.

A different beat and feel. and energy. deeper. calmer. more concentrated and intense. but also more relaxed. more advanced. the real deal. you could tell. right away.

A few I recognized from certain days when Andy's was closed and they'd come to Rama.

The room was smaller than Rama. but full. more people. Not crowded. but just enough to keep it full. six across. three deep.

Once in a while one or two waiting by the changing area for a spot to open up. someone else to finish. rise from the shakti dream state. where you go in *sivasana.*

The road I'd run on in Maine striped by early morning shadows of trees. like bodies lying across the road.

My father in the woods. white shirt. sleeves rolled. among the black column spruce. standing in the tall room. listening.

His yellow chain-saw anima. same yellow team as the lawn mower. my department. white rubber sneaker toes greened.

Me standing in the tall room morning listening. bodies lying around the room.

When it arrives the great blue heron lands below consciousness. this light agency. settling in.

It stays. moves mysteriously. but barely. like you're not alone anymore. stays all day. all days. barely there. never gone.

Inside the body is the subtle body. And inside the subtle body is this.

Be still and know that I am God.

The practice is real. The process is real. This again.

It's not a thinking thing. It's relinquishing thinking. recurrent. this letting. like blood-letting. life-blood.

Something happens, like this, in the practice, in the life. In the nine-gated city. the body. (each hole a gate in. nostrils. eyes. mouth. et al. count 'em.)

In the mind. aswim. *klesha,* afflictions. negative thoughts, *vitarka.* all its swarming distress. *dukha.*

You don't need Sanskrit words to know and name fears. desires. words. visions. delusion.

The mind the king of the nine-gated city.

Is crowned by life when the kingdom is ready. the unnameables line up. when the subject is willing. and blind. they blend.

And each night blended with the sweet next and the next and the sex-dreamy next. in spite of the shifts and kinks. reality settling in.

Continuous touching fed continuous anticipation. desire the self-feeding driving force. overriding. underlying. We were in that other blessed dimension lovers live in. for a while.

We were only apart when we had to be. weekdays. and then we talked on the phone. often. like every hour.

Before we were together I went around in my Rollerblades. Before that I'd walk to yoga. or jog.

Ludlow. before it went SoHo. rock-and-roll rising

from a basement practice space. stop and listen. keening glorious electric guitar benediction scribbling up and radiating outward.

Washing over day-shy Pink Pony. Max Fish and Luna Lounge. waiting for night. hipsters&co. getting younger every year. if not hipper.

A had her rattletrap English-type bike. Skinny tires. knocks. arrhythmic clicks. One brake cable disconnected. tied to the silver-blue frame. Fuji.

Now we went around together. biorythmic. I'd skate behind her. admire her voluptuous form. switching in steady rhythmic bicycle action. work that seat. arms straight to handlebars. Pinup pose.

I'd come up beside her. hold on and glide. or pull her faster. Get her going. quick choppy little steps. holding her handlebar. The horse pulling the cart.

I'd show off. fly ahead. I went backward on smooth streets. fast. Two blocks of St. Mark's Place was the smoothest surface on our routes.

"Do those backward crossovers."

I'd sweep around corners. cars. people. In and out of cars. people. cruise in a crouch. slalom quicker than a skier. swivel hips. like a daredevil kid.

"You're happy in motion," she observed. back in our enhanced beginning. enhanced.

We'd dance in the Lake. Floor painted turquoise. high-gloss.

The Lake! (my addition. plus red trim. walls white. first time she saw it she made a face that tried to hide its smile in faux disapproval.)

We danced in the Lake. to raucous rock. We'd make the same into-it expression. Lids hooded. Lips pressed in. Faces blithe moons. Holding hands and leaning back. arms straight.

Slow dance to Al Green. Her long thighs measuring up nicely against mine. She'd stand on my feet. hold on to my handles. one inch. my butt. barely there. her bare feet on mine. around and around. starting in clothes.

Her father used to dance with her. drunk. but so what. she loved dancing with him.

Neither of us drank. anymore. But we sure got drunk on sex. Those first days. weeks. on each other. on the third thing. My mouth on her pussy. wetly glued there. her other mouth. lips licking lips. flickering tongue.

My cock in her mouth. she looks up at me and our eyes lock. sexiest thing in the world. she pauses. continues. eyebeams complected.

She giggled or moaned until she giggled when I stuck my tongue and dart in the comma of her ear.

A comma is the heard pause, formed in the special mind inside the ear, delicate receptive tympanum conductor, reading the pulse of a pause that doesn't stop. full stop. but slips along more glibly, silky, surfing the liquid text, supple as sex, birdsong, the risible mercury in the music, linking into a living pattern the next pause and the next, the liquid or choppy or otherwise rendered rhythm the heartbeat and breath, the pulsing, rippling meter and jazz logic and genius embedded in language, each felt beat gingerly heard by the ear, and instinctively held, briefly, appreciatively, ingeniously tasted, ingested, invaginated, instantaneously, in the nice little curve, as in a mold, hence its spermy shape.

Charlie Parker lived right near us on Avenue B near Ninth Street. there's a plaque. near the corner of Tompkins Square Park.

Before it was bad and got good again. manufacturing in his avian inner-outer space his special kinds of comma. his quiddity. sonic flight and song, dreaming, spirit extending, sending, expanding, still here emanating strong in our inspired little corner of the world.

Your mind in the delirium of sex streams free-form afflatus, fusing tumbling images and thoughts not thoughts, thoughts almost words with not-word emotions teeming in unedited profusion. unending.

We kissed fiercely, bodily, gently. we kissed totally, tenderly. That sleepless marathon. unconscious continuum. fueled by the love drug.

The love dimension. all streaming images and sensational, weightless intergalactic sensation. Her face in *ecstasy!* Time a sweet cosmic joke, this high holiday gift we happily accepted. *This was real!*

We held each other, you get the picture, touching, exploring, tasting, etc. in the countless different ways. unceasing variations, involutions. and also more repetitious than yoga! conjuring together the beginning of time and a new life. together.

Holy nights. We hid in each other. pulled each other in. down. We kept each other afloat, we pulled each other under.

The open mouth. the egg of air between our open mouths, long gone now. and gone her oral distance, or lesbian otherness, the gaping initial open o. Now my cock went there. Now I understood!

Our wild tender circus act. acrobatic, pornographic, anaerobic. nonstop fantastic sex.

She wanted my cock inside her as much as possible. which was great, because that's what I. it. wanted, too.

In her mouth. her in mine. we made delicious love in

all the ways lovers invent anew. in those first days. off the charts.

That bonkers first phase extended. lucid. fecund. blessed. lured. lost and found. realm of the senses. sex equals spirit. expanded.

Marathon fucking sessions that seemed effortless, endless, attenuated ecstasy, improvised, energized, plugged into this amazing third thing between us. the welter, the wonder. the sacred mount. shared sport.

Like a long multi-layered favorite rock-and-roll song you travel off and dissolve into. merging. creating together. weaving guitars. again and again. mounting the waves. the wall of sound and sense and mind. riding the crazy sacred horse rocking between you, our own mind-manufactured music, spirits and samples lifted from your day. your genes.

Stray fragments. imagined fleeting things. feeding us, leading us deeper in.

A loved hearing the music that would arrive, clouds getting louder, down on the street. She always turned or lifted her head, stopped moving, tuning in.

Hyper salsa, polytonal, sexy-ass, hyper-synthesized. hip-hop jeremiads. scary posses kicking out car windows. chucking horses off buildings. and the car would slide away, samurai sneaky, dialing down our live sample. They kept coming. especially in warmer weather. cars like bombs of throbbing sound. some pop riff. one of those shimmery divas. Eminem. that year. Slim Shady. beat box on wheels. *Please stand up.*

We went out and did whatever we had to do in the day. what beautiful forgotten days! and returned to each other as soon as possible.

Glued together, arms over shoulders, mine on top,

no mine on top, no mine on top, windmilling competition, how many times did we do that. perfect it. over our time?

Fitting together, (high) hip to hip (low), wit to wit, walking/talking as one love creature through the polymorphous East Village streets.

Globally mixed gene pool. living remainders of world history. the crazy past century. or two or three. or all. speeding up. the entropy and the end. spinning this blue-skinned world into an insane final frenzy.

When we thought maybe we should get out of bed and go do something, guess what. we went to a movie. I like to sit pretty far up front, center, fourth to sixth row, depending on the place. size of screen. distance from screen. She liked to sit in the *back!*

"Why don't you just stay home and watch it on TV, then, it's so small?"

"Cuz, we're at the movies!"

"The screen's as big as a postcard back here."

"No, it's nice. You sit back here and . . . relax, enjoy the show . . . See everything . . ." Between your feet.

Our first negotiations as a couple, toward compromise, outside of bed, landed us in the exact center of the theater.

"This is good," I said as we settled into our seated positions (slumped, interlocked) for takeoff. "Are you happy?"

"Yes, I'm happy." She tapped the back of my hand twice reassuringly with her other hand that wasn't already holding it.

"I'm happy, too."

I kissed her. We twisted in our seats. really made out. still in our bedroom. Her flesh under her clothes was so soft!

We had the whole blind slug thing going with our tongues. engorging. wrestling. pink vs. red. like thumb wrestling. but slimy. This was not French. this was live-food carnivorous.

A pace game. now slow it down. okay. we eat. we wait. then the jabs disport. faces shift. speed it up into competitive ardor..

We made out more than we watched the movie.

You feel like. fear. things are getting worse. fading. and then they. get better. you settle in deeper.

"Who's that guy with the gun?" she asked. We had no idea what was going on.

When you see people making out all the time you feel like, why do they have to do that? So teen.

But when it's you there's nothing else.

"That's the guy getting out of the car," I explained. "Now he's going into the dark bar . . ."

The usual angry, sourpuss New Yorker. petty. lonely. turned in her seat a few in front of us and hissed, *"Shhhh."* like a viper. pent rage like steam, vitriol, out her ears. eyes. nostrils.

"She needs to get laid," Amanda didn't really whisper. "Poor thing." Our new solution to everything.

Every time they kissed in the movie, I kissed her. I did that as long as we were together. At least one of us held the other's crotch at all times.

We laughed at things that weren't supposed to be funny. or weren't funny to anybody else, but were hilarious to us. because we had the gift! the laugh and lift and inherent ease and spring and lightness of this other dimension.

"Wait—why did she . . ." A was still trying to follow the plot. Even when she totally paid attention she didn't always get what was going on. in the kinds of movies I liked.

They kissed in the movie, and we kissed. longer. "Why don't you two just go back to bed!" The pissy New Yorker turned and practically shot us.

"Why don't we?" I slid my tongue (I win!) in her ear and fattened it. splat wet fat comma. She pushed me away. *"Ewe!"* Still holding on.

"I want to see what happens!"

"Too late for that, Man!"

On the screen I see my mother. her sunglasses. in her helmet hairdo. a school day. my brown boy shoes. round sharkskin toes. we eat. and where in the boy-dream does everything go? God has no bottom. We die.

The witness (*purusha*) arrives. the observer. becomes part of the process. within. of thinking, of being, of responding to emotions.

You find yourself responding differently. to anger, to difficulty. sometimes. More calmly, by degrees of growth. more kind.

To life and what happens. asana to asana. scene to scene. breathe smooth. right action. at least has a chance.

My practice, and the consciousness it fostered, had shifted now to the place where the series of separate asanas now seemed one long, continuous song. of life. scene to scene. one long, continuous, connected sentence.

When had this happened?

In love, first. then that quantum quicksilver jump start fades. the liquid love continuum hardens back to ordinary love life wax. wood life again. world again. sometimes softening.

Then in the process, in the practice. on the floor. in the room. in the mind. in the body. in the something in between or beyond. or linking here and there. death and grace in the repetition devotion. the leap of faith life. unconscious. sort of sensed. more and more so. stronger. more sustained.

Then noticed. vividly. seen, registered, assimilated, in the seismic shifts.

The psychic correction or magic that gives you your life back. Gives you back your narrative. Back to your old tricks. But no! No longer spinning wheels. so it seems. In synch. with life. more. Your tricks are skills. You get a good rhythm. Cycles of this. getting closer.

You carry this quiet boon within. into the day. your scenes.

"Push me up the stairs, B." She took her ready position on the fourth step, not even looking back. ready for the chairlift.

"So what's the big secret?" Atlas grunted. She was wobbling. She was heavy. "What happened at work?"

"You have to promise not to tell anyone."

"I promise."

"I, Billy Winslow," she said. She often did this.

"I, Billy Winslow."

"Do solemnly swear . . ."

The big news was that Rama was being sued. sexual harassment.

Yoga's a very sexy thing. the yoga center's a hot place. who are we kidding? Some perceive as sexual what others see as yoga. Boundaries are blurred. distinctions subjective.

Some students feel violated. Some teachers touch *inappropriately*. Some teachers are total lech creeps.

"What's a deposition, B?"

On the menu tonight we had millet-quinoa (pr. *keen-*wah, people). collard greens and bok choy. a nice dal (red lentils. yellow split peas). three-berry kanten.

Welcome to Chez Billy.

Amanda said she wasn't hungry. During her bath she spoke to Sarah1. I read in bed.

Nice to be home. No underlying tension tonight.

After her bath A filled the African (wooden) bowl with food. covered it with *gomasio* (sesame seeds toasted and ground with salt). glugged carrot ginger dressing all over it. wrecking it. and ate it up. beside me in bed. with chopsticks. and her fingers.

The sesame flecks, the food bits fallen onto the bed, didn't bother me tonight. And it didn't bother her when I picked them up. flicked them away.

May I get you something else tonight?

And it didn't bother me when we watched VH1. In fact, I enjoyed it. it was good. It was about the brothers Gibb. The Bee Gees. at it since they were boys. Brit upbringing.

The cats got in on the action. the good vibe. "The whole family's on the bed," A observed contentedly.

Nobody took them seriously. though everyone loved their songs.

"Hey B, pass me the puke bowl?" I was cleaning the kitchen.

We had a designated (plastic. Chinatown) bowl. for her occasional regurgitation.

She fell asleep before the best part. disco. A loved disco. as a kid then. part tomboy. part glitter-girl. glam. still. dancing in her bedroom mirror. school dance.

She became a kid again when she fell asleep. Her

chaos of sheets. Bunched pillows packed under her head. Her beat-up yoga books, unopened. one open, in the scrambled nest.

She looked a bit like Barry Gibb.

Her needed rest. Home was bodily. like animals nesting, nestling together. We had a good home. Even with the blips. A good love. What you wait your whole life for. longing for it.

I pulled off her shirt. tucked her in. The TV clicker. the phone. her vital black plastic devices with buttons. I cleared her dinner. her puke bowl.

The stuff she spat up seemed to have blood in it. I took it close to the light at the sink, inspect it. I didn't cook anything for dinner that color. She didn't have a juice with beet in it. or any smoothie after class.

It wasn't just a bit of blood. Like when your sinus and snot get bloody. from dry winter apartment air. Maybe she'd had a bloody nose?

I smelled it. sure smelled like blood.

I tasted it. Blood gravy. It was blood. like, a lot.

"I don't feel so good, B."

She didn't look so good. Waxy. wan. etiolated. Sick.

She'd been feeling shitty on and off the whole time we'd been together. Always tired. Lately she'd been outright sick. weak. dispirited.

She called me from the bathroom. She stood with her head hung, chin to chest, belly sticking out unself-consciously.

Her toilet paper was bloody. She didn't have her period. The bowl was full of blood.

I made her go to the doctor.

"But you don't believe in doctors."

"I do for some things. They're good for diagnosis. You have insurance."

"Will you come with me?"

The doctor was a woman. short blond hair. like A's. except prim. not a curl. professional, trim, perfect bangs. A's was a wilder flower. the laughing helmet. lotus face. not laughing now.

The doctor called in a few days with test results. She sent A to see another doctor. An internist.

She agreed she didn't get enough sleep. Enough *downtime.*

It was like Seinfeld said about daytime resolves to go to bed early. At night it's like, "Well, that was day guy. I'm *night guy!*"

"Yeh, like that," she agreed. But it didn't change.

I tried to help her find a balance. I wanted to be part of the solution. but I felt like I was part of the problem. like I was in her way. Same old thing.

So I gave her her space. Stayed in the studio late, tended, or just sat in, my own ragged garden. tumble-down. build it up. sort it out. strip it down. make piles. lists. pieces. did my art, pretended to. tried to. tried to let it. Read late, went to movies.

Now that the doctor said she needed rest she believed it, more. But still it didn't change. Habit energy is more powerful than we are. all those drives. instinct. seemingly beyond us. but within us, zooming. driving us.

Her life was zapping her. I felt like I was zapping her. And she felt like that too.

How many times had she heard herself say to her class *Yoga's about energy.*

How many times had she heard herself say *I'm tired.* Her (h(om)e) mantra.

Kind of sick. or *getting sick.* sort of a flu. down with a cold. for the last year. more.

When we were first together she was sure she was allergic to my sperm. She was so wiped out all the time.

(Not from *not sleeping* for weeks on end.)

It never changed. *beat* became the norm.

More tests. Another doctor.

"B, what's an oncologist?"

~

Felix was playing at Tonic. He toured the country and Europe, played all around the city. Tonic was his home. and we were his peeps.

Tonight he was playing early. "So you yogis can make it." A felt obliged. They were good friends. pre-me. He came to her classes.

In fact I was jealous of him. early on. and still. a bit. though I liked him. He was my friend, too.

Early on, when we were discussing attraction to others, the deadliest subject in love (after indifference), she shrugged it off when I mentioned Felix.

"That's just not where it's at." But she was smiling tellingly. her expression more honest than she.

(She could never hide the truth when it came to attraction to others.) (Nor could she tell it.)

Circumstances. timing. initiative. Was that all that had held them apart?

Felix had a girlfriend. Shula. long-term, over ten years. They lived together. made music together.

He was in two bands, sometimes more. One was with Shula. She sang. superslowly, softly, like seductive heroin jazz.

She was a sexy doll. pale night-owl diva. She had the whole persona down. They were great.

Shula wore a long black evening dress with shimmery scales. She was busty and full-hipped. knew how to work it. reveal, more than just *suggest.* make it personal. real.

She was busty and full-lipped. A dark-haired beauty. dark eyes, dark trouble and mystery. feeding on same. looking for more. attracting it. in her act. and her life.

Felix sat on a stool, shaved head tilted over his red guitar. He plinked away. postrock. postjazz. like ancient Chinese royal court music. preelectric. but electrified. fizzing a little. amplified. when he turned a knob. woozy. another. some nice underwatery reverb.

Calmly concentrating, leading the drummer, leaning close to his cymbalsecrets. reading and sending out minute Morse code. *tss*-touching them wetly. splashing dots and sizzling dashes into the mystical mist emanations.

Shula's voice was breathy sweet alto Marilyn. but also suggesting, almost licking, voluptuously, darker brassy lewd acid lows.

She moved and sang so slowly and languorously, and with that detached weird artificial mien. A swore she was on smack. (She should know.)

But she wasn't. Maybe she used to be. developed her act then. now she was clean. She just kept the magic strangeness. inhabiting the fantasy. the way as the persona and act become real. in the world. they also become a real part of the performer's personality.

Or she was a true borderline. She was a yogini. Kundalini. Another whole scene. trip. practice. cult.

All about releasing the coiled snake kundalini bliss spring-loaded at the base of your spine. (*!?!*)

Like a cosmic orgasm crashing spiritually up through the chakra piano keys of your spine in a life-changing jolt of crashing whitelight enlightenment. (*?!?*)

Her singing, her bearing, this whole dark Marilyn seduction trip, was all about orgasm, too. leading up to. unabashed. leading you. teasing. She was a cocktease. She was a primitive. in that best sense.

I was mesmerized. A elbowed me. I grabbed her and held her in a bear hug. She was wearing Faux Bear. her thick fake fur coat we loved. (Canal Jeans.) And which I wore too, sometimes. like her pimp. sleeves up my forearms.

We sat in the front. Folding wooden chairs. (My assertiveness, or whatever (*Excuse me*), though it bothered her often, often also served her well. as now.)

As my knack and need (okay, compulsion) for order. tidiness. drove her crazy. and/but also created her cozy (our humble) home nest.

It was smoky in there. (before they outlawed it.) Packed. most people standing. like we were all in a ship. (as in *ashtanga*.) (but different hold.)

We lived in New York for a reason. We met. We were here tonight for just this. We felt it here.

I describe this particular night out of a thousand, because, whatever the combination of factors, tender intangibles, we felt really good together.

The love was in the music. the spell. and as ephemeral. A leaned and nestled into our embrace, and we were happy.

She seemed to be thinking of something else when the doctor told her she had cancer. She didn't seem upset. She didn't seem to quite be there. She didn't seem to get it. or to mind.

A glint of that giddy Amanda surfaced, strangely (or not), looked around the room for some goof to play on. But it was only me and the oncologist. and what he was saying. and it was not a joke.

He began to address me as much as her. seeing I was the one who was listening. who would take this in. She was the one who had to live it. Survive it.

He spoke in generalities about treatments, rates of remission, recovery. cure. The recent leaps in chemotherapy. How fine-tuned..

A surprised us both by saying, softly, "Am I dying?"

Dr. Stern's considered pause said far more than his considered reply.

"*You're* a lymph."

More tests. It was winter. A was always cold. She reluctantly wore socks. I put my socks on her, on top of hers. like she was going skiing. she didn't have any heavy enough to keep her warm.

I got her an orange parka from The Gap. for her expedition. She picked it out. I bundled her up and bounced us out the door.

We/she didn't tell anyone for about a month. No treatment had begun. yet. Life went on, not as normal but without any outward change.

Still practiced. still worked. Curiously, though, the work load had lessened. the way this kind of thing happens. when it has to. (divine hand. cat's paw.) The pressure was off. (that pressure.)

F&J were gone for six weeks. Giving workshops on the West Coast. then Australia. Then to India.

Before they left it was crazy. Now A was in charge. It was smooth sailing. pretty much. Everyone at Ram-Ananda was happier, lighter.

Even A. She liked going to work. The office became like a reception area for friends. Cats away.

The doctors gave us material to read. A didn't look at it. She didn't want to read about chemotherapy and radiation. She didn't go online to "research" it.

"You read it, B." She read her Buddhist books. *When Things Fall Apart.* About transforming suffering into joy. however the fuck you do that.

She didn't meditate. But she read about it.

I thought she should ease up on her practice. She refused. We agreed to tell Andy.

He said stop doing *ashtanga.* immediately. Gave her restorative poses to do instead. A sequence that generated only mild heat. *Pranayama* (breathing exercises).

And then sitting. He told her to meditate. Practice for half an hour, sit after that for another half hour. up it to an hour. He hugged her. We cried.

She did what he said.

"Does sitting in front of the TV count?"

But she had trouble sitting for that long.

"B, will you sit with me?"

Meditation. *Don't just do something. Sit there.*

Treatment would begin in a few weeks. Just chemo. No radiation. Meanwhile, more tests. Barium enemas. colonoscopy. catscans. blood work.

"B, what's systemic?"

Cab rides uptown to Sloan-Kettering. Clean corridors. blond birch paneling. blue letterheads and labels.

"Like we're here for our audition. Stage Three." Or, rather, rehearsal. practice. was over, kids.

Long waits for short meetings. quick tests. Nice nurses, doctors, technicians.

"Everyone's so nice there, B." In the cab ride back downtown. Her head rested on my shoulder, A watched the city dream by.

"Is Stage Three bad?"

We went to lots of movies. On with the show. no cancer talk. this is it.

Had only one dinner, friends over, during that time.

Neither of us really wanted to have it. But we did it almost out of habit. meets right action effort. Like we should. And we were right.

A still went to dance class on Saturday afternoons. The doctor demurred on that.

"I don't care what the doctor says," she said about that. "I'm going."

She still had plenty of energy. Just ran out of gas fast. And slept like there was no tomorrow. woke cooked.

Sometimes in the morning so devastated from the rough sleep she just needed to rest. get some sleep.

I made my African groundnut stew, big favorite, while she was at dance. Baked marinated tempeh. Golden rose (medium grain brown rice) and Canadian wild rice.

She dragged friends back with her. Others, yoga friends, trickled in, out of their various and vague time frames, over the next two hours.

Shoes accumulated outside the door. I made the place nice. Swept, mopped. Flowers from the farmers market.

Blooms on the altar. Square blue candles like bricks we were always saving for later. Burgundy candlesticks.

The good family plates. my only heirlooms. Zen materialism. (reduce it all to just this.) blue with a pattern and a thin gold border around the rims. This was my life. Here. Now. her.

Cushions and folded mats arranged around the low table. Tamari-toasted pumpkin seeds in a bowl. Cashews. raisins. carob raisins. Hers. ours.

The food in the pots on the stove, warm. A little Nag (incense) to mingle with the homey vegan food smell arrivals said hit them as they came up the stairs. (The smell moved down as it got later.)

"Yum!" someone called from the stairwell.

I was in the bath when A got home with her friends. She gave them cider, Evian, settled them on the bed. They all lay long, with the cats, watched Britney Spears. squealing.

When Britney was done A slid the bathroom door shut behind her and said, "Move over, B. I'm coming in." We bathed together. the others out on the bed. The buzzer rang.

It always seemed like there wouldn't be enough room around the table, more people than planned always came. but we'd always fit.

The apartment was small, full. like a transport plane we were settled into. and conversation and company lifted us off.

The fuel the food, the quips and laughter passed around. Faces bathed and animated in the candlelight, sated.

"Thanks, B." A leaned back into me like I was her armchair. "This was really nice."

Some people left. Felix sorted through the CDs. deejay.

"Looks like you guys got hit with the Zen stick," Sarah1 said. recent casualty. again. bruises under her eyes. the brutal love wars. rounding forty. single woman. New York City.

"Yeah," Stacey added. roundly thirty. "Whatever you guys are doing, you should bottle it. I want some."

A and I exchanged a glance.

Both cats were on the table, soliciting and receiving attentions, the golden hands, with come-hither head-nudges. Self-serving little hookers posing as cute, useless little waitresses. curious about the candle flames. whiskers in danger.

(Live here rent-free, lounge around all day, food paid for. for life. Good scam, kitties. All cats. Keep it up, do your act. get yours.)

"A round of charades?" Adam suggested. Some faces lit up. I was always up for it, they knew. But I knew my Man was wiped out.

"Sorry, you guys," I told them. "Not tonight."

"Yeah, they've got other fish to fry," Stacy singsang, and started the movement to leave.

"C'mere, B," A creaked from the bed. she crooked her finger, beckoning. The French doors were open. I was finishing cleaning up.

She'd started to help but I led her to bed by the pinkie. Our friends were trained, they knew the routine. Before dessert the dishes were mostly done.

She pulled me in for a nice, sloppy, sleepy kiss. When I returned from closing up shop, shutting off the lights, this and that, she was long gone. way asleep.

One arm over her head, bent, like she was raising her hand in school. her mouth open in midanswer.

I loved our mornings sitting together. meditating. We tried different places. The front had street noise. a bit. The kitchen was the kitchen.

So the bathroom. big for New York. Under the framed little Buddha. always right there. sitting in lotus. showing the way. patiently waiting for now.

Where first she practiced. Where she'd always done her warm-ups, before practice, running through the sequence, abbreviated, for her class that day. Now that was her whole practice.

Mat at an angle away from the tub. where it just fit. Me in the tub, very helpful, giving her shit.

We sat facing each other. We tried back to back. A with her eye-blue sweater, with the very long sleeves that taper open out like lily bells. pistil fingertips. over her hands. over her bathrobe.

Her striped Gap hat with the earflaps. The cats circled and settled with us. Whitey on the towel shelf. paws hanging out. presiding. Big Guy would prowl and pretend to decide. little punk. prod and prod, then sit in my lap.

She didn't cry. She didn't want to tell her family. She didn't want to tell her friends. At first I tried to persuade her. then stopped.

Of course I had to let her do this her way. When she asked my opinion I gave it. When she didn't ask I tried to get her to.

I took care of her in the obvious ways. The little things. basic needs and details of the days. and nights. plus frills.

We talked on the phone five times a day. I'd pick up a video, and we'd watch it. She'd fall asleep before it was halfway over.

The next day she'd ask me to please not return it yet, so she could see the rest. My cutoff was three days. (Like Two Boots. Kim's.) (Blockbuster was five.)

We talked about going to the country for a weekend before she began chemo. but y'know..

One day at lunch Sarah2 was going on about herself. her troubles. A had a hard time staying with her. She interrupted her. told her she had cancer.

Sarah burst into tears. So did Amanda.

I didn't want to, I didn't feel good about it, but I took this personally. I couldn't help it. I'd been crying a lot lately. Alone and with A. She'd hold me. but wouldn't cry.

"It's not about you, B." Punctured me.

But. sorry, Man. what I was going through was intense! It *was* about me. and her. It was fucking terrible. *She had cancer!*

Though obviously I wasn't the one with the cancer. The next morning she punctuated her remark. it echoes still.

"You have to be strong, B."

"Where do you get your strength?" I cried. Floodgates. really tapping the deep stuff.

She shrugged. "From you."

I wish I could say she lived. and I can. For what is my dogged ragged devoted marginal independent film East Village vegan lost and found free spirit free artist keep-it-simple yoga guy life worth. bachelor of art career of girlfriends, master of sex, postdoc in applied post-pomo, pro bullshit artist, this aspiring self-referential ragtime doggerel spiritus, art-walled, self-willed, self-trapped, tragicomic, appetitive, dream-fictive, wonder-fueled, lovelorn, word-drunk, image-intoxicated, if the high Himalayan intention and base animal burrow and grope, the artifice, narrative, animus, reach and truth of art and the soul's exquisite invisible divine extensity and complete connectedness can't in fact touch and feed and influence supple and hard-edged real life in real time, others', yours, here, or hers, even hers, let alone mine, right here, wordpainting now at the pained core, the inner elusive quiet place, and in the not-so-great transitory real world where it's really lived, where the selfish knotted song of self versus the play of God (*leela*) is lived out for each of us, so that we can maybe get beyond the reader to the realer reality ostensibly there, eternal, etc., behind the battered concept tattered tissue *veil of maya*, lighter-than-life psychic projection screen, which always seems and sounds nice and deep but also unreal and cliché, meaningless, pat, maybe wishful thinking or desperate projection, like all faith, religion, theodicy, conjured out of primal need and mortal fear, of death, of meaninglessness. of the famous emptiness. until experienced. It's not just as an idea, a metaphysical conceit or spiritual maxim to be touched. tasted. tested. awkwardly embraced, nobody's looking, though that's a start. But you get there through pain, desperation. and through repetition. of the life mistakes and also the practice that stills the mind. tries, does. clears the muddy waters, fosters *samadhi.* allows the other lotus dimension to rise, bud, flower. *atman-brahman.* the ways of saying and seeing it are many, but the thing itself is the same, you get the idea, the paths are many, but the way is one, death is one, God who goes by many names.

~

"I don't need a wheelchair."

"Come on, Man. That's just how they do it."

The guy let me wheel her. She wore the standard-issue outfit. The paper/cotton smock that opened in the back. "You'd like this," she said. She was right. easy access. And a skimpy bathrobe. Foam rubber slippers.

The guy led us down a quiet corridor to a corner section divided by curtains into private areas. Her "cocktail" was added to the IV bag. In twenty minutes. less. A's hand in mine went limp.

She twitched in her sleep. a little snort. Head fallen to the side. drool pooled and spilled from her leak. a little death. (practice?)

"I saw him notice my scars," A said in the cab home. The scars on her arm. from track marks. like from cigarette burns.

That was all she said about the experience. her first round of chemo. That, and, "I really feel like shit."

The third round wasn't as bad as the first two. According to A. They adjusted her *cocktail.*

But from where I sat, beside her, reading to her, observing closely. reporting on the day. how practice was, who was there. until she shut me up. who asked about her, sent their love. she looked a lot worse.

She looked haunted. Wiser. Drained of life. Her skin was a weird color. dead fish gray. oily wax. She was really spacey. Her face was elongating. She looked like a Martian.

Chemo happened (usually) on Mondays. For the rest of the week she was out of commission. In and out of sleep. just lying there. I fed her soup (miso. squash. lentil. carrot).

Veggies, way overcooked. rice cooked with lots of water (3:1) till mushy, like oatmeal. She added lots of *gomasio.* (too much) Then would hardly eat anything.

Or she'd go right for the fruit kanten. the cashew whip. maple-sweetened. Just jab at that. She'd apologize. eat the rest.

"Sorry, B. I'm not very hungry."

When she did eat a little, it wasn't long till she said, "B, pass me the puke bowl?" The joke of it long gone.

Things line up in advance. like they know. and want you to know, too. Clues accrue.

The TV was on all the time. Stuck on VH1. when she wasn't surfing. places I'd never go. She kept nodding off.

The Sarahs would visit on the weekend. Tell her again everything they'd told her on the phone. What was going on at Rama.

Then other friends came by the following week. I spaced the visits out. chief of staff. Early afternoon. Two or three a day. tops.

They energized her. also wore her out. People brought flowers. CDs. magazines. little statues of Dancing Shiva, her aureole of flames. and portly Ganesh, fat on his sweets.

(God of the year. of the new millennium.)

(After Shiva the Thug Destroyer. thus far.)

After the fourth round she looked like herself in some pictures when she was younger. except older. old. More wasted. Like her brother. sharp nose.

I'd see that odd/off self in photographs, but could never reconcile it with the Man I knew. It always unsettled me when I saw this in photos.

Now I saw it in her. And it *really* unsettled me.

"B, will you rub my feet? They're cold."

I was scared.

She was being great.

We had it down. Taxi to Sloan-Kettering. Ordinary workaday Midtown, swirling, rushing away in all directions, tautly choreographed pedestrians. The duffel bag with her things. We knew the people at the desk.

She wore her own bathrobe now. thick and comfy (unbleached cotton, Terra Verde. Xmas. B). which I brought each time. in my green canvas bag. (Mysore. gift. heavy-duty, rigid.)

And the red Moroccan chemo slippers, toes curving up, I got from the guy with one leg with the shop on Eleventh Street. almost never open.

A was holding up great. Sometimes at night, the TV on but the sound off, she'd wake me. Face puffed and bleary. Eyes all red, lids swelled. In a mortal panic.

"I'm afraid, B." Her eyes fucking terrified. focused, bleary, feral.

I held her and held her. She gasped and quivered. We cried and cried. It seemed like if she cried enough like this she'd cry the cancer out of her.

The chemo was working. The tumor in her colon had shrunken in half. Same with strands in her duodenum.

The lymphatic white blood cell count was up. Another one I didn't understand was down.

The numbers were good. This was all great. Except she felt like shit all the time. And now a new tumor had appeared.

You think a tumor is hard. like an egg. or at least a boiled egg. It's not. It's soft. like jelly. Nestled in the lovely waiting declivity of her collarbone.

She took this news as if she expected it. When the doctor had finished saying what he had to say, she took him aback by saying, simply, sincerely, "What is cancer?"

It was like when we were first in love. In bed all the time. together all the time. in our own she-referential world. Once in a while going outside, when necessary, and there was the day. the night.

New York out there, going on with its incessant, urgent business as usual, vivid and strange, relentless, alive. The traffic. the endless flow of people. energy. the stream of stories and complications you don't have time or emotional space to even begin to imagine.

But do for a second when they pass. like glimpsing inside an apartment through the window from the sidewalk when you're walking past. the whole life in there.

A came out for a walk a few times a week. When she was up for it. We'd go, slow, to the park. Rest on a bench. Visit the dog patch.

The bounding circus of doggy energy in there. the littlest ones racing around in circles, making up for their short legs. and no nature. The owners standing around talking. smoking. cups of coffee.

Like people outside an AA meeting, I said to A. Same people, she said. The dog patch was a big ashtray.

We almost always ran into someone we knew. A

knew everyone in the East Village. From meetings. back when. then from yoga. That covers most. and the rest hooked up with them.

You could tell which ones knew she was "sick." She didn't like seeing people she knew. Or so she said before we went out. that she didn't want to see anyone she knew.

But when she did she was as affable as ever. but with a flatter tone. happy to see them. Mandy was a people person. one of many neighborhood mayors. much loved.

"Don't you get tired of taking care of me, B?" she asked as we strolled along. her arm in mine. or hand in crook.

"Nope. I love taking care of you, Mandy." She knew it was true.

"You're a good man, B." It took very little these days to get me crying. Though usually not in front of her.

"You're just a big sap."

We held each other in a loose but close way on the bed while it gradually got dark. each fingertip felt.

We'd answer a question. esp. she. Want some water? with the slightest nudge or tap. We let the machine answer the phone.

The safe place we conjured and held on to and climbed into together, her first, was like a tree house, our secret club, the deep held time-shared holiday home of wordless love and sappy sleep. in the pines.

And I can tell you she taught her classes, got more confidence in that, and in herself.

Kept going to James, still in the Chelsea Hotel, her hairdresser, every couple of months for a cut and dye. let her hair grow out. like she always wanted. parted on the side. cute. simple. some days the middle, wet-combed. wore it up in a puny bun, back in a ponytail sprout. that grew into an actual sustainable ponytail. (spout)

Got some Save Humanity jeans. new nice shirts. more colors. new century. middle age. the new not. had a little more money. not much, still. but still. People stay the same. What else? Wore dresses more often, in summer almost always, also the side seasons extended, ambling along, no rush. beautiful New York woman walking on the street. makes you believe in life. if not God. Got an iPod. but never used the earplugs. *buds.* used it only for music in classes.

Bare feet most of the day, most days. Still hated winter. still cold the whole time. not enough light. Got some Uggs. Went south as often as she could in the winter. to Cali. to the beach!

You just can't decide. still. what happens. commit. Just like you couldn't decide if you really wanted to be with me or not. You wanted both at the same time. And you still do.

Led retreats to Mexico, this cool place with open bungalows. white beach like a long arm a little bent. where, other times, they had bikini boot camp for models. lots of jokes about that. especially by the guys. Organic vegan meals. mangoes galore. great veggies and margaritas and music. Everyone kept calling everything "Mexcellent!" and laughed. and when they got back to New York, recharged and tan and connected to each other in that special way that feels like will last forever. and does and doesn't last. that grounded, peaceful, lifted feeling and the new friends. and when people asked them how the yoga retreat was, they'd say, *"¡Mexcellent!"*

Like all people with animals, we spoke to each other through the cats.

"They're poisoning me, Big Guy."

I'd recently reminded her, when she asked why she felt so bad, B, that besides having *cancer,* chemotherapy was poison therapy.

They were trying to kill the cancer. Poison it. by poisoning her.

She stroked Big Guy, chin raised, stretched long against her. "You don't look so good yourself, kitty," she added.

I'd noticed. His eyes were watery, gunk in them I'd pick away. He didn't like it, ducking and pulling his face away, when I did it. but he let me.

Diarrhea. splattering, more than once, past the rim of the kitty litter box beside the toilet. He'd been sick for a week. I hadn't mentioned it. *What is going on around here?*

"B, he's getting skinny," she said. "I'm worried about him." His spine had gotten bony. pushing through.

In the last year he'd kept growing and growing, getting longer and longer, stretching into a weasel from the original mitten-size kitten punk, his pink petal tongue licking and licking. minutely prickled sandpapery surface. little nips with the little teeth.

We'd joke about *how long could he get?*

Now he was growing backwards. inward.

"It's a sympathetic reaction to you," I suggested.

Two days later Big Guy took a turn for the worse. Trying to take the hit for Amanda. Fall Guy.

When I came home around noon, laden with produce, goodies for A, she was sitting up in bed, crumpled limp Big Guy cradled in her lotus lap.

Amanda was really skinny now. Long limbs. long hands. New blue veins. milk skin. I (horribly) thought she looked good. except she was. um. *dying..*

Her thinner body, revealed at last, was sexy, what can I say? Her face, however, was drawn, bruised, sallow, scary.

Her nose was sharper, more prominent. She looked exactly like her brother. Her eyes were bigger. bluer. glassine baggy. puffed in the a.m.

She used to look like Ellen DeGeneres. Now she looked like Rod Stewart.

We talked to the Humane Society vet. where we got him. She said bring him in. today. now. We did. A insisted on coming.

Cab uptown. our routine. Up First Avenue. further uptown this time. This time A holding the little dying deity patient.

He was skinnier than she. He couldn't hold his head up. eyes bigger. He didn't move.

After a waiting room wait among cats and dogs and owners, pet people, fellow feeling, the shelter smell, the vet spoke gently to Big Guy. She remembered us. she remembered Little Guy.

She pulled at Big Guy's skin. It was baggy. slack. He was dehydrated, she said. She had to get him on an IV.

He had to spend the night. They had to keep an eye on him. Take blood. do tests.

"He's never coming *home*!" A cried in the cab. big gasping sobs. like she was out of emotional breath. out of patience. time.

She was not wrong. Big Guy declined over the next three days. He had "cat AIDS". since birth. just kicking in now. They gave us a choice.

Individual cremation. or group cremation at the end of the week. There was little choice but to "put him to sleep".

"Sleep!" A bawled.

Did we want to see him again? they asked. We did. We wanted, we decided, to be there, to hold him, while they did the injection.

The injection, the vet explained, wouldn't hurt him. And it wouldn't hurt him to die. he'd be unconscious before he died.

And because she was a woman, it was easier to accept. to believe her.

Cab back up. next morning. Big Guy was in a cage in a room with a few other unfortunates. He lay on his side. unmoving. We crouched down and spoke to him.

His legs immediately started moving, in a pathetic, mechanical simulation of running. kind of spastic. Like his nervous system was on motor control. either off. or, like this, on..

Like Dad's eyes at the end. beacons homing back and forth. except no one home. Except here, spasms. then stop.

A gasped. hand to her mouth. cried the whole time, wiping her eyes with her sleeves. I carried him to the examination room.

Emaciated, ears enlarged, he looked like E.T. a puppet. He didn't open his eyes. We spoke to him gently.

"Hey, Big Guy . . . We love you, Big Guy . . ."

He lay on his side on the stainless steel examination table. limp. We had our hands on him. A minute after the injection he was definitely dead.

I wish I could say she didn't die, that she lived and went on living her life. And I can say that, that she lived, she moved on, and I moved on. I'm saying that.

Because art, after all, is not life. So while the symbolic work and psychic play, my letting her go, all this solipsistic necessary stuff, might mean I have to let her die here in me. in the art box map. in you. How about the place she goes on to goes on? Here but not here. Death is not the only other place. Because why do so many women have to die. in books and movies. in male minds? Our evolution, our survival, requires they live. The man-made world vs. eternal feminine life force. The only solutions are living. as in live and let live. How about Live and *help* live? Maybe the necessary myth of the artist for this crashing swan song century should include *Stop killing the girls, boys!* Our battered smoky blue-faced mother, above all, choking to death. our sorely mismanaged home planet miracle. above us only sky.

B—

And so lotus life stands up and says she lives. and so she lives. For the fictive dream we share here holds and allows both. The art opening. Shiva's deliverance. (death.) otherness. space. nothingness. (unto new life. love.)

And. the yoga center she and Sarah (and Sarah) opened did well. She thrived. but of course still struggled. stayed living in her same little apartment. kept practicing at Andy's. As the yoga levels rose around us, she rose with the tide, and their *shala* became a fixture on the downtown map. the pink flag soon sullied, proudly hanging like a humble offering, silky, sooty, out over old Broad Way, our mercantile Mississippi, the secret yoga world no longer secret. at all. in fact became fad. cliché. in every other ad. everywhere you looked. then came the copycats. bogus fakers out for a buck. And meanwhile their place. known for its good energy, down-to-earth, simple, authentic, pure, no bullshit. just the practice and a good feeling. good people, the real deal. became a vital place on the mental maps, daily tracks of the inner and outer lives of many seeking perspiring souls. A bunch of the old RamAnanda faithful came over with them, happily, oxymoronically eagerly, relieved and grateful to be able to get away and to keep that original tight group *satsang* feeling alive, from the Old Place, before it went overboard, too popular, commercial, diluted. the typical mainstream decline. and rise Amanda became known as one of the top yoga teachers in New York. humble and normal and friendly. sweet. cool without that weird chilly haughty thing. She had her own needy fishies and chickies now, and she acted toward them, or tried to, the way she learned at RamA you should, and always vowed and imagined she would. and she did. And she was rewarded with a warm, cool, living place with a really good vibe. And regulars brought their friends and attracted others, the way it works, the garden grows, new people came, wherever they come from, all these downtown New Yorkers, Billy-burgers, uptown mentalities who work Midtown, they keep coming, our numbers and spirit are strong, gentlemen. our mission of peace is building, girls, winging its vital way, quietly winning hearts, bodies, private and collective mental ethical momentum. witness. quantum critical mystical mass, a quiet but real millennial moral quorum breathing and chanting the all-powerful *om* against the omnivorous amoral forces of runaway capitalist Shiva the shit-faced destroyer—

B.

Yeah, so.. she moved on in her life. as people do. learning and not learning, like all of us, same cycles, new people, same old friends, habits, hopefully growing with practice, awareness, letting go, again and again, the permutations, vicissitudes, steady extensity. the witness. the practice a daily habit, holy intention, holy New York, holy repetition, stumbling toward grace, sex, the next cycle. love. She got an iPhone. and after a month felt like chucking it under a taxi. We can't measure or really see our own progress or path. Dharma. Growing, groping, also regressing, repeating mistakes, intentions, repeating our imaginary insights, staying the same. We just keep going. offer it up, turn it over. all those things they say that add up to holding pattern *sadhana*. progress. of the soul. our actions, our lives. as best we can.

Versus

A got worse in the next week. She stopped talking. She stopped eating.

We put a picture of Big Guy on the altar. Standing up on his hind legs like a little black bear. his dipped white paws raised. pink pads. Our sacrificed son.

His eyes, in the photo, were red, like the devil's, the way it happens with eyes in photographs. (Human eyes, anyway. Who knew, cats', too?)

"Cats are people, too, B," A had said. a running joke. from Jonni and her cats. Lingam and Yoni. (*ahem*) animal identification. advocacy. PETA. (*ahimsa.*)

Which to me was why it was so funny Frankie looked like Fred Astaire. our cat growing up. and seemed. ever elegant. lines. ease of movement. effortless precision.

It seemed like all the people in my life were increasingly dream-related. and what and how it was all happening. living symbols and metaphors. mystery. death.

Was this part of the big shift? into awareness. action.

Or a kind of mania. my hungry artist mind devouring itself. Or just the mind observing life. itself.

We watched TV. together! Instead of just her watching. and me resenting. Rented movies. Old ones she hadn't seen.

I brought home *Love Story*. She hadn't seen it. But she knew the story.

"But B, she dies."

"An Affair to Remember."

"Thanks, B-B. But she dies in that, too."

How could I do that? I really didn't realize. I should just go back to Steve Martin. I didn't tell her I'd ordered *The End of the Affair* and *A Farewell to Arms* from Netflix.

Movie therapy. By Billy Winslow. Cure all ills.

The chemo was working, they kept saying. But the cancer was also growing. seeping. gnawing. elsewhere.

Before, A was on this side of the disease. and of mortality. Now, such an extreme change, almost overnight, heralded by Big Guy. intrepid little guide. our Mesopotamian death-god. or selfless offering. propitiate. obviate. Now she was on the other side.

She was alive, awake, cognizant. But her soul, her attention, the restive, adamant girl-angel that was Amanda, was facing the other way. slipping. draining away. toward sleep. "sleep".

She lay on her side. knees bent. curled fetal. Like my grandmother in her last days. We went in for an emergency appointment.

They kept her overnight. as a *precaution.* They wouldn't let me stay with her.

She'd been chastened, quickened, *scared.* by the night in the hospital. Her eyes the next morning were fierce. crystallized. not calm.

"Get me out of here, B. I am not spending another night here. Ever."

They let us go home. Equipped with our own IV bags. Tubes. She had a stent in her arm now. You just stuck the IV tube into it. it clicked into place.

She was in pain. You could tell when it hurt. Her body tightened. her face masked and glazed over. Then she'd breathe.

She'd always been kind of a wimp when it came to bodily pain. a bit of a hypochondriac with little things. forever popping Advils. her back always hurt. (thanks to yoga!) But now she was strong. stoic. uncomplaining.

No more visitors for now. Just us and the TV. and this growing, unbelievable, unacceptable unmentionable. And Whitey, sniffing, casing the mystery. looking around everywhere for Big Guy. clues.

Every day, a bath. She lay there, bony. exhausted. I softly soaped her.

"Don't get fresh." Little jokes still kept bubbling up between us.

Her hand groped and hit and grabbed me awake in the middle of the night. Her nails dug into my skin. She was sweaty. bent.

"It hurts, B."

She pushed me away when I tried to hold her. She

smelled not like herself. She smelled like a science lab.

I held her hand. She gripped it hard. held on. She groaned. on and off for a couple of hours.

Through a low hoarse tube at the back of her throat. hollow, vibrating, animal temple. connecting her lungs and heart to the little cow sound. ominous *om*. fucking fed up.

She stumbled after waking up from the next round of chemo. fell but I held her up. It took her hours longer than usual to wake up.

When she did wake up, she wasn't really awake. *"F-u-u-ck,"* she moaned. When she was ready to go, we went.

I had my arm around her. She didn't pass out. but she kind of buckled. collapsed. again. again I held her up.

"Maybe we should get the wheelchair," I suggested. taking her over to the row of wheelchairs. like high-end shopping carts at this strange sort of spa supermarket.

A candy striper accompanied us to the curb, took the wheelchair when we got in the cab. waved. watched us go.

The driver was Indian. bearded. ebullient. His long Hindi name, on his taxi license behind the Plexiglas, like a Sanskrit asana. invocation. Indian music played. between devotional and Hindi pop. A perked up.

I asked the driver to turn it up.

"I'm going to India, B," she said.

She asked me to read to her from the *Bhagavad Gita. again.* Krishna on the battlefield with Arjuna. again. explaining meditation. again.

Difficulty concentrating? Keep at it anyway. each return counts. back to the breath. toward the end of all suffering.

She barely became conscious the next day. It was scary. Especially when she did wake up enough to speak.

She asked for some water. then for some OJ.

"What's the cancer and what's the chemo?" she wanted to know.

The sicker she got, the more economical her utterances. Her original impressionism compressed and adapted to less is now.

Now she was becoming, under extreme mortal duress, an unconscious minimalist poet. (*OJ, B.*) newborn avatar of economy. of barely spoken word. of emotion. intention. gesture. in one sapped minimum.

I couldn't give her an answer. She alone had it.

"It's killing me."

She woke with Whitey on her neck. The doctor had said to get rid of the cats. She refused. (So Big Guy volunteered. to go.) Whitey was like me. He saw the exposed skin of her neck, above tornadoed sheets, and wanted to cover her, keep her warm. so he laid himself there, splayed.

"Hey, White Man," she croaked. distress deferred. duress disguised. "I'm going to India."

The friends were great. As soon as she wanted to see people, they were there, eager to see her. The steady love-stream.

They'd lie or sit with her on the bed. or beside the bed. It was a total love-in. Overlapping groups hugging hi/bye. Whispers.

Holding A's hand. her hands. Her many arms, like Shiva. her Destroyer. They stayed awhile. Talked about work. guys. girl gossip. pop gossip. told her they loved her. and left.

Visits from the god-men. When they were in town. The Das family. Westerners wrapped in Indian cloth. *Bhakti* (devotion) yogis. Seeing and offering up to God through devotional chanting.

Shyamdas. Inspired, Sanskrit-saturated New York Hin-Jew. Lived half the time in India. The other half in the Adirondacks. (Nice work if you can get it.)

"Good *bhav* today." He'd nod, leaving. "Good *bhav.*" Hands in prayer under his chin. "Beautiful *bhav.*"

Krishna Das. Black T-shirt. Silver earring. Former lead singer for Blue Oyster Cult. Then did the India thing. deeply. Got a little fat there. spiritually plump.

Now released CDs of his devotional singing. (*ragas.*) successful. tours. Got the girls (*yoginis. gopis*) to sing backup. if you know what I'm saying.

Cried easily. (which the gals loved.) Spoke about letting go of the ego. Always the same message. Clinging to opinions. emotions. Grasping at right and wrong. Clinging to life.

Let go of these things, give your actions up to God. Your thoughts. your intentions. your heart. your life.

Tears streamed as he spoke gently. as when he sang, after. We're only visitors here. tenants in time. in this place. in this body. we rent.

Gopala-a, go-pala-a . . .

Different friends would come with different Das guys. Gopi gals also with Bhagavan Das. Big, gentle bear of a man. familiar now. dear, savage. always broke. never-washed ropes of hair piled on top of his head. taking up the whole doorway. talking. (often about sex. sacred. tantric. of course.) (and about money. scheming like a junkie.)

Pulling out the harmonium and chanting. after talking for a while, covering A's whittled fingers with his big soft hands. explaining some Sanskrit lyrics. which she already knew.

All our human dramas are leela, the play of God . . . All is grace . . .

Which she lived. now. This *letting go!*

Big Bhagavan bear hug at the door. He had to duck so his dreadlock beehive wouldn't hit on the way out. mindstuff extended. (*chillam.*) extruded. wormy ropes.

Sarah1 also played the harmonium sometimes, and they'd chant. lovely, soft, heartbreaking singing. Just them/us. whoever was there.

Bedside *kirtan*. the girls. Felix with his acoustic guitar. Someone with tablas. 8-shaped. A with her little hand cymbals. sitting up in bed. slumped.

Sarah would nod at A when it was her turn to solo, and she'd sing her part, as when they led night *kirtan/ satsang* sometimes together at RamAnanda.

Her dangling voice was clear, high, soft, lovely, rising to the occasion like a waning canary spirit freed from the phlegmy mine of her throat and thwarted downward-pulling doom. lovely as hell. dangling dwindling life. It broke my fucking heart

Jaya Ga-nee-sha,

Jaya Ga-nee—ee-sha . . .

"I never knew I had so many friends," she said after a few days full of visits. wiped out. And,

"I feel like I'm already dead."

I knew what she meant. I had that feeling, too. everybody soft and loving, coming together around her. grieving.

There's a Buddhist idea that you should live as if

you're already dead. picture it every morning in meditation. focus intention. for we practically are. I didn't say this to her then.

Why not, B? That Buddhist stuff helps.

I came home and she was sitting at my desk. online. Wrapped in the comforter. Gap hat on, with the earflaps and pom-pom.

She hadn't gone near the computer in a while. so I noticed. She signed off as soon as I came in. like she had something to hide.

The music was on. the TV was on. all the lights were on. the computer. Sandalwood incense, mixed in with the sour sick smell.

"Looks like all systems are go in here," I observed.

"That's right, Captain. Time to turn this spaceship around."

She looked, frankly, worse than ever. She looked like a different person. Bony. Wasted away. Like a concentration camp victim.

But here was this vivid will-to-live. *Samsara hala-hala!* Surging through those ghost-hungry eyes.

It was snowing outside like a crazy person. Big fat wet flakes, a zillion of them, flying around in all directions. It was inspired. exhilarating. Riding the bike was like going up a chairlift.

I left my parka, hat and boots in the hall, to drip and dry. I pulled back the curtains, let the insane show out there leap into the room.

"That's great, B." She was back on the bed, bundled. "But I hate winter."

"Yeah, but you gotta love this. Tell me you don't." Swirling white slashes and mad polka dots. hilarious, ecstatic, manic energy on vivid avid display.

You're on vivid, avid display.

"Whitey, tell Daddy we don't like winter like he does."

She had taken herself off the IV. She asked if she could have some miso maybe.

"You say hop I hop."

"What's that supposed to mean?"

Why did I say that? "I don't know. I'm sorry. I was joking."

"I guess I missed the funny part."

"I'm sorry. I didn't mean to say that." Really. I was happy to get her some miso.

"Yeah, but you did."

"Yeah I did . . ." Bosnian Serbs on CNN. Now what? "But that wasn't me. That was my evil twin talking."

"The one who's tired of taking care of me? The one who would rather be with Sarita than a dying corpse?"

"Mandy, that's a terrible thing to say." Oh boy. here we go. "Where did that come from?"

"Same place your *hop* came from—" She started coughing and couldn't stop. peak. The more she wanted to stop. to speak. the more she kept coughing.

I offered her her Evian bottle. I hovered near, an annoying hand on her back.

"Like maybe the *truth*," she finally gasped.

Sarita and Sarahl came by that afternoon, dripping, laughing out in the stairwell. stopped when they entered. in a cloud of active world energy.

They piled onto the bed with Amanda. She wilted like a plant before our eyes.

As it got dark out the snow turned to rain, lashing,

trashing the frosting. the delicate white delineations on the urban scape, the branches, the fire escape.

The night was lacquered black. the street slick. Our sick-bay time warp was under invasion. Thunder rumbled, crashed over the great collapsing evening cake.

Winter thunder. lightning flashing behind soggy low cover. sagging onto the pointed buildings, smothering their empire state auras.

We hugged goodbye. S&S left crying.

A was awake, but silent. in a way that was not peaceful. in a way that did not welcome me.

I didn't *go there.* I didn't know where to go. What to do. I felt terrible. I took a bath. Ate cashews. carob raisins. (grain-sweetened.) 2:1 ratio, ideal. (c.r. to cashews.)

All my addictions reduced to this. (and love. sex. and art. and *ashtanga.*) (and the (empty) longing. and the (long) emptiness. and self-—.)

My mother was afraid of thunderstorms. lightning. And she didn't want to transfer her fear to us.

So she'd take us to the window while the storm wailed and crashed her celestial cymbals beyond. behind our ghost-floating faces in the panes. pounded the great God kettledrum. stretched over the riled sea.

And she'd say, "Isn't that beautiful?"

I wanted to tell A this. Had I told her already?

Yes, B. Tons of times.

But now wasn't the time.

That night was the worst. A was in agony. moaning and crying. and later more crying out. like never before. For the first time I felt like she didn't want me there.

I was no help to her. I tried to put my *hurt feelings* aside. tended to her. but I felt helpless. I cried more than she did. when she didn't see me.

For about a half an hour, deep into delirium, in the middle of the night, she yelled out in pain. in terrible, endless repetition, *"Aagh . . . aaagh! . . . agh! . . ."*

I gave her more (a lot) of her painkiller (Dilaudid) in her IV bag. Finally she passed out.

You can see how people want to die. When the pain is way too much. When the pain is all there is. and it's un-fucking-bearable.

But A didn't want to die.

But she was definitely dying.

"I can't do this anymore, B."

Her diarrhea was bloody again. At the next meeting, to review the latest blood test and chemo results, the doctor spoke, for the first time, the dread phrase *quality of life*.

My father had responded stoically, simply, when it came to this stage. He opted to stop chemotherapy and go and stay home.

I don't think the phrase stood out to A. and I didn't mention it afterward. But she knew. in her way. for sure. more than we. what was up.

She seemed, still, oblivious of the medical side of this whole ordeal. She just let them do their thing. She was busy doing hers. I was the go-between. the *caregiver.*

Only when she asked did I tell her things. Like when she asked why she had diarrhea all the time. I explained that chemo targets the cells in the body that reproduce fastest. most readily. Which includes the cancer cells.

This was the point. the aim. To stop the cancer cells from reproducing. If the cancer cells don't reproduce, the cancer doesn't spread. is the idea.

Other cells in the body that reproduce readily, daily, are the cells lining the intestines.

The chemo zapped them, also. Hence, the nasty runs. Hair (follicle) cells also reproduce daily. Chemo got them, too. sometimes. Which is why people sometimes lost their hair in chemotherapy..

"Why haven't I lost my hair, then?"

"Because they've *fine-tuned* chemotherapy in the last few years. People in chemo used to—"

"Okay, B." She put her hand over my mouth to shut me up.

The danger, of course, in trying to poison the cancer, is that you poison the person. to death. also. instead.

A's tumors weren't shrinking anymore. The treatment had reached that *critical plateau.* where eradicating the cancer is no longer a possibility.

Keeping it from growing, spreading, is the new game. the endgame. More time, maybe, poisoned by chemo. vs. less time, but not feeling so fucking awful all the time from the chemo.

This was not happening. It didn't seem possible. But also seemed superreal. like my father dying. It seemed like the same thing. continuing. (like my unconscious overflows. spreads too far into life. takes over.)

Each cycle, after the first week of recovery, feeling totally shitty the whole time, A would start to feel better, as the toxins left her body. got some strength back. Then it would be time for another dose of poison.

~

People piled on the bed to watch the Knicks. Man felt sorry for the guys who missed free throws. or who lost.

Spree! the crowd chanted. *Spree!* His zigzag cornrows, different do every night. The gals livened up at the ads. That lasted fifteen minutes.

"Nix that," Scott quipped. (Get it?)

Instead we watched Peter Brooks's *Mahabharata.* Sunday afternoon grading into evening. Fleet youth into middle age. Five girls and two guys. Scott and I the oldest there.

He was in heaven. kept the gals entertained. his pitch-perfect Indian accent. head-wobble.

No one wanted to leave. Sarah1 and Sarita lingered late, till A fell asleep.

"She seems good," Sarah said, over a mug of mu tea for the road. "Too bad she has to do chemo again tomorrow." Stating the obvious. but stirring pent depths we felt in the long well-held hug.

In the morning, lovely surprise, there was snow everywhere, like a clean taut bedsheet over the city. It was bright out, clear, the light sharp, that boldest New York sky blue sky.

On the ground it was crisp fresh winter. in the air spring rose. promoting melt, sprout. glare. lust. slush.

A was at the computer again when I woke up. She came over and pretended to be me, straightened the comforter, tucked it around my shoulders. Touched my temple, my brow, smoothed my imaginary hair.

"Can I get you some miso," she asked in her simulation of B-brightness, "with arame and scallions and shiitake and shredded daikon? Good for your blood . . . your colon . . . give you energy."

"B, you are too much—" I wasn't very good at being her.

Meanly, I felt like moaning. I could have enacted her

perfectly. *Shit!* the time. I looked at the clock, ending our little game.

"Man, we've got to go. We'll be late."

"Not going, B."

"What? Why, did they—"

"I'm done with all that."

I was speechless. for an instant, as all the responses, arguments, urgencies converged. pressed.

A nodded no. finger raised. please don't speak. don't say no.

"I'm sure, B. I feel good about it."

"Wow." I suddenly felt not just us in here, in our bubble, but the whole world out there—

"I'm at peace with it."

And all the possibilities, people, unfathomable energies came rushing in, burst through. I started crying like crazy.

She climbed in under the covers, bulky in her robe and her layers, skeletal, fragile, beneath. But strong.

"Shhhh," she soothed me. "It's okay."

"It's not okay!" I blubbered, in the vortex. surprised at my spasmodic convulsions. I buried my head, let her mother me a minute.

"Shhhh . . ." She stroked my head. "It's going to be okay."

That wasn't all.

"There's two things I want to do, B. Three."

"Okay. Tell me. How can I help?"

"You're a good man, B." She smiled. and her head looked like a skull. She had this eerie new calm. Like she was a different person. Like she was possessed. or dead and alive at the same time.

Like the real her was no longer there. Or now the real her was here. And the familiar vague her was gone. It scared me. it freaked me out.

This whole thing scared me. Dealing with it day-to-day was not hard. You did what had to be done. tend to the details. to her.

At times it became too fucking much. But not really. that would pass. You stay calm. carry on. She was the one with cancer. not me.

My own agonies over it I thought were self-indulgent. but I couldn't help it. I was glad they were mostly at bay. mostly came out at night.

Right now I felt totally overwhelmed. crushed, terrified. But I kept it back. for now.

"First, I want to get a new kitty for White Man. He shouldn't be alone. He needs someone."

"Okay."

"Second." She had that voice and face she had giving her talks. She had memorized this. "I'm going to India. For real."

"Wow. Are you sure—"

"Hear me out, B." She coughed. *Winced?* "And I want to borrow six thousand dollars from you. So I can go."

"Okay," I said. Big breath out. "Of course I'll give it to you. But can we just talk about this?"

"Yeh, sure. But I've decided. Can you respect my decision, please?"

She was right. I wanted to dissuade her. My immediate, unconsidered reaction.

"Yes. I respect your decision. I'll help you however I can."

She had that impersonal deliberateness I wanted to

zap, dissolve and melt into our softer togetherness. where I was included. where I had a say. But no go.

How did I know she didn't want me to come with her?

"Can I come?"

She hesitated, downcast. Her nose a blade. Her separateness nonnegotiable.

"Do you *want* me to come?"

We'd talked about going to India together since our first predate. D's slides at India Night.

"I need to do this on my own, B."

I knew it was selfish. solipsistic. etc. but this upset me. a lot.

"You've helped me so much. You've given me so much. Always. And I totally appreciate that. But this is just something I've got to do on my own."

I couldn't even say *Wow.*

I hated my reaction.

She took my hand. Looked me in the eye. too close. She looked like an old hag. my pain trying to slither away, disguised as the serpent revulsion.

"You have to start to get your own life back, B." She squeezed my hand. her bony claw.

The more she said the more devastated I felt. Suddenly desperate, unmoored—

"You have to start to let me go."

At this I started wailing. shaking my head through its arrival and persistence, apologizing. "Sorry," I spluttered.

"It's okay to feel your feelings."

"I know—" I had no problem there! "I just—"

"I love you, too, B."

"Aghkt!"

I knew she did. But she seemed cold. remote. No matter how close her face was. her waning physical presence. waning.

It felt like her intention was already elsewhere. It felt like she was already gone.

Instead of going to chemo we took the cab uptown to the Humane Society to get a new kitty.

She'd been planning it. on her own. Why did she feel she couldn't tell me before?

In her way she did tell me before. *Yeh I did.* Did she think I'd be opposed?

She needed to act independently. I understood this. I guess. But understanding didn't *obtain* emotionally. didn't ease the terrible feeling she was cutting me out. she had cut me out.

Let alone that *she was dying!*

Sarah1 and Sarita were going, too. for part of the time. A was going for three months, she said. at least.

We'd hardly spent the night apart since we got together. a few times. Those times felt like a big deal. then.

I asked when she was leaving. It was now mid-March. This was a big deal. now.

"Two weeks advance purchase," she smiled. She smiled.

"Mandy—" My feet sank into the floor. the legs of the low table I sat on shot down through the building and basement into the middle of the earth. dizzied my feet.

"Billy, you've got to let me do this." She was eating. She was *eating.* "I really need your support in this."

I breathed in. "You have it. Totally." Breathed out. "Just tell me how I can help."

"I need to buy a backpack."

I'm a practical girl, B. What can I say?

We went to Paragon. She looked so pale and intrepid, *insipid,* out in the shitty, slushy, booming city day.

Bruised sky. wet wind. suggesting the frothy, sloshy sea. not far. behind the black buidings. we were on an island, after all. moving forward, steadily, like a boat.

"It's so noisy," she creaked. bag of bones in the back of the cab. She watched her city jogging by out the window. gloomy. raw. great. amply peopled with people. going nowhere.

"You've been in quarantine."

She stopped at the top of the stairs to catch her breath.

"Boy, B. Am I out of shape."

She took a canary yellow ski jacket off the discount rack beside her. put it on. It was way too big.

Went to the rack of goggles. took an evil reflective pair made for a big bug. put them on. Then put on a silver racing helmet. Also way too big. it wobbled. antic.

She looked like a little kid. You're supposed to put the helmet on before the goggles. *I know, B. Duh.* so they were kind of crushed, twisted sideways. Grinning her leaky grin.

Like if she was the captain, we were going to crash. Arms out like she was floating in outer space. slow time. Cut loose. on her way away from the world.

Her neck was slender. lovely. *Scrawny. gross.* like an arm. *Gross!* Corded at the throat. nice spoon declivity. She never had that before. so well-scooped. I could fuck it. *You would!*

Suddenly she fell down. The jackets on the rack swished, swayed together. stopped. She didn't move for a second. Then looked up at me, like *Help.* through the twisted goggles. helmet askew.

The night before we saw a thing on CNN about Indian troops mobilizing in Kashmir. One of the soldiers held a submachine gun (Kalashnikov).

He was just a boy. brown. White, brown eyes. A pretty, slender boy. He wore a bulky bulletproof vest on his front, like he had his backpack on backwards.

(Like if he'd just put it on the right way, it would have books in it, and he'd be a schoolboy on his way to school. and there would be no hostilities. no ever-looming war.)

His black helmet was too big. the chinstrap tight, holding it skewed. She looked like that. Like, *he was going to war?* Like, *she was going to India?*

As I helped her up a guy came over from behind the Swiss Army Knives and travel clocks.

She said she didn't pass out, she just tripped.

"Good thing you had your helmet on."

Funny guy, B.

There were *a lot* of backpacks to choose from. The world is overrun with travelers, trekkers. scraggly kids in cargo shorts, caps, dirty socks. with half-baked rebellious notions and their Lonely Planet guides from Barnes & Noble. *out there.*

You see them, like flies, in the airports. in the plazas of the tourist towns. at the beaches. the mountains. parks. sacred sites. infesting sticky wonders of the world.

And here, clearly, was where the backpack nation came to buy their backpacks.

We were narrowing it down. I favored the smallest of the three. still plenty big. rigid. light. padded straps.

lots of straps. zippered compartments. and a day pack attached to the butt.

"You're not being very helpful, B."

I thought I was.

"Baby, you just have to decide. It's for you . . ."

"It's for *us*."

Anything can be laden, charged, misconstrued, in love. It's always the little things. And so everything, in the end, is important.

"Okay. I choose this one. How about you?"

"Did you call me baby?"

"Yeah, I—"

"You never call me baby."

"Just came out."

"It's nice!"

I was sorry I didn't call her baby all the time. Why didn't I?

On the way out we picked up a travel clock. cheapest flat one. from the guy. She wanted one.

He looked at me keenly. nodded once knowingly, sympathetically. He was gay. not young. knew this dwindling chapter.

❧

And so Amanda went to India. She'd had enough of the chemo. the suffering. the dying.

And so she folded up that sad tent, packed her bravely hopeful show into her/our superior new backpack, and off she went.

Everyone was supportive of her decision. Friends. family. yoga family. cat family. even the doctors. The doctors surprised me. shocked me, in fact.

They and I were the only ones who knew how sick she was. They see so many people. all going through essentially the same decline.

Though of course, in the deepest sense, she knew more than anybody.

And though she liked to think, to say, she was a practical girl, she always went on intuition. And so she was going. End of story.

Our parting was the saddest good-bye in the history of airport farewells. We were both total wrecks. I knew I'd never see her again.

When I tried to say that the night before, she reflexively covered my mouth. as when you cover the other guy in basketball. or reach over to turn out the light. shut your significant other up.

It was three in the afternoon. Traffic getting there was not bad. The trouble was within, between, us. We couldn't speak. I held her the whole way.

Half the ride she had her eyes closed. It was not just fatigue. It was the pain expression. her blithe, blank mask. Hardened. departed.

She didn't want to, but when we saw the line at the airport, she agreed to play the sick card. The scene at Kuwait Air was already Asia.

The crowd bursting past the cordoned cutback. People and possessions, passive urgency, packages, bundles, boxes, overstuffed, woven plastic bags, baggage, extended families, fat, short women in saris, children.

"Okay, B. Let's get the wheelchair."

Sarah1 was taking the flight with her. but was nowhere to be seen. Hopefully already past security, at the gate.

Wearing her backpack, I wheeled Amanda to the

front of the line, led by a helpful svelte ticket hostess. who seemed to be twelve years old. like she was playing at working at the airport.

The pack was heavy. How would she manage? What was she going to do? Where was she going? What was she doing?

I knew I'd never see her again.

It was strangely not hard to accept. Now that the moment was here. It was as true and easy and unchangeable as any moment or scene unfolding. or oddly more so.

She fixated on the backpack. the ticket. her passport. her pureed meal I made her. her seat selection. finding Sarah1 inside.

This was really happening.

We sat for an hour away from the security entrance. Facing the movie screen–size plate glass. showing the usual tarmac tableau. parked huge planes. geometry of fins and fuselages. lined up in diminishing perspective.

Baggage guys bombing along out there, wearing orange headphones, jumpsuits. farther away, planes landing and taking off. a scrawny little plane bumping along, looking lost, buglike, about to get crushed.

We sat hugging, crying, and not crying, the whole hour. Except when she had to pee. Gasping, blubbering basket cases.

We just kept saying *I love you.* More than we ever had. Nodding. Wiped the sea splash off each other's tormented, demented, never-fading face.

I'd never see her again!

The young hospitality hostess touched our shoulders. I wheeled A to the entrance. Her breathing was caught in spasmodic crying. She coughed and coughed and stopped.

She looked really scared. She was being so strong! I wheeled her to the security entrance.

We kissed one last time. Not really a kiss. One more killer hug. at a weird angle. I wouldn't let go.

"You're choking me, B."

She was a scarecrow. with the will of a god. her eyes twin lake souls. unafraid! I gave her an envelope.

I told her she couldn't open it till after takeoff. It had a ring in it. My grandmother's engagement ring. And an original document.

A signed, certified, fully official Declaration of True and Everlasting Love.

You only get. and get to give. a few of these in your lifetime. if you're lucky.

"Take care of yourself, B-B. I love you!"

"Did you call me baby?"

She cough/laughed through her crying, nodding *no-yes-no.* The hostess wheeled her to the security entrance.

She looked back. I punched my heart twice and pointed to heaven. like Sammy Sosa. rounding first. when he hit another home run.

Like we always did parting on our bikes. the mutually timed backward glance. a block or so apart. heading off in our own directions.

She did the same. Her little hand, curled, waved *bye.*

5. Broome & Crosby

H von Braunhut, 77, Inventor

Harold von Braunhut, who used comic books to sell mail order creations like Amazing Sea Monkeys, tiny shrimp that pop to life when water is added, died November 28 at his home in Indian Head, Maryland. He was seventy-seven. His wife, Yolanda, said he died after a fall, but the exact cause was not known.

Von Braunhut also created X-Ray Specs and the Amazing Hair-Raising Monster, but his pièce de résistance was Sea Monkeys, which come from dried-up lake bottoms, not the sea, and are not monkeys but brine shrimp.

Amanda would have liked that her obituary in the *Times* was beside this guy's. She loved comic books, as a kid. And she managed, instinctively, to stay, always, close to that fun, loving, fun-loving place.

I read every inch of the paper like a rabid editor-in-chief every day in my studio after practice. I stayed up late working or doing my things, effectively suspended in the art box, I knew the tricks, blindfolded. but feeling awful the whole time.

I ached for her like crazy. I wrote her an e-mail (from the apartment) telling her it missed her. and everything in it missed her.

The rounded rice paper sliding door misses you. the curled-up corner of linoleum in the bathroom I still didn't fix misses you. the cats don't really but the cat door beside the French doors. their private low-down entrance. misses you . .

In her absence I felt amputated. cut off. floating in inner-outer space. in my near-sleep holding my raw red dick. severed umbilical to the gone mother ship. I read a lot. hit some events. lots of movies. Film Forum Film Forum. with whomever would join me. or solo. Also a little tomcattin' with Buddy. but nothing really, no fucking around.

Practiced at eleven. not full. at Andy's new place in SoHo. above a corner restaurant Orange Bleu. bigger shoe box room, nice. second floor. long wall lined with windows overlooking Crosby. sheer sari curtains. slender woman's toes of a breeze tickle in. come-hither hand.

Dripping heat like India. (Why go there? when this is here.) Deep summer voyage in the sweaty hold. half-empty city. absentminded. Andy's firm knowing touch. as ace and intimate as it gets.

SoHo architecture upside-down out the window in headstand. the inversions. volumes lined up.

Amanda returned from India. healed.

We went to Maine. Ease back.

She didn't want to talk about India. the miracle of her healing. any of it.

"It's not about words."

Okay.

She wanted to carry it, silently, inside her. She was a vessel carrying the mystery. sari-wrapped. careful not to wreck it.

While she was in India we had a few faraway calls. the two-second delay. wavery. as if underwater. outer space. lots of *what's* from her side.

Some touching not-long e-mails sent from an outdoor place, rickety table on the crowded Mysore sidewalk. mosquitoes. the noise. monkeys. a kid Ajay. women in their saris.

Not a word about herself.

I asked again when the moment was maybe right. We were sailing. like lying around in our lake, but real nature around us this time. not just ours. our magic fake lake. the walls of the apt. fallen away in the interregnum, spat us out in this paradise spot.

It was calm, a gentle cobalt breeze. invisible cat's paw. pulled us silently along. little wavelets lapped audibly, delicate little plashes, the cat drinking, playing, at the plying bow, her tan bare foot trailing in the green water *co-hold,* nice knee over the gunwale.

All she said was *"Pancha karma,"* shrugging. and added "Chanting." As if that said it all.

Chanting is prayer. after all. to God who goes by many names. devotional singing. repetition. in Sanskrit. Exotically other. new and anciently novel. acceptable to a stray unconvinced Christian. like this whole yoga thing.

All is coming.

Ayurveda was one of yoga's many sideshows. The diet. (*dal. ghee. lassi.*) the chakras. massage. (warm oil poured on your forehead.) weird, complex astrology. symbols, triangles.

You learn your *dosha.* (Body type.) *vatta. pitta.* But then what?

And I didn't push it. for once. and was rewarded with a few more crumbs of nonrevelation.

"The guy was amazing. The whole thing, it was—I don't understand it . . . Like you're a plant again. You had to be there."

We got up really early, at first, to practice. still dark, sometimes foggy, the stillness a holy spell. lovely as hell. She had me doing second series with her. all of primary and well into second.

Picnics. naps. boats. My meals. Reading on the window benches. lying there. in two seconds she'd fall asleep among the cushions. shored up, mouth agape. leak back in business.

First sex on a smooth stone beach. ravenous! Gulls passing over. cycling back. *Raw! Wah!* Lobster boat at one o'clock. Flat round stones stuck to her back and butt. as we rolled over. Let Mandy take over! riding the waves.

She looked different. the same. Slender. not skeletal. strong. luminous. her eyes. no longer scary-looking, feral. that hungry ghost gaze. desperate plea. last-gasp search. gone.

She said this island was her favorite place in the world. (That's almost *I love you.*)

She ate ice cream like there was no tomorrow. Any time of day. she'd get up and go. announced or unannounced. slip down to the Lobsta Shack down by the ferry.

Came back licking her chops. Repeating overheard

snatches, phrases. *You know it.* the delicious accent. *I doubt it.* her gathered Maine mantras repeated, at random.

How you doin'?

Computah.

Dot calm.

And so yeah.

Old patterns resumed.

Back in the city. the routine. the apt.

The disconnect. the frustrations. built in.

I suggested therapy. not for the first time. For us together. A couples therapist.

She said she didn't have *time.* couldn't afford it. as usual.

But when I said this time either we go to therapy, or I'm breaking up. I got her attention. she found the time. and money.

While she was gone I missed her like crazy. But if it was more disturbing with her than without, what was that? Why stay together? Work it out. or move on.

Shouldn't living together be, like, *living together?* instead of apart together.

Our therapist looked like Virginia Woolf. Tall and thin. aesthetic pallor. (more milk and paper than night and anguish.) appropriately offset by dark clothes and black flat hair precisely framing like a parted curtain her concern-hungry eyes.

Her eyes were also dark, ink-intense, psychic punctuation-mark stewards to a firm yet sweet gaze that was almost aggressively present, compassionate, attentive, penetrating.

You had to look away. I felt like I'd done something wrong, just sitting there in front of her. Time stopped. guiltily. I stared at her long, elegant hands the whole time. folded on her lap. gesturing economically.

She asked what was going on in our relationship. Amanda smiled. demurred, squirmed. didn't say anything. So I answered, began to describe our problems, let's get to it. until Virginia Woolf stopped me and asked Amanda what she thought of what I'd just said.

When Amanda said she didn't know, I cut in. cardinal original sin. demonstration. and said, "See? This is exactly—"

"Billy." She cut me off again, kindly asked me to let her guide the conversation. to let Amanda speak.

So I did that and looked from Virginia Woolf's tapered hands to the dark window hole in a vine-infested ruin in the framed photo on the wall across from me, to the view out the one window, over the London-seeming arrangement of rooftops and eaves. actual angled, slanting *roofs,* one with dormers like triangular cat ears, one stately old mansard, rounded slate shingles. instead of the usual bizarre New York architectural omission, the hatless, headless tradition of flat black scab tar beach "roofs", in lieu of actual real *roofs.*

Her questions were delicately proffered. but devastatingly astute and direct. at times. She welcomed uncertainty, she said. when Amanda said she wasn't sure about how she felt. what she thought. I left the first session feeling like we were much worse off than I'd thought. A, to my surprise, seemed hopeful.

"I like her," was all she said afterward, navigating Sixth Avenue on our bikes, going with the flow, the herd of crazed taxis stampeding furiously uptown between

Balducci's and the brick Victorian library, whose handsome clock tower always drew the eye, used to be a prison for women, or asylum, shrieks and otherworldly screams pealed at night amid civil dulcet bells, and howled in the lovely silver lunatic silence after the bells selved, resolved, stopped, under many moons, born of the bells, each launched and lit by each successive, almost respiratory *gong*, history conceived in the candled eggs, fatally, fetally curled in each, waiting to happen, other worlds, floating there, clouds that look like anything you want them to, dreams emanating from the surrounding West Village/Old London moonscape mind, whose rhyming diurnal roofscape details and repressed, hysterical-era patterns the (my) eye drew, traced, repeatedly, habitually, escaping out the window, during therapy sessions, unconsciously etched into place an emerging, impressionistic map of our abiding conflicts, patterns, the elusive jazz composition of our brief emotional history, already too complex, blending with the neatly overlapping, compact, nearly cubist concentration of roofline delineations, slopes and planes and spaces in between punctuated by pipes and chimneys and wrought iron details that taken together comprise the supercinematic, brick, richly poetic and peopled, altogether impressive, pretty and pretty cool, cooly understated and wonderfully over-written (and -written about) West Village (NY) abstract expressionist imagination.

Billy? Are you with us?

At subsequent meetings it was somehow established that I'm *angry*. Virginia Woolf asked me why I was angry. I said I wasn't. But if I were, the profile fit. I explained I had an alcoholic absentee father. My mother was loving, but too busy. So the quality and depth of her love was great. But it wasn't enough. it was intermittent. there and not there. or at least not enough for little Billy. or at least it felt that way. Hence the big huge hole in my heart I'm always trying and trying and failing to fill.

"Amanda?" V Woolf asked her for a response. None was forthcoming.

So V Woolf asked me to continue. so I continued, "So now, brilliantly, I've found someone whose love is just as wonderful and also limited as my mother's. So. I'm angry because the woman I love will hardly talk to me! She has withdrawn her love! She's gone! *Again!* It's breaking my heart!"

"See?" A cheeped.

I didn't see. But Virginia Woolf did. She pointed out I didn't really answer her question (I disagreed. but kept it to myself.) and suggested that my *style,* as she put it, was shutting A down. I was too aggressive in my speech. my tone. my forthrightness. my demands. Language and expression for me could be a gift, Virginia Woolf informed me, another time, but also a weapon.

At least that's how it felt/seemed to A. Who was quietly thrilled to have an ally and a witness to this assault and dynamic.

Amanda came to see. did she, really? *Yes, B, really.* that her *withholding,* her withdrawal, was what made me so angry. Abandonment all over again. My, maybe everyone's? primal wound. core fear.

The opposite of what I wanted. needed. (I thought.) (Because we think we know what we need!)

"I. me. my," A's (mean) mantra. when I talked about my unmet needs. before. But in therapy that didn't fly! I was allowed to have needs! What a fucking relief. That alone was worth the (high) price of admission. Even if they weren't being met. still. yet. ever. it felt like.

I had a joke with A about therapy that she didn't think was funny, but so I kept at it, hammering it home, which becomes the funny thing about it. maybe. or not.

Instead of the ticket you get at a movie that says ADMIT ONE, the ticket to therapy (both are projection) should say ADMIT IT. Amanda didn't think it was funny.

We learned lots of things about each other. And ourselves. At least I did. *I did, too.* (We're still arguing. well after.)

The main thing was communication. No big surprise. Turned out I wasn't as good at it as I thought I was. This was, *I admit,* a revelation. I resisted for a while. sure that V Woolf was imagining rather than observing this, that she had me pegged from the start as the usual angry overbearing guy who couldn't communicate his feelings, and she wasn't paying attention to how responsive, sensitive, singular, etc., I really was. In short, that *she* was *projecting!*

If you've never done couple's therapy, here's the *dealio.*

None of us knows how to communicate well. effectively. In terms of mutuality. (Equal partners. vs. Perpetual power struggle.)

If you don't really listen, you're not really a partner. This I could accept. in myself. I *admit it*! and work on myself.

But we both had to be doing that. to get anywhere. And we both had to work on our own conscious inner gaze. *What are you feeling right now, Amanda? Billy?* What the practice was about!

The problem wasn't that she didn't care. I learned in

time. though I don't think she did. It was that she wasn't capable of this intimate conscious inner gaze. Let alone reporting from there. calmly within. let alone joining me there. Joining me in the effort to learn to do this. Let alone listening.

"What about that, Amanda?" Virginia was careful not to accuse, but only to gently suggest, compassionately *inquire.*

"I don't know." Man laughed nervously. "I care about his side . . ."

"Guys." V called us *guys.* Was she a lesbian? A and I often speculated on her orientation. Her life. beliefs. weekends. diet. lack of. Was she a Buddhist? (So spookily calm. present.) A Wiccan? Bulimic. anorexic?

"Guys. You don't have the tools to communicate with each other effectively. Who does? When do we learn? I can help you develop the tools."

She said this many times at the beginning. *The tools.* Once a week. sometimes double sessions. if we missed one the week before (i.e., because A *didn't have the time.*)

Basically, we had to learn to listen to each other. You had to listen. really listen. Then repeat it back. It was hard. You'd forget parts. Get caught up in your own side. your boiling, overflowing reactions. my response bubbling up and building, by itself. V would bust us. both.

"Billy, what did Amanda just say?"

Or, "Amanda, are you with us?"

I liked this, and would say it to A sometimes, in V Woolf's tiptoeing, compassionate, annoyingly soft and sweet but to-the-jugular tone.

We'd practice in the sessions. listening and repeating. then your turn. And then we had homework. five minutes a day. to start. Each. The problem was. one problem was. surprise surprise. A didn't ever want to do it. We'd return to the next week's session. Me dark. A lighter.

"So. How're we doing, guys?"

I'd shrug. Emit an "Okay."

A'd smile. "Good!"

"How about the exercises?"

"We didn't do it," I reported. retorted. Virginia Woolf's long hands held fleeting still life in them. poised just so. or cupped together like there was a little voodoo chick in there. Little Fluffy Chicky Mandy. in safe*Eep!*keeping. *Eep!*

"Yes we did!" A protested. She wore her fluffy chicky sweater. To go with her hair, freshly cut and licked blonder. Washed, blow-dried. *Cheep-cheep!* Totally cute.

"Yeah, once."

"Amanda?"

"Yeh . . ."

Amanda squirmed. chirped. complained five minutes each was *too much.* (Too much *time?* Too much *effort?* I wasn't allowed to jump in and ask.) Five minutes to talk. Less to repeat it back. Then more to respond, discuss . . .

So V cut it down. (We went from kindergarten to pre-K.) (And I felt like I was postdoc. experienced, sage, supersensitive worldly-wise, well-endowed mutual fellow. (im)patiently jumping up and down over here. waving my arms. my.) From back and forth to just one person talking per day. Still A was reluctant.

"Every day?" She tried to joke her way out of it.

And since I was always the one initiating. or trying to. as in sex. (The Initiator. textbook.) our homework, V suggested/decided we alternate days. One day I'd say let's do it, when do you have time? The next day would be A's turn to *initiate*.

Only problem was. on my days, practically upon waking I'd say, "So when do you want to do our five minutes?"

When it was her day to initiate, she wouldn't bring it up. I'd call her during the day. as usual. give her a chance to bring it up. *Nada*.

"Amanda, I think Billy really has a point here. I have to say, you're not participating in the exercises."

"I'm here at least," she peeped.

"Yes. You are here." V paused. "Can you see how Billy feels shut out? How he feels you don't want to participate in the *relationship*?" God bless Virginia Woolf.

"Yeh." Cute, downward-facing mouth. contrite downcast gaze.

My roving eye fell into the dark hole window in the derelict stone building in the photograph across from the couch.

Sometimes the sessions were rough.

"Billy, how can we get you to be less angry?"

"Get Amanda to stop ignoring me! To desire me! Talk to me! Care how I'm doing! Ask once in a while! Besides *How ya doin.* Slash-cut to *Love ya, mean it./ Seeya. I'm not doing so well!*"

They helped, though. a lot. the sessions. I guess. somehow. even the homework, sometimes. When Ms. Fluffy Chicky was emotionally present, I calmed down.

This showed me how right I was. for what that was worth. about her distance. But also revealed my role. demanding. needy. domineering yet dependent. trying to control. steer, direct, fix everything.

"What would happen if you just let everything collapse?" Virginia Woolf challenged me, her nerves-of-steel attention and directness sheathed in the velvet voice of lovingkindness.

"Then everything would collapse!" I answered, exercised. as if pleading with the gods. the fickle gods of relationship. to *please let this love work!*

We pay her one-twenty an hour to say this? I felt at the time. (But now see her wisdom.) (Maybe a nudge. suggestion. advice.)

(admonition. adumbrating.)

Stop it, B.

I *admitted* my eye wandered when her attentions dwindled.

Amanda accused me of wanting to fuck Sarita.

Virginia Woolf looked at me to respond. "Billy?" So I told the truth.

"I'd love to fuck her. But I wouldn't, I haven't, I'm not trying to, and I won't."

Amanda crumpled, her devastated face I'll never forget. (And to this day I'm sorry I said that.) Except that actually I can't remember it, it was too painful to really register. retain.

V Woolf winced and sort of recoiled, too, her expression and head movement telling me I'd crossed the line, you fucking idiot, my brutal frankness was brutal only, not helpful honesty. certainly not the carefully crafted response we were supposed to be learning here. tailored for the ears and hurt heart of the delicate, imperfect, imperfectly acceptable significant other.

One session Amanda said, "I feel like I don't have my own space to breathe or live in."

Virginia Woolf pressed her, gently but firmly (a good assist), to explore further what she meant. Amanda shrugged and said something that shocked me.

"Ever since my sickness. I don't know . . . Maybe that was, I don't know, pulling us apart. And we never really got back together. In the old way."

"Guys," Virginia Woolf responded without hesitation, and then paused. as if she had considered this and had her considered response ready-made, locked and loaded for the appropriate moment to pull the trigger. now.

"The cancer wasn't pulling you apart. It was keeping you together. You survived that, went through that together, and now comes the hard part. Living an ordinary life. Together. Learning to get along—to see, hear, accept, and love one another."

It all showed how disjointed indeed we were. Did the therapy in fact help?

"Amanda? Are you with us?"

Lunch with Andy. Teany. cute waitress. after T&R's wedding. (their wedding. note. not our wedding.) malas. music. food. dancing at the party-pretty *shala*. silk-wrapped Ganesh-festooned, decked out. the whole deal.

"I was watching you guys at the wedding, and I've gotta say, Billy, she's not there for you. I can see you're unhappy. She's not at your level, and she never will be."

I didn't know what to say.

"I'm sorry. I probably shouldn't say anything. I probably should keep my big mouth shut. But I just hate to see you suffering."

"Yeah, no, I'm glad you said something."

Man would often, still, ask me to pick her up after work. I'd sit across from the fountain wall. The girl at the desk or someone heading back would tell her I was there. After ten minutes she'd stick her head out, down the corridor, and say, "Five minutes. Okay?" In fifteen, twenty, more, she'd emerge.

I'd read. take the wait as an exercise in patience. Not-so-slyly watch the girls go by. lots of looks. lots of heys.

Knee talk with Pat, my knee club protégé. fierce yoga striver brother. completely drenched from his practice. Showed him how to do half lotus if you can't really do it, move toward it, without fucking up your knees. ankles. for life. Do ankle-to-knee. for starters. daily.

"Sorry, B. I thought I'd be ready at seven."

Pat came out of the men's dressing room. trim fifties parted haircut wet-combed. flat pie-face. parboiled pink.

"Pat! You're our hero!"

He'd been on the news the night before, all sweaty (as after practice. but soot-begrimed), after going into a building and saving a kid. He was famous in the FD. living legend. for doing this. countless times over the years.

"You guys are my heroes," he said.

Riding away down Lafayette. Cabs ripping by. A crowd outside Blue Man Group. Not New Yorkers.

Lucky's for a juice. our old routine. She'd reach into the overstuffed desk spilling out of her pocket and I'd slip her a folded twenty. While she ordered I'd discreetly move her bike away from where she parked it, her rickety, scarred, skeletal trusty pony, blocking the entrance.

We'd sit on the bench outside with our Reggae

Rumbas. Watch the light lilt and die softly in faces. in the architecture. in-between spaces. the characters parading by, noting trends, admiring efforts, sympathy for the sad cases. *Look at this one.* Who was having sex and who wasn't. Deciding which ones were wearing the fashion, and working it. and which ones. most. the fashion was wearing them. (or most, really, even in New York, no fashion sense.)

She'd tell me things that happened at work. So-and-so's pregnant. (*Do not. Billy Winslow. tell anyone.*) The magazine shoot, everyone crazed. How she got blamed for everything. as usual. How Jonni was a crazy bitch. again. How few people came to her afternoon class. How nobody liked her classes. I listened, made cracks and assorted supportive replies.

I'd have food waiting at home. She usually said she wasn't hungry. and then she'd look. taste. *Mmm.* and eat.

"This is *really good.* What is this?" Miso tahini. y'know. hijiki, arame.

Onto the bed, for the TV drama. She'd turn it on, settle in and surf. in and out of VH1 and MTV, her homes of the heart. If I didn't say anything, still she knew it bothered me. If I complained, no matter how ironically or sheerly eggshell-diplomatically I framed it, she didn't want to hear about it.

And so there we were again, at odds again. or whatever this was. It was just TV. so so what? But it was the TV instead of conversation. connection. TV instead of sex. She just wanted to tune out. Okay. unless the phone rang, and she was suddenly all energy and Amanda sweetness.

I'd shut off the TV. try to read. But listened,

instead—no choice!—to her (whole, long) phone conversation. So I'd turn the TV back on. NewsHour. Bravo, AMC. Dave. nicer now, less acerbic. now that he had a son? or since he almost died of a heart attack..

What can you do when the other person wants to tune you out? Tune out with her? Even though the whole point of my life now. supposedly. was to do the opposite. Connect. within. with you. and you. with her. with God. with life.

The one show I liked was *The West Wing.* For her they talked too fast. about issues and stuff she didn't know or really care what they were talking about. and the lighting was too dark.

But the one thing we both liked was when our fantasy good president Martin Sheen (in that alternative intelligent-universe effectual presidency), ready for action, put his jacket on with a sudden decisive smooth movement over his head, both arms raised and—*shoop,* it's on. We'd try it in the morning with our parkas and laugh, get all caught up like idiots in a straitjacket. (My five-year-old nephew could do it. first lay the jacket down on the bed. the table. upside-down. arms out.)

The apartment was too small. We were on top of each other. Same old thing. I was waiting for her to want to talk to me. want me. Do our therapy homework. But she wouldn't. she didn't.

We went on for weeks like this. months. This is what it was like. She'd sleep facing the kitchen through the French doors. chilly East Coast. I'd be over in my California. (our role reversal.) miserable.

There were good times interspersed. still. *true love!* don't get me wrong. We'd laugh till the back of my head hurt. Made love like we used to. We could always return to that. Amanda's instinct for sensing when the distance standoff was too much. she was losing me. had sharpened. she'd open up and reach out.

Maybe this was all you could expect? Maybe the problem wasn't the relationship, but the expectation? *my* expectation.

Literally reach out and touch me. Or look at me in that mischievous way, and beckon me with an upright, crooked forefinger. Like pulling a trigger. Or scan my semiclad body and boing her eyebrows up and down. Or call me into the bathroom, where she lay marinating in the tub, a stream of hot water running constantly. Or she'd take a running leap and pounce on me where I lay on the bed, our raft, reading away.

All winter and spring we went to therapy. We seemed to make progress, in the sessions, in the process. As far as it went. which wasn't very far. Certainly I learned a lot about how controlling or demanding of a response I can be, needy for affection, contact, connection, sex.

But communication exercises didn't become part of our relationship. Amanda didn't want to do it. the homework. the *work.* cultivate the intimacy. the careful gardening, slow as growth.

It didn't matter what we said or realized with Virginia Woolf. What mattered was what happened between us. at home. in our time together.

We'd come a long way. *had we?* from the beginning, when I was the problem, the angry needy controlling guy. It was good to be seen, validated, in my abandonment. her intransigence. For what that was worth. But it didn't help. Didn't solve or dissolve the problem. change the dynamic. This was the way we were.

Instead of telling me I was aggressive and selfish, and controlling, Virginia Woolf suggested maybe I tried too hard to have my emotional needs met. I ended up forcing things. which didn't work. sounds obvious. but it wasn't to me.

Virginia Woolf's kind, nonjudgmental way of holding the mirror up to us. our movie. to me. to Amanda. was helpful. (to me.) even if it didn't really help. (us.)

Instead of telling Amanda she was repressed, damaged, thwarted within, her heart locked, or some such. Virginia Woolf diplomatically said, in what turned out to be one of our last sessions, "You two have different, opposing pictures of intimacy. You want two different things."

It was true. I wanted us to blend into one. She wanted us to stay near, but not too close. *Nothing too deep.* as the girls joked. their mock motto. except real.

Us in bed. making love we're one wonderful love animal. souls like that all the time. you carry it with you. when you're apart you're together. as in the early days! minds and lives meshing in that deepest way. connects you to all creation.

Or us in bed, sitting there, side by side, like dead couples everywhere in the world, doing our own thing, in our parallel separate lives, resentful, separate. resigned, except not really. me reading, her watching TV. me unable to concentrate because the TV's on, and I'm upset, and she doesn't desire me. she unable to enjoy it fully because I'm there reading and wanting sex and the whole deal, *love,* disapproving of the TV, of her, even if I don't say anything, she knows, and she's exhausted, just wants to chill, zone out, *what's wrong with that?*

And of course she'd have new boyfriends I wouldn't want to hear about. but would, inevitably, bit by bit, we had so many friends in common. and my fierce shutting-out capacity was well equipped, as well, obversely, backside, perversely, with keen periscope radar that relentlessly picked up details, clues. I know her so well I knew without knowing, just from looking at her, or from something someone said, something someone said she did, that she was down again, hurt heart, or way into some other guy again, fucking all the time, you know, loving him and loving life, and without wanting to I'd meet him, see her with him at a party, a friend's wedding (another. another not ours), thinking, yet again, in spite of myself, or precisely because of myself, but in spite of my better judgment and all if any insights and growth and plain old pain and suffering (are they different?), in spite of myself I'd think again this might be like a renewal date for us, this time, at last, funny how love goes, like the song says, I kept remembering in an e-mail once, from the middle place, she said we had unfinished business, and since she asked me twice, three times, if I was going to the wedding, we'd been getting along sweetly lately, if sparsely, and then when I saw her there with this other guy, she with him, I realized why she'd asked me repeatedly if I was going, and instead of avoiding them the whole time, I did that Buddhist thing I'd learned, with and without her, go straight at the thing you fear, that you want to avoid or find yourself running away from, and so I went over to them, after seeing them, and getting zapped by the stun gun, the worst part, I thought, life is suffering, like they say, and if it's happening now it's almost past, maybe, so chill, persist, be still, let it be, I look at them again, look down from the three-sided balcony above, dancing a sweet slow dance embrace after the vows, first dances expanding to lovers, parents and creaky spirited crones, geezers, her head resting on his shoulder, eyes shut, her face in her angelic repose, touched by the magic wand of early love, her addiction, perhaps, no doubt, love, early love, the easy erotic part, I'm one to talk, now here with this new guy, life is renewal, *all love is good,* and so I said hello, and I spoke to them, kissed her cheek and shook his hand, she invited me to sit with them, on the floor, she, we, remain in character, and we're talking and I like the guy, I mean, enough, okay, though also of course I could kill him with the glass in my hand, crack his nose, *Om shantih*, motherfucker, ram it into his brain, high five hard, with my palm, and Amanda gets up and goes for another glass of wine, she used to not drink with me, we didn't drink, leaving us guys to speak, civil and what have you, without tension or *attachment*, the way we're supposed to be, *Be the change you want to see in the world*, she loves this guy, love is good, loving her means accepting this, accepting reality means accepting this, she loves this fat fuck? who hasn't uttered an interesting word, I'm sure he's rich, and there you go, the house in the Hamptons pops up, inside a minute, the beach, we're talking along and he goes, now Amanda's back with us, he jokes about something about her, like of course I think it's funny, too, I can't remember what it was, maybe how she sometimes sneaks smokes, or loves her chewy power bars, I don't like where this is sliding,

I veer it over to sports, but he's not sporty, but he likes to eat, so I steer it into food, anything away from her, her and him, the ol' diet card, general health, a little balance, there, big guy, but he, in blinders, emboldened, keeps going the other way, this time deeper, on sleep, with, "Well I haven't been getting much sleep since I've known Amanda, if you know what I mean!" which hits me sickly, thickly, in the gut, and deeper, I look down at my drink, swallow, breathe, contain, defuse, maintain, deflect the sucking burning sensation incursion by saying something, "I don't know—you're talking to the wrong guy about that," staring a hole through the rising teeming misery, downward-staring cuckold, stunned again, fuck me, and Amanda, blessedly, but too late, but it wasn't her fault, what could she do? except how could she love someone who could say something like that? she bluntly contravenes, "I think we should change the subject." Not exactly the *Gotta love Amanda* exchange her ex before me and I managed, he managed, I just sat there, but still, be still, when we crossed paths, that time, going around, the stone steps, the dance in the church, an amicable changing of the guard, it was just right, acceptance and the implicit *I'm good, you're good,* take care of her, good luck, and friendly enough greetings when we'd cross paths after that, coming around, as opposed to this time, this guy. and my not great, but not un-gracious reaction.

~

Sarah2 was going to LA for the summer, so Amanda took her apartment in Little Italy. for the summer. The *space* she said she wanted.

"That's not what I meant, B. I'm talking about *give me space.*"

Not very nicely, I did what she did to me sometimes, it always annoyed me, made a W with my hands, thumb tips touching, forefingers raised, angled outward. meaning *Whatever.*

I wasn't glad she was going, and it wasn't really like we were breaking up, we were just separating, not even. living apart, get some perspective, hopefully she would, but seeing each other as much as we wanted. But I did push her to go. Because it was clearly the *right thing* to do.

All this talk about *right action.* it's not just a nice-sounding principle. The point is to really try to live that way. which means doing what you don't want to do. I kept telling myself. meaning choosing a course that is painful. Like telling Amanda I wanted her to move out. That unless she wanted to love me, open up, do our fucking therapy homework. *Talk to me! Fuck me!* I didn't want to continue like this. Though of course I did want to. So I chose what was right instead of what *felt* right. or what I wanted.

It felt awful. I was relieved, sure, in a way, to have peaceful silence at home, instead of the tension or disappointment building unbearably. No doubt. I'd read, work, practice, hang out with friends more. I didn't like it. but I didn't like it the way we were going. I could no longer choose that. We had crossed a threshold. of what's working. or workable. And on my own I'd crossed a threshold. of awareness. clarity, thanks to therapy. the practice, repetition, cultivating *purusha* the witness. where to continue wouldn't be generous perseverance. love's ever-giving duty. but weak folly. perseveration.

I didn't have the strength of my conviction, though. Though I knew you can't wait for that. That's procrastination, rationalization, any -nation but free. I knew I couldn't wait till I felt more ready. The yogi learns to act without pausing to think. So they say. Not that I didn't think. and think. and think about it. I'd heard friends in recovery say *Fake it till you make it.* And *Act as if.* So I just did it.

Really I hoped this would crack the coconut shell of her stubborn resistance, her distance, that hardening and unfriendliness, her defensive shell and shield, magically lifted, and she'd come running back to me with open arms. and legs, and mouth. *As if!* Right now, for some time now, she resented more than wanted me. I'd become the nemesis instead of the Siamese ally. the problem, to her mind or heart or gut feeling, no longer the welcome, desired solution. whereas before it was, as dreamy Marilyn Monroe said in some movie we once watched under the warmth of the down comforter. winter out there and new love in here. (when we felt that way together), *creamy.*

6. Disaster Place

Guruji was in town. Big deal for the ashtangis. came from all over the country, the world, to practice en masse with Guruji. We in New York were lucky. where everything comes to you. all we had to do was roll out of bed, as usual, flip our jackets on like proactive President Bartlet, and pedal on over. Except, um, A wasn't living with me anymore. for now. Everything highlighted the lack of her.

He was at the Puck Building again this year, the ballroom on the top floor, emptied out. Bikes locked to the black wrought iron fence along Lafayette. Arrivals. nods, greetings. familiar, similar souls from other corners of our cult. many strangers. Solemn, sleep-puffed faces. yoga clothes. out-of-towners more colorful. everyone carrying a rolled-up mat. one loud person talking in the elevator.

Arched, mullioned windows on three sides onto sky, looking east, uptown and west, over rooftops. the stepped composite building block composition, the brilliant cubist New York density, everywhere you look, the sense of so many souls out there, packed into so many expensive, sleeping privacies. the traffic and life flowing below. an early-morning respite up here in our clear cloud, quietly peopled, filled with murmur and walled by morning rising in the wraparound glass. Looking out the window I thought again what I'd recalled at therapy, mooning, musing out Virginia Woolf's window, what Gertrude Stein said about cubism, after visiting Spain with Picasso and Juan Gris, that cubism wasn't cubism, cubism was realism. The villages in Spain, where those guys came from, really looked like that.

Out the humid-whitened windows an astonishing invasion of crude, cool wooden spaceships. a few new, the wood blond. most blackened, weathered and sealed by city soot. had landed overnight on the rooftops, squat, on spindly spider legs, cone hats. the attack of the wooden water towers.

And in the room an intense, distilled, collective intention, the sense of so many souls, each unique, we are gathered here today for some reason. as if each had arrived here in the sky ballroom for check-in to heaven, bring nothing but you and your celestial magic carpet yoga mat, one of those romantic comedies. all the girls and guys, most in their twenties and thirties, the fleeting prime of life. this is it, kids. each with their own complex, many-peopled, many-chaptered personal histories, their clothes, jokes, fears, yearnings, discombobulated finances and philosophies, half-baked, crumbling and nevertheless ascending lives reduced to here and now on their mats in their bodies moving together in these set movements, holding a pose, in breathing unison, acting out before seven in the morning this ancient healing body alphabet and active meditation transportation.

I put my mat down in the front row, left side. Where the two walls of windows come together. it felt like a fat arrow of sky, lifting you astrally outward. In the grid of nine larger panes I counted the water towers, crammed like homemade toys on every available surface. twenty-three spaceships. the invasion from Vermont. In dot-com New York. these stalwart anachronisms. antiquated relics. still standing. serving their purpose.

In mountain pose over Houston-on-high, airy, eastward. the airports, the world. Standing strong, arms spread, warrior two, front leg bent to a statuesque right angle, you were planing, flying immovably through celestial imagination. beyond the Manhattan rooftops. childhood lawns and trees and bodies of water, bodies of air, breathing awareness, divine intention, dimension. *samadhi?* something.

A was practicing after us, the uneasy overlap, the select group, second series.

The room filled with voices, a headful of murmur. Bubbled gradually louder, crisp vegetable greetings, muted, mumbled, swallowed replies, chewier exchanges. chatter. God the day. making the mundane miracle. the fleshy wonder and mind. cooking into being all things.

For instance, Ms. Robena. surprise arrival by my side. long time no see. always in India.

"Can I practice beside you, mister?" Her incongruous carnival barker's voice. deeper than husky. always struck and amused me. could not possibly come from this open flower face and happy floppy puppy body.

Then Hair-dog descended, practically drooling, hot

on her tail. He spoke to her first through talking *woof-slurp*, to me, over me. Down, boy. too early in the morning to grin like this. and thus we joined the babble. new day rising. simmering, bubbling animal anima soup.

Guruji sat glumly, as if sitting for a portrait, in a folding chair just off the big room, surrounded by his entourage. He looked like someone Lucien Freud would paint. years of sitting. of painting. He looked like Gertrude Stein, as painted (realistically) by Picasso. Even her manner his manner somehow. their gnomic, authoritative utterances. The gnostic, very Vedic *There's no there there.*

When he was ready, Guruji got up and walked to the front of the room. Everyone shut up. Practice began. at Guruji's gruff command. First the gravelly opening Sanskrit incantation. invocation. Call and response. Guruji and then all of us. everyone standing in prayer at the fronts of their mats. (Nobody knew what it really meant.) (Or. only a few knew.)

We got warm fast. In the openness over the roofs, here, aloft, when you got going in the practice, the mat went from a meager flimsy camping mattress to your flying magic carpet ticket to ride.

Up-dog. *"Sve."* down-dog. *"One!"*

Soon we were really cooking.

Guruji was scary. (but not really.) Harshly calling out the asanas, the *vinyasa*. gravelly Sanskrit mixed with English (numbers). counting the (slow) breaths. it was like he stepped out of that ancient yoga world himself, hobbling solidly around the postmodern planet in his rugged eighty-six-year-old body. crusty, severe, serene. seeming embodiment of Sanskrit.

A demented expression. his deep-set eyes. like some

depraved Third World dictator. before he so warmly smiled his full, bald-headed smile, winsome, innocent, wise. before psychotically slash-cutting to a dead long look and chopping your head off with a machete. Wearing his black Calvin Klein underwear (X-Large. Big man!) pulled up high. (Last time. this world tour. And after this, Adidas.) (As if he signed with a new sponsor.)

His ancient, leather, clay feet, earth-flat. swollen, worn. nasty thick nails. crusty claws. fat callused primate toes apart like finger stubs.

"Ash-to!"

He was also very sweet. to the women. the girls who kissed and hugged him every day. when everyone lined up to greet him. after practice. after *sivasana.* people peeled themselves up and got in the line snaking around the perimeter of the room.

Touch the dust of his feet to your head. three times, those who knew to. The girls who didn't mind when he grabbed their ass to drop them back. held their pussy in certain hoisting assists. *Ahem.*

He stood near you. meaty, powerful presence. intense gaze (you didn't look back. *drishti!*). a bit bent. mad, disapproving? Intimidating, disgruntled, great-grandpaternal. It was like he was your father. your father's father. everyone's father. everyone wanted his attention. approval. but of course you never got it.

Even if he wasn't looking at you, you felt him watching closely for flaws. psychic eagle eye. X-ray vision. His stern strong presence looming. pushing your effort and frail practice to levels you couldn't reach before. You'd feel the depth. liberation. meted limits melted through. what the practice was always supposed to be about.

His meaty hands were adept and hands-on direct as a

butcher's. His assists were precise. severe. legendary. Stories of knees popping. backs, necks cracking. He'd put a hand on you and you had to just surrender. *Here we go..*

He moved among the rows of people like an aged general (the original *Warrior One!*), inspecting his troops. the latest batch of shabby recruits. steadily calling out the orders.

Sage old gardener of bodies. of souls. kicking at stumps. plucking deadheads. yanking. picking away at our imperfections. no there there. we human weeds.

Checking e-mail after practice. One of those unidentifiable city sounds you always accept. wonder at and edit out. seemed to bang out from the buildings across the street. slow percussive boom. not a gunshot. not as loud. but broader, deeper, slower. whatever. carry on.

Toweling off after my shower, as Whitey stepped gingerly into the wet tub to like and lick the residual water, his wont, the phone rang.

It was Buddy. He couldn't talk right.

"Uh . . . you . . ." he sputtered . . . then finally spat out, "Turn on the TV!"

One of the World Trade Center towers had a gaping hole in it, at the top, like a shark's mouth. smoke pouring out.

Apparently a stupid little commuter plane had crashed into it. crazy city.

Buddy lived a few blocks away from the accident. He was watching it, like a movie, out a south-facing plate glass window.

"It's incredible . . ." He coughed. *Indelible?* I wasn't

sure what he said. but he repeated. ". . . Incredible . . . I hope there aren't too many people in there yet, shit."

The word soon switched from a lost Piper Cub to a hijacked airliner. The Pentagon had been hit by another. The White House was next. How did they know? We were under attack. It didn't seem possible.

Buddy was watching it smoke. burn. out his window. when the other tower was hit. He didn't see the plane. coming from the other side. just the explosion. Nobody knew what was going on. on TV. or in New York.

People were jumping. Buddy called back. He had been up on the roof. watching. A big white cloud rose up around the tower on the left. He reported to me on the phone as I watched the image on TV.

"I've gotta say, Billy, it's not there anymore!" He could see. through the top of the cloud of smoke. in and out. smoke. air. the building was gone.

I was on my way out. to meet Buddy. to go see everything. when Gully called. He pleaded with me not to go. that was why he called. He was sure I'd head right down there. He was right.

Then A called. She'd been remote these last weeks. She was at RamAnanda. was heading out with the Sarahs, Jules. We agreed to look for each other on lower Lafayette. fifteen to twenty minutes.

Outside, sirens everywhere. different whoops, computer-quick blip-bleeps. looping, blaring. near, far. the alarming sound composition was more frenetic than the activity on the street. people moving around, lots of people. some cars, vans moving predatory through the crowd.

Not everybody in the East Village, not surprisingly,

seemed to know what was going on. Some people were up on the roofs. like snipers. peering southwest. binoculars. visored hands.

At Astor Place they definitely knew what was happening. fewer cars, more people. Groups converged on the sidewalks. around the radio of a parked car, door open. Cop cars, emergency vehicles, going in all directions, as if searching for the action. or fleeing from it. sirens weaving.

An odd, relaxed urgency in the air. strange sudden holiday. Delivery trucks acted like nothing was out of the ordinary. except they had to slow down, to get through the crowds.

Lafayette was a river of people, below Tower Records. Everybody heading uptown. Like someone had tipped the giant game board Manhattan.

Like as a kid, when you stomp an anthill. out they flow. you imagine the ant news guy on ant TV, radio. announcing the emergency. *We've been hit!*

A massive, majestic exodus. No big rush. no panic. Even this doesn't faze them. The usual impassive New York expressions. as inured to you as you are to them. except now vivid floating faces. superseen in this hejira upheaval parade. The sidewalk thick with flowing heads. shoulders. Just as many walked in the street. though not as crowded together. A few rushed as if to catch a bus.

The odd ghost-car nosed its way through the crowd. the roof and hood and windshield laden with gray dust. like snow. swirling off it in capes, veils. chunks that would lift off and hit the road in puffs. little smoke bombs behind.

Some of the people, too, were covered with the gray

ash dust. One guy in a pinstripe suit, tie still tied, dust over his shoulders. like shoulder pads. and a cake of it on his head. like a joke. like the Three Stooges. His white shirt bloody, his chest, under his tie. A bandage wrapped around his head. like Axl Rose. gauze wrap saturated with blood. His expression business as usual. not dazed. not upset. heading uptown like everyone else. carrying his (oddly) dust-free briefcase.

Someone had lifted our island by the downtown tip. first stomped on it. then shook it, sending the people uptown. *En masse.* calmly. quietly. the steady flow of the living. Up Centre Street. up Church. up Broadway. thick with thousands. Lafayette. University. Mercer. Greene Street. Wooster Street. West Broadway. LaGuardia. This was Tolstoy. the grandeur. Sixth Avenue (*Avenue of the Americas*). the mass movement uptown. up Varick and Seventh Avenue. Hudson, Greenwich. the path between the river and the West Side Highway. the main route, already, for emergency vehicles. heading down. Fire trucks. howling. ambulance after ambulance.

A mountain of white smoke. where the left tower usually stood. one of the two fingers in the monolithic peace sign New York gave the world. and ourselves. Manha'an's bowsprit. (mainmasts missing. first the first. now.) at the tapered tip of downtown. (Lady Liberty the floating figurehead.) big paper cutout goal posts at the end of the broad up- and downtown avenues. now clotted channels of escape. People were saying there had been a bomb in the foundation. (like last time. when they found it.) The smoke a dense, mountain-shaped mass. leaning to the left. muscular billows. already acrid. pulling toward Brooklyn. The bottom part grayer, shadowed. Like a mountain-fresh beer ad. the Rockies looming right there behind the Wall Street skyline.

Below Canal it felt like an emergency. though still without panic. not chaos, but dire urgency. military movement. Everybody seemed to know what to do. feet of wheels. head uptown. People were saying Federal Plaza was gone, now, too. another bomb.

There was no way I'd find Mandy down here in this mass exodus, *somewhere on Lafayette, in the next half hour.* But then there she was. between Broome and Canal. Chinese stores and tool stores. Riding between people. as slowly as you possibly can ride, without falling. Her face grave and lovely. taking it all in. I felt that welling when I saw her. the lift I always got after not seeing her for a while. even only a day. Enhanced here by the Tolstoyan tableau. She had on her turquoise Birkenstocks, the soles layered black and white stripes like a dessert. Her hair blow-dried back from her forehead from riding the bike. even that slowly. looked like Farrah Fawcett. Barry Gibb.

"The building's gone, B. All the people in there."

We went together to Spring and Broadway, where I was meeting Buddy. He was going to go out to Wainscott to join his wife and kid. as soon as he could get his car out of the lot at Pier 19. if he could.

Buddy looked wiped out. haunted. agitated. like he'd just seen a ghost. He'd seen far worse. He spoke unusually softly. A went into the deli to get a bottle of Evian. He told me he'd taken binoculars back up onto the roof. You didn't even need binoculars. They were right there. He'd been watching people jump from the upper stories of the remaining tower.

"Like fucking *lemmings.*" We hugged. squeezed the life.

Buddy breathed. sucked it in. spoke more. "Some were *holding hands!*"

He coughed his crying into his hand. "There's paper falling like a ticker-tape parade. It's weird. It just keeps coming. Paper and ash, endless, in the smoke." He opened his eyes wide and blew into the trumpet of his fist, cheeks ballooned. "They keep climbing out of the windows, standing there—*and*—."

A cluster of people inside the deli gazed up at a TV. glued to it. A came back out. hugged Buddy a long bear hug.

I moved to hug her. changing partners in a crowded sidewalk dance. The smell of industrial smoke was intense. She acted like I was in her way. between her and her bike.

"There were lots of firemen in the building, B," she blurted. "I know Patrick's dead." A soprano birdy chirrup leapt out of her crumpled, miserable face. as from a cell phone. hiccupped into crying.

I held her. she waited it out. like it was my fault Patrick might be dead. I didn't try to draw her. pull her back out. I let her be.

But enough time passes. and enough separate experience, life and love, layers over and separates us, that we can be friends, in that way you swore and swear up and down in top secret court of love testimony resolve you never could be, never wanted to be, that would be relinquishment, repudiation and violation of the higher love you refuse to downgrade from exalted/excellent to regular sad sack ex status, you can violate and offend our beautiful love, but I, die-hard devoted true lover, steadfast and honorable (duty. honor. country. *sir!*) truer lover than you, stubborn, angry/resentful romantic, never, ever, ever will, would. refusing, in spite of all the arduous, painful letting-go, refusing, really, really refusing, to really let go of her, of our love, because how do you really do that? Because for us die-hard romantic warriors of the heart, yes sir, be it for love or for art, or some kind of service or passion, semiotic, myopic, semantic, pacific, psychic, antic, to move on is a betrayal of our highest love, our gratitude and self-evident duty, this gift from God, commitment to God, fuck it, say it, a lie of the heart and an affront to love, again, to God, for us tenacious desperados, for relinquishment means abandonment, we/I refuse to suffer or inflict that again, and giving up is quitting, is wrong, is not possible, closure is a myth, goes this solipsistic line of desperately clinging defense, love, devotion, goes on without us, *You're losing me, B,* whether you're on board and embrace it or leave it, neglect the garden, the estate lives on within us, in the protean, always active and deep-sleeping, sly, deep-pocketed silverlake unconscious, that sly potent depth-charged reservoir of emotion, skillfully or randomly imagined experience, reflected, distorted, reimagined in art, love, loss, exists outside of time, beyond volition, the glowing ember eye in the dark, winking unknowingly, recurrent, eternal flicker, amber fire, within, recombinant, all of which of course is just attachment and pride and who knows what other sticky unresolved strands of ignominious unevolved selfishness, self, the danger and beauty of love and art lies in this timeless suspension, allure, retention, power, we can never escape what we've felt, known, experienced most deeply, the trenchant catcher and deft genius of dreams draws on this insistent inner reality, and art flows from here, like love, we're just the liquid medium and chosen conduit, its means of escape from mere thinking and being and that inchoate rolling recess process building, rolling behind thinking and being into color, into air, life, actual abundance, luminous motion, accumulation, marks or objects arrayed just so, an access of music, arrived out of nowhere, pleasing or puzzling streams and strokes, a great wall of words, a vision rendered, a flush return on assiduous investment, an image appears, recycled, of its own, that happened, and now it returns, a shard or chip to be shredded, or saved, charmed into imaginary life, shared, a custom movie clip, her red butterfly barrette, present and real enough, accounted for not in consciousness, the wet surface of your eyes, tired, confused little earths, the easy seen skin of the water, liminal, stretched tight as a drum, the clinging edges slightly smiling, delicate swelling capillary action binding beauty and pain, *You lost me, B,* good, go, bye, I'm busy, but you're right here, sorry, in second grade, cooking creamed corn, pretending to, all organized, apron on, got the can open, narrating the scene to yourself as it unfolds, beside clapboard lines, the house and lawn a nice morning nook of warm morning sun, the smell of warm macadam driveway and mud rising from the cake earth under the grass, wet from the rain last night, the house a bright book of life waiting to be written, along spiritual lines, who will give us a boost, help a tomboy up into the tree, a girl just wants to have fun, we want to go to the show, we want cash and prizes, not a language of the unconscious, or the soul, boring riddles of

God, this continuous wrestle for meaning, significance, access, the ever-shifting game, the artist knows what the mystic knows and the lover knows, what others know in other ways, the ways are many but the path is one, submission, your job, your family, your fond found form, devotion in music, radical prayer, tantric fucking, even surfing, or walking, or walking on coals, extreme sport, Ignatian exercises, *vipasana* meditation, the long inner-life wish list, the ways in and the different merging explanations, particle physics and Vedic cosmology are the same, vibration, uncertainty, wave theory divinity, what teens all know keenly, and philosophers nearly, but ruin by prodding, tampering, touching, naming, the tissue tears, disappears, trying to identify and define, hold and break it down, reduce or deduce, into words or logic, analog or metaphor, concept or construct, what is insubstantial and experiential, not logical or expressible in words or image merely, if at all, if anything the words must be arrows, images assistants, pulsing, indicating action, direction, motion, *thataway,* right action, devotion, as religions know, the molten soul core they're based upon, spring from, but manage to mangle, the most personal mystery, faith, lost in mass transmission, what the moment-intoxicated child, and the panting dog, and the dying man in his lucid, back-of the-eyelids omniscience-senescence knows, that time is our necessary fiction, our miraculous invisible medium, we angels planted in animal flesh, human mind and not-great condition, culture, appetite, that pull in us always, multifarious, away from the central simple spirit truth, to forget what we also always know, that love is all, erotic love, love of life or food or some stupid sport or art, of God, of nature, people, name them all their different names, but know they're all the same, God is not complicated, in the end, we are, God is God, God is love, love is love, is everything, and by the time you get to this and say that it means nothing, no more than the tattoo on the dude in Mysore Amanda mentioned more than once, and it made me want to gag, and break up that she liked that, liked that stupid guy, *Love is the answer.* But so what if high spiritual truth comes to us in the popping bubbles of sticky-sweet pop songs? or from less-than-intellectual yoga teachers saying *so yeah* a lot, making up words like *equanimous.* That's where the message belongs. everywhere. out there. in the mud. in the cracks. drummed home where we live, in the high-low everyday, the city buzz, the so-simple, endlessly repeated, easy, one-size-fits-all solution to all that ails you and all humanity and—

Emotional transparency on a mass scale liberated Lower Manhattan that morning. Soul descended. burst, overflowed, extended out from each to each. the living and the dead. connecting everyone. acceptance and enhanced awareness. It lasted three days. We were all one. like the teachings say. however cliché. it doesn't matter. it was real. It was beautiful. also, of course, terrible. People wide open to one another, to the emanations. looking at one another, and seeing and feeling and being the sameness. sticking together. strangers familiar. instantly. this streaming festive-solemn suspension. no borders of separation. so intrinsically New York. groups spontaneously forming everywhere. No cars. except the occasional death-dusted vehicles moving ominously uptown, trailing their blizzards and capes of ghost. While the rest of New York (above Fourteenth Street. the boroughs. the suburbs. beyond), the country, the wired, bewildered, overexcited world, were glued to the TV. looking into the fire. the video loops. redreaming the devastation. the impossible, magnificent violation.

We were mammals roving in the country-quiet aftermath toward safety. warmth. home. family. our families of friends. It felt like a sudden holiday. awful, awesome. visited on us. instead of you going somewhere, it came to us. by force. this monumental collective release. grace flowed freely. goodness and sympathy flowered in faces, in gestures, general open intention. a benevolent aura. and the shock and the grief. everyone equal. emergency and death the equalizer. distinctions acid-washed away in the mortal collapse. fear in the air. the pervasive dread. and love. this dire mystery. ominous. the smoke smell. acrid air. like burning tires. something chemical in there, too. foul. Jersey. ferrous. numinous. nefarious.

Also a pervasive peace. immediate, apparent haven. our familiar streets. safe and abounding. blesséd New York faces. normal and numinous. Everyone just wanted to be out and around. circulating. in the buzz of being. and momentousness happening. amid the collective felt unbeing. suffering unseen. but ubiquitous. the nearness, the hereness. the unknown, shaken from the hive. from the quotidian. to kneel before this amazing, horrible moment. walking around in this collective shock and awakening. as to a humming awesome body. more than mere aura. hovering over our suddenly sacred city. this great subtle body. colossal, electric, kinetic and tender. densely human. and spirit descended. decided for us. manifested in this unimaginable morning unfolding, afternoon. made of all the heart energy so suddenly zapped. released. offered up. a body of millions. supernatural. soft-skinned, pierced by the mangled steel. melted into agonized forms by the supersonic heat. ripped and crushed like paper. like bodies. pulverized lives. partners falling. thousands vanished. atomized.

Among the living the invertebrate mandate. to walk in the air among the living. over the exploded ground of being. the sentient soul to enter the sudden violent transportation. stoppage of time. the oversoul bell of the tainted day. Be with loved ones.

Three times on her cell Amanda moved our meeting till later.

The smoke and the smell. a pall over downtown. unreal city. odd spell. death and untold suffering. unseen among us. Both towers were gone. buried the day. The Pentagon burning. The president (presumptive) bumbling somewhere in the air. over North Dakota. (heart of the action.) acting out his own fumbling, private farce on our *Air Force One.* The rest of the air traffic over the country, like so many racing thoughts, was suspended. except for birds and bugs and the arrows and long-tailed excursions of prevailing winds. political currents hyperventilated, whispering unusual through the usual actions. the awakened workaday consciousness of every stunned field marshal fieldmouse American hyperextended, cowering puny and proud, collectively indomitable, pulled up, blindly, unconsciously transforming, during this jarring shadow pause. fire-breathing, nation identification. into a single dragon, winged, rising, righteous, wicked, compensatory, hyperinflated hawk, seemingly commensurate, upright, broad-shouldered, hulking, mobilizing beneath our violated skies.

We met in the afternoon. Since we parted in the morning I was thinking about A the whole time. feeling her, inside of everything going on. wanting to be together. in the long view. waiting to be with her today. But when I saw her, her chin led away, gaze gone. She had the shut-down A expression. big-time. down demeanor. shoulders down-rounded, somehow padded against me. protectively, defensively poised in no thought. access denied. eyes downcast and hurt. no words heading my way. evidence of our great love inverted, here now, converted into hard impenetrable and overwhelming evidence against.

We pedaled together/apart to Bronwyn's, where Bronwyn and a certain Miranda were watching TV. Replays. rumors. Bronwyn was a painter. an old friend. her art star rose in the eighties. like mine and Buddy's. wavered in the nineties. somewhere between mine. majestically petering, silently crashing. and Buddy's, magically fixing itself firmly, comet-wise, blazing, first fast and now slow, steady, permanent, on the unchanging upper-echelon art world firmament.

Bronwyn took Amanda's yoga classes. They were newish, maybe lunch-once-in-a-while friends. Bronwyn sometimes showed up when A was doing *kirtan*. A once mimicked the hand movements Bronwyn made while chanting. arms snaking out like Dancing Shiva. Indo-funky/New Age free-form. *Go, Bronwyn*. She had coiled copper hair, springing out from her high forehead. housing formidable mental machinery. long legs. long strides carried her boldly, almost gawkily, exotically, to the next point of interest. She was tall. always inquisitive. absorbed. she drew you, absorptive, into her lively subjectivity. many wheels spinning. she thought and spoke quickly.

In the midnineties she had a career. a husband. baby on the way. She was delighted. (Smell trouble?) Her husband was Bryan. my and (more so) Buddy's friend. Brit bad boy art star. Since it wasn't a good idea for her to fly, she didn't go with Bryan to Paris for a show he had there. The day after he returned she called him at his studio (no caller ID) on her cell from Balducci's. long line. to ask which of two choice gourmet unpasteurized (illicit. FDA-disapproved) *fromages* he preferred.

"It didn't take very long for you to call," he said saucily.

Sickness, sudden, shot through her. morning-/sea-/air-/home-/heart-..

"Bryan, it's *me.*" *Soul-*.

"Uh, *yeah!*" *Duh.* "I know! Hi."

She left him that night. In the divorce settlement she got the dog, Barn. big, dumb, happy, drooling Newf. and the Bank Street town house. Chipping pale blue painted brick. Windows with that lovely swirly flowing outdoor-distorting old glass. tiny elongated bubbles.

Bronwyn was undone. We hugged in her vestibule. she clung to me for dear life. (as when she'd miscarried.) Barney jumped up to get in on the action. knocked us. slobbering.

"Get down, you big *galoot,*" she blubbered. spluttered into a laugh.

Bryan's sister, Miranda, was in town. Bronwyn and she were still close. Closer than before. Miranda was staying at the SoHo Grand. some production paying for it. down at the edge of the war zone. the smoke. So with

Bron for now. part of the huddling together happening everywhere. family, loved ones. primal.

I liked Miranda. a lot. We'd had a flirtation going for years. neither of us was ever available or living in the same place at the same time, and we'd never made the leap. She lived in London. was in New York now and then.

Amanda had never met Miranda. She hardly looked at her when introduced. Amanda had shy person's ESP, plus telepathic, laser-sharp woman's intuition, combined with sheer mistrust, when it came to me and other women. especially certain (easily identifiable. to her) beauties. She could always tell who I liked. (or would like. even if I wasn't there!) I could have told her she was paranoid. insecure. etc. all the times she felt like I had a crush on some woman. except she was always right. almost always.

Buddy showed up with his assistant. twenty-eight year-old knockout tomboy artist from P-town. Ariel. not lesbian, but dressed like one. like she wanted to disguise her voluptuous form. (Smith College zippered hoodie. torn worn jeans.) which of course only enhanced it.

In the kitchen Bronwyn and Amanda were talking about her when I came in. Bron had never met Ariel.

"Is he fucking her?" Bronwyn asked me point-blank. disgusted.

I laughed and said *no-ho way*. They looked at each other. complicit female acknowledgment. vs. inherent/instant male denial. solidarity. Like my laugh told the truth. what *guys* do. and the universal guy code. don't tell. admit nothing.

Takeout from Bennie's Burritos. grapes from Integral. the disaster on TV. Then we went outside to watch it. live.

On TV it was the twin towers. Outside, the great numen. spreading its toxic doom. everyone walking around felt the loosed mystery. the great rupture. the power. rapture. Greater by far than the colossal cloud piling up and pulling away from the vanishment.

The firefighters barreling down the avenues. the screaming numbered trucks. first responders. storming the scene, in the helmets and heavy boots. running up into the burning buildings.

We crossed Houston with a southward-roaming herd. the stirred tribe. stricken awake. alive. aware.

People stuck together. love emerged. chastened. strengthened. in this sudden, extreme reality check. Also stress test. worse. All around the city (and beyond?) relationships came crashing down.

A was spectral. Buddy was silent. Ariel also. sexy minx. by his side.

Ahead of us, pushing up the middle of the street, as up history's long-haul slope, an old Chinese couple, dogged, wiry, tiny, from the next neighborhood. another world (rural Sichuan province). and time. another war. without end. each pushed a shopping cart full of stuff, most crammed into pink and orange Chinatown plastic bags, white deli bags. green. a few blue, the man a good ten yards in front of the woman. both bent. slippered. small. she like a scarecrow in plaid pants, striped shirt, floral sweaters buttoned to her scrawny neck, where a mop handle balanced (second/third cervical) across narrow, frail chair shoulders. clear garbage bags full of cans hung suspended from either end of the pole. The man didn't once look back.

Miranda nodded as Bronwyn spoke. A pushed her bike beside me. trailed back. She was preoccupied. heavy.

unwilling. or unable to converse. not even the slightest twitch or signal of connectedness from our talented bag of tricks and battered arsenal of jokes or signs of life or clues of love. We were like the Chinese couple. mute. brute. together/apart. I was trying to hear what Bronwyn was saying. Miranda wore braids. a hoodie with a dragon on the back. whose head went onto the hood. so that when she put the hood on she wore the dragon head.

Beyond the SoHo Grand (formerly a rat field. the border wall blazoned I AM THE BEST ARTIST). was the police line/martial barrier of Canal Street (formerly a canal. now a barricade). We waited in the lounge above the lobby. on the plush couches and easy chairs, NY outside under siege, sipping eight-dollar orange juices. while Miranda went up to her room to get her things. do whatever women do. during that half hour. and counting. they keep you waiting. under siege. or normal life.

Back at Bronwyn's. I said I'd cook dinner. A left. Bronwyn and Miranda and I went to Balducci's. Crazy-crowded. frenetic. like Christmas Eve. lines going back around the diminishing islands of fruit. Tried Lifethyme. People were stocking up there, too. ditto, Healthy Pleasures. like there was no tomorrow.

"The hoarding instinct in full force," Miranda observed. in her irresistible British accent.

"Gone haywire," Bron replied.

We walked west, carrying the bags of food. crossed Fifth Avenue, magisterially empty.

I said I thought she said *whoring* instinct.

"You guys never stop, do you?" Bronwyn shook her curly copper head. springs popping out all over the place.

"You have no idea," I conceded. mumbled.

"It's a known fact that historically, in tumultuous times, people have more sex," Miranda observed. "For instance in the Middle Ages, during the *byoo*-bonic plague. Apparently everybody was madly bonking all the time . . ."

We unloaded the provisions. laid the food out on the nice old barn-board table. put on some music. put on some tea. Phones rang. sirens hiccupped. whooped outside. We had to close the window. that nasty acrid smell.

We shut off the TV for now. Various dishes for dinner. six of us. Amanda arrived. wilted. worn. tilted. worse. I took her ever-overladen, formerly turquoise backpack/bag (JanSport) from her shoulder. help unburden her. For a split second she resisted. held it to her. She said there was no word at the firehouse (Ladder 33. Thirteenth Street–Fourth Avenue) about Patrick. nor the others. his twelve guys he led to the site. this morning. among the first there. I hugged her. She didn't respond.

She sat on the far other end of the table from me. diagonally opposite corner. I let it be. My new approach of letting her go when/wherever she went. not try and pull her back like I always used to. Was this growth? accepting the sad distance. She was off on her own punctured planet. I let her be. after serving her portions of what I knew she liked. She talked with Bronwyn, hunched together down there at the other end of the table.

Miranda wheeled in when we were pretty much finished eating. I served her a plate. She *ooh*-ed. *ahh*-ed. Did I cook like this often? she asked with a new person's enthusiasm, awe. Bronwyn said *Oh yeah.* world-weary. mixed with a flattering hint of *you-don't-know-the-least-of-it.*.

"You're so lucky to have a boyfriend who cooks for you like this all the time!" A didn't respond.

Miranda had no idea she was this lurid divisive arrival. vivid wedge. sharp-edged. inserting herself so guilelessly. or not so. but so fatally, between me and A down there at the other end of the table. done. (or did she?)

Her avid freshness. filling the room. her maybe-too-open affection. (un-British.) (or not?) borderless enthusiasm. maybe unleashed, unfettered, by the shock of the day. the grief in our air and death. right there. here and not here. Her too-voluptuous flesh. Her face you have to look at. that looks back at you. me. with an irresistible energy. even if you don't look. so much lovely action, nature, affirmation, in so small and well-designed a place. shape-shifting, lusciously formed, mouth-sent words. imparting fresh new life messages. For even the imagined pulse or glimpse or hint of new love is new life. Any flash. And life, hunger, craves, creates, invents connection. invents, creates itself. life. love..

Miranda sat beside me. She told the table, with spotlit storytelling expansiveness, anima, magnetism, lip gloss, how this morning she'd been running on the path between the West Side Highway and our murky mighty Hudson. She was looking up at a huge billboard of Arnold Schwarzenegger as a fireman charging heroically from a great conflagration (as she put it. I love. I admit. those bright Brits. Do they know they're smarter than us?). when a remarkably identical fireball bloomed just behind it. up on the World Trade tower.

She'd arrived in New York the night before. woke up this morning and went for a jog.

Everyone else had finished. I served Miranda dessert. a nice crimson few-berry kanten. (agar agar.) ("That's the one you say twice," Jules once mused. at one of our dinners.) cashew-maple whip. (kuzu.) flecked with grated nutmeg and cinnamon. topped with a few uncooked berries. sprig o' mint.

Buddy described the scene downtown by his building that afternoon. They let him back when he told them his dog was inside. The building. the block. the surrounding blocks. all of Tribeca had been evacuated. He didn't talk anymore about the people jumping. He described the ash-covered emergency vehicles. the firemen. the cops. stray souls. the roadblocks. the ash. the smoke. the smell. the empty expectancy. the sick excitement. the martial activity below Worth Street.

He stopped in mid-description. Ariel put her hand on his back. tapped a fond beat. Bronwyn looked at me with a particular female expression she specialized in.

A did the dishes. her stubborn back to the room. wordless. impervious. a human shield. impenetrable. head dropped. shoulders rounded downward, forward. cold/hurt mountain pose.

We watched TV. the same images again and again. around the world. Amanda said she wanted to go to the firehouse to see if there was any word on Patrick.

I didn't go with her. She clearly didn't want to be with me. She was acting like she hated me. Bron said she'd go with her. They went.

Nothing happened more than this. between me and Miranda. between me and A. She returned an hour later in the same shocked state. worse. racked face. wrecked.

"They think he's dead," she said. There was no word of any of them. him and his guys. Apparently they'd gone up into the tower.

We all stayed together that night. all of us in Bronwyn's apartment. Nobody wanted to leave. like people all over the city. on couches and beds. a collective spontaneous comfort slumber party. And the suspended snow day feeling continued for a few days. heavy and light. Everybody kept calling all this *surreal.* Unbelievable, horrible, etc. but mostly: *surreal.* (Which it wasn't. It was superreal.)

We walked over to the West Side Highway the next evening. down toward the site. the Arnold sign. Between low shocked buildings our head was missing. The smoke was lifting off to the left, eastward, white and slow. toward Brooklyn. Lots of people out. strangers talking to strangers. or there were no strangers. the usual barriers gone. All kinds of emergency vehicles backed up from the checkpoint. fire trucks from all over. the boroughs. upstate. quaintly named Jersey towns. CT. beyond.

We went our different ways. to go field our calls, e-mails, feed our animals. shower, change. then came back together for dinner. Time was a long slow song.

After dinner was a replay of the night before. repetition opportunity. A in cold/hurt mountain pose, doing the dishes. There was a playoff game on TV. The Yanks were out to show the world New York was strong. undeterred. They sacked our temple. shook our tree. but the motherfuckers can't stop us from living our lives! This became the battle cry. *We can't let them stop us from living our ordinary lives.* If we stop, they've won. we're terrorized. fear wins.

The guys sat on the couch closer to the TV. really watching. The women kind of watched. watched us watching. Miranda was fascinated. amused. mystified. by baseball. our sudden complete absorption.

"My God, men are like this everywhere, aren't they?"

"They sure are." Bronwyn shook her head. They watched us from the Balinese bed. Amanda and Sarah sat in the kitchen. through the always open pocket sliding doors.

Scott was way into Miranda. He/we told her the Rivera story. Cuban refugee. rags to riches. milk carton glove as a kid. baseball as national lifeblood in Cuba (*Koo-ba.*) (as opposed to *Cuber.* JFK.). like the music. She was enthralled. folded herself at our feet.

"And that one?" she asked about Jeter. of course. All the women like Jeter. men, too. Chewing gum with his mouth open. lazy, Elvis orgasm eyes.

"He went out with Mariah Carey," Scott informed her.

"He didn't!"

"He makes seventeen million dollars a year."

"He does not."

"That's something like twenty thousand a game."

"Five thousand per at bat. A thousand per pitch."

"He's brilliant," she concluded.

The Britney Spears Pepsi ads came on. Britney with Pepsis in different eras. outfits. Beach Blanket Bingo. etc.

The guys were transfixed. Miranda, too.

"I love Britney," she confessed unapologetically.

Scott commanded the remote. switched to network coverage of our disaster in progress. PBS. cable. Rudy stepping into unlikely sainthood. last-hour grace. redemption. milk it for all it's worth. at the end of an ignominious reign. (crushing the disenfranchised. the weak and the poor. the usual heartless bottom-line *quality of life* Republican stuff. profit over people.)

Scenes from Washington. The bombed Pentagon. smoking. The White House empty. The field in Pennsylvania. The president (acting. presumptive. missing) finally spoke. deer in the headlights. a scared kid. who hadn't done his homework. ever. cameras rolling. Not even a remotely close second fiddle to Rudy's virtuoso swan song.

"I don't understand how America works," Miranda said. hair bunched up on her head. tumbling and tumbling (deathlessly) down and up all night.

Miranda was one of those people. women. who asks a lot of questions. innocent, charming. verging on stupid or ignorant. but that everyone wants to answer for her. A ready question was one head-tossable coin of her realm. the answers, the men, the benefits, the goods accrue. line up. jostling.

On the couch Scott leaned into her. overready to explain how everything worked. I, too, I admit, felt like, *I'll explain to you how America works!*

When she wasn't busily fascinated between me and Scott, Buddy and the Yanks, Miranda was pacing the rooms. poking and pulling at her hair. working those trendy jeans. orating into her cell phone. (which worked.) Fielding calls. sporty line drive laughs. pop fly sigh. going deep. going, going.

Getting up for another beer Scott asked her if she wanted something to drink.

"Woo-tah," she tossed, without breaking stride. Water.

I repeated her pronunciation. *Woo-tah.*

A heard and did not think it was funny. Looked quick daggers at me like I was an evil slut. (Was I?) Bronwyn explained to Miranda I was just kidding. not mocking.

"I adore loving mockery." She didn't look at me.

A wanted to leave. I wanted to wait till the end of the game. when we'd all unglue ourselves and disperse. Long hugs. But I left with her.

On the street A said nothing. a tacit static. brooding walking bruise. I tried saying something gentle. *You okay?* Tried my arm around her. her hard shoulders said *Go away.*

I asked what was up. as if I didn't know.

"Why don't you go back there? It's obviously where you want to be."

She was right. It was where I wanted to be. But my duty was (still) to her. in spite of the shutdown. my place was with her.

Near the corner of Tenth Street and Fifth Avenue we stopped and had it out. I didn't want to fight. But she went from saying nothing. for two of the most intense, unusual days either of us had ever experienced. to a rabid torrent of acid words spewing out uncontrollably. I'd seen her upset before. plenty. but never raging like this. torrid. apoplectic.

"Right in front of me!" Hair on fire. her face her brother. feral, flinty. pushing out of her skull. sharp nose. sharp rapid-response eyes. possessed. straining to escape.

"You put the extra berries on her dessert! You follow her around like a fucking puppy! Why don't you just go back and fuck her!"

"Mandy, Jesus." Now I understood. I did before, too. but pretended, to myself. feigned baffled accepting dismay. how you can do that. (How can you do that?) Her at the sink. both nights. all our time together. But it pissed me off she was putting it on me. I didn't do anything. wrong. I was waiting for her to let me back. for two years. plus! waiting for her to let me love her. Even still. in this moment. Instead, we were the couple you see arguing on the sidewalk. she screaming. he silent, downcast. pleading, looking past.

She was really fucking pissed off. I'd never seen her like this. She hated me. It had crossed over.

"I can't do this anymore," she said. She was shaking.

"Good. Me neither." I meant argue. She meant the whole thing. the relationship. I knew what she meant.

"Okay. So we're breaking up." She was like the girl in *The Exorcist.* head spinning around.

"Not like this," I muttered.

"So you're free. Go on."

Her face was angular in the orange amber streetlight. No traffic. the occasional cop car. official vehicle. state of siege. I was doing my Buddhist best to let this moment pass. hopefully flip into peace? Instead she said,

"Go fuck her."

"Are you insane?"

"You're free now. Go ahead."

"Oh, we just broke up right now?"

"Yup . . . I'm relieved."

"Yeah, you look relieved."

"I don't want to do this anymore."

"Okay."

"So you agree."

"Agree what?"

"You don't want to do this anymore."

"No, Man, I hate this."

"Okay, you're free."

"This isn't the way to do this. The world's crashing down around us. We're out on the street at night . . ."

"But you want to be free."

I shrugged. agreement. maybe. noncommittal.

"So take it. You're free."

"I also want our love to work. I love you."

"You also want to fuck her. I can't take this anymore."

"Come on. That's what they say all the time in the movies. Next it'll be, *I don't know what I believe anymore.*"

"Well, I don't. Sorry I don't say the right lines you want me to say. Why don't you write the script and—"

"Why don't we give this a rest. This isn't the way to do this. Let's—cool down. Give this the space it needs. You go back to your apartment and I'll go back to mine."

She rode off on her bike. slow hurt bell. her butt and form solid on her seat like she was on a horse. without a final parting word. like she was the horse. heavily clopping away. without looking back.

We didn't really agree right then, or after, to really break up. but that pretty much did it.

7. The Middle Place

Patrick's funeral was held at St. Patrick's Cathedral. on his birthday. five weeks after he was killed. Like Rudy and Father Judge, the priest who seemed to know, and went in, he'd been beatified by public opinion, the press, the rank and file of the city's and the nation's firemen, cops, blue-collar workers. all the stricken, grieving souls. flying flags now from their pickups, cars, cab antennas. flags popping up everywhere, like flowers after rain: but these were not flowers of peace, but the knee-jerk first chest-pounding jingoist drumbeats of war.

Fifth Avenue was blocked off for four blocks in either direction. The afternoon was cold and clear. the eternal sky, filled with spiraling footballs, bullets, phantom jets. long bombs. glazed blue eye. uncracked. above the tall proud buildings crowded up and down the Midtown canyon, street-striped, by distinct, long shadows. sharp light. An army of firemen from around the country. also cops. formal dark uniforms, rows of shiny brass buttons, filled the avenue in rows of impressive martial order. The flag on every uniform, the town and city. From other countries, too. Canada. Finland, Australia.

Two glossy lipstick-red fire trucks faced each other across from the crowded cathedral steps. ladder distance apart. Early arrivals watched as the living firefighters strung a flag between the ends of the opposing long extension ladders extended diagonally toward each other from the two trucks. Everyone watched. and everyone watching took satisfaction in the gradual reaching, the fine tuning, a hand lifted, the incremental success of the easy operation, flag centered, a fist, in place. High above them hung another flag, suspended from the top of a skyscraper under construction, most of it built, except for the top floors, which were still open to the sky.

Sarah1 appeared. Sarah2. Their heads borne toward us upon the slope of heads and shoulders massed on the cathedral steps, the crowd spread over the sidewalks in all directions. Amanda's absent attention returned from the (unreachable) reaches of private sorrow when the girls arrived. her face returned to life. before my eyes. but not for me.

The cathedral was lit. ranks of candles wrapped in red, white, and blue ribbons. on the sides, banks of votive candles blinking in their red glass jars, painted with gold diamonds and beribboned. gold sconces spiffing up God's Grand Central Terminal.

We sat near the front. behind Patrick's best friend, Jack Somebody, an actor who plays cops, detectives on TV. Soon, no doubt, firemen. Often took A's class with Pat.

The last time A and I had seen Pat was after her class at Lucky's. He was with Jack. Pat was in a gruff mood. didn't speak. I showed him the story, the picture, I was reading on the front page of the *Times*. or front of the Metro section. Instead of sending them to eastern Europe, or Pennsylvania, they were dumping old subway cars off the Jersey Shore. They'd become reefs, homes for fish, officials said in the article. Pat didn't think it was funny and didn't think it was funny I snickered at this. He and Jacko left with their juices, nary a word, nor nod. late for a meeting. or on time. so time to go.

Jack kissed A, made some remark like the *gopis* are playing in heaven today. He was movie-star handsome in his suit. groomed. teeth white. hair funeral-formal, slicked with a smart part. Give the man the role. His daughter, maybe ten, beside him, was pretty. dark shiny new hair in a grosgrain memorial ribbon. The wife was Asian-American, ex–model/actress.

When A had something to say during the funeral, she murmured it to Sarah, on her other side. We were there together, but we sure weren't together. When I spoke to her, or touched her, for comfort or contact, *nada*.

Cardinal Ryan read the Mass. Ex-governor Carey spoke.

Followed by the man of the hour. many of the hours, recently. Mayor Giuliani. self-appointed saint. who said what a legend Patrick had become over the years. saving so many lives, throwing himself in harm's way. the most decorated fireman in the New York City Fire Department. Yet Pat was humble. On formal occasions, he would only wear some of his *salad* (medals and commendations), not to appear proud, boastful. If he wore them all, they'd have covered the whole front of his suit and pants.

Then a fire chief. friend. old boss. white leonine hair. bearish bearing. beaten working-class warrior face ruddy with Irish anger and alcohol. bushy white eyebrows pitched in pissed-off resignation.

Then Pat's best friend (the other one). his sponsor, you could tell. Got a few laughs. and a lot more tears. Talked about how religious Pat was. though he wouldn't let on to most people. Then Pat's brother, who looked a lot like him. a lot. but bigger and softer, with glasses.

The night before, at the crowded wake, in the upstairs rooms of a Madison Avenue funeral parlor, among firemen in formal uniforms, holding their hats, and wives, and old folks, almost everyone Irish. pie faces, flushed. canny, familiar eyes. Amanda and I spoke to Pat's brother. and Pat's ex-girlfriend. and another ex-girlfriend.

Each room had a display of photographs of Pat. action shots, blown up. him hanging over the edge of a building. formal portraits in uniform, different stages of his life. He seemed to be twelve years old in his military uniform. He was a small man but built. His face boyish, even approaching fifty. He was one of those teenagers who looked like he was twelve. At seventeen he was in the marines. Vietnam. Volunteered for a second tour.

His father, an ancient, shriveled version of Pat, goggled in magnifying glasses, sat in a wheelchair, surrounded by people who went up to him, crouched down, offering condolences. The old bastard used to beat the shit out of Patrick when he was a kid. Pat found shelter, haven, up the street at the fire station, where they welcomed him. and practically lived there. from then on.

Pat's altar from his apartment was set up in a corner. A picture of his mother. His black belt. A Bible. a couple of other books. A little Dancing Shiva statue. An incense boat. Lined up like a few cherished baseball cards, laminated photos of fallen brothers. When a fireman died in action, these memorial cards, with his picture on it, were given to those who knew him. On the table in the room where we entered from the elevator were stacks of similar cards, with Patrick's face on them. his name and dates. Fellow firemen put these cards behind the inside bands of their hats, which they held, thick fingers tapping the drum..

These cards with Pat's picture were also distributed in the pews at the cathedral. Pat's brother, the night before, said he didn't know yet what he was going to say at the funeral. When he got to the microphone he looked like he still didn't know what he was going to say. And the first thing he said was that he didn't know what he was going to say. He explained that he was a doctor, and Pat would call him out in Utah to ask him medical advice, questions, like, How does Advil work?

The whole cathedral rumbled in gentle laughter.

I wanted to tell Amanda how my own eulogy of Patrick Brown would summarize what he described to me, different times, of his life leading up to yoga, where our paths met, curious brothers, his path nothing less than the rough, ineluctable progress of his soul, by stages, toward God.

How after the war he decided to fight to save lives, rather than kill. Now the fire was the enemy. He redirected his anger, and attacked fires with a selfless, if not demented, passion. He put down his arms and took up boxing. Then he gave up boxing in favor of karate. a step closer to a gentler spiritual discipline, the balanced inner-outer philosophy of the martial arts. He got a black belt. taught karate to blind people at the Y, so they could defend themselves alone in the city. Then he took up yoga. Taking the fight within. toward peace. warrior one. He said he'd done a lot of intense kinds of workouts in his life, and yoga was by far the hardest. He wanted to, and started to, bring guys from the station over to yoga. I offered to teach yoga to the guys at the station. He said maybe later. These guys were macho, definition of, thought yoga was gay, and he had to go carefully, give them time. In our knee club circle of trust I felt like I was his new world confessor. I felt honored. I knew he loved Amanda. I mean really loved her. but when I got to know him I didn't mind, much, I didn't blame him, and he was always supersweet to her, respectful of us, cool with me, me with him. He told me he was tired of the whole macho life, tired of being a firefighter, was thinking of quitting. His pension was right there. This stuff no one in the nave would want to hear.

At the end everyone stood and faced the center aisle and waited while the opposing front rows one after another moved toward each other and merged in the middle to stream out through the heart and gaze of the congregation. Amanda and Sarah moved out our pew in front of me and slid together in the center aisle. I was faced with the next person coming out the other side, a woman in black looking down. When she looked up, her bleary, seafaring face changed completely, resolved in a smile and release in the eyes, a lift of recognition or plea or both before I recognized her. It was that woman Colleen, from Patrick's wake. She took my proffered elbow, her hand a desperate claw, and leaned her head for an initial instant on my shoulder. I touched her hand holding my bicep, *I've got you for now.* She hiccupped a spasm, a sob that slipped down to a little laugh, and she took my hand, like someone afraid to fly, and we held hands, too hard at first, then warmly for the hundred civil yards to the door, where with a squeeze and no glance she slipped away. Mourners drained out of the cathedral in pairs to a gooey, too-peppy dirge tooted from the three-story gilded pipes of the great organ serried in back above the entrance, now the exit, red doors clipped open, central and side doors, pouring us out, each shaken New Yorker carrying in her breast the shared public and private grandeur and shock of death, historic moment, profound and questionable, the puzzling sense of fleeting, fragile mortality seeming instantly to dissolve or flee once outdoors in the sunlight, on the banks of Fifth Avenue, the stir, the annoying lack of movement in the overflowing hillock of people, the crowd stopped on the steps and filling the sidewalks. The firemen and police officers in formation on Fifth Avenue responded to the incomprehensible calls of an unseen officer. (*Attention!*) Three fighter jets screamed at us, passed low overhead, above the standing buildings, the assembled survivors, raced off to strafe the wrong country. bomb the next decade into global ruin. (*Right face.*) A row of marines fired off a twenty-one-gun salute. Pigeons rose and arced away in a harried, scattered cape, a fat Africa shape that morphed with a shimmer as it turned, elongating, into South America, before an abrupt northern exit. edit. uptown. Amanda was holding Sarah's hand. Sarah2 saw me crying, gave me a kiss and a sympathetic squeeze. Behind the buildings, across the silver, mindful, seen-it-all river, the fantastic industrial meadowlands of New Jersey, the stunned, depleted continent beyond, the tireless, blood orange sun had dripped, timeless but always on time, dropped, was already gone.

Time to go away. get away for a bit. get some perspective. Emotional genius that I am. *Run away!*

Now was the time for immersion: solitude. work. reflection. still the waters. search the spell. mark the movement. read the rise and fall and psychic swell. make that map. (this.)

Rented a house on the beach edge of Tuscany. (*Maremma.*) Shared it with a friend of a friend of Buddy in Rome. He came on weekends, with the Romans. women. packed in a Jeep Grand Cherokee. They'd show up at midnight. laughing. arguing. and make dinner. Lots of laughter. voluble banter. their lovely mellifluous language. so raucous and loud and reckless. after my string of days of solitude. stillness. immersion.

A path to the beach. feral cats in the shrubbery. shiny leaves. dirty fur. Set up a few workstations in the house. different light and vibe at different times.

Practice first thing. *Ashto!*

Mornings facing the shrub scrim, leafy light, beach and sea glimpsed behind.

Afternoons upstairs, the one room, more sea, bluer with wind. Elba on the horizon. Napoleon scheming.

When the sun sank into Elba, an evening walk on the beach, then to the dinner table. press on, darkness dissolving out there. make dinner and eat. keep going after dinner.

In the slow time stillness sitting and walking around thinking about the map I wanted to make my mother returned to me one night swimming in the moonlight.

I'd thought of this scene often, but not for a long

time. I'd always thought that if I were a real painter, in the old-fashioned, pictorial-representative sense, I'd paint this scene. Since there it was already, hung clearly in my mind. Trying, of course to tell me something. And instead of listening I'd argue with it, in my ways.

Because I can picture it. Like the Milton Avery painting of the swimmer on the pthalo sea. All you see is the arm. bent. This would be like that. but night. my equivalent. Mum. But I can't paint it. Because I can't paint. like that.

It brought me back to my beginnings as an artist. I always thought of myself operating somehow in the fictive dreamspace between writing, literature (and music!) and art, paintings, pictures, all the rest. I can't paint it, but I could bullshit about it. But where does that get you? I was done with that.

Amanda and my mother were the presiding guardian angels ushering in what felt like this profound and momentous return to myself as an artist and to Amanda and my mother.

And the feeling lasted, like a season that arrives, a breakthrough access, there's no question it's here now, a magnificent boon, release, subjective explosion of creative energy and love.

I can't paint it but I can wordpaint it!

So I let the work begin, if work is the word. happen. arrive. happen to me. through me. like taking dictation. I worked and slept in a blessed bliss, and awoke and a sentence was writing itself.

And so I got to it. And so I began to make the map, review our love, let it accrue, through me, surge, visions and details flooding, pouring out my fingers and into your eyes. your own movie screen mind remaking them. differently. Let the sentient cinematic catalogue arrive. rain down. radiate.

It flowed like a dream. a dream you believe in. relish and participate in. steer it and make it as you watch it arrive. proliferate. There was almost no loneliness to contend with in those ripe first days, weeks. Amanda was more present than when we were in the same city. She was with me all the time, totally there. Clear source and subject and amusing muse.

I just let it all come. memories, scraps, scenes. All I had to do was sit inside the welling, watch and catch and record it all, or as much as I could, as it arrived. accrued. evidence. details. a turquoise crumb.

And so as I returned to our beginnings I returned to the old place on Second Avenue. the immersion. It seemed clear that to render us fully I had to fully render the early days of RamAnanda as well, first. really take you there, really get into it, the way it happened, take you in deep. the new commingled dimension. the practice, the new life, the new love. her sleeping cashew body.

It felt like being on a team. The deepening connection you felt with the others in the room. In the room every day. It felt like being in a dream.

Affinity. The fluency of feeling carried.

Strangers at first. Mixed bag of characters.

Energetic familiars now. Strangely intimate.

Everyone's essence revealed. Your own included.

Deeper than through fumbling superficial conversation. The usual limited path of getting to know someone.

You didn't even know their names. Names came gradually.

The pace of growth.

Written on the mat in Magic Marker. Called out by the teacher.

People you never even talked to. Maybe *hey.* A nod.

But you were getting to know these people well. In a way.

In a very real way. This was part of the powerful appeal. True selves stripped down.

Engaged together in this ritual almost mating dance.

Like endangered cormorants on a Galápagos rock.

Communal. Singular. Both.

Forms reaching. Moving in sync. Breathing together.

The sound and rhythm of the sea. The fathomless feel of the ground.

Poses held. Preposterous positions. Arching. Bending.

Twisted to the sun. Necks elongated.

Bodies stretched to limits. Quivering. On the rack.

Upside-down. Contorted. Limbs extended. Torture/ pleasure.

Wings weak. Hidden sides nakedly exposed.

Eyes slide around the room. Meeting fleetingly. Energetic connections shooting around. Leaping field of nature.

Faces flat.

Exchanging. Sharing the moments in the dimension. Feeding. Feeling.

Enhancing each other. Pushing it together.

Gaze fierce.

Drawing each other further. Into the pose.

The gaze soft.

The slipstream effect.

Pulling along. Pulled along by. The person beside you.

Their supple flux. Their bounding energy.

Precision. Flex.

Sweating like mad.

Surfing on so many magic carpets.

Into that solo zone of inner stillness.

Destination created. Discovered. In the process. The whole point. The dimension within.

Clarity. Evenness of mind. The peace motive.

Breathe in.

The body. Mental. Emotional. Energetic. Peace initiative.

Breathe out.

How do we grow? What is the body? What is the body for?

Making love! Moving around. Making art. Getting you there. Getting to God.

This beautiful ancient ritual. Peace process. Mystery. Physical. Metaphysical. Psychological. Wisdom. *Samadhi.*

In postmodern dot-com New York. *Samsara.*

Day in.

That sunshot freedom of a child at the beach.

Day out . . .

Roll out your towel and lie on your back.

Amanda smashing into the waves. Gull-white grin.

The way kids play. Power politics. Imposed improv.

One announces the rules. The others obey. We were like that.

The child's direct knowledge of God. Simple. Clear. Hi, God.

Before belief. Automatic.

And before we smartened up. And lost faith.

You wondered. Looked around. Others seemed to buy the teachings.

Tolerance. Compassion. For your*self!?* First..

Eyes closed. You see your mother. Your places. The swarming endless little things. (*Chitta vritti.*)

Yoga is not a religion, Rita stressed imperiously. In her *Cherman* accent.

Rita's regulars definitely got more attention than the others. Most were men. In her class. Her guys.

Though it is a way to directly experience God..

She'd press the back of your pelvis away from the spine. Sacrum. With the heel and palm of her hand. In down-dog. (*Adho mukha svanasana.*)

She'd drape herself over you in seated forward bend. (*Paschimottanasana.*)

Full body weight. Squeezed exertion. Female sexual mammal. Concentrated.

She'd press with her pelvis and squash you deeper into the pose.

Her pussy, let's face it, Scott would insist.

Dinner. 3:1 girls to guys. More. On the floor. Around the table. Barefoot.

Yogis practice and yogis talk about the practice.

As men and women talk about men and women. Yoginis.

~

The map made itself. it was brimming. overflowing. The days one mind expanding, suspended, in the process. fresh ingenuity flourished and blessed the progress, ran the scenes and images into the nights. I was reliving the early days with A. falling in love. feeling clearly their rare gift and precious worth. and also transfiguring the context into something equally valuable. hopefully. also a gift. In the art box I was living in the love bubble. (doubly unreal. beware. Or doubly blessed? blissed.) life stopped in her slippery tracks, making glorious meaning conjuring and recording our vanishing moments and images appearing.

I felt really close to her. We spoke on the phone a few times. Once she said, "Do you have a new girlfriend yet?"

"No, of course not. I'm here alone. I told you."

On another call—as if we were in the same place, next room, and were together in our old way, just as I'd been imagining and feeling it—she said she was having trouble with her talk for her class, and could I help her figure it out, and of course I said sure. Love demands. exacts. we pay. we give and do the work. or live alone. pay that way. pay either way.

She ran it by me. The theme was expectations. future-tripping. Her example was, Say you like somebody. You're looking forward to seeing them. You think of what you might do together. Imagine things you might talk about, etc. But this would only lead to disappointment, because things always turn out differently than you imagine they will.

She'd first said Sarah2 was seeing a new guy, totally into him, and I'd said I thought that was sick. weak. She and George had been living together, thrashing it out, until just recently. (I assumed they were still at it. still *together.*) I assumed that A's talk idea came from talking to S2 about her and her situation.

The mound of shoes. Impromptu art installation. Street-fashion gold mine. Urban-archaeological site of interest. Pedi-portrait of the East Village. Foot soldiers of the downtown scene.

The temple door. A millennial memorial. Mass murder remainders. Down the centuries. Soon a city near you.

Under the benches under the coatracks. The crowded corner L. The first shoes were parked in pairs. Almost comically. Considering the pile-on to come.

The next layer was considerate. But it was hopeless.

On top of those were the scofflaw latecomers. Scuffed shoes. Like their people. Scattered everywhere.

Laceless. Stylish. Clueless. Distressed. Sneakers. Shoes. Sandals. Boots.

Each divided pair a signature of the various souls inside the big room. Stripped down. Barefoot. Each removed from his and her shoes like souls separated from their discarded bodies. Like reincarnation.

Between bodies. Time for some new shoes. A new body.

New life. Born breathing within any given moment. The yoga streaming through the channels of energy/consciousness (*nadis*). Out of the body and into the new.

Shoulder to shoulder. Totally solo. Surfing through space on our magic carpets. Arms out like an umpire.

You're safe. God will take care of you. (*Krishna* will take care of *me?*)

Hold. Breathe.

Thoughts all over the place.

A moment's peace. Extended. Flowing from the quiet place. Into your scrabbling runaway life.

Return to the child. Lowercase ease. Intimate little voice talking to inanimate things. Kite on the open sky. Squiggling upward. Animating everything.

Open arms. Release. The sense of wonder. Receive. Breathe in. Relief. Breathe out. Awareness. Awe. Is the idea.

Return and return to the still point of calm concentration. The true self. Hidden in there. Always right there. The higher Self. *Samadhi.*

It goes on for too long. You want to escape. Then time falls away again. The resistance is gone. You're back in the flow. Or whatever it is.

You keep hearing the same things. Again and again. Doing the same things. This way it will maybe sink in. And it does. And whatever it is is pretty great.

East is east and West is west. And now they meet. At last. In this.

Before it is too late. Global union. Start Here now. In you.

It's already too late. Global yoga? Begin where you are.

This kind of thing.

There was gossip. Lower self. Frankie and Jonni never had sex. Except with their adoptee yogini daughter. Who was with whom. I had my purview.

Now there were rumors. Rama was moving. Rita was leaving. A power struggle?

I found an apartment. In this shuffle. Subtle quantum shift. An apartment found me. Is this how this god works? Nice.

Squatting over a puddle of sweat. After an inspired Rita journey. I found an apartment in New York. Downtown Manhattan. The most impossible real estate accomplishment in the real world.

Rita was picking up her book. Folded blanket. After class. Zomboid yogis. Yoginis floated out of room.

She spoke to the dwindling room. Personal afterthought. Putting it out there. Trailing after them.

"Oh, if anyone knows anyone looking for a sublet, let me know . . ."

I lifted a finger. She saw. Came over.

"I need a place," I said.

"Okay, it's yours."

That simple. Zipless transaction.

East Village. Not far. I checked it out. Nice place.

If ugly-ass paint job. Swirly purple bedroom!

We made an agreement. Sublet for the rest of their lease. Then likely get the lease. (*Likely.*) Nice Irish landlords. Live in the building. No problem.

I was still sort of living with my not-really-my-girlfriend-or-my-assistant-anymore.

When she was back from California. Or Europe. Or Brazil for some reason all the time. Time to get out. Get out of that. Get her out.

I could get some income (much needed) from renting the floor of my building I lived in. If I stayed there I'd have to get a *job*. So..

This was perfect. I was ready for a change.

The universe provides.

And reconstructing and reviewing our story, our progress, our path and dynamics, the things that worked and the ways we got stuck I returned, in a way (in a pure way. undisturbed! (by reality. the other) in the abstract.) to our therapy.

I found myself almost lecturing myself. as if opening and laying our case out for inspection. to appraise and analyze and formulate. to explain and understand everything. To make the right decision moving forward! What did I learn, really? What can I say, almost clinically, about our case? our chances..

I learned a lot, actually. For instance how almost structurally incompatible we were—not as man and woman (lovers), but as man and woman partners. partners in mutual dialogue. mutuality. *We're just different,* you hear people say, hitting a wall or resigned to a relationship not working. or *too different.* But difference is not the problem. Everyone's different. Difference is not the same thing as incompatibility. Some differences enhance compatibility. Others disenhance. or outright preclude compatibility. You have to look at what you have here. in any given relationship. Because loving someone or each other isn't enough. Just because you love each other doesn't mean you should be together. doesn't mean you're compatible. (usually means the opposite! structural incompatibility. imago theory.) Take a good look at what type of person each is, and their assets and weaknesses. It amounts to nothing short of *facing reality.*

For instance, some (A. though usually the man) don't know how to talk about their feelings. Often don't even know what they're feeling. They/we either act out or shut down. or both. and more. They project. act out. close down. etc. all to protect themselves. from feeling the pain they've been paradoxically holding and running from their whole lives.

Indeed, the whole character, what we see, the apparent personality, almost all ego, is structured around this self-protection. The inability to feel, grasp, and talk about what they're experiencing emotionally. Many have no inkling they should be in touch with themselves. let alone that they're not. This is basic psychology. but still. We're all human.

Then there are those who know full well what bothers them. or so they think. and have no trouble articulating it (B. me). They/we think they/we know how to communicate. and they do. in a way. we do. But only in terms of themselves. ourselves. It's way one-sided. solipsistic.

Just as protective and neurotic as the passive, withdrawn other. Even more so. Controlling! They know how to broadcast their woes. Yet the report is more limited than they know. This is not mutuality. The other is eclipsed. worse. Nor is the effort to draw the other out into dialogue, to manage the moment, act as therapist.

One withdraws, the other reaches out. overreaches. Both are selfish.

This insistent, incessant, and exhausting (for both) performance does not create the gentle, safe place for the other to begin to unburden. be. grow toward trust. This is a one-man/one-woman show. Or a competition between the two. Between two children. two over-needy children.

Mutuality. effective, two-way communication and compassion in a couple. means hearing the other person's side. Not just hearing it (*Yeah, yeah.*) to your own satisfaction (*I get it. I hear you.*). But. and this is the key. bear with me. (for this is where almost everyone fails) to the satisfaction of *the other.* She needs to be heard. She needs to *feel* heard. She needs to feel *held* (in the kindergarten parlance of couples therapy).

If you ever interrupt, you suck at communicating. (B.)

(I interrupt all the time. *I get it. No I know, but that's not what I said, I—* Turns out. I humbly submit (though I don't really believe it! (*I admit!*) is the problem) I was as bad as a talk-show Republican. at times. But I'm learning not to! I'm trying!)

(Life the practice. at the edge of what you can do. can't.)

(But see? I even interrupt myself interrupting myself.) (and answering myself.) (I could do a whole 'nother novel of only that.) (I will. I warn you.)

If you ever interrupt, you suck at this mutual, two-way communication. which basically *is relationship.*

Without that, what do you have? A slipshod operation. tense opposition. fragile house of cards you try to protect, hold up. the temporary comedy, degrading all too quickly into farce. grinding, inevitably, all too soon, into a wretched, corrosive, crumbling bitch of a tragedy..

Why are you angry, Billy?

If you ever counter what the other says with your own side of the story. or with something you feel sure is more important, insightful, more to the point than the obvious thing the other just said.

Who are you fighting with?

If you respond with anything other than a patient, sensitive recapitulation, *holding,* in the parlance, the other, and what she just said, then you fail. as a *partner.*

If you don't put aside your knee-jerk, self-defensive, self-obsessed reactions, and instead listen. listen deeply to the other, hold your fucking tongue, keep focused on what the other is saying. and when she is done, if you don't repeat what she just said, in your own words, without a twist, or blink, or reductive slight, or ironic snort, or impatient twitch. better yet, if you don't repeat, in the words you just heard, to the expressed and unforced satisfaction of the other. so that she says, with a nod, even a *smile* (*?!*),

Yes, that's what I meant . . .

If you don't do this. every single time you discuss something, emotions or any other important or seemingly trivial thing, then join the club. You are emotionally immature.

You have not yet learned the art of loving: the essential (tedious. frustrating. impossible) practice of *holding* the other. your beloved. So that he/she feels *held.*

So that you can then go on to *your* precious points. (Or, the inconceivable, more advanced state, *Letting your precious needs go.*) So long as he/she asks. otherwise. beware. you'll be accused. you'll be guilty. of *not really listening.* (Which translates into *not really loving.*) But if you're going through the motions of listening. of *holding* her. only so that you can get *your* holy point across. This cancels out all preceding efforts.

This is what happened with us. I learned how my insistence felt to her. Overbearing! Too fucking much! Like I was banging on her chest with my forefinger. as she once vividly displayed. hitting herself with her finger. how it felt to her.

If she hadn't already been closed for business, I surely would have shut her down.

You weren't so bad, B. You were sweet. I want to hear. *You were good to me.* so I hear it.

I also learned. bear with me here. our time is almost up. (If you're not gone already!) how she wasn't interested in hearing my side. almost ever. didn't have the capacity. like a container, vessel, tank, full, that has no more space. physically. psychically. I already knew this. But wow. how this really revealed it. Relief! But not really.

And yet the answer to the question *Should we get back together and keep trying, or really break up and let it go?* appeared, so far, overwhelmingly, emotionally if not rational to be *Get back together and really try. again.*

Every relationship hits a wall. Maybe that's when the real relationship. the real love. work. (if work it is.) giving. etc. loving. begins. *Right, Virginia Woolf?* Surrender. or give up. Either you walk away. look for something/someone else. start all over again. Or stick with it. face the troubles that will come up every time. work through them. that's why they're there. that's why we're here. Embrace them as sacred givens. accept your reality. go deeper into the love. into yourself. your shadows, core fears. into life. *Go!* Be bold *Grow!*

E-mails weren't easy because it was Italy. where instead of wires (silica), the Internet service (dial-up) is transmitted through spider threads, strung vaguely between trees, waving languorously in the coastal breezes.

An exciting thing happens when you live for a while in isolation with your work. if you don't deteriorate from loneliness. and you manage to actually get into the work. the deep process. not just tapping at the task. text. material. In the same way that your daily encounters and conversations gather and travel with you during the day, and then fuel and people your dreams. when your only encounters and conversations are with your own work and words, thoughts, reveries, inner visions, the dreams absorb and refract these instead, and ramify, amplify the dimension and content, exponentially subjective biofeedback loops. so that you're truly inhabiting your art. living in it.

I was inhabiting this rarefied, deepened and deeply satisfying dimension. this ridiculous, lovely, avid *active* subjectivity, seemingly selfless, love-infused, feeling like *this is why I'm alive.* this is the immersion in work that gives meaning and ardor to life and love. and that life and love give meaning to, the sense of significance flowing through you, sacred, as in yoga, as in love, except this connectedness to the inner amaze, *anima mundi,* this utterly subjective theater of creation, wonder, quiet delight, supreme release, is at the same time connected to the world, the closest you can get, to others, in the tenderest center of their beings, and also the vital, infinitely involute heart of our living collective culture. and the connectedness, the mystery, obtains, somehow, universally, radiates into the imaginary but sensed universe out there, flows, even, seemingly, palpably, to God. And if the art or attempted record or rubbings or marks or map of this psychic or spiritual penetration translates its power and mystery effectively, here, as a bonus, you had not only a palpable product, something to show, evidence, or a boon, would be great, or imperfect accumulations toward something substantial, would be wonderful. a hybrid equation, vision, structure and abstract or inner-wordly animal approximating, signifying, celebrating, sanctifying existence, the quotidian and also the magnificence. because art is a gift, a spiritual offering, linking the world out there unlimited and our sore worlds within and within reach with the perfect spirit world, we're at a loss and art erases the void and all rises in her mind, lifting, pulling toward expansive future. a gift. of hope. In late afternoon gazing over hazy hat Elba, into which the blood orange sun dropped each dusk when it was good and red, I left off writing the moment before our first kiss. save it for after dinner, when I stayed at the dining room table (my night station), reentered the afflatus to write the kiss, and on into our coming together. first sex. The instant I touched pen to paper to kiss her, the phone rang. It was Amanda, interrupting our first kiss. Amazing, perfect timing! Auspicious. or ominous..

There are no coincidences, only appointments, Frankie would say. Or,

Coincidence is God's way of remaining anonymous.

Evidence. clues abound.

I don't remember the first part of the conversation, because she was calling to tell me, she just thought she should tell me, she was *seeing* someone else.

Either God was everything, or nothing. The teachings, the practice, the path: spirit, God, all the above, vanished brutally. That dread awful feeling again. the real reality. that always returns. and asserts its awful primacy. raw pure ungod.

And the art box? *Art?* Dead dust. bits of paper. dead leaves and chicken scrawl. suddenly totally meaningless. vanished visions. soul banished. bashed in.

Everything stopped. It was me who'd been future tripping. wonderfully. And now for the violent inversion. brutal comeuppance. pathetic unpoetic justice..

I followed the old pull back down the stairs. She was gone. The chain clanged against the hollow aluminum of the streetlamp's base as I unhurriedly unlocked my bike. It was like the deal I made with myself was that I'd go after her, but not chase her, I'd take it easy and let us come together like that. I rode after her through the park, ineluctable, up the next block. The light went green, and Amanda had moved into the tree-lined corridor of the next block. The little bald guy you often see right here walked his funny duck-walk across the street, heading for the Korean market (Lime Tree), the *Times*. He carried himself with strange, mechanical, extra care, as if to make sure he wouldn't pop a spring or tip over.

Man slipped from view at the top of the block, whose boutiques were stillshuttered. Midblock the superfat super was already out on his stoop, his cassette deck, beside him, holding his pent blues, not yet released into the still Atlantic-fresh morning air. the waking city stream of consciousness.

A peripheral shout-out from or to the old RamAnanda (its windows curtained now, inhabited). The apple falls close to the tree. or whatever that saying is. between Whiskers and the Starbucks across the louder racing river of Second Avenue, taxis bounding, Amanda was poking along, her sky-blue shirt a fluttering flag. She was in the middle of the street, heedless, her torso swayed with the heavy horse rhythm of her slow pedaling. Again she slipped out of sight ahead. It was like she was towing me, but didn't know it, on a long rubber umbilical I still couldn't cut. Instead, like bungee jumping, you went way away, got small and terrified in the fall, then it pulled you back.

Where the little dogleg in front of St. Mark's Books (Wanamaker Place) hits Third Avenue I saw her sliding past the knot of people waiting for the light at the corner where Astor becomes St. Mark's Place. between another Starbucks and the massive handsome brownstone edifice of Cooper Union, whose too many street-level arched windows were perpetually hidden behind a blue plywood shell. I nosed out past the waiting, roaring bus and went against traffic to the intersection, where I had to wait. Another bus sat at the curb in front of Cooper Union, so I couldn't see Amanda.

When the light changed I slid in front of the pedestrians closing ranks, and then in front of the east-coming cars to slip across the hairy intersection. I'm used to this maneuver, I do it every day. Eighth Street and Astor Place converge here, after that black cube public sculpture on the median triangle where the skateboarder kids begin, together, their long scraping skid in the wrong direction. Eighth Street and Astor converge and all the cars funnel into St. Mark's, three lanes merging, helter-skelter (*Look out!*), into one. Every day, every morning. except moon days. for three years, we'd make our way against this rush of traffic on our way to practice. Once past this mess, you were home free. down Lafayette (against uptown traffic).

When I got past the bus I saw A just ahead. There was another bus on the corner of Fourth Avenue. (Curious convergence this morning. all the buses at their stops . .) The red light over her head, God's eye calmly winking over the tumult and flow below, turned green. The angle of the intersection there is steeper than ninety degrees. Usually at that spot at that time there aren't many or any cars coming from the left up Fourth Avenue. If the bus is there. and the bus was there. you can't see past it to see what's coming.

A didn't look left. She ambled onward, in her hard emotional bubble. A beat-up white van smashed into her. Her right arm shot up like a rodeo rider's. Her body banged against the flat front of the van like a crash test dummy, and flopped to the side. The bike bounced and landed beside her. The front wheel mangled, the rear wheel spinning beside her immobile body. The sound of the crash was not that loud. A little metallic crunch and a terrible thud. There was no skid. The van kept going.

A number of pedestrians, halted in their flow to and from the Astor Place subway stop, noted that it was a plumbing and heating van. The sloppy, hand-painted lettering on the door, in red paint, included Chinese characters. No one got the license plate.

Amanda lay on her side. knees slightly bent. One of her Tevas gone, so that foot was bare. She had scarlet polish on her toenails the same color as the puddle of blood spreading under her head. Her right arm was out, palm up. Her face didn't look mad. Her eyes were open, about to ask a question.

8. The Quiet Place

If you're the New England Patriots, you're thinking pass right now, you're thinking deep, and to the sidelines, get out of bounds and stop the clock, get within striking range of the end zone for the final series, or play, which, if you're Tom Brady, Bill, is anywhere inside the fifty-yard line.

Amanda loved when commentators did that, said if you're New York City, you're thinking Jesus H. (W.) Christ, if you're Al Qaeda, you're thinking Jesus H. Mohammed, maybe I'd better, uh, hide, the kind of amusing construction my father liked also, chortled at, *Indeed,* the human mind revealing itself in common sleepwalking words.

B, what's meta? she once asked, a toe in my zone, late in the game, and I said it's narrative self-consciousness. a narrative that's aware of being a narrative, and its voice expresses that awareness with commentary, wisecracks, like hers, ironic asides, hedging tangents, other verbal curlicues, or questions questioning itself, Bill.

You mean self-conscious, like me teaching my classes or me almost all the time with people, maybe most people most of the time with people, self-conscious but just putting it out there anyway. and I said yeah, no. except talking about it makes it meta, like I do. too much, guys do, instead of keeping it to ourselves. letting it be. go.

Dad had this new boyish expression sometimes, in his final days, rapt, soft, lips kind of cookied flat, he was simple, present, enchanted, also crafty in there, still, shifting beneath the surface back to the better-place sleep he was half in, the ageless play and love there, so easy and complete.

The sudden shift of the season from summer to fall in New York, if you're Al Qaeda, you're thinking punt right about now, nice pent word, the compact thump of the kick, nice sexual fillip, release, on TV, before the family, country, duty, penis and cunt in one nice compact word and act.

Hey, B, what's the meta? she'd then say sometimes, getting a real kick out of herself, mocking me, and she was right in a way, better just words on a line, birds speed-walking on a beach, the boon out over the water, blue and windless, where minds meet and merge, here, words carry, whisper, obtain, allow.

Or a presence that's conscious of being the leafy Northeast, happens the morning of September first, every year, right on schedule, a magnificent conscious presence, vivid, sentient, invisible, it's unmistakable, it's nostalgic and bracing, the focus, shadow, attention to detail, the lovely cool clarity like a great numen anyone can walk freely into.

If you're Amanda, you're moving on right about now, Bill, so how about it, how about you, too? how about we meet for tea, and so we do, a stainless steel table at Dean & Deluca, when we decide let's do something together, instead of just this quick hi-bye every few months, and seeing each other at practice. she suggests we go to the beach.

If you're a character in a novel right now, you're wondering if you're alive, is how I began to explain it to Rose, holding a microphone like a cock in front of her mouth, then my mouth, test test, pivot to Rose, ready to roll, she placed the mike on its little stand on the surface of the round table between us, blue and white Moroccan tile, smoothly laid.

The ferry goes slowly at first, prowls past neglected Governors Island, Amanda in her shades, in her shade, some megaproject looming, they'll talk green development, argue, delay, as with the gaping World Trade Center, the massive omission, raw nerves still exposed, we look at Lower Manhattan like it's the boat, the stern, and we're watching it go away.

From our box seats on the observation deck up here, the Circle Line, Ellis Island, Lady Liberty, which New Yorkers never visit, who knows what she's thinking, feeling, credits roll like a prayer unfolding, as open harbor excites the ferry's imagination, the purring engine growls, we speed up, the boat lightly, potently lifts.

She wonders why she had to die, *You couldn't just move on like everyone else does?* I guess not, or I guess yes, this is my way of doing that, words move, are actions, a gull alights, cause actions, Mum arrives, always there but now here in person, out of the blue like this, Dad goes by in his boat, doesn't even look over, up at us.

Yoo-hoo! Mum yells, voice high, trying to get his attention, she always thought her soprano *yoo-hoo* could cut through any sound, massive motor, distance, dimension, death, waving her right arm, left hand holding her floral turquoise kerchief, sort of Ukrainian, onto her head, hair, also Jackie O, Catherine Deneuve, in her sunglasses.

And Rose, also here now beside Amanda, in her Rose sunglasses, a lot like Mum Deneuve's, retro, round, O, I want to embrace them all and see and show as one lovely female vision the cobalt harbor morning, zipping toy boats, tipped little daedali moth wings. a plane high in the sky looks like a boat, its white wake, seen from above.

Amanda sits slumped in the deck chair in her imitable way, saying not much. her beat-up Birkenstocks slipped off her feet, her feet and shiny shins and calves in the sun only, the rest of her inside the indigo wedge of cabin shade, out of the wind, the almighty blue-skinned deity day, Mum on the ledge, Rose to the right.

Dad plows on past, oblivio, in his dimension, squinting in the velocity and sun, toward Ellis Island, the brick compound growing, mechanical, skeletal horses of the Port of Elizabeth encroaching behind, begins to arc away toward the big Colgate clock like the Swiss Army pocket watch he used to carry, gave me.

The whole family's here, Amanda said that time on the bed with the cats, before Big Guy died, after Dad died, when we were there on that floating bed, before Amanda died, or dwindled, and returned to life, our moment a raft mortally afloat and appreciated, felt, resembling a future we could imagine, feel, but who would clean the house, keep it all together?

If you're Ellis Island, you're thinking holy shit these days, this century kicking off, what hath ye huddled masses wrought, yearning to be free, boyo, with a bang, the mighty Hudson has a silver memory, the river writes and history slides by, fast and slow, in boats, planes, commerce devouring ideas, meaning, nature, little wing souls, buildings.

So we have Rose on one side, talking, listening, Amanda on the other, saying nothing, Mum on the Vineyard ferry, and me, Billy, twelve, wearing my baseball cap I always wore, pulled way down, Mum grabs my cap by the visor, bill, and flings it overboard, pissing me off, my seventies long hair lashing around.

A card she she left on my desk, a severe saint, I forget which saint, grim, glowering expression, *Billy after I wouldn't let him go ice-climbing,* she wrote in her Mum handwriting, I was angry she wouldn't let me climb the ice face but was I angry, Virginia Woolf, when she, a week or so later, um, *fell off the planet?*

Over the stretched canvas harbor the ferry moves like a hand across the surface of a table toward another hand, Rose says something to Mum and Amanda and they smile, Mum mumbles something to Amanda, in tonally smooth unison with the trembling engine, the vibrating low *om,* Amanda inside the spell, home.

Mum was hit by a van coming from the right, barreling through the red light blinking God in the middle of the leafy busy intersection, she was late for aerobics, Jazzercise, witness accounts varied, but all agreed the guy was amped, drunk (enough) on beer after work. didn't even see the light.

And how about the plane landing on the Hudson, Bill, God the novelist, writing large right on the river so no one could miss the message, bold headline declaration, low over the Hudson, the same route to the first Tower (AA 403), emergency landing, everyone safe this time, the day before our new calm smart competent president (innate yogi) is sworn in?

Words, boats converge to take the survivors off the wings (USAir 1459), chilled by the winter water, but nothing worse, wrapped in blankets and taken to hospitals, the captain an unassuming hero, old Norse, sage argent wings neatly combed back above his ears, applied his skill and experience to his given duty, *We're going down.*

The boats on the river each anniversary morning converge at the exact time the first plane hit and sit and float together in silence, in bobbing memoriam, and at the moment the second tower collapsed they honk and blast and toot their horns for a full minute, then disperse, with spontaneous military precision, plow and zoom off over the silver loss.

The ferry arrived at the other side, a lull of a place, the room with tinted windows on three sides in the belly of the boat where we waited with our bikes to disembark by the opening framing the landing area was like a bar with the bar removed, sunlit wall-to-wall industrial-tough teal carpeting.

This was what it felt like to be retired, I said to Amanda, to be in no big rush, content together but not much to say, like we'd made it after all, together, visiting this lush pocket in the afternoon, calm cathexis, a breath of nature, while everyone else was at work, the greenish pressure-treated wharf planks weathered gray.

The map of the area mounted behind plexiglas beside the white stripes and numbered parking lot, only the front two rows filled with cars, one lone wolf one, crafty commuters who'd figured out they could treat New York like San Fran and go to work by ferry every day, return to the beach vibe every night, the world simplified.

And at the same time to feel like you're already dead, I didn't say, but still alive, moving toward nothing but nothing, or sudden-death overtime, so every moment is vital, or everything's meaningless, take your pick or fuse the two, savor your sandwich, a good way to be, to see and live every day, you're off the hook, let it be.

Colleen told me that the night before the attack her husband woke in the middle of the night from a nightmare he told her right then, that the World Trade Center was hit, they were called in, they went, and went in, and the building collapsed on them, killing everyone in there. and in the morning he got the call. he looked at her.

Except then you wouldn't really make plans, if the mortal pressure were off, or do anything difficult, you'd forgo delayed gratification for the good life, now, adolescence extended, a good definition for many yogis, so-called, self-nominated, living in the yoga bubble, with like-minded shirkers, if well-intentioned, latter-day idler-saints.

Who would cook, make the beds, make the plans *You would, B!* make them/help them do their homework, *you're a good dad,* brush their teeth, *I'd help, too,* we fully felt the budding family between us, that sacred thing, welling and immanent, why every love story matters more than all else, love and her place in nature.

We pedal along, away from the ferry landing parking lot, palpably free of all the cars and crazed density of NYC, the great magnet you can't pull yourself off of, until you do and you feel instant peace and freedom, the stillness upstate for a weekend, night, no wonder we need yoga here, how else can you ever cope, everyone else?

All our time there, riding on bikes in traffic, to and from practice, work, lunches, friends, all those days and nights, vanished, replaced by this single placid sunny beachside road, not death, empty pleasant noon, it's my birthday, she gave me a Ganesh sticker for my bike, out of our lives, in childhood, America, instant irrelevance, lightness.

Relief, release, from the nonstop urban scrimmage, our long-running balancing act, this was all it took, in the end, to get this, a plan and an enjoyable half-hour ferry ride? true transportation, to get here, mythic, at last beyond conversation and the need to talk and understand, this peaceful little heaven where all you do is pedal along, be.

Amanda's body lying along the edge of the bed is the beach at the end of the road, stray gulls also off work, mean little heads, Beckett beaks, float along, look around for something to steal, peck at, as talismanic Dad divides the brackish inland waterway past the marina, towing behind his boat a rowboat. that looks like a coffin.

B! Amanda calls out behind me, as if in my head, she has stopped by the side of the road, diminishing, as if the invisible bungee cord line between us has snapped (at last!), her bike aslant, we're almost at Oz, the opiate field the bridge to the dunes and beach and piddly sniffling Jersey surf, I circle back to see what's up.

Her mouth is clown-downturned, more doughy on one side, *It broke,* she says in why-me mock-dismay, also real, a sigh and comical resignation lifts her brow, the chain came off, I assume, without looking, no biggie, just put it back on, but it's worse, her chain broke, one part is dragging, the other part wrapped around.

Maybe the shift happens by itself (the chain comes off), not in a flash of enlightenment, but a letting go into non-attachment, maybe enlightment means illumination (*prakasa*), and you have many light lifts, many small enlightenments, and there's peace now, this is nice, where before was a rush. a plan. a need. another.

A jolly, two-tone dog comes jogging along, black pointed ears from another model, but no car to help, no magic man, that would be me, mr. doggie joins us happily, nosing in, his tail flagging supine eights, sideways infinities, sniffs the uneven equals sign of black chain grease beside the double freckle carob colon on her ankle.

So we push ahead, toward the beach, something will happen, we'll figure it out, first let's go to the beach anyway, and in one of the pleasure crafts lapping, sleeping in their slips after summer, mid-September stasis oasis, I see a bandana, tanned back, beer belly, I see my other self, a road not taken, bent over the open inboard.

I go to him, tell him what happened, ask if there's a bike place around, sporting goods, anything, there's a fishing and sort of surf place, he says, before the beach, up ahead, still open, we go, it's just tourist junk, sunscreen, water wings, folding chairs, the woman's a peevish old prune, so I return to the guy, maybe me, our one hope.

I ask him if he has a spare line, some old rope he doesn't need or if he knows where I could get some, and without hesitating, as if he were waiting for this and already had the solution in hand, or like a scene that has to be reshot because the actor forgets to pause a beat, to consider, *act,* he tosses me a bunch of rope he has right there.

It's nylon, like new, I say how much do you want, he shrugs, bring me a six-pack next time, and I resolve to really do that, I look at the name of the boat to remember, I forget what it was, I never returned, but when I return to Amanda with the rope she says, *What are you going to do with that, cowboy, tie me up?*

I'm going to tow you, I say, *You can't tow a bike, B*, she answers, big smile, guffaw, like everyone knows that cardinal universal bike rule, but I persist, tie a good bowline around the post under her handlebars, I loved rope as a boy, and tell her her job is to keep the line taut, mine to pedal, if we both do our parts it'll work fine.

And it worked fine, it was funny, she jeered and balanced with her legs apart, cheered me on on the hill, *Faster!* living it up back there, making the best of it, always happy to kick back and not to have to do anything, be served, but when we went down the slope to the back of the beach, *Hey!* she didn't do her job.

I yelled for her to put on the brakes, she laughed me off and she was right this time, it didn't matter, she could just glide up to me and the fence where we locked the bikes, but when she messed up on the way back, after the beach, on the way to the ferry, her bike jerked, she yelped, when the rope went taut.

At the beach Amanda says what a drag the bike broke, and I say but it's classic, it's like a myth, let's look at the meaning, the living dream, we create our symbolism, I can spew these things all day, every inconvenience is a misunderstood adventure, there are no coincidences, only appointments, she shushes me, says she's going for a swim.

I join her, the sand is large granular Jersey sand, low grade, and the beach drops off abruptly, a ledge, not designed for wading into the sniffling surf, you're up to your knees and then it drops off and you have to go in, or out, and instead of bowling broadly ashore each "wave" raises a little fist and punches down its spiritless rote protest.

Weedy ribbons float around us as in miso soup, Amanda's nicely browned tofu head seals around, delicious, her grin says, she does round dolphin dives under, then just floats, bodiless, bodiless, me, too, we both tread water as if it's a mental or soul activity only, nice cool green depths flow in from the living art dimension.

Lying on our towels (as on our mats) side by side we hardly talk (as in bed), I wait for her to, I know she likes this silence under the open sky and sea, and I would, too, if she weren't there, if I didn't want to talk to her, now that we're finally together for a bit, and I feel exactly why we broke up, and also, still, how I love her.

I watch a couple of teenage girls negotiate the steep rim of the beach and the waves, a fat white girl who lets it all hang out and a self-conscious black girl with a beautiful body who keeps her shirt on over her nice new breasts and bikini top, unintentionally eroticizing her talented Olympian lower half, look away, it never ends.

Just as just because you love someone doesn't mean you should be together, also it's easier to love someone when they're not there, or dead, or asleep, or you can look and look at her and she won't look back, which is why we love movies, you can gaze at her face and she won't look back at you, so you don't have to look away.

In the middle of the Amanda movie screen Amanda opens her mouth and yawns, *but do you yawn when you're already asleep?* she just did, she's a little heavy, a pear, I can inspect her body, though I already know it, inside and out, but still I inspect, we're middle-aged, face it, getting there, I can accept that, but looking better than most.

The beach is almost empty, maybe eight people total, in range, spread out in couples, like a board game, but no one goes, no one moves, just the gulls and the girls in the surf, they stand at the cusp to their knees and touch-taste enough spittle, a white power boat moves across the Rothko scrim of sea and sky from the left on a long curve.

I imagine I'm my father, imagining life, he drives his boat, Amanda dead asleep, Mum sits in front of the console Dad stands behind, driving, like a Chinatown couple, together and not, at the middle of the screen he steers away, Mum is eclipsed, the boat heads away, toward the too-painterly horizon, the uneven long edge of absence.

You wouldn't know it grazing at the horizon dividing and binding the open resting place ocean and sky but if you went straight up in the air here as high as a gull or a building you'd see across the water the amazingly always named Fresh Kills landfill holding forever the sacredly forensically sorted and bulldozed debris and cremains.

But so we get it down, our little act, in the almost empty Jersey lane, our practice zone, which is good because when we get to Manhattan we have Midtown to deal with, because the ferry we got on, why not, why wait, nice river ride, lets off near that helipad pad beside FDR Drive, not far from our little corner of the world.

There's a bike path between FDR and the East River, not really a bike path (yet) but a footpath, for joggers, and bikes are allowed, too, right on the river, it's great, like being on the boat still, but on the massive solid immovable boat Manhattan whose belt rim wall bellies back the waves from barges, tugboats, stinkpots, the odd fiberglass wedge.

As long as it's flat, and mostly it is flat, I can keep up a kind of momentum that feels like we're going downhill a little bit, the velocity I create helps keep the velocity moving, the way life works, but if I let up at all it gets much harder, fits, tugs, yelps, the trick is to not stop, living symbolism aside, keep pedaling, strong and steady.

And to do this, it sort of makes sense, but whether it makes sense or not, it works, I do it. you hold the handlebars strongly, hands squeezing hard and arms straight, to stabilize the steering, and to do this best you sit exaggeratedly erect, hold the whole body like that, ramrod slightly arched, strong seat, *gluteus maximus.*

Why are you sticking your butt out like that! she jeers, I ignore her, Bulls cap on backward, plug along, steadfast, a tugboat pulling his spewing old stinkpot wife, carefully pass joggers, this one a slowpoke, determined, this one a champ, in a cap, on a mission (of mercy or self-hate), she messes around behind me, yukking it up.

We pass a beefy cop on his bike, stopped, emasculated in shorts and a helmet, he shakes his head at us, secret poet fly in his iridescent mirror shades, smiles at the spectacle, this bountiful city, a couple of adult children of the American Century on rattletrap bikes, southbound on the East River path, one towing the other.

High school kids in red sweats out running, the last two, in steel-rimmed glasses, way behind, walking, talking, the glass and steel edifices slide slowly by on our right, cliffs and looming presences, conformist design, huddled together, fates shared, in bled dark blue shadow, the river wrapping, lapping, the rapid-firing FDR racecourse.

I'm sweating but cool from the breeze of motion and it's not as hard as it maybe looks, to A, or who notices, nobody registers our caper, New Yorkers let New York flow past, without batting a lid, until an elderly lady walking her terrier stops and waves like she knows us and loves us, Amanda, pinup girl pulled on her bike, grins, waves back.

We see things you otherwise wouldn't see, an Italian restaurant you can see through to the river, no one inside, but cabs outside, a hospital that sits on the path, squat over it, so we thread through the arrival area, past Emergency, out again, *seeya,* curve back to daylight, free a Japanese pocket garden, bamboo, a bench, a trim bonsai.

We pass the UN, Hitchcock and old white telephone movies set in Sutton Place, *Give me Knickerbocker six-*

five-hundred, please, Amanda's voice says to the operator in that cadenced way they spoke, in movies at least, mischief playing on her face, satin dress and drapes, Amanda now inhabiting that blithe coy spirit.

The nightclub music explains a lively xylophone complication, and then the immediate horn section solution, the silver trumpet moon fades to her face, bestirs the city rhythm of the next scene, outdoors, Fifth Avenue, day, flowing along the sidewalk, the stores, a gent in a hat, a suit, absorbed, strides by, glances, does a double take.

Across the reflectively patterning pewtery water we see the stacks and steeples of Queens and Brooklyn amid the fewer newer towers and the old low warehouses and hulking industrial shells, the four fat Con Ed polluters painted white, with bold wide red (guilty conscience? corporations are people) barbershop stripes. *B! Stop it.*

We see the Rikers Island orange and blue and white convict transport bus in the traffic, thickened and slower further downtown, at least I see it, the windows reinforced with black wire mesh, three rows of unmoving heads within, large heads, imagine those lives, unimaginable, we're so fucking lucky, I want to say to A.

Because even though we're cruising along in this adventure together and passing through the same series of streets, sights, *maya* revealed, scenes unfolding toward some end, now as ever I'm seeing what I see, and she's seeing what she's seeing, separately, though attached by the rope, a couple, tenuously together, love on a string.

A gang of choppers, loud-rumbling low-riders, leather Angels, comes up behind us, their throaty low boil and mild menace surrounds us at the light at Houston where we stop, now I'm tired, want to quit, back in our home zone, one of the big guys offers me a line, a clip, to tow me, us, I decline, the light goes red, I press on.

As their collective resentment roars off in a proud testosterone cloud of chrome and black leather, a harmless urban road toad, muscles and fat seared with threatening tattoos covering quivering little boys' fears like textbook psychology coloring books, their receding chopper rhythm turns sibling helicopter chopper.

The 1010 WINS traffic copter beats into the picture, top of the screen, as it trolls up FDR, then out of frame behind the dun brick projects, as the vibrational beating wanes, ushering in, as its aerial spirit lingers with us, its philosophical overview, as I pull her along, past Bowery, past our past, tracked from higher and wider.

We see the traffic go molten and the buildings hunker down, *ready,* it's all about people, meaning all about love, *set,* or people are lost here, we've lost our way, depending on the floating bird's-eye view on the matter, *go,* watching from above the fragile process, also within, the mystery progress of us tender two souls unattaching.

I say good-bye to her outside the bike place on Lafayette she likes, dreads, if bald, skinny, tanned, ropey calf muscles, jumping around in his bike shorts, fixes her bike for free, telling how it is while she waits, super-stressed, you wouldn't know it, looking at her, you'd think she has all the time in the world without end.

So many times I've said good-bye to her, maybe in too many ways, all this included, forgive me, thank you, but so how about, Bill, the time I overheard her, like catching someone praying, signing off on her computer, the AOL voice says *Good-bye* in his upbeat, robotic two tones, and she softly replies, just as upbeat, if a little softly-sadly, *Bye.*

And so back in my studio I stop. sit. for a moment extended, expanded, still, at last, in the quiet place, always there, let go the grip, the conscious weight, and shed the world, the welter, volition, barbed, willful vision, revealing the sacred ancient secret of love and art: look at anything long enough and you see a woman's face.

ACKNOWLEDGMENTS

For the help and support and love, gratitude and more than many thanks to:

Mike Diamond, Eddie Stern, Milo Minot, Willem Dafoe, Joe [Torczon], Victoria Wilson, Melanie Jackson, the crack team at Knopf, Dad, Helen Hannon, Martha Snowden, Richard Stewart, Carla Waldron, Woog, Wah, Doodle, Whip, Wham, Tough, Li, Can, Tati, Jason, Nati, John Guare, Claudia Palmira, Giulia, Kristin Schaumleffel, Lea, Steve Spretnjak, Francesco D'Intino, Stephan Crasneanscki, Elka Krajewska, Johanna, John Heinman, Sherri Dougherty, Michael Bonomo, Bruce, Scott Sommer, Amy Hempel, Carolyn, Cy, Ned Herter, Bea Magee, Lee and Miles Herter, Josuph Kosuth, Alissa Quart, Peter Maass, Shaila Dewan, Paul Breen, Spo, George Bell, Gary Shteyngart, Kath, Roberto, Myra, Barb, Ira, Kent, Jeffrey, Dorothy Senecal, Anne W, Angie, Inti, Peter J. Smith, JC Smith, Barbara Carleton, Adams, Richard Price, John Mahoney, Larry Cuddire, Carlos Dews, the Bramhalls, HR Coursen, Alec Wilkinson, Nick Witte, North Haven, AYNY, FAO, Mark, Marie, Sharmilla, Maria, Ruth, Katchi, Roderick Romero, Sharon Gannon, David Life, Sharath and SKP Jois.

A NOTE ON THE TYPE

This book was set in Adobe Garamond. Designed for the Adobe Corporation by Robert Slimbach, the fonts are based on types first cut by Claude Garamond (c. 1480–1561). Garamond was a pupil of Geoffroy Tory and is believed to have followed the Venetian models, although he introduced a number of important differences, and it is to him that we owe the letter we now know as "old style." He gave to his letters a certain elegance and feeling of movement that won their creator an immediate reputation and the patronage of Francis I of France.

Typeset by Scribe, Philadelphia, Pennsylvania

Printed and bound by Berryville Graphics, Berryville, Virginia

Designed by Iris Weinstein